Maddie Please was born in Dorset, brought up in Worcestershire and went to university in Cardiff.

Following a career as a dentist, Maddie now writes full time, and lives in Devon with her exceptionally handsome and supportive husband.

Also by Maddie Please:

The Summer of Second Chances

A Year of New Adventures

Maddie Please

avon.

A division of HarperCollins*Publishers*

www.harpercollins.co.uk

Published by AVON
A Division of HarperCollins*Publishers* Ltd
1 London Bridge Street
London SE1 9GF

www.harpercollins.co.uk

This paperback edition 2018
1

First published in Great Britain in ebook format by
HarperCollins*Publishers* 2018

A catalogue record for this book
is available from the British Library

ISBN: 978-0-00-825345-5

Typeset in Minion by Palimpsest Book Production Limited,
Falkirk, Stirlingshire

Printed and bound by CPI Group (UK) Ltd, Croydon, CR0 4YY

For Jane

Best friend, writer, and matchmaker.

Chapter One

It was the third writers' retreat Helena and I had run and the previous two had gone like clockwork. There was no reason why this one shouldn't have been just the same.

And then Oliver Forest turned up.

It was a dark, wet day in February and, believe me, his mood made it seem even bleaker.

*

It didn't take long for things to go wrong.

It was ten-fifteen and people had been asked to turn up after eleven, so Helena and I were sitting with our feet up in the gorgeous kitchen of our rental house eating cookies out of the first batch I'd made; some of them had broken when I'd burned myself and dropped the baking tray.

Although she is my best friend, Helena is nothing like me. For example, she believes any meal taking longer than seven minutes in a nine-hundred-watt microwave is a waste of time. I love cooking and have been known to sleepwalk into the kitchen to make an omelette.

She has an immaculate and much-loved pale-blue Morris Minor called William, whereas I have a beaten-up old Land Rover, which isn't called anything except rude names when it refuses to start. Actually, I'm petrified it needs a new cam belt, something that was mentioned in hushed tones last September when it had an MOT. I hope it wasn't listening. I didn't dare ask what a cam belt was, but it sounds expensive doesn't it?

Even though it might be on its last legs, my car had more space than hers for all our provisions. I had removed the Tesco bag full of muddy shoes, a box of books to take to the local telephone kiosk library, and the cracked first-aid kit that now contained only a triangular bandage and a box of corn plasters. Still, if we'd met anyone with a broken arm and bunions on our drive down to the lovely house we'd rented for the retreat, we'd have been ready.

'So I hope you're going to tell me you've got your money back from Matt?' Helena asked with an innocent air as I reached for another cookie.

'Well no, but he promised he would sort it out,' I said.

This was an ongoing conversation that had started before Christmas when Matt – my now very ex-boyfriend – had gone on our romantic holiday without me.

'Oh for heaven's sake, Billie!' Helena said. 'When are you going to toughen up with him? He owes you money! He nicked your towels! Why are you letting him get away with it?'

God knows.

But then why did I let him move into my cottage on the understanding he would replace the skirting boards in the kitchen when he obviously had no intention of doing so?

Why after two years did I keep hoping he might stop being so inconsiderate in bed – not to mention untidy, lazy, and thoughtless?

Why had I allowed myself to believe that a crap boyfriend was better than no boyfriend?

'I'm going to go and see him when I get home, I really am,' I said, trying to sound resolute.

Helena huffed a little. 'You won't because you know he'll just get round you again. He never was good enough for you. I did tell you ...'

Suddenly there was a mighty banging on the front door, followed by some irritated bell pushing. Helena inhaled a chocolate chip and began coughing and spluttering, tears streaming down her face. I thumped her on the back and went to fetch her a glass of water. Meanwhile, the racket at the front door continued.

I decided to give the bell pusher a piece of my mind. We had made it quite clear that door wasn't used because it opened directly onto the street. It was locked, the key was hidden somewhere, and it was secured with four pretty sturdy bolts. We were in the middle of a gentle little village in Herefordshire and I don't think it was a hot spot for crime so all this security was perhaps a bit excessive.

'For God's sake! I'm trying! Stop pushing the frigging bell!' I shouted as I located the key on top of the doorframe and wrestled with the bolts. After a few minutes – hot, sweating, and red-faced – I managed to open the door.

'What?' I shouted.

Outside was a dark-haired man standing propped against the wall. He had one leg in a big plastic surgical boot and behind him an exceptionally glamorous blonde was wheeling his suitcase towards me. She was making heavy weather of it too given the unequal struggle with her stilettos and the cobbled street.

'It's raining. I want to come in,' he said. 'Is that too much to ask?'

He limped past me, and stood watching as the blonde lugged his case over the doorstep. What a gent, I thought as I went to help her.

'Who are you anyway?' I said as we hefted the bag inside and closed the door.

The blonde gasped, horrified. 'But this is *Mr Forest*.'

The man himself ignored me and began giving rapid-fire instructions to the poor woman.

'So, make those calls, do as I asked with Gideon, tell him I'm not prepared to talk to Patterson and he'd better sort it or I won't go at all. Tell Jake I've got no bloody mobile signal so let's hope the broadband speed is reasonable.'

He looked at me, one eyebrow raised.

'Well is it or isn't it?'

I gulped and started to panic. 'I did explain in the information we sent out ...'

He rolled his eyes in exasperation. 'Did you? Fascinating. Look, can I talk to William Summers? I understand he is the organizer here.'

This happened all the time; thanks, Mum, for giving me a weird name.

'I'm Billie Summers,' I said, 'and I'm the organizer. Well I'm one of them, you see ...'

Organizer? I should have been struck by lightning.

Oliver gave me a look that clearly showed he didn't believe me and turned back to his hapless assistant.

4

'Pippa, put my case in my room. It's over there behind the kitchen. I checked on the floor plan. And then put my phone on charge. It might be useless but ... well.'

He limped after Pippa as she rolled the case across the flagstone floor and into the downstairs bedroom, which already had 'Elaine' printed on a picture from *Swallows and Amazons* that Helena had taped to the door.

'Um, sorry this isn't your room,' I said, scurrying after him.

He pulled Elaine's name card off the door, looked at it, and then handed it to me.

'It is now,' he said and went in, closing the door behind him.

Helena and I stared at each other, gobsmacked.

'What!'

'He can't do that!' Helena said. 'It's Elaine's room. She asked specially.'

'Well, I know!'

We went up to the door and listened. We could hear Mr Charm rattling off instructions to Pippa, telling her where to put things. After a moment's hesitation, I knocked and opened the door. Mr Charm turned to look at me.

'Er, do you mind?' he said.

I hesitated; he was a lot bigger than me.

'This is Elaine's room,' I said bravely, 'not yours. You're Oliver Forest aren't you? You're in the upstairs front room. I told you so in the email.'

Pippa drew in an appalled breath at my insolence. I swallowed hard and waited for the full force of his bad temper to fall on me.

He sighed and pointed to his leg. 'And how am I to get up the stairs?' he said.

'I'm sure you could manage,' I said. 'If there was a winning lottery ticket up there on the landing you'd get to it wouldn't you?'

'Is there?'

'Well no, but I was just making a point. If there was ...'

'You're expecting me to get up and down the stairs with my leg in a boot? Really?' He fixed me with a hard stare.

It was only the utter unfairness of his attitude that kept me from running off. 'Well, Elaine has arthritis.'

'Who is Elaine?'

'The person who had ...'

He waved an impatient hand at me. 'I don't know what you're talking about. I haven't got time for this. Now would you excuse me? And by the way, I don't want these.'

He limped across the room, put the dish with the bedside chocolates into my palm, and closed the door in my face.

I turned to look at Helena.

'Bloody hell, what a rude sod!' I hissed, unwrapping a Belgian truffle and handing the other to Helena.

'Sssh! He might hear you.' Helena is always more concerned about other people's opinions than I am and she pulled me away. 'What shall we do?'

We stood and thought about it for a moment.

'I've no idea. He's bigger than us,' I said. 'We could wait until he comes out and then move all his stuff?'

'We can't do that!'

We looked at the closed door for a few minutes until we realized there was nothing we could do. Not without a couple of beefy companions and a cattle prod.

Suddenly the oven timer beeped and I dashed across the kitchen to rescue the second lot of cookies.

'What can we do?' I said, darting a fierce look at the closed door and trying to get the cookies off the baking tray without burning myself again.

'We must keep cool and think,' Helena said, stretching her hands out in a calm-down sort of gesture. 'He's a paying customer after all. He did pay didn't he?'

'Yes he did,' I muttered and made a different sort of gesture. 'Unbelievable. I can see this week's going to be a barrel of laughs. Didn't you say he was allergic to shellfish? Well let's hope I don't accidentally buy a lobster.'

Chapter Two

I once made the mistake of telling my boyfriend how hard it was to write a book and get it published, and Matt sneered and said writing was just drinking coffee and making stuff up. Why would that be difficult? He then added some pithy comments about how many Mint Clubs I had been getting through recently under the guise of plotting. In my defence they were on a BOGOF offer, and of course once they're in the cupboard ...

We broke up soon after that – I put up with a lot from him in our two years together but even I have my limits – still, I think he was partly right. I like Mint Clubs. I'm not ashamed to admit it. OK, I like most things that mix chocolate and biscuits, if I'm honest. Perhaps that's why my figure is always slightly out of control.

It wasn't a very merry Christmas last year. We had been about to go to New York as he had finally persuaded me there were holidays to be had outside Europe. I was fizzing with excitement. These sorts of trips were few and far between but Nan had left me a small inheritance that I'd been hanging on to and I'd just been paid for some private pre-Christmas catering, so for once I had some savings.

Unfortunately, I gave the money for my part of the holiday to Matt and I still haven't got it back. Swine. We had been living together in the tumbledown Cotswold stone cottage my grandmother had been in the middle of renovating when she died. When we split up he left with my holiday to New York, most of my DVDs and all the decent towels.

New Year's resolution: never do anything spontaneous.

My sister inherited the picture-perfect holiday house in Cornwall. Typical. In her will Nan said Josie 'needed' it more than I did. I guess that's because Josie and Mark have two boys and their school has longer holidays than some members of the British aristocracy, while I had no kids and no prospect of any.

*

I started trying to write when I was doing English A level, and had just read *Forever Amber*. I quite fancied being a writer of historical fiction. After all, it didn't need specialist equipment, formal training, or a particular level of physical fitness; the only thing it did require was aptitude.

Unfortunately, I was rubbish at it but for some reason I just couldn't give up. I've been trying for eleven years. An eleven-year apprenticeship for God's sake! I could have got a PhD. I could have learned how to rewire a house or renovate a canal boat in the same amount of time. Or at least had something to show for it other than a dead laptop and an unhealthy interest in stationery shops. I was always looking for that magic notebook that would make all the difference.

So, there I was at twenty-nine, living in the front bit of

Windrush Cottage, Lower Bidford, while I waited for a miracle that would allow me to afford the renovations of the back part. The only increase in my net wealth was locked up in the value of the cottage. I still hadn't got a proper career path mapped out. I was working part time in my uncle's bookshop, and doing some occasional catering and cake decorating.

I suppose I still assumed I would one day magically produce a saleable book to make my fortune. Meanwhile, I had joined forces with my genuinely talented best friend Helena to run occasional writing retreats. And that's what I was trying to do when Oliver Forest turned up at the last minute with his seafood allergy, his aversion to perfectly good chocolates, and his dark blue eyes, hell-bent on wrecking everything.

OK, the dark blue eyes bit shouldn't matter; I don't know why I mentioned them.

*

After he had rudely slammed the door in my face, Oliver Forest and Pippa stayed closeted in his bedroom for the next half-hour.

'Perhaps they're having sex?' Helena whispered at one point, when it had all gone a bit quiet and we couldn't hear him barking out instructions to the poor woman.

She edged closer to his door, crouched down, and angled her ear towards the keyhole. 'Perhaps they're doing it really quietly.'

'I doubt it!' I said. 'I don't think people like him do anything quietly.'

At that moment Pippa opened the door and stuck her head out. She looked down at Helena and seemed rather startled for a moment.

'Could we have coffee?' she said. 'And I'd love one of those cookies.'

'Of course,' Helena said sweetly, pretending she had been about to re-tie her shoelaces, which was the wrong thing to do as she had slippers on. She recovered quickly by picking up a bit of fluff on the floor. I saw her checking to see if Pippa was in any way dishevelled. 'Just come out when you're ready.'

'We'll have it in here,' Oliver said loudly.

Pippa gave a weak smile. 'I'll pop out in a minute for a tray shall I?'

'Yes, yes of course,' Helena said.

The door closed and we exchanged a look.

'This is going to be a very long week,' I said.

Helena, as is her way, tried to make the best of the situation. 'Well let's try and make sure he has nothing to complain about.'

She went and found a tray and wiped it over before she put out two matching mugs, a sugar bowl, a milk jug, and two polished teaspoons. Then we scrabbled around looking for the cafetière and some real coffee. I selected a pretty plate and put out some cookies before Helena found a nice little wicker basket and tipped them into that instead. Then, we took them all out again and this time lined the basket with a paper napkin. At last, after a bit of artful arranging – because there is only so much one can do with six choc-chip cookies – we took the tray up to the closed door and I knocked.

Pippa came to open it and took the tray from Helena. We both peered round her, trying to see what was going on.

'Everything OK?' I said cheerily, craning a little.

I could see Oliver Forest sitting in the armchair next to the window with a large notebook on his knee. He was writing, his dark hair tousled as he ran one hand through it. Almost as though he could feel my gaze on him, he looked up. His eyes really were beautiful, and he stared at me for a moment in that funny way writers do when they are deep in a plot and they aren't actually seeing you.

Bloody hell.

#Rathergorgeous.

He was beyond handsome. How had I not noticed this before? He could have been a prototype for any dark and brooding hero. His long legs, one of them in the plastic boot, were stretched out on a footstool. He looked to be in his late thirties, had a clean jawline, strong straight nose, and rather kissable mouth.

He blinked a couple of times and came back into the real world with the rest of us. 'What now for heaven's sake? Is there a problem?'

'No, no, no, absolutely not,' I said, covered in confusion.

I backed away and trod on Helena's foot, making her yelp. She started hopping around – her knee held very high – and I hopped after her, apologizing. We must have looked a right pair of clowns.

Luckily there was a knock on the back door and we scurried off to welcome the first of our other guests.

Happily it was a couple of old friends from our first retreat: Nancy and Vivienne, both retired teachers who had travelled down together from Shropshire.

'Well the roads were really clear,' Vivienne said, shedding her soft silk scarf and folding it neatly into her coat pocket. 'We made excellent time. Have we missed anything?'

'No, you're the first to arrive. Apart from our unexpected

extra,' Helena said. She lowered her voice to a theatrical whisper. 'He's in his room. His name's Oliver Forest.'

Nancy frowned. 'Oliver Forest – that name's familiar. Has he been before?'

'No, believe me you would remember him,' I said with feeling.

'Did we ever teach a boy called Oliver Forest?' Vivienne asked Nancy who had spotted the coffee and was already halfway through a cookie.

'Maybe,' she said through a mouthful of crumbs. 'Short boy? Ginger?'

'No, he's dark-haired and' – *ridiculously good-looking* – 'quite tall,' I said.

'Nope, doesn't ring a bell. Come on, Nancy, let's go and get settled in. It's always the exciting bit, finding out what our rooms are like. Are we next door to each other again?'

We took them upstairs and along the corridor that divided the house in half. The floorboards – centuries old and polished by time to a wonderful patina – were warped and uneven. The house was scented with wax polish and wood smoke and bowls of potpourri in odd little nooks. I began to calm down again. Oliver Forest was only one person. There was no reason why he should monopolize the week. It would be OK.

I trundled Vivienne's suitcase into the front bedroom where a high four-poster bed was waiting, piled high with snowy bed linen and pillows. There was a built-in wardrobe whose doors lurched unevenly to one side, wedged shut with a scrap of cardboard, a huge tapestry armchair in one corner, and a rickety Indian carved table.

'The bathroom is down there, between your room and Elaine's.'

'I thought Elaine was going to have the downstairs room,'

Nancy said. 'I remember because it's got an *en suite*, and I wanted it.'

'She did, but Oliver Forest has a leg in a boot and he commandeered it before I could stop him. I don't know how I'm going to tell Elaine,' I said.

Nancy went into her room – a large single with an exceptionally ugly turquoise sink in one corner.

'Goodness, this is a ghastly thing,' Vivienne said, evidently pleased that she had the better room. 'How did they get away with putting this in? I thought this house was listed?'

'Ah but just think! This could be the very sink where Charles I brushed his teeth before the Battle of Bosworth,' Nancy said.

Vivienne snorted. 'Oh for heaven's sake. So what time is lunch? One o'clock? Good, there's time to get freshened up and have a power nap.'

Nancy went into her room and closed the door and I went downstairs to help Helena with lunch. I was going to make soup and she had arranged a fresh fruit platter. There's no point loading people up with large meals in the middle of the day; they only go to sleep and miss out on good writing time in the afternoon.

Suddenly the door to Oliver Forest's room opened and Pippa came out, handed me the coffee tray and started struggling into her coat. She looked like a condemned prisoner seeing the cell door left unexpectedly open.

'Are you off then?' I said.

Pippa closed Oliver's door quietly behind her and came towards me, her eyes slightly wild.

'Yes, I'm ... absolutely ... I'll avoid the traffic if I go now ... Paris ... I might ...'

14

She had already missed the armhole of one sleeve three times and I went to help her.

'Are you sure you're OK? Would you like a drink of water or something?'

'Yes fine. No. Really. Absolutely.'

She had an outstandingly pretty face, but it was clouded with unease. I could almost feel the stress coming off her in waves.

'I wonder if you could take Mr Forest in some more coffee in a minute? Black, no sugar. And don't bother with those silly little mugs – I think he'd prefer a bucket if anything. He has lunch between one-thirty and two p.m. But no shellfish and definitely no cheese – it makes him sleepy and grouchy.'

'No cheese; thank you for the warning. I don't think we'd want to risk *making him grouchy* would we?' I said. 'But surely he'd want to come out and meet everyone?'

Pippa shot me the smallest smile. 'Good luck with that then.'

I trailed after her as she edged towards the back door. I was curious to find out more before she disappeared in a flurry of angst.

'Back to London are you? I expect you'll enjoy a few days off,' I said.

'Yes, I mean no … I have plenty to keep me occupied. Paris – I should – Oliver's work, difficult, you know how it is.' She stopped to blow her nose on a tissue and take a deep breath. I swear she was about to burst into tears. 'And, of course, the blasted launch has been postponed. It's far from ideal … but then needs must. Anyway, I'll be along on Friday to collect Mr Forest.'

'We have to be out by ten-thirty, remember? Don't be late! We don't want to have to leave him on the doorstep!'

'Yes of course. God Almighty! No, please don't! He'd go mad!' Pippa said, wide-eyed at the prospect.

'I was joking,' I said.

'Oh. Were you? OK. Well you've got my mobile number. Right, I'll be off.'

Pippa shot out of the door and round the corner of the house. I closed the door after her and went back to my vegetables, wondering what it would be like to work for someone who was so terrifying.

Five minutes later Oliver's door opened and the man himself stood there. 'I thought you were bringing me coffee?' he said.

Ah! I had of course forgotten. I gave a nervous little laugh.

'Yes, just coming. Awfully sorry, you see I was a bit busy with ...'

'In your own time,' he said and closed the door again.

I pulled a face at where he had been and went to flick the kettle on. Black, no sugar, and in a bucket. Right, I could do that.

There was a knock on the back door and a worried little face at the glass peering in. She gave a big smile when she saw me.

'You must be Elaine!' I went to open the door and helped her in with her suitcase that was almost as big as she was. 'How lovely to meet you at last. Come on in and make yourself at home. We're very glad to welcome you. Helena is upstairs with our other guests Nancy and Vivienne, although I think Vivienne was going to have a nap.'

Elaine took off her fingerless mittens and unwound her woolly scarf.

'What a lovely house – lots of character in these old half-timbered places. You can almost feel the history can't you? If

16

these walls could talk eh? I bet there would be a few tales. Do you know, I was saying to Frank the other day ...'

Oliver's door opened again at this point and Oliver stood there, his face dark and irritated.

'Ah,' I said.

'Coffee?' he said. 'Today?'

'Of course, sorry I was just getting Elaine settled. This is Elaine by the way. She's ...'

Oliver closed his bedroom door again with a noticeable slam.

'... the one whose bedroom you nicked,' I finished.

'He's in my room?' Elaine said, and turned her worried round face to look at me.

'I'm sorry; it seems he's injured his ankle. He's in one of those boot things. He just went in there before I could stop him. I would have got him out but he's not very friendly.'

'No,' Elaine said looking at the closed door thoughtfully. 'He's not very polite either is he?'

I stood up and went to make a cafetière of coffee and poured out a cup for Elaine. She was busy looking through her handbag and pulling out paperwork, charging cables, spectacles, and all sorts of odds and ends.

I found one of those awful oversized mugs decorated with a slogan for chocolate that usually come with Easter eggs and are really only useful for storing pencils. I put it on the tray with the cafetière and went and knocked on Oliver's door.

'Come.'

I went in. He was still sitting with his feet up on the footstool, writing in his notebook. He didn't look up as I came in.

'Leave it on the table,' he said.

'Please,' I muttered.

He seemed not to hear.

'Anything else I can get you?' I said.

'I want lunch at one-thirty,' he said.

Oh do you?

'Yes, Pippa said you did. Well we generally have it ready from one, as we explained in the joining notes. But just come out when you're ready and help yourself. Everything will be out on the table. I'm making vegetable soup ...'

'I'd prefer it in here,' he said.

Oh would you? *Would you indeed?*

Well I'd prefer to be a stone lighter and six inches taller.

I'd prefer to drive an Aston Martin.

I'd prefer to have swishy, glossy hair instead of this unmanageable brown mop.

I plastered a smile on my face and moved the table closer to his chair so he could reach it. I'd made him an eight-cup cafetière in a rather sarcastic way; if he got through that lot before lunch he'd be crashing off the ceiling.

'Fine, of course. Whatever you want. It would be nice to meet the others though wouldn't it?'

He looked up, his expression stony. 'What others? I didn't know there would be any others. Is that what all that noise is?'

'Oh, but I told you ...'

'Pippa assured me I would have the house to myself. I made it perfectly clear what I wanted. I assumed she had listened. I assumed you had.'

Assume? Hmm.

I started to edge away from him and towards the safety of the kitchen. 'Pippa must have misunderstood. I could give you a hand to get to the table if you need one?' I said.

He looked up and fixed me with a dark blue stare. The sort my school sports teacher used to give me when I said I had forgotten my gym kit for the fourth time.

'I don't need a hand,' he said, 'just lunch. At one-thirty. Is your name really Billie? What's that short for then? Wilhelmina?' He gave a snort of amusement.

'No, actually it's short for Billericay,' I said sadly. 'It's been a complete nightmare all my life.' I bit my lip and looked away.

He had the grace to look embarrassed. 'Really? I'm so sorry, I mean I didn't mean …'

I took pity on him. 'I'm kidding. It's short for Sybilla, which is just as bad really isn't it?'

He didn't answer.

I went back to the kitchen and when I had closed the door I'm afraid I stuck my tongue out at him.

Elaine was still rifling through her capacious handbag and pulled out some printed emails with a little harrumph of satisfaction.

'Look, I did ask for the ground-floor room. I thought I had. Is there another one perhaps?'

'No, I'm afraid not, Elaine. I am sorry. I feel terrible. Obviously, I will put you into a really nice room as near the stairs as possible and refund the price difference you've paid. Sorry.'

Elaine smiled and cocked her head towards Oliver's bedroom door. 'It's fine, dear; I can see how you're fixed. I'll just have to manage. Don't you worry. I expect it will do me good; I'm getting very lazy these days.'

'Well thank you for being so understanding, Elaine.'

I took her case up to the room. It was at the top of the

19

staircase, a pretty room above the kitchen with a delightful leaded dormer window overlooking the garden. The single bed was high and stately with a deliciously plump duvet and pillows. I was suddenly tired and I could have crawled in for a power nap myself given half a chance.

Elaine was delighted. I introduced her to Nancy and Vivienne and I left them to settle in while I went back downstairs to finish off blending the soup and unwrapping the cheese. I took a glorious wedge of Stilton and waved it at Oliver's room in a gesture of defiance – and of course at that precise moment he opened his door and caught me in the act. Oh FFS.

He stood and raised his eyebrows at me and I froze, the cheese in front of me like an axe head.

I started to wave it around. 'Just airing it,' I said, 'like you do.'

'I've not seen that done before,' he said, narrowing his eyes.

'Really?' I put it behind my back. 'Can I get you anything?'

'No, I was just wondering what the Wi-Fi code was?'

'It's all on the welcome sheet,' I said, briskly efficient. 'One was left on your bedside table.'

'Was it? I hadn't noticed.' He looked around vaguely.

You mean you didn't try looking. Give me strength, why do I bother?

I went to fetch it. 'Here we are. The Wi-Fi code is there under the section headed Wi-Fi code. See?'

His mouth twisted a little. 'So it is.' He went to close the door and then hesitated. 'Thank you.'

Good grief!

Helena came downstairs.

'Everything OK?'

'Perfect,' I said, arranging the cheese on a slate platter with some grapes and celery sticks.

Helena started wiping down the worktops. 'Nancy says she's got into such a muddle with her WIP, she's almost tempted to start again. How's the soup coming along?'

'It will need seasoning I expect. I haven't been able to concentrate on it. There's still no sign of Nick Fitzgerald. I hope he won't be long. It's twelve-thirty.'

Helena started opening the cupboards looking for side plates while I ran two French sticks under the cold tap before putting them into the oven to crisp up. There was a fresh block of butter in the dish; we were just about ready. I went rummaging through all the cupboards and drawers to find glasses and cutlery so I could set the table. It's always difficult the first few hours in a strange house because no one knows where anything is and it's a steep learning curve.

Suddenly Oliver's door opened again. By the expression on his face he was not happy. 'Do you have to make such a bloody racket?' he said. 'Shouting at each other! Opening and closing doors! Crashing around. I'm trying to work and it sounds like there's an elephant on the loose out here.'

Flaming cheek! I know I might have put on a couple of pounds recently but there had been an offer on Wagon Wheels and I'd forgotten how much I liked them.

'So sorry,' I said, 'but of course that's the disadvantage of a ground-floor room. You could always go into the big sitting room. It's right at the front of the house, very quiet and there's a lovely wood burner in there. Very cosy.'

The oven timer beeped and I went to get the bread out of the oven.

'I don't want to be cosy; I just want some peace and bloody quiet,' he said.

There was a knock on the back door and Oliver rolled his

eyes in exasperation before disappearing back into his room.

Helena went to open it. It was a young man, rather attractive in a tousled, geeky, sports jacket sort of way.

'Hello,' Helena said, rather breathlessly, 'you must be Nick Fitzgerald?'

He stepped into the room, bringing a swirl of rain with him. 'I am.' He shook her hand.

It was obvious he liked what he saw. A lot. I swear you could feel the electricity between them crackling across the room.

'Filthy day it's turned into. And it started out so well. Still, it's looking up now I've got here.'

He gave Helena a wide grin and shrugged off his coat. Helena fussed and twittered around him and after a few introductions took him away to show him his room. She came back a few minutes later still rather dazed and silly. Most unlike her usual Miss Sensible demeanour.

Great, just what we didn't need: Helena flirting with a guest. She'd never done anything like that before, although thinking about it we didn't get many men as guests. And we'd never had someone with an unruly mop of tawny curls, smiling brown eyes, and the hint of a rather muscular frame under his tweed exterior.

There was soup to be served and bread to be sliced up and arranged attractively in the wicker baskets we had found. I fixed her with a steely look and willed her to calm down.

22

Chapter Three

At one o'clock on the dot everyone appeared in the kitchen. Well everyone except Oliver Forest of course, whose bedroom door remained closed. I swear I could sense the chill of his disapproval seeping underneath it.

Nancy and Vivienne fussed for a few minutes about where to sit while Helena went to fetch a glass jug of iced water and a pile of paper napkins. Nick Fitzgerald came downstairs and sat at a non-contentious place halfway along the table, trying to watch Helena without appearing too obvious.

He half stood up as she came across the room towards him, his long legs still under the table so he was trapped in an odd crouch.

'Can I help?'

'No not at all, we're all under control here,' Helena said with a bright laugh. I swear if she'd had a spare hand she would have twirled her auburn hair.

'I'd better go and check on Elaine. She's not very good with stairs,' I added a shade louder.

As I reached the hallway I saw Elaine was well on her way down.

'Lovely house,' she said. 'Very inspiring. I'd like to work in the little space under the staircase. But only if no one else wants it? Comfy-looking chair, very pretty lamp.'

'Consider it yours,' I said. 'Now come and have some lunch and meet the others.'

'Even Mr Forest?' she said with a wicked twinkle.

'Well who knows,' I said.

Elaine went to sit next to Nick, who gallantly stood to pull her chair out for her.

'Perhaps we could start by introducing ourselves?' I said. 'Just to fill in the gaps? I'm Billie Summers. I love to cook and I work part time in my Uncle Peter's bookshop. I've been trying to write a book for most of my adult life. This could be the week when I suddenly gain the necessary inspiration! Helena?'

Helena coloured prettily and sat up a bit straighter in her chair.

'Helena Fairchild. I write children's and YA. I'm a librarian. I sold a short story once, about a million years ago. It was about Bonfire Night. I'm not exactly setting the literary world alight just yet but I'm going to keep on trying. Nancy?'

Nancy was cutting a slice of cheddar and she paused, her knife halfway through the block.

'Nancy Gregory, retired RE teacher. I write murder mysteries. The latest one has taken three years and I haven't the faintest idea what I'm doing with it. I get so muddled I am quite capable of making the detective in charge of the case commit the murder.' She looked thoughtful. 'Perhaps that's not such a bad idea!'

Vivienne sniffed; her aquiline nose a beak of disapproval.

'I'm Vivienne Noble. I'm a retired chemistry teacher. I've

self-published a couple of novels on Amazon to mixed reviews. I write contemporary erotica. Nothing too outré, just a bit of S&M, some bondage, and some role-play.'

'Really?' Nick said.

Vivienne loved it when this sort of surprise was voiced and was inclined to play up to the audience and show off.

'Well I may not have been married but it doesn't mean I haven't lived. And I think I've got a pretty good idea of what does and doesn't work.'

The table fell silent at this point until Helena cleared her throat and we all jumped.

'Nick?' she said. 'Your turn I think?'

I kicked Helena under the table. She sent me a cross-eyed look in return.

Nick fidgeted a little and pulled his chunk of bread in half.

'Blimey, I don't quite know how to follow that. OK, I'm Nick Fitzgerald. I'm a contractor specializing in IT. I'm trying to write thrillers with a sort of international edge. Dan Brown, Ross Black, John Grisham – that sort of thing. I've had some technical papers published on subjects too dreary to go into, but as yet I don't have an agent or any sign of one.'

He seemed to run out of steam at this point and he looked down and started buttering his bread.

We all turned to Elaine.

'I'm Elaine Weston. I'm a partly retired doctor and I write paranormal romance. Not very successfully I'm afraid. There doesn't seem to be the market for it these days. Unless there is, and I just don't write it very well. I had an agent but unfortunately she retired. I'd love another one, but well, we'll see.' She hunched her shoulders and gave a little excited smile.

'I can't wait to get going! Lovely soup by the way. What's happened to Mr Forest? Isn't he joining us?'

Oh God, I'd almost forgotten about him. Should I make up a tray of stuff for his lunch?

'He always eats at one-thirty apparently,' I said.

'Well he'd better hurry up or we'll have eaten everything,' Nancy said tartly, taking another piece of bread. 'That'll teach him.'

I looked wildly around gauging how much food was left and what I would do if he came out to find nothing left but a few crumbs and some Stilton.

We all looked towards the closed bedroom door and waited for a second in case Oliver was about to come crashing out, snarling and looking for food. Nothing happened so we all took some more cheese and grapes and carried on chatting.

'Well have a good look around the house. There's an interesting book about its history on the desk in the hall. Find yourselves a nice spot to settle down and write this afternoon,' I said. 'There are plenty of armchairs in the sitting room, and a dining room if anyone prefers a table. I'll be making cake for tea and sorting out this evening's meal if anyone needs anything.'

'And I'll be going out to the local shop later if there's anything you need picking up,' Helena said. 'There's a newsagent, a grocer, and a couple of other gift shop sort of places. The church is fourteenth century with a fifteenth-century rood screen if that type of thing interests you. The tower is open on Wednesdays. I checked.'

I took a sneaky look at my watch; it was one-twenty-eight. Was Oliver going to be so precise? If so, he was verging on the obsessive-compulsive spectrum in my opinion.

His bedroom door opened and Oliver stood there, still looking rather rumpled, almost as though he'd been sleeping. Surely not?

'Ah, this must be Mr Forest,' Nancy said. 'Pleasure to meet you. Do join us.'

Oliver favoured the group with a bad-tempered stare and it was obvious he hadn't had any intention of sitting down, but then Nick stood up and pulled out a chair for him, shaking his hand and introducing himself. Oliver was rather blindsided into it.

'I was just going to have something in my room,' he said.

'Oh that would be a pity,' Vivienne said, patting the chair next to her. 'We're all writers. We spend more than enough time on our own. Come and sit down. Tell us all about yourself.'

Oliver darted a rather accusing look at me; like it was my fault he had no social graces. I don't think so.

'Well if I'm not interrupting anything ...' He came and sat down, handing his stick rather arrogantly to Nick who hung it up on the back of the kitchen door.

'How did you hurt your leg?' Nancy asked.

'Bike accident,' Oliver replied tersely. 'There's supposed to be soup? I presume all the crashing about and door slamming resulted in something?'

'Oooh yes, sorry.'

I darted off to the stove where, thank heavens, the remains of the vegetable soup were still steaming. The others, still not properly aware of his prickly nature, were polite and engaging – asking him how far he had come to get here, was it his first time with us, what sort of thing was he trying to write?

Oliver replied with resolutely monosyllabic answers until

I brought him back a bowlful of soup and some more hunks of French bread.

'You didn't go to school in Godalming did you?' Nancy asked. 'Your name is familiar. Vivienne and I were teachers there.'

'No.'

'And you didn't go to Oxford?'

'Born in America, educated in Scotland.'

'I was going to New York just before Christmas,' I said. 'Tickets bought and everything. I even had an ESTA and then ... well I didn't.'

I tailed off into stuttering silence. I hadn't gone to New York because of course Matt had dumped me and taken someone else – but that might be a share too far.

Oliver shot me another look and this one was far from friendly although what I had done to annoy him this time I wasn't sure.

'Anyway, Oliver, tell us what you write,' Vivienne said.

Oliver didn't look at her, but concentrated on his soup. 'Thrillers.'

Nancy didn't think much of this answer. 'And?'

'Political, and sometimes aspects of espionage.'

'Sounds good,' Nick said. 'Are you published?'

'I have a paperback out fairly soon.'

Everyone sat up a bit straighter, me included. Of course! Pippa had mentioned a launch. A book launch! This was exciting stuff; it was what we all aimed for.

'And what are you doing at the moment? I mean why are you here?' Nancy said. She was persistent – you had to say that for her.

'Working on the next one.'

'And how's it going?'

'OK.'

There was an uncomfortable silence for a moment while we all thought what to say next.

'None of the demon writer's block then?' Elaine said. 'You don't find yourself sitting there not knowing what on earth to write?'

'No,' he said with a little snort of laughter as though the very idea was too ridiculous.

'Oh I do. It's awful when you sit there in front of a blank screen and your mind is equally empty isn't it?'

The others made general noises of agreement and sympathy.

Helena took up the thread. It was a useful topic of conversation to get things moving. 'I mean it happens, doesn't it? I wonder how we all cope with it?' she said.

We looked around the table for suggestions and unexpectedly, Oliver got in first. 'There's no such thing as writer's block.'

'Really, do you think so?' Elaine said.

'Have you ever heard a girl in a supermarket complaining she had checkout block? I used to be a teacher and we all know what a thankless job that can be but ever heard of a teacher with teacher's block? Basically, it's a fancy name for laziness and lack of discipline. People moaning about their pathetic word count when they've spent most of the morning on social media looking at pictures of kittens or playing games.'

Well that told us. I mean I've looked at pictures of kittens – of course I have. And everyone likes Candy Crush don't they?

Oliver finished his soup, the spoon scraping on the bottom of the bowl. He looked up at the unexpected silence. 'I seem to have spoiled your flow,' he said.

I felt it was up to me to get things going again. 'OK, what does everyone do if you find your story has stalled into a soggy mess in the middle?'

Nancy chipped in. 'My book is such a muddle and I know it's because I work in fits and starts. I might leave it for a couple of weeks because I'm doing some tutoring or I'm on holiday. Then I can hardly remember who is the main character, let alone who are the suspects or who actually did it.'

Oliver looked at his watch, a chunky, expensive-looking thing on his tanned wrist. I think he was keen to get away. 'You've solved your own problem. Write every day and plot properly. It sounds as though you haven't plotted your book at all, so it's not surprising if you get in a muddle, is it?'

'Do you write every day?' Nick asked, squaring his shoulders as though going into battle.

'Yes,' Oliver said, pushing his chair back, ready to get up. 'And where do you get your ideas?' Nick said.

Oliver suddenly realized he was the centre of attention and everyone had stopped eating to listen to him. He looked very uncomfortable. 'Well where do *you* get your ideas?' he fired back.

Oliver for some reason then had second thoughts about leaving, pulled his chair back to the table and unfortunately began to focus on the cheese in front of him. 'Nice Stilton,' he said. 'Well aired.'

I hoped he wasn't going to eat too much of it if it made him grouchy and sleepy as Pippa had suggested. He was bad enough already.

We all started talking at once to cover the difficult pause in the conversation. Elaine and Nancy liked to scour local papers for ideas. Vivienne liked daytime TV shows where unappealing people aired their dirty laundry to whoops and cheers from the audience.

Nick liked the broadsheets. Helena listened to the children who came into the after-school reading club she had started at her library.

'And what do you like to do?' Oliver said, turning his laser gaze in my direction.

My mouth went dry. I took a sip of water. 'I don't know. Go for walks. Visit old houses,' I said at last, sounding rather dull even to myself.

'Go for walks,' Oliver said thoughtfully. 'Visit old houses. Hmm, wouldn't you like to do something more *exciting*?'

He looked at me again and I swear I could sense him reading my thoughts or certainly seeing through my noisy bravado to the insecure specimen underneath. It wasn't a comfortable feeling.

'Or maybe do something more daring?' he added.

I could feel a blush starting, so I began to gather the dirty plates together to cover my confusion.

'Don't you ever do anything thrilling? Don't you have crazy moments?' Oliver continued, waggling jazz hands.

I thought about it.

The craziest thing I had done recently was having XX Hot Sauce at Nando's for a dare instead of my usual choice of Mango and Lime. And I won't be doing *that* again in a hurry, I can tell you.

Exciting moments? Exciting moments?

I tried to think of an exciting moment I was prepared to share with the group. One not involving last summer's final reductions at L. K. Bennett.

'I don't think I do,' I said at last.

Elaine gasped. 'What, never?'

Vivienne sighed. 'That's one of the saddest things I've ever heard. How old are you, Billie? Thirty-four, thirty-five?'

'Twenty-nine,' I muttered standing up a bit straighter and trying to look younger.

'Well you should be doing exciting things on a regular basis. Daily or hourly if at all possible,' Vivienne said with a knowing look.

Nancy chimed in. 'Let's think of something exciting for Billie to do.'

This was terrible. Everyone was looking at me. I suddenly felt like the most pathetic, most boring person in the universe. My hands weren't working properly and I dropped a couple of spoons onto the floor. Bending to pick them up I was sure my arse must have looked the size of Pluto.

When I stood up I saw the smallest of smiles flickering across Oliver's face. I realized he had done what he wanted: changed the focus of the conversation from himself to me. He hadn't finished yet either.

'So you don't ever do anything crazy or exciting? I wonder why not. Perhaps you should? Take some chances. Have some adventures. Do something wild and irresponsible before you're thirty.' Oliver gave a broad white smile, changing his face from brooding Mr Rochester into something rather glorious. 'I mean, have you travelled much?'

I began to stammer a bit, a childhood habit I thought I'd grown out of.

'I've been here and there, you know G-Greece. And- and- and the Isle of Wight. I can't afford to go too far.'

'You could have come to India with me. I did ask you to, several times,' Helena muttered. 'It was really cheap.'

'Could we talk about something else?' I said rather heatedly. I began collecting more plates and bowls, making a lot of noise and clatter in the process.

I went over to the sink, still blushing furiously, and ran some hot water over the plates before stacking them in the dishwasher.

Helena followed me. 'OK?'

'Fine.'

Oliver stood up, collected his stick, and made his way back to his room. 'Right then I'd better get on with some work. That's why we're here after all isn't it?'

The others watched in silence until he had gone into his room and closed the door, then an excited whispering began between Elaine, Nancy, and Vivienne while Nick sat looking thoughtful, gnawing at his thumbnail.

'I must have met him somewhere because his face is so familiar. But I can't have gone to school with him because I've never been to Scotland,' Nick said at last.

He stood up and started collecting the water glasses until Helena came across with a tray and stopped him.

'There will be cake and tea at four-thirty,' I said. 'You're all free to do what you like. Do some writing or editing or plotting or just have a sleep.'

'Well if you're sure?' Nick said. 'Although I like the idea of a quick walk into the village later if you don't mind company, Helena?'

Helena fidgeted a bit and the glasses on her tray rattled. 'No, super! I mean it would be nice. In about an hour?'

'Perfect.'

Nick darted off upstairs and we encouraged the others towards the sitting room where the wood burner was throwing out an immense amount of heat. I would have opened a couple of windows, but they seemed quite contented. Elaine went to her nook under the stairs and was soon tapping away on her laptop while Nancy and Vivienne picked their places on the sofas and settled down to spend the rest of the afternoon dozing and chatting, hopefully with a bit of writing thrown in at some point.

I finished the coffee preparations and made Helena take the next eight-cup cafetière in to Oliver. She reported back that he was standing looking out of his window into the garden and didn't say much except a vague thank you.

I can only assume he suffered from raging insomnia with so much caffeine inside him on a daily basis. Still, in the immortal words of my long-gone boyfriend, writing was after all only making stuff up and drinking coffee. Oliver must be writing *a lot* – that's all I can say.

Chapter Four

I spent the afternoon chopping yet more vegetables ready for the beef in red wine casserole we were going to have that evening. I made sure I did all I could to keep the noise to a minimum and didn't slam a single cupboard door. I even turned the radio off; usually I sing along. I have an unusual voice. Matt once described me as singing in a bunch of keys. I think he was trying to be funny?

Why did I put up with him for so long? I have no idea. He wasn't funny at all I eventually realized, just rather spiteful. You know the sort. One of those men who make themselves feel better by making you feel worse. And, of course, I'd been pathetically grateful just to have a boyfriend so I was one half of *BillieandMatt* instead of being a spare part that people were always trying to find dates for.

Helena went upstairs to get a coat ready for her walk into the village. She came down with fresh lipstick and her red hair tousled artfully into a messy chignon, two things I'm sure weren't necessary just to go and get milk and low-fat spread.

Helena then remembered she had forgotten the coat so, giggling, had to go back upstairs again to fetch it.

The two of them shuffled off into the village like the Start-Rite kids, not holding hands exactly but definitely connecting. Well lucky Helena, I thought. I could see he was certainly rather cute. And Helena – like me – had been going through what I think is referred to as a 'dry spell' over the last few months. Heaven knows why Helena should be unattached. She's really attractive. Trouble is she's never really realized that and she spends most of her time in libraries surrounded by elderly newspaper readers, young mothers, or school-age children.

And me? I'm lying fallow, like a field that's recently had all its vigour drained out of it through over-cropping, courtesy of my last significant other. Matt was really gorgeous-looking, a skilled carpenter and furniture restorer who was more than happy to spend a week buffing a table but didn't bother to spend more than five minutes polishing me.

My mother said he was a Neanderthal and I would be better off buying furniture from IKEA rather than expecting him to do anything for me. He also chiselled away at my self-confidence with horrible precision, alienated most of my friends, and laughed at my feeble attempts to diet, manage my hair, and find a serious job.

I can see all of that now, but at the time of course I just put up with it. The trouble is I have the memory of an elephant and I never forget any slight no matter how small. (I think I might be developing the figure of an elephant but that's another story.)

Anyway, I did learn something; when we split up I realized how much easier life could be. I could do what I liked when I liked, and no one said *should you be eating that?* I didn't have to do his laundry, and my hoover no longer clogged up with the wood dust that fell out of his clothing. I decided having a serious boyfriend was far too difficult and time-consuming. Not to mention expensive. I wasn't bothered about being alone. Well not much.

I now qualified as what the government describes as 'just managing'. Good job I could type and was a whiz at conjuring up incredible meals out of very little. I really should find a proper job though. A route through to the future and my perilous old age. It was a topic that, often in the stilly watches of the night, bothered me a great deal.

I finished assembling the beef casserole – with button mushrooms, baby onions, bay leaves, and a bouquet garni – and sacrificed a whole bottle of red wine in the process. Well, minus a tiny bit.

I'd brought the apple pie with me so all I had to do was knock up some duchesse potatoes, prep some green beans, and I was done. I began clearing down and arranging cutlery in the formal dining room.

It was a glorious setting too, with twelve chairs and a highly polished table; it would have had Matt dribbling with pleasure.

If the cheating bastard had been here to see it.

And if he'd had the brain to actually write a book in the first place.

And needed to go on a writing retreat, which obviously he didn't – having the brain the size of a peanut and the attention span of a woodlouse.

#Arse.

The two alcoves either side of the fireplace were filled with shelves and a wide selection of books. It was a room just made for huge family lunches and a coterie of rosy-cheeked little girls in sparkly Monsoon party dresses.

Helena and Nick didn't return until an hour and a half later. Considering the local shops were five minutes' walk away, I guessed they had been wandering about aimlessly, casting shy glances at each other. It seemed highly unlikely they had got lost unless they had both developed the most diabolical sense of direction.

Nick went off upstairs to unpack and do some writing in his room and Helena mooned around, fiddling with her hair and going over every detail of their unremarkable and entirely predictable conversation. It seemed to consist of tedious teenage topics.

Favourite colour, best subject at school, ideal holiday?

I fully expected them to progress over the course of the week to deeper interests: preferred biscuit for dunking, favourite film, and best chocolate bar.

I left Helena tidying up, collecting coffee mugs, and putting out slices of the fruitcake I had made the previous day. I went to get changed out of my food-splattered jumper and pull on a new shirt, dithering about how many buttons to undo. I eventually did most of them up as I thought it was a bit early to be showing off my rather generous cleavage on purpose. It makes a surprise appearance fairly often; perhaps I should go for a proper bra fitting one of these days? My mother was always trying to get me to do that. I shuddered at the thought.

I spent ten minutes applying a fresh layer of eye shadow – blended in for that smoky-eyed look that obviously is important when you're about to make tea for seven people and open up a packet of chocolate digestives. Then I messed about for a further five minutes with lipstick. I eventually wiped most of it off and went down into the kitchen and slunk into the pantry to have a sneaky glass of red wine before anyone caught me.

I grabbed my laptop and returned to the corner of the kitchen I had earmarked as mine. It had a comfortable chair and it wasn't overlooked, which meant in an instant I could swap from writing my deathless prose to checking Facebook undetected.

It also had a nice view of the garden. It was probably filled with colour in the summer but now at the tail end of February it was dull and rather ugly with the straggling stems of last year's plants drooping over the borders. As the last of the frail light of the afternoon faded, a thin fog began to form over the lawn, hovering and curling like smoke.

I shivered although the room was warm and glanced over towards Oliver's room. I wondered what he was doing in there and why he was so irritable all the time.

Helena went to look at the guidebook on top of the sideboard, left by the homeowner, and flicked through a few pages, humming tunelessly.

I looked up. 'Go on then,' I said.

'Go on then what?'

'Tell me some more about Nick.'

'Oh ...' she waved a careless hand '... he seems lovely. Nothing more to say really. He lives quite near my mother.'

She put the guidebook down and went to look at one of the dull watercolours on the wall next to the telephone.

'And? You like him don't you?' I said.

Helena shrugged, feigning disinterest very badly.

'Oh he's easy to talk to. You know.'

'He likes you,' I said. 'Pity we've just missed Valentine's Day.'

Her face brightened. 'Do you think he likes me? Really?'

Finally the floodgates were unleashed. 'He's so funny too. Do you know we both went to the Slimbridge Wildfowl place a couple of years ago at Easter? He was taking his nieces and I went with my mother. Just think, we could have met then, or passed each other on the way to the bird hides.'

'Just think!' I said.

Helena stuck her tongue out at me and went to fill the kettle.

*

The writers left their lairs and returned to the kitchen promptly at four-thirty for fruitcake, biscuits, and tea.

Everyone was happy with the house and how comfortable it was. Nancy had been reading through her book, trying to sort the muddles out and attempting to plot it properly. Vivienne had read the house guidebook and discovered the tale of a shocking relationship between a gentleman who lived there in the nineteenth century and his ward, a girl more than half his age. They seemed to have produced three children who were passed off as foundlings and when the girl had threatened to confess the truth to the local rector, her guardian had strangled her – a crime for which he was hanged. Vivienne was thrilled and determined to transpose the tale into the twenty-first century, adding more scandalous detail and possibly some bondage.

There was no sign of Oliver for which I was grateful and eventually people went off to their preferred chairs to continue writing. I was washing up and about to wrap the remnants of the cake in foil when Oliver's door opened.

'Oh! Have I missed tea?' he said looking around rather bleary-eyed.

I swear to God he'd been sleeping again.

'No problem, I'll make some more if you want it,' I said. He was doing this on purpose. Just to be bloody difficult. 'It won't take a moment.'

'Go on then,' he said, pulling out a chair and sitting down.

I flicked on the kettle and made more tea, rinsing out the pot and dropping in fresh tea bags. No sooner had I dowsed them in boiling water than he said, 'I don't want tea. I'll have coffee.'

I gritted my teeth, chucked the tea away, and made coffee instead.

Back at the table he was looking into space. I put the cafetière down in front of him and offered him one of the giant mugs.

He looked at it for a moment and then pushed it back across the table to me. 'I don't know why you always give me those. I'd really prefer an ordinary one.'

'But Pippa ...' I bit back the protest and went to find him another mug, which I placed in front of him. 'Sorry.'

He didn't answer but poured himself some coffee and took a slice of cake.

'What have you been doing?' he said.

'Cooking, clearing up, washing up,' I said cheerfully as I put some dirty mugs into the dishwasher.

'Nothing exciting then?'

I swear he was laughing at me and I felt my hackles rising in annoyance.

No, I would be calm and not lose my rag. I would take a deep cleansing breath and think nice thoughts. I would not knock the milk jug over accidentally on purpose so it soaked his legs.

'I like doing it. I like looking after people. And I might get some writing done later, *after I've abseiled off the roof*,' I added under my breath. 'And you? What are you writing about?'

Oliver topped up his coffee.

'Sandstorms. War. Nothing to appeal to you. I mean there are no cupcakes or shoes. So you really enjoy doing this?'

I bit back my annoyance at such a patronizing attitude.

'Do I like running retreats? Yes I do.' *Otherwise I wouldn't do them.* 'Are you enjoying being here?'

He shrugged and took another bite of cake.

'I mean are you sufficiently relaxed to write? No plot holes or – you know – writer's block to worry about?'

'What?' he looked up rather sharply.

'I said plot holes and writer's block. You don't suffer from those then? Oh no that's just lack of discipline or something isn't it?'

He stood up, favouring me with a hard look, and without a word stomped back into his room, taking his coffee with him.

Well someone was grumpy. I mean grumpier than usual. It must have been the Stilton.

Chapter Five

That evening Oliver didn't come out to join us for a drink before dinner. And he still hadn't come out when we sat down to eat.

Helena and I did Rock, Paper, Scissors and went to the best of three. She lost so I made her go and knock on his door. She returned very quickly, pulling a face. We went and had a muttered discussion in the hall out of earshot of the others.

'Blimey, he's in a mood. He practically growled. He's writing. He says he'll grab something later.'

'It's gone eight o'clock. We'll have tidied up and set the things out for breakfast by the time he comes out. Does he want something in his room?'

'I don't know. I didn't ask. He's looking very thundery – I couldn't wait to get out of there,' Helena hissed.

'Jeez. Come on, let's get back to the others.'

'I'll open some more white wine. The red is already on the table.'

Oliver Forest must have been in the middle of a really determined sulk because the aroma of the beef casserole was wonderful. It would have persuaded anyone else out into the open but not him. I almost felt like wafting it towards his door with a tea towel, but undoubtedly he would have caught me doing it, so I didn't. It wasn't as though I minded that much to be honest. He could eat when he liked really; it was just his attitude that got me going.

'No Mr Forest this evening?' Elaine asked as we came back into the dining room. 'Perhaps he's finding the distance from his bed to the dining room too difficult as well?'

I looked at her and caught the twinkle in her eye before she returned to her meal.

'Lovely casserole,' Nancy said. 'Really delicious sauce.'

'It should be – it's ninety per cent red wine,' I said.

'Fabulous. So how have people got on today?' Vivienne asked, helping herself to more green beans. 'I did awfully well. I'd been having trouble with the scene involving a pair of handcuffs and some tangerines—'

Nancy put her knife and fork down with a clatter. 'Viv, leave it!'

Across the table Nick laughed. 'I've been researching sandstorms. My main character has parachuted out of his plane in the Western Desert; well, he's been shoved out. Do you know sandstorms can blow at one hundred kilometres an hour? And in the sixth century an army of fifty thousand soldiers was lost in one?'

'You ought to ask Oliver Forest if you want to learn about sandstorms,' I said acidly. 'He's writing about them too. Well he said he was – he might have been winding me up. He thinks all women ever read about is cupcakes and knitting—'

'I love cupcakes,' Helena said, 'although I'm not so hot on the knitting.'

'And running teashops. I bet if I asked what he was writing about it would just be bombs and submachine guns.'

Nick stopped and looked thoughtfully at me for a moment and then shook his head and carried on eating.

'So how about you, Elaine? How is your work progressing?' I asked.

Elaine was staring into space and jumped as she realized I was talking to her.

'Well this house has given me a marvellous idea for a plot twist. Do you think it would work if my *doctor* – who's just married the vicar's daughter, remember – was the one to poison the squire because he found out the squire was actually her father ... and after the wedding ... no, of course the squire was in India for twenty years so perhaps not. Although he could have just *stolen* the child couldn't he? Or found her at the end of the garden? I wanted to use a bit of folklore about the fairies and how awful they are. Always stealing babies apparently. Oh dear, if I imply he found her I'd have to re-work the whole of the first part yet again. I need to think it through properly. I'm beginning to wonder if Mr Forest isn't right and I should plot the whole thing out properly. It goes against the grain though.'

'I saw someone do a plot sheet once. It looked very complicated,' Nancy said. 'There was something to do with Post-it Notes and different-coloured pens. I don't know what all that was about.'

I passed round the wine again and went to get some more water. In the kitchen I glanced at Oliver's door. It was still closed. I filled the jug and found some ice. I began to worry. What if he was unwell or – encumbered by his plastic boot – had fallen over?

I imagined him prone on the bathroom floor, his head banged up against the radiator, lying in a pool of gore. I'd have to phone an ambulance and there wasn't any phone signal. I could almost see myself running down the road waving my mobile above my head like an Olympic torch ...

I'd better check.

I edged over towards his room on tiptoe and stood listening. Nothing.

I stepped closer, cleared my throat and made sort of 'goodness me I wonder where Oliver is' noises. Nothing.

I knocked and received no reply, so I knocked harder.

After a moment's hesitation I opened the door and looked round. No sign of him anywhere. The room was immaculately tidy, the curtains closed, the bed tightly made, and no sign of Oliver or any of his possessions. I relaxed a bit; perhaps he had left? No, his suitcase was still tucked in next to the wardrobe.

He must have gone out. But how? And why? After insisting he couldn't manage the stairs, would he just go off for a walk? Bloody cheek of the man! I had a good mind to get all his gear together and just move him into another room upstairs and put Elaine into the room she had booked months ago. I'd have to change the bedding though. I mean, I wouldn't want to sleep on someone else's sheets. Even if he wore pyjamas.

I bet he didn't.

I bet he slept with nothing on.

Shut up! Shut up! Stop thinking such ridiculous thoughts! He'd probably kept his clothes on during his nap. Hadn't he? I would.

I didn't think I could bring myself to do it. There would be all sorts of man stuff. I remembered only too clearly what it was like when I went on holiday to Cornwall with Matt. Clothes and shaving kit and personal things with plugs and chargers. I couldn't just, you know, *rummage around in his drawers*. I snorted with laughter despite myself.

There was a sudden movement just out of my eye line.

I turned.

There in the shadowy corner was a naked, one-legged man.

I screamed and instinctively clutched the water jug to my chest. In the same second that the iced water splattered all over me and a couple of ice cubes sneaked down my top into my bra, I realized it was Oliver with his injured leg in a black bin liner. He'd been having a shower. The only correct part of my assumption was he was naked.

Don't look! Don't bloody look for God's sake.

Too late!

Jeeezus!

I shut my eyes as tight as I could and took a step back and of course fell over something. And tipped the rest of the water over myself.

I heard myself yelping like a trampled puppy and someone roaring with laughter and then I fled out of the room. Nancy and Vivienne, alerted by the noise, had come out of the dining room and were standing there. Nancy was still chewing.

'Are you all right?' Vivienne said reaching out a kind hand. 'You're soaking wet. What on earth have you been doing?'

I babbled for a second and then thrust the empty water jug towards her before sprinting upstairs.

I stripped off my clothes, trying hard not to wail too loudly. After all, when you have a house full of guests it's not the done thing. I found a towel and some dry clothes by which time Helena was rattling on the door trying to come in.

'What the hell have you been doing?' she called through the door. 'Are you hurt? Are you OK? Let me in!'

I struggled into a clean top and some jeans that I preferred not to wear as they were a tad tight, and unlocked the door.

'Just don't ask,' I said. 'I'll tell you when you're older and I've stopped cringing.'

'Well obviously you're not going to get away with that. Have you had a shower?'

I rubbed at my wet hair with a towel and glanced in the mirror. I had mascara running down my cheeks. My hair looked as though I'd stuck my finger in a light socket.

'No, I haven't had a shower. Look can you just go back downstairs and keep them all happy for a few minutes? I'll explain later!'

'Well come on and stop messing about,' Helena said chucking me a comb. 'Oliver's just turned up and he wants his dinner.'

*

Oliver didn't even look at me, not so much as a sly glance, a cocked eyebrow, or a supressed snigger to imply he was at all bothered by the last half-hour. I on the other hand was puce with embarrassment. I went to fetch a clean plate for him and placed it on the table before scurrying off, pretending I was checking something in the kitchen. I went back into the pantry and had another sneaky glass of wine to bolster me up.

The apple pie was on the worktop looking glamorous and golden, its sugary top glistening in the kitchen spotlights. There was crème anglaise and vanilla ice cream to go with it, so I pretended to mess around with jugs and saucepans to give myself time to calm down. I was feeling quite hot and bothered and quickly realized my long-sleeved sweatshirt had been a bad choice. I should have gone for a cotton shirt. Or a T-shirt. Or just stayed in my room with a paper bag over my head.

I tried thinking about something else – the plot of my novel. I was writing a scene where the hero meets the feisty young heroine and rescues her from a flash flood. Or should it be from a dangerous dog? Or a dastardly villain with evil intent?

One thing I would not do was allow my hero to continue morphing slowly but steadily into Oliver Forest. With dark hair curling onto his neck and eyes the colour of a summer night sky. White, even teeth. Skin tanned and taut over just the right amount of muscles. Tall, broad shoulders, long legs, narrow hips.

And no clothes.

Blast.

Shut up.

*

I couldn't hide in the pantry forever, obviously. And to try and do so would be really immature and pathetic. I put the pie on a tray and decanted the crème anglaise into a pretty blue and white jug. Then I took the plastic box of vanilla ice cream out of the freezer and carried the lot into the dining room as Helena carried the dirty plates away. Oliver had just finished his casserole and the discussion around the table had moved on to one of our favourite topics: the difficulty of finding an agent.

Elaine was talking.

'I used to have an agent, back in the day, but then I lost her and no one else wanted to take me on. So I was cast out into the literary wilderness. Since then I haven't had much luck finding a replacement – and getting a book published without one is impossible these days. I did wonder about self-publishing and then I didn't have the nerve.'

Nancy nodded vigorously, her grey curls bobbing. 'And the utter shame of a load of one-star Amazon reviews. People can say the nastiest things. And sometimes it's for ludicrous reasons. I read one once where the person had given one star simply because the book had arrived late. And someone else gave five stars because they liked the cover. Nothing to do with the standard of the writing.'

Nick was looking very thoughtful. He threw Oliver a curious glance. 'So what do you think, Oliver?'

Oliver made some sort of non-committal noise and took a sip of red wine.

It was Helena's turn to look pensive. 'Hang on; Pippa said your launch had been delayed because of your accident?'

'What did you do?' Vivienne asked. 'We never did find out.'

'I told you, a spill off my motorbike,' Oliver said.

For some reason I'd assumed he had fallen off a bicycle. There's nothing I find remotely appealing about neon Lycra, padded gel saddles, or aerodynamically designed bike helmets. But motorbike leathers? Big biker boots?

Yummy scrummy! Now you're talking!

I nearly had to grab hold of the back of a chair to steady myself. For heaven's sake what was the matter with me?

Helena wasn't going to be distracted. 'So, this launch. Have you written *other* books? Or is this your first?'

'I'd love a slice of pie,' Oliver said, ignoring the question.

Helena cut him a piece and slid it onto a plate. She pushed the jug of crème anglaise across the table and I handed over the tub of ice cream. 'Anyone else?'

She was busy for a few minutes sorting out the dessert and it wasn't until she was sitting down with a small serving of her own that Helena returned to her question.

'So, Oliver? About this book and the launch? How incredibly exciting. I mean we would give a lot to be having a book launch – small, medium, or otherwise wouldn't we?'

We all nodded in agreement.

'Oh, you know,' he said vaguely.

'Where is it? Can we come?' Nancy said boldly.

'Ludlow. I'm not organizing it,' Oliver said. He jabbed at his dish with his spoon. 'This is delicious by the way. Excellent pastry.'

I don't know if anyone else noticed but I certainly saw what was going on. Oliver was very keen not to talk about himself. He was in a room full of writers and they are some of the nosiest people on the planet, so he was on a hiding to nothing.

'Ludlow is a lovely little town,' Vivienne said. 'I remember going there with the WI years ago. Lots about Catherine of Aragon and Prince Arthur I think.'

I ambled around the table, heading back towards the kitchen, and was almost knocked over by Nick who had darted out of his seat leaving his dessert half eaten. He skidded out into the hallway and I heard him running upstairs to his bedroom two at a time and slamming his bedroom door.

Flipping heck, I hope it wasn't anything to do with our cooking? I mean we had both done a load of online training and certificates about hygiene, food preparation, and handling, but there's always the fear of someone coming down with salmonella or botulism or something isn't there?

I stood at the bottom of the stairs listening for sounds of

retching and heaving but couldn't hear anything, so perhaps he was all right after all. I carried on into the kitchen to start loading the dishwasher with the dinner plates.

By the time I returned to the dining room Nick was back in his place, his hands clasped between his knees. He looked a bit pinched and pale around the mouth.

'Are you OK, Nick?' I asked.

He nodded and didn't speak. He was looking at Oliver with a strange expression.

'Anything wrong?'

He shook his head. Not a sudden attack of typhoid then.

'I know who you are,' Nick blurted out.

We all looked at him, a bit startled.

He was still staring at Oliver.

'I knew your name was familiar. I knew I'd heard of you,' Nick said.

Nancy and Vivienne looked up from their dessert, their synchronized noses scenting some unexpected excitement.

Oliver didn't say anything. He just looked a bit irritated. No it wasn't that – he looked resigned if anything.

Nick went on, his face still pale and determined. 'I just went upstairs to google you. And I can't think why it took me so long. You're one of my favourite writers. I've got your books. I've seen your photo on the dust jackets. You're Ross Black aren't you?'

There was a split second of silence and then an audible intake of breath from the others. Everyone turned as one to look at Oliver, waiting for his reaction. He finished his mouthful of pie and put his spoon down.

He gave a crooked grimace. It was almost a smile but it didn't reach his eyes. 'Ha!' he said.

Chapter Six

We sat in silence for a few seconds and looked at him. In a moment he had changed from being just a disagreeable guest with a leg in a boot to one of the country's most successful writers of thrillers.

Oliver Forest was Ross Black. This man in his perfectly ordinary-looking dark-blue sweater and jeans was *Ross Black*. Seven years ago he'd been teaching maths in an oversubscribed comprehensive, writing a book in the school car park during his lunch hours. It was snapped up by the agent of the day who organized a bidding war and he'd become a literary sensation in the space of a year.

A Hollywood film of his first book, *The Dirty Road*, had been made, with Channing Tatum in the lead role, and there was another one planned for the sequel: *The Fool in Charge.* I had even been to see it. I couldn't remember too much but without a doubt there had been sandstorms, a brilliant car chase, heroism against all the odds, and men with scarves wrapped round their faces. I think there had been a woman with a twisted ankle too come to think of it. I'd been too busy watching the hero's muscles rippling to remember much about her. Except her clothes kept falling off.

His books had topped the bestseller lists; he had been nominated for several prizes and awards. He was a success. His next two books had been bestsellers too. The fourth one, *Death in Damascus*, was due out sometime this year; Uncle Peter had an order in for it.

Oliver Forest would have been all over the celebrity pages if he hadn't been so reclusive. What the hell was he doing with us in the middle of nowhere, eating our food and wandering about with no clothes on?

For a moment it was as though the air had been sucked out of the room. And everyone just sat and gawped at him for a few minutes, waiting for him to do something unexpected and unusual. As though he was a juggling dog.

He didn't really do anything; he just took a bit more ice cream. At last he looked across at us.

'It's no big deal, you know,' he said at last.

'*The Dirty Road* is one of my favourite books,' Nick said at last, hero worship glowing all over his face.

'I bet there are at least four people in this room who haven't read it,' Oliver said.

Elaine fidgeted a little. 'Well I've *heard* of you obviously, but I've never read any of your books.'

'Me neither,' Nancy admitted. 'Not really my thing.'

'Nor me,' Vivienne said. 'I did try one once ... but ...' She tailed off in embarrassment as she realized what she was about to say.

'There you are, told you. Helena? What about you?' Oliver said.

Helena blushed and shook her head. 'Sorry, no.'

'And you, Billie?' He looked at me, his eyes dark and unfathomable.

I would have given a lot to have a heated debate with him about the merits of his books.

I imagined myself musing how the plot had been a bit patchy in places, whether or not a macho, dirty vest-wearing, gun-toting hero was politically acceptable these days despite my secret crush on Bruce Willis and my addiction to the Bourne Trilogy. And was the use of explosives and destruction to solve a political crisis really OK in the twenty-first century? Unfortunately I didn't have the knowledge or the nerve.

'Well, yes ... no. I mean I've always m-meant to read them and I think ... I mean I'm sure I would enjoy them. I think ... I did see the film, well I saw a bit of it once. I went with Matt. My b-boyfriend.'

I have/had a boyfriend. See, I'm not completely pathetic.

I'd been in a crabby mood through most of that film actually. Matt and I had been heading downstream towards the end of our two years together and we both knew it. We'd gone to the cinema because we didn't feel like having sex and it was easier than talking to each other.

I would have preferred to see the latest chick flick playing in Screen 1. All my friends had enjoyed it and my mother described it as nauseating garbage to set the feminist movement back fifty years. So I know I would have enjoyed it. Still, Channing Tatum's rippling muscles were quite enjoyable too.

Now I was a gibbering wreck. It was all I could do to stop staring at Oliver in the first place; now it was going to be hard not to ask for his autograph at some point. I glanced away from him and looked at the bookcases. And yes, there were his books. Three fat hardbacks, immediately recognizable, lined up on the middle shelf. Books the owner of the house obviously liked and had left for guests to read. They were all well thumbed, the dustcovers cracked and discoloured, the gilt of the title letters was tarnished. *The Dirty Road, The Fool in Charge, Glory 17.*

Bloody hell. There we had all been, chattering on about writing and plot holes and word count and our piddling little WIPs. Droning on about how hard it was to get an agent, writer's block, and how was it that pathetically ordinary novels became bestsellers, and in our midst was one of the most successful authors of the last few years. It was one of those cringing moments when you just want to hide behind the sofa. Except there wasn't a sofa to hide behind.

'Well you've just proved my point haven't you?' he said.

'You should have put some cupcakes in or had a fete and then we would have found it more appealing,' I said before I could stop myself.

He bit his lip. 'You could be right,' he said.

Horrified at myself, I stood up and put the lid back on the ice cream so I could put it back in the freezer. We were all crippled with unusual politeness for a while. We chatted quietly about non-contentious issues: what holidays we had planned, how Elaine's recent house move had gone, whether or not Nancy's three sons would ever get around to producing grandchildren. Oliver sat at his end of the table, eyes down, and finished his dessert.

At last he looked up at us. You could tell from his expression he was expecting something. I couldn't imagine what.

Nick was the first to speak to him. 'Um, Oliver, sorry but would you ...'

Oliver put his spoon down with a clatter and gave a humourless laugh.

'Here we go. Now it begins. I knew it wouldn't take you long. There's always something. Would I what? Put in a good word with my publisher? Take a look at your manuscript? Talk about how to get an agent to your writing group? Chat to your book club? Give you a signed hardback to auction for your school? Open your village fete? Speak up to stop your library being closed?'

Nick fidgeted uncomfortably. 'No, I just wondered ... would you pass the red wine, please?'

I stood up and began collecting the dirty pudding bowls together. 'Coffee, everyone? There's more wine here if anyone wants it?' I said, my voice shaking with laughter.

This suggestion met with tremendous approval and everyone started talking at once very loudly. I went out into the kitchen and began making coffee and putting cutlery into the dishwasher. Helena wasn't far behind me.

'Well what do you think? How amazing! Ross Black here! *Ross Black!*'

'Well yes but you've never read one of his books have you?'

'No, but I know a famous author when I meet one. Even if he is a—' Helena struggled to find the right word.

'Rude, self-satisfied twat?' I whispered.

She nodded. 'Yes, I suppose rude, self-satisfied twat would cover it. And we have to put up with it all week. We've always wanted to get a really famous author too. What a pity we got him.'

She finished loading the dishwasher and shut the door. She turned to me, her face thoughtful.

'It's a bit of an opportunity though isn't it? I don't suppose he would do a workshop, do you?'

'What on? Being obnoxious?' I said. 'You must be joking – you heard him just now. I wouldn't give him the satisfaction of asking. He'd only say no and do the sneery thing he does.'

'I haven't seen a sneery thing,' Helena said, puzzled.

'It's just me then. Come on, let's get this coffee into the dining room although, let's be honest, he's had enough caffeine today to run the Grand National.'

I took the tray back into the dining room and found Oliver Forest, or Ross Black, or whatever he wanted to be called, had gone.

'He's in his room,' Nancy said. 'He said he wants his coffee in there.'

'Oh does he? Right then.'

I went stamping back into the kitchen and set out a tray for him with a second cafetière I had found and a second unattractive mug.

'Here,' I said to Helena, 'can you take this to his majesty? I'll start on the saucepans.'

Scrubbing saucepans was the job both of us detested and we went to considerable lengths to avoid doing them, so my offer was unusual in the extreme.

'Bloody hell, are you OK?' Helena said.

'Perfectly,' I said, rolling my sleeves up and getting stuck in. 'I'll get rid of some of my irritation this way. God I wish we could go to the pub!'

Going to the pub was out of the question, of course. We had to be on hand in case there was a food crisis or wine bottle needing to be opened. It would have been very bad form to leave our guests, and anyway it was usually fun to get to know new people and enjoy hearing their writing stories. Adding Oliver Forest into the mix seemed to have affected everything somehow. No it hadn't; it had ruined it. Helena and I were going to have to work hard to get everyone relaxed and cheerful again.

*

We ploughed on, and gradually everyone began to enjoy themselves. This might have had something to do with the unexpected bonus of Oliver taking his coffee and staying in his room for the rest of the evening. Occasionally I went into the kitchen to fetch something or stack a few more dirty dishes on the worktop. Once I heard him shouting into his phone but on the other occasions it was eerily silent.

I tiptoed around as though there was a sleeping tiger behind the door and put the crockery down with exaggerated care. I dropped a teaspoon and waited with bated breath in case he came out roaring, but nothing happened and I slunk back into the sitting room.

'No sign of our celebrity?' Nancy said in a stage whisper.

I shook my head. 'Perhaps he's writing.'

'Or maybe he's gone to bed.' Helena said.

I fought back the mental image of Oliver Forest in bed and asked Nick how his novel was progressing.

We all chatted happily enough until after ten-thirty, which was plenty late enough for me, and then Helena and I set the breakfast table in stressed silence in case we disturbed him. Shortly afterwards I went upstairs. I was quite exhausted. And this was just the beginning.

Helena came up a few minutes later and rummaged around in her suitcase for her pyjamas and her sponge bag. We were sharing a bathroom with Elaine, so we did a bit of polite dodging backwards and forwards until we were sure she had finished her nightly rituals and was safely tucked up in her bed.

I wanted to talk to Helena but as usual she was snoring gently in minutes, the product of an untroubled mind, whereas I lay in bed, unable to sleep at all.

I tried to put Oliver Forest out of my thoughts, but instead I remembered what we'd talked about at lunchtime. I knew everyone was right. My life did need an adrenaline shot. What could I do to make my life more exciting?

I needed a list.

I know, a ten-point plan!

I sat up and reached for my notebook and the pen that lights up in the dark that Helena had given me for my last birthday. What would someone put on an 'adventure list'? Climb mountains? Hmm I'm not really great with heights. Explore foreign lands? That takes money. Learn how to do something dangerous ... Did adventurous have to mean dangerous? I'd prefer it not to. Not only was my budget limited, if I was honest, what I really needed was to take a few more adventurous leaps in my own life. Maybe if I kept to things that were easy to achieve I might actually do it ... because there was no way I was going cliff jumping! Right then ...

1) Go on an ~~expensive~~ unexpectedly cheap holiday. Somewhere I've never been. Take masses of brilliant photos that are not obscured by other people's heads, own finger, or phone case. Win photographic competition.
2) Lose a stone before 1) happens by starting a new clean-eating regime. Raw vegetables instead of chocolate. Fruit instead of ice cream.

3) Declutter wardrobe in manner of impossibly stylish woman. Put all remaining clothes into order using limited colour palette so I don't look as though I've dressed in the dark. Become known as elegant, sophisticated person whose clothes fit. Get measured for bra.
4) Declutter kitchen cupboards. Check use-by dates on <u>all</u> items and <u>discard where appropriate.</u> Do not replace on the off chance I will be using a lot of ground nutmeg any time soon.

I paused to think and chewed the end of my pen.

5) Get second bedroom cleared of all junk. Ditto garden shed. Do not scream and hop about; woodlice are harmless. Find out what purple flower thing in garden is.
6) Find a proper job that pays proper money, has a pension scheme, and paid holidays.
7) Do 6) first. Before all the other things.
8) Get a tattoo. A really small one I can hide.
9) Consider eyebrow waxing.
10) Rethink shoes. Ugg boots – while comfortable and cute – are only suitable for children and people who go to the supermarket in pj's. Wear heels more often so am forced to be elegant and stand up straight and not scuttle around like a beetle on speed.

I read back through the list. It sounded manageable, but also a bit outside my comfort zone – when was the last time I had allowed myself to imagine I could ever be stylish? I'd never been stylish. But wasn't that the point? And a tattoo? I wasn't even sure I approved of them.

And could I start a new career? Even just thinking it made me shiver with anticipation.

Maybe it would be possible. But doing what? For the moment I needed to concentrate on tomorrow. I was going to make a Victoria sponge and a chicken carbonara sauce. And two quiches for lunch.

Would Oliver approve of that?

Real men don't eat quiche.

Matt said that the first and only time I made it for him. I should have known then it was never going to work out between us. He didn't like salad either and only tolerated fruit as a decoration.

Did Oliver eat fruit? And salad? Would he like the cake I was going to make?

I clicked off my pen and lay down again, impatient with myself. I'd just written a list of all my big adventurous plans and I couldn't stop thinking about a man! And an annoying man at that. Anyone would think he was the only guest here; the others were equally as important. Just because he was famous didn't mean I should fixate on his needs.

His needs.

Did Oliver Forest have *needs*?

What sort of needs?

Was Pippa his girlfriend? Was she in love with him? All the evidence pointed to no.

But maybe she was and that was why she was prepared to tolerate his moods?

Not a chance in hell. Surely not, considering the way he spoke to her! Even I wouldn't stand someone treating me like that and my self-esteem had been flattened over the years.

Did he have a softer side when they were alone together? Was he sweet to her when no one else was looking?

Perhaps he was bad tempered because he was missing her? Perhaps he was sex-starved.

Was he good in bed?

FFS! Shut up, woman!

I thumped my pillow and tried to think about something else.

It struck me that: *11) Finish the book and get it published* hadn't figured in my thinking at all. That was a bit of a surprise wasn't it?

There was no denying it: my work of so-called light-hearted Tudor romance had solidified into a turgid disaster over the last six months. I think it's very hard to write about love when you're not in love yourself. Perhaps I should shift to writing about revenge killings?

There was a soft glow from the street light outside the house but at midnight it went out and the room was intensely dark. As my eyes grew accustomed to the gloom I looked through the open curtain next to my bed and saw a clear, dark sky studded with stars.

I tried the usual methods of getting myself to sleep. What would I do if I won the lottery? One million? Ten million?

Nope, nothing worked.

Perhaps I should try and read one of Oliver's books?

My eyes snapped open.

Now that was a thought! I wondered if there were any rude bits? You know, *sex scenes*?

For God's sake, how childish was I?

I could certainly remember some erotic scenes in the film; the sight of Channing Tatum with his shirt off was the only thing that made the film worth seeing in my opinion. Had Oliver written them, or had they been put in by Hollywood? I couldn't wait to find out. I lay wide-eyed in the gloom and considered the possibilities.

I'd not read many sex scenes by male authors. It wasn't as though I went looking for them, but I was intrigued. Would Oliver's style be realistic? Would his hero dump his sub-machine gun behind the bedroom door and do erotically slow and explicit things to some silky-skinned beauty who had been panting for him since their first meeting?

Or maybe his sand-encrusted hero would be forceful and determined, sweeping women away on a tide of lust and pheromones? I could almost imagine him, pulling his scarf off his face with a devilish laugh and ripping her flimsy garments with his strong white teeth? Coo er, actually that sounded rather good to me.

Or possibly he would close the bedroom door behind him in a flurry of asterisks.

Perhaps by the end of the week he would be swapping tips with Vivienne about alternative names for body parts? Maybe I could sneak downstairs without disturbing anyone and get one of his books off the bookcase and find out? It suddenly seemed a really exciting prospect. And then I fell asleep.

Chapter Seven

The following day I woke late to find Helena had already dressed and gone downstairs. I hurriedly dragged some clothes on and ran a brush through my hair, wondering how I had managed to sleep through her departure. She wasn't usually so considerate. If she was up then generally her view was I should be too.

She was in the kitchen prising frozen croissants apart with a knife and putting them onto a baking tray. She had already sorted the juices and jams ready for people to come down for breakfast.

'Afternoon,' she said rather tartly.

'Sorry. I slept really badly,' I said. 'I didn't hear you get up.'

'I chucked a pillow at you and even that didn't work.'

I jerked my head towards Oliver's room. 'Any sign of himself?'

'Nothing yet. I expect he's still asleep. I've tried to keep the noise down.'

I looked at the kitchen clock; it was nearly eight o'clock – breakfast time – and I could hear someone coming downstairs. It was Nancy, swathed in a strange voluminous garment of various shades of purple topped off with a jaunty cerise beret. She was certainly eye-catching.

'I can smell coffee,' she said. 'Exactly what I need.'

Helena put a tray of clean mugs and a freshly filled cafetière on the table in front of her and Nancy helped herself.

'So? Any sign of our celebrity?' she hissed.

'Nothing yet,' Helena said.

I went to fetch the milk and yogurt from the fridge only to find they were already on the table. I began to fidget. I remembered last night, wondering what sort of erotica Oliver was into. The thought still made me feel rather odd.

How casually could I go into the dining room and take one of his books from the shelf?

'Was everything cleared out of the dining room last night?' I said airily. 'I'll go and check we didn't miss anything.'

I took a damp cloth, went into the dining room, and pulled the curtains back to let in the pale morning sunshine. The room smelled of old beams and dust and I would have opened the window if I had been tall enough to reach the catch. There were a couple of wine glasses on the mantelpiece to take and I wiped a handful of crumbs off the table. Then I went to the bookcase and pulled out *The Dirty Road*.

The cover was pretty much what I had expected. A dark-haired man, his forehead smeared with dirt, squinting against the sun, a scarf around the lower half of his face. It's called a shemagh by the way – I looked it up. In the background there was a well-endowed woman in need of a bra fitting, crouched on the ground looking hopefully towards our sandblasted hero, and what looked like an oil refinery on fire in the distance. So far so predictable.

I heard a burst of laughter from the kitchen and the unmistakeable sound of Vivienne's hooting laugh. I winced. Oliver would love waking up to her racket.

I stuffed *The Dirty Road* up my jumper and dashed up the back stairs to put the book under my pillow for later.

In my absence everyone, except Oliver of course, had arrived. It's like being on holiday; at home you'd skip breakfast and have two cups of coffee but in a hotel you feel honour bound to go for it. This morning we were offering Danish pastries and croissants and by the looks of things our guests were hoovering them up as fast as possible. Jars of apricot and raspberry jam were flashing around the table at high speed and the new block of butter was covered in stab marks and flakes of pastry.

Helena was already making more coffee and the chat was all wonderfully lively and book-related. Which is one of the great things about writers: they will talk for hours about their work in progress and other writers will listen and make helpful suggestions. Everywhere else people's eyes glaze over and they ask when your book is going to be in Waterstones.

'No sign of Oliver?' I asked as I took a new batch of croissants to the table.

'Not a squeak. Do you think he's dead?'

'Well if he is I'm not going to look. Not after the last time!'

'Oh yes, you never did tell me what happened,' Helena whispered. 'Go on.'

'I made a complete tit of myself in every sense of the word,' I said.

'Huh?' Helena's face screwed up in confusion.

'I fell over and spilled a jug of water. Remember? I was soaking and you thought I'd had a shower?'

'Yes that sounds like you. More coffee, Nick?'

Helena sailed off to where Nick was sitting happily larding slabs of butter onto his croissant and she topped up his mug. They exchanged a shy smile and I shook my head at her. Everyone knows you shouldn't mix business with pleasure, don't they? I speak from bitter experience; I went out with an electrician once and my immersion heater never worked properly again after he mended it.

At last everyone was sorted and we sat down to join them, eager to hear everyone's plans for the day.

Nancy was going to resume her plotting; Vivienne was still busy with the handcuffs scene and was wondering if it was possible for her heroine to unlock them with a safety pin in her teeth. Vivienne admitted when she was seventeen she had once successfully picked a lock with a crochet hook so she could get at her father's sherry.

'I'd quite like to go up the church tower tomorrow if anyone fancies it?' Nick said.

Helena jerked in her chair with the prospect.

I saw Vivienne and Nancy exchange a meaningful look.

'We're not very good with steps either are we, Nancy?' Vivienne said.

'And it's a bit wet for me,' Elaine said.

Helena tried to appear casual. 'I'd love to ... if you didn't mind ...'

'No, it would be lovely,' Nick said, his freckled face flushed with pleasure, 'so I'd better get on with some actual writing today. I promised myself I'd get past fifty thousand words this week and I've got a way to go.'

He jammed in the last of his breakfast, made some half-hearted attempt to help Helena tidy up, and went off upstairs to get his laptop. Several cups of coffee later the others followed suit and Helena and I were left to clear away the breakfast things. It was nearly nine-thirty.

'What about Oliver?' Helena said.

I shrugged. 'I'll arrange some things down this end of the table and wait and see if he comes out.'

I set to with my cloth, wiping up jam and making the table look reasonably attractive again. Helena loaded the dishwasher and washed the baking trays. Still there was no sign of him. I rinsed out a cafetière, loaded it up with fresh coffee, and put Oliver's hideous bucket-mug next to it. Then we both went upstairs to get our laptops and tidy ourselves up. I for one had a blob of apricot jam on my shirt.

'So you're off with Nick Fitzgerald again?' I said.

Helena tried and failed to look cool.

'We're just going to look at a church and go up the tower,' she said. 'That's all. Not as though we're going clubbing is it? OK if I grab a shower?'

'Of course, and I don't think he's the sort to go clubbing any more than you are,' I said, scrabbling in my suitcase for a clean shirt. There were three, all of them a bit crumpled. I never seemed to get properly unpacked at these things. The week always ended with my clothes in a big untidy heap as though someone had stirred the contents of my suitcase with a giant spoon.

Helena on the other hand had hung all her tiny clothes up in the wardrobe and filled two drawers. Perhaps that's why she always appeared neat and crisp and I usually looked as though I'd just come back from a jumble sale?

(Point 3 on my to-do list would soon sort this out.)

Anyway, it was early days so I still had a chance of appearing relatively tidy. I had yet another cake to make too – better get on with it.

Downstairs the kitchen was pretty much as we had left it except the cafetière and the bucket-mug were missing. I think there were also a couple of pastries fewer. So Oliver had taken the opportunity to come out, grab some breakfast, and disappear back into his room again. Honestly, we weren't so bad were we? Did he really need to sneak about avoiding us? How childish.

I worked on in silence for a while until the cake was in the oven and I was taking the first batch of cookies out when Oliver's door opened.

He stood there for a moment watching me and then he held out his cafetière towards me accusingly. I waited for him to say something, but he didn't. He just shook the cafetière towards me as though I was psychic. I wiped my hands on a tea towel.

'Can I help you?' I said.

I knew I was being stroppy. I knew exactly what he wanted. Personally, I would have thought he'd had more than enough caffeine for one day and it was only ten-fifteen.

'What do I have to do to get this refilled?' he said.

I went over to where he stood, and took the coffee pot from him.

'You could ask nicely?' I said with a saccharine smile. 'It's usually a good starting point.'

'I assumed you would have been a bit more on the ball by now?' he snapped and went back into his room, slamming the door behind him.

'Well you know what they say about assume,' I muttered.

I made coffee, put it on a tray, took it with some of the fresh cookies to his door, and knocked.

70

'Yep.'

Do come in, thank you so much.

'Your coffee and some cookies.'

How kind.

'I don't want those,' he said. 'You women are obsessed with cake and biscuits. Take them away.'

You women?

He hadn't even looked up from his laptop. I felt rather like tipping the whole lot over him. Except it would probably result in a legal claim for actual bodily harm; not a good idea if you think about it.

International bestselling author in burns unit.

'I swear she did it on purpose,' said Ross Black, his face and both hands heavily bandaged. In the background I was being led away in handcuffs.

I put the tray down on the table, picked up the basket of cookies, and turned to go.

'Lunch is at one o'clock,' I said encouragingly.

'One moment,' he said.

I stood with the basket held out in front of me like a begging bowl as he typed on, his fingers rattling the keys at great speed. What was he going to say? Was he going to make an effort to be polite?

Maybe he would say something to make up for his rudeness.

Sorry if I sounded a bit brusque back then. I'm on a tight schedule. My editor wants this by yesterday.

I looked around the room as I waited, hoping for some clues into his character. Maybe a photograph, or some personal items. Everything was still extraordinarily tidy. It didn't look as though anyone had slept in the bed. Perhaps he hadn't;

maybe he slept bolt upright in the wardrobe with his sweater hooked over a hanger? The waste paper basket was filled with tightly screwed-up bits of paper and on top of the chest of drawers there was a mobile phone on charge.

'I can come back later if you prefer,' I said.

He held up an index finger and then carried on typing. He was evidently on a roll and the words were flowing.

At last he stopped, poured some coffee out into his mug, and drank some while he scrolled back to check something. He made a sort of harrumph, annoyed noise on a couple of occasions and sipped his coffee. I stood there like a spare part fidgeting from one foot to the other. I cleared my throat to remind him I was still there, and he looked up at me.

'I've told you, I eat at one-thirty,' he replied at last.

I took a deep breath, ready to give him the benefit of my opinion, and then bit back my rising temper. He was the paying guest after all. He was perfectly entitled to his preferences. I shouldn't be so dogmatic.

'I'll bring something in for you then,' I said and left him to it.

I think I saw the sudden movement of his head as he looked up, but I didn't wait to hear what he was going to say and I had the feeling I was being rude and unprofessional. I like looking after people; I like it when they are happy. Nothing seemed to be working with Oliver Forest.

I closed his door with care despite longing to slam it off its hinges and was about to tell Helena exactly what I thought of him, but she wasn't in the kitchen. The timer was making apologetic bleeping noises, and something was burning.

My beautiful cake was ruined thanks to Oliver bloody Forest. I grabbed a tea towel, yanked the cake tins out of the oven and chucked them in the sink. It was half past ten now, time to think about elevenses for the others.

Helena came into the kitchen frowning, her hair still damp from the shower.

'I can smell burning,' she said.

'Yes I know, it's my cake. It was going to be lovely too,' I said mournfully. 'Flaming Oliver bloody Forest – he kept me in his room for so long it burned.'

Helena giggled. 'My word, what were you doing?'

'Nothing like *that* I can assure you! He was writing and kept me hanging on while he rattled out another scene of death and destruction and bombs and feeble-minded women.'

I gave a growl of fury.

'I suppose the others are panting for their coffee? I'll stick the kettle on,' I said.

Chapter Eight

We didn't see Oliver at all for the rest of the day. The others were quite happy writing and occasionally chatting. Most of the time all we could hear from the three in the dining room was the tiny machine-gun rattle of laptops. Elaine was writing in a notebook with a propelling pencil and sighing.

There were occasional book-related groans of '*I'll never get this damn book finished*' or '*Why did I set this book in the nineteenth century?*' but that's another great thing about writers en masse: they love to make a helpful suggestion or take ten minutes out from their own problems to offer suggestions about someone's synopsis, plot holes, or character names. In fact, they love it because it means they can procrastinate, which is the other thing writers love doing.

I made a successful replacement cake and a cottage pie for tomorrow's dinner, then I went upstairs for half an hour with *The Dirty Road*. I have to say it really was very good: one of those books that grabs you by the lapels and drags you off on a roller coaster ride of unexpected phone calls and safe deposit boxes and strangers in dark rooms. I flicked through to find a rude bit and enjoyed reading about the hero doing some imaginative things with his love interest (the flexible Selina) on a couchette whilst the Orient Express thundered suggestively through some tunnels.

Lunch came and went and I made a tray of food for Oliver and left it outside his room on a small table I had found in the hall. He'd taken it and two coffee offerings without so much as a comment. It was like having a permanently hungry poltergeist in the house. Or like *The Man in the Iron Mask* when the jailers leave food for the prisoner and take the empty tray away later without actually ever seeing anyone. Weird.

The three ladies returned to the front room to write and Nick and Helena left at two o'clock as the tower was due to open at two-thirty; excitement was reaching fever pitch. I don't know what they were expecting to see from up there: a lofty view over the Serengeti plains perhaps, or herds of elk migrating across the tundra? I settled down to a quiet afternoon at the kitchen table with my laptop and was just getting into things when Oliver's door opened.

He stood and looked around as though he was only half awake. His eyes were sort of distant and unfocused. Perhaps he was deep in his work and not really with it?

'Can I get you anything, Mr Forest? More coffee?'

Blimey, surely not?

'Can you come in here a minute?' he said and he flapped his hands in a 'come here' sort of gesture. I stood up and went towards him.

'Now turn round,' he said.

I did so, mystified and looking around for a suitable weapon in case he was going to have a funny turn. There was an umbrella in the stand by the door and the usual fixture outside his room – an empty cafetière. I could fetch him a nasty whack with either if the need arose.

He stood behind me and put his hands on my shoulders.

'Good heavens, you're very short. How tall are you?' he said.

'Five foot three,' I said, standing up as straight as I could.

'Really?' He laughed.

Why do people always find that funny? I wouldn't laugh at him for being – what – six foot two?

He positioned one forearm in front of my shoulders. All the time he was hmm-hmming and making notes in a little notebook. Then he put a forearm around my neck. Nothing uncomfortable but he was obviously trying something out for size.

He smelled delicious. I hadn't anticipated that. A sort of man/warm skin/slightly spicy aftershave sort of smell. It made me feel a bit weak at the knees to be honest and I had to make myself think about something else so I didn't blush.

Tax returns, grouting, Brussels sprouts.

Oliver was pushing me gently to one side by this point. 'What do you weigh?' he said.

'I'm not telling you!'

What sort of question was that to ask?

He tutted a bit.

'Ballpark?'

'I'm not as big as a ballpark! Oh I see what you mean. About nine and a half stone,' I lied.

'Hmm.'

He came round to stand in front of me and put his hands under my elbows. He lifted me off the ground very slightly. It was very unnerving.

76

'I'd say nearer ten and a half,' he said.

'Bloody cheek! I'll have you know—'

'Shush. If someone did this what would you do?'

He put his hands very gently on my throat, his thumbs in the classic strangling position.

I pushed him off. 'Do you mind? You're freaking me out here! What the hell are you doing anyway?'

'Look I'm just having a bit of a problem. I need to know what an average woman would do.'

'Speaking as a far from average woman, I'd say she would knee him in the nether regions. And scream.'

'Hmm. And if she was shorter than you?'

'You'd have to ask a shorter woman,' I said acidly, '*if* you can find one.'

He put his hands back near my throat and hmm-hmmed a bit more.

'Look, what exactly are you doing?' I said.

'I'm trying to work out what would happen if a sensible woman of average height and weight was put in this position. She's in a ruined house in Istanbul, in the dark with a man who has been following her on and off for about five chapters.'

'Your basic premise has significant flaws. No sensible woman would put herself in a ruined house in the dark. We're not stupid you know.'

'I didn't say she was stupid—'

'But she would be exceptionally stupid if she allowed a man to follow her for five chapters, presumably intimidate her, and then chase her into a ruined house in the dark. It's like every version of *Dracula* ever made. They set off for Dracula's castle just as it's getting dark. Why don't they go after breakfast on a sunny day? All they would need to do is find Dracula asleep in his coffin, open the curtains, and Bob's your uncle.'

Oliver pinched the bridge of his nose and closed his eyes. 'But there would be no story would there?'

I raised an index finger, unexpectedly confident. 'Exactly, so in fact Mary Shelley had a plot hole of mammoth proportions didn't she? The whole thing relies on the people being irresponsible and heading off in the dark. Just like your heroine. Why doesn't she phone the police?'

'Actually, it was Bram Stoker. Mary Shelley wrote *Frankenstein*. My heroine has lost her mobile and the local police are corrupt – she knows she can't rely on them.'

'Then get on a plane and go home,' I said.

'She's lost her passport.'

'Explain to the airport staff; buy a new ticket out.'

'She doesn't have any money.'

I rolled my eyes at him. 'She's stranded in Istanbul, with a man following her for five chapters into a ruined house in the dark *and* she's managed to lose her phone, her passport, and her bankcards. She's a bit bloody useless isn't she?'

'Look—'

'And you're just worried about whether she could fight off a man in a dark house and whether it would make any difference if she was nine or ten stones? She's got pathetic loser written all over her. I'm guessing her only hope is the sandblasted hero with his Shaman over his face—'

'Shemagh.'

'Yes whatever.' I was off on one now. Brain engaged. Mouth in gear. 'Women these days are pretty aware of their surroundings you know, and taking personal responsibility for their own safety. I've already clocked an umbrella in the stand over

78

there and an empty cafetière in case I needed a weapon.'

'Why the hell would you need a weapon?' he said, his brow creased with confusion.

'Well you might be a complete nutcase who has fits of irrational anger, or a closet drug addict who's just had a sniff of something.'

'I'm neither of those things!'

'Well you're not going to admit it, are you? I bet you any money your heroine has gone in the dark to a ruined house in a cocktail dress and stilettos, hasn't she?'

'Well—'

'Although if she had they would be a pretty good weapon. Whack him with a stiletto in the eye and it would make him think a bit.'

Oliver sighed. 'I wish I hadn't asked. Look, this is supposed to be a thriller. The woman is in danger. He has to save her.'

'Oh well, I'm sure he will. I expect she'll turn out to be another of your drippy women who are little more than a walking pair of tits—'

'Walking pair of tits!'

'Now if *he* went to the ruined house with a submachine gun and some hand grenades and *she* had already planted a few land mines and then swept up in an armoured car with a bottle of Bollinger so they could escape to the airport where she had a private jet waiting, it would all be tickety-boo wouldn't it? Now, did you want anything else?'

'You did mention coffee,' he said faintly.

'You drink far too much coffee,' I said. 'It can't be good for you. Did you eat your lunch?'

'Yes,' he said looking vaguely around for the tray.

'I'll bring you a cup of tea and a piece of cake. Yes, I know you don't want cake but it's a jolly good one – better than the one you made me burn – and it would do you a lot more good than shedloads of caffeine. OK?'

Oliver rubbed a hand over his face and sighed. 'God Almighty. Fine if it will stop you talking.'

I smiled. I felt a little shiver of triumph. 'Oh not many things do that I'm afraid.'

Chapter Nine

Oliver went back into his room with his cake and tea and I heard no more from him. I'd read some more of *The Dirty Road* and, as yet, hadn't found any more rude bits – not even by the tried and tested method of letting the book fall open at the most viewed page. That only resulted in an exciting section where the hero (Major Harry Field) took out a nest of snarling insurgents single-handed. Probably with only a catapult and a bucket of water to defend himself.

He then laughed '*like a devil contemplating sin*', lit a cigarette in a leisurely fashion, and disappeared into the night. Presumably to go home, find his romantic interest (the generously endowed Selina), and roger her senseless although this time there were no sexual calisthenics in confined spaces.

In fact, there was no mention of what they got up to other than '*he took one look at her and knew what she wanted.*'

Well now that made me snort with laughter.

We all know in real life *no* man can take one look at a woman and know what she wants so I thought this was very unlikely. After all, Selina might have wanted Major Field to take the bins out or move his car so she could go to Pilates. Hmm.

I skipped a few pages and found another scene of a romantic nature when Major Field was taking Selina out to dinner and he was admiring her choice of outfit: a red satin cocktail dress '*tight in every place*'. Every place? Really?

This would suggest to me:

1) Selina had body dysmorphia;

2) She hadn't really thought her outfit through regarding space for her impending meal; or

3) She'd been tucking into a few too many pies during the Major's absence. If Harry Field was anything like Matt I could just imagine him slapping her on the arse and suggesting she get a bigger frock.

Anyway, who was I to judge? Oliver was the one with the books on people's shelves and presumably a lot of fans and oodles of money in a Swiss bank account. I was the one who needed to go downstairs and set the table.

When Nick and Helena came back from their trip up the church tower they were both a bit giggly. I tried to catch her eye, but she didn't seem to notice – she was too busy fidgeting about and flicking her hair. Nick went to help her in the kitchen and you could tell there was something going on. I mean a grown woman doesn't usually need a man to 'help her grate cheese' does she?

'Now what have you and Mr Tweedy been up to?' I said later. 'I can tell you've been doing something.'

Helena grinned. 'We went up the tower.'

'Yes?'

'And he kissed me. Just my cheek.'

I gasped. This was definitely un-Helena-like behaviour. She'd always been a slow starter and since Ghastly Greg had broken her heart last year, she'd been in a sort of self-imposed purdah. Even when the engineer who came to service the photocopiers in the library had asked her out, she'd said no. And he had been buttering her up with company pens and notebooks for weeks. Like those bowerbirds who like to fill their nests with trinkets to encourage the lady bowerbirds in. This sort of gauche enticement cut no ice with Helena.

'And? And?' I said, eager for more details.

'And he asked me out. He's going to take me out for a meal when we get home, and there's a car museum near where he lives. He says it's really good for a visit. Apparently they have a really rare Bugatti—'

I put a hand to my heart. 'Stop it you're killing me!'

'—and one of the Queen's Rolls-Royces.'

OK, just because I wouldn't have thought this was an interesting date, didn't mean Helena didn't.

'Do you fancy him then?'

Helena blushed. 'Of course! Wouldn't anyone? He's so incredibly handsome' –

Well he was reasonably nice-looking. Beauty in the eye of the beholder I suppose.

– 'and we talked for ages about everything. He really makes me laugh.'

'Then that's great news. I couldn't be more pleased.'

She looked a bit dreamy. 'And he did such a brilliant job grating the cheese.'

*

Oliver came to join us for the evening meal – late of course, stomping out of his room and sitting at the end of the table. He didn't talk much, just shovelled in his pasta and a couple of glasses of red wine, then declined dessert – with more than a hint of sarcasm – on the grounds he had eaten cake earlier and didn't want Type 2 diabetes.

He even mentioned the obesity crisis in Great Britain and I shuffled sideways a bit to hide my arse behind the sideboard. Talk about sucking the joy out of an evening. I was looking forward to some of that dessert too; it was crème brûlée with fresh mango coulis. Instead I sat on my hands watching the others eat it, murder in my heart.

Nick, still slightly star-struck, badgered him to know how his work was going and Oliver muttered something about rewriting. He then refilled his wine glass and went back to his room, closing the door firmly behind him.

'He's not what you might call user-friendly is he?' Vivienne mused, her chin in her hand. 'He must be a barrel of laughs to work for.'

Helena huffed. 'You didn't see his secretary when she dropped him off. She was a wreck. She couldn't leave fast enough.'

'But maybe he gets fed up with people pestering him,' Nick said. 'It can't be easy being so famous.'

'Well he walked in here and we didn't immediately climb all over him,' I said, 'and you're a fan of his. He must be quite disappointed we aren't paying him more attention.'

Helena went round the table topping up people's wine glasses.

'I met quite a few celebrities when I worked for BOAC,' Elaine said. 'I used to go all over the world.'

We all turned to look at her.

'Did you? How fascinating.'

'I was part of the medical team, looking after the staff. We hardly ever did any actual work, but we used to get free travel. I met Audrey Hepburn and Bette Davis. A number of genuine Hollywood stars. People who definitely wouldn't have been able to walk down the street without being recognized. And without exception they were charming. It was part of the price of fame I suppose. Being pleasant to the fans who paid for your ritzy lifestyle. Doesn't take much does it?'

'I saw Graham Greene in Fortnum and Masons once. He was buying a pork pie. No one took any notice,' Nancy said.

'I once saw Nigel Mansell buying petrol,' Nick offered.

No one seemed to think much of this.

'Why don't we do a bit of sharing on Thursday evening?' Vivienne said suddenly. 'So we can show what we've been doing?'

The others discussed this and agreed it might be fun although Helena said she didn't have anything worth reading out. Nick came to her rescue, gallantly insisting she had made her latest book sound wonderful. We discussed how many words and decided on five hundred maximum.

'So what about Oliver?' Nancy hissed, jerking her head in the direction of his room.

I got up and started stacking the dessert plates. 'You ask! I'll bet he says no.'

There was one crème brûlée left and I scarpered out into the pantry with it before anyone could nab it.

*

Well I was wrong. He didn't say no.

Vivienne nabbed him when he came out of his room for more refreshments and asked him. He tilted his head to one side and considered her suggestion and a rather strange expression crossed his face.

'Maximum five hundred words to show what we have been doing this week? What an interesting idea. I think I might have a piece to share if you're really interested?'

'Oh we are, of course we are,' Vivienne said, nodding enthusiastically.

'It would be a real treat,' Nancy added.

'I'll see what I can do,' Oliver said.

Well this little exchange was more than enough to cause a minor sensation in our group. I don't think there had been a more keenly anticipated literary offering since the last *Harry Potter* book came out.

*

We always do a curry on the last night of a writing retreat. It's a sociable meal with lots of sharing and it's always popular. Well, other than last time when one guest, having been inhaling curry spices all afternoon, smugly announced she was allergic to garam masala ten minutes before the meal.

Trust me, there are few things more depressing than watching someone eat a cheese omelette and saying no it's fine honestly while everyone else is troughing away at Chicken Dhansak and Vegetable Biryani and all the side dishes imaginable.

Anyway no one had voiced a similar reluctance so the curry was well under way and smelled fantastic. Outside the weather had deteriorated still further and the rain was lashing against the windows. We lit all the wood burners, and everyone settled down for an industrious last day, typing fit to burst.

Nancy, Elaine, and Vivienne shared the dining-room table; Oliver of course was cloistered away in his room; and Nick was pretending to work at the kitchen table while sneaking looks at Helena and occasionally offering to help her with some mundane task. It's one of our rules that guests shouldn't have to lift a finger while they are with us, but Helena was flagrantly disregarding this and eventually she and Nick sat at the breakfast bar, firstly slicing tomatoes and onions and then making raita. And giggling.

In the end I left them to it and went to do some writing of my own. What was I happy to share with the group? I read through a few pages, trying to find something that didn't make me cringe. It was awful. Why was I doing this? I wasn't any good at it. In fact, I had the growing suspicion that I was just trying to go along with Helena and she was the one with the talent. I preferred the catering and the fussing around people.

What would Oliver read to us? I wondered. Some shoot 'em up, bomb-blasting heroism? Perhaps we would learn more about how he made his books so successful, even if I didn't fully understand their appeal.

I was already determined to get *The Dirty Road* on DVD when I got home to watch it again properly. Perhaps I would watch it as a research project and not as an excuse to buy a tub of Häagen-Dazs vanilla and a jumbo bag of Maltesers?

If I didn't have Matt next to me, ignoring me and crunching away on a jumbo bucket of sweet popcorn when he knew I preferred salty, perhaps I would find it more entertaining?

That evening we made the table pretty with two candelabra and some silvery tablemats and sprays of artificial holly left over from Christmas that we found in a bin liner under the stairs. By the time we had finished it looked rather smart and we began to bring out the many dishes of chutney and accompaniments to go with the meal.

'Can I help?'

It was Oliver. I don't know which of us was more surprised. *Can I help?*

'No, no, I'm *fine* thanks,' I said, more than a little flustered. *You just sit down and keep out of the way!*

Well this was a turn-up for the books. Firstly he was on time and secondly he wasn't snarling. Thirdly he had changed into a glorious cobalt shirt that contrasted well with his dark hair and brought sparks of light to his eyes.

At this point I had to scurry off to the kitchen at speed and stop being quite so mushy. His shirt was tucked into chinos, accessorized with a well-worn leather belt. He looked presentable. Well more than presentable actually. He looked bloody gorgeous. And he must have just had a shower because his hair was still wet ...

Shower. Mmmmm.

Shut up, woman, for God's sake.

I pretended to check I'd turned the ovens off to give myself a few minutes to recover. Then I rinsed out the end of a tea towel in cold water and pressed it to my throat.

Calm down, Billie; stop being such a prat. He wouldn't look twice at you.

Why was I being so ridiculous? I didn't fancy him did I? Did I?

Oliver had been nothing but a pain since he got here. He'd been rude, disruptive, unfriendly, and pompous. He'd be leaving in the morning and I'd never see him again. There was no point developing a crush on him now.

Crush? I didn't have a crush. I was just a bit distracted.

Chapter Ten

Although Oliver was sitting in what I had come to regard as *my* place at the end of the table, it turned into an enjoyable evening. For once I was feeling quite happy with my appearance. I'd saved a rather nice gypsy sort of blouse to wear. Perhaps I would keep it when I did my clothing cull. It hid the muffin top I seemed to be developing for some reason.

We had done everything we could to make the dining room attractive and welcoming and we had some nice wine to finish up. It was definitely getting colder and the rain was battering against the windows behind the thick curtains.

'I've had such a lovely week,' Elaine said. 'Really set me up. I honestly think this might be the year I get this book finished. It's only been three and a half years since I started it.'

'Oh God!' Nancy said. 'Don't! I'm just as bad.'

'Right so are we all ready for the sharing our work bit of the evening? I for one can't wait to start showing off,' Vivienne said.

Everyone started chattering at once and collecting plates up except Oliver who evidently considered himself exempt from domestic drudgery. Instead he swivelled around and pulled his laptop out from the bag he had looped over the back of his chair. I felt a tremor of excitement despite myself. I had the feeling we were in for a treat; after all it's not every day you get to hear an internationally successful writer share their first draft of something.

Helena and I spent the next ten minutes clearing the table and wiping off the rice and splatters of food from the silvery placemats; it was like a posse of toddlers had been over for dinner.

'Go on then, Viv, if you're so keen,' Nancy said. 'Let's get the rude stuff over with.'

Vivienne looked haughty. 'It's not rude *actually* – it's a thoughtful piece about Zen, the meaning of life, and existentialism.'

'Is it?' Nancy said, her eyebrows disappearing into her fringe.

'No of course not! It's the bit with the tangerines and the handcuffs.'

'Oh God.'

Vivienne chuckled and started reading her piece out while we all braced ourselves. It really was quite alarming what her brain had come up with and I don't think any of us would ever look at a fruit bowl again in the same way. I could see Nick slowly sinking down in his chair, his shoulders up by his ears.

Nancy was next, and she read out a piece from her detective-led mystery. It left all of us, including her, confused.

Oliver made a couple of suggestions and asked a few questions.

'I have a really great plotting sheet I've used in the past,' he said. 'You can have one if you think it would be any use. Just let me have your email address and I'll send one through.'

Nancy sat back, her face one big beaming smile as though she had won the lottery.

Then Elaine gave us five hundred rather spine-chilling words about a man living behind a mirror. It was a sort of time slip thing and just as she got to the climax when an avenging warrior lifted his head off his shoulders, the wind gave an extra blast and upstairs a door slammed somewhere. I nearly had a heart attack.

'And who have you sent that to?' Oliver said.

'Oh the usual suspects,' Elaine said. 'I went through Agent Hunter and found all the agents who claimed to like paranormal and no one was interested. I had some nice refusals but it's still a refusal isn't it?'

'You shouldn't give up,' he said. 'There's a home for it somewhere. You should enter some competitions – ever thought about it?'

'Well no, I haven't. You think I should?'

'Why not? It's certainly as good as some of the winners I've read.'

She fiddled about with her laptop before closing it with a snap. 'I jolly well will. Now come on, Helena, let's see what you've been up to.'

Helena took a deep breath and read out part of her children's story, a sort of adventure mystery set in Scotland. There were some lovely details of castles and a potential sighting of the smaller, shyer cousin of the Loch Ness monster. It was really lovely and when she finished we gave her a spontaneous round of applause.

'Oooh thank you! I'm glad you liked it! I know there's a

problem with the middle section. The bit with the monster needs to happen more quickly too.'

Across the table Oliver reached into his laptop case and fished out a business card.

'When you've finished editing, get in touch with this lady. Maryam is a friend of mine; she's just started an agency on her own. She's very good and looking for YA clients. You could do worse.'

We all gasped our approval and Helena clasped the card close to her chest.

'Golly thank you,' she said, close to tears.

'Can't promise anything – mention my name by all means,' Oliver said rather gruffly. 'Now come on, Nick.'

Nick hummed and haa-ed for a bit, undecided which bit to share with the group before launching into a segment that was littered with hand grenades, the rattle of machine-gun fire, and doors being burst open by burly shoulders. I sneaked a look at Helena and saw she was enraptured. I began to think this wasn't just a bit of a flirtation but something more serious. As he finished, Nick looked across at her for her approval and she grinned at him.

Nick looked across at his hero and Oliver gave him a thumbs up.

'Good work,' he said. 'I liked that a lot. Very claustrophobic.'

Nick scribbled in his notebook, his eyes wide with hero worship. 'Cool, thanks, Oliver.'

Oh God, now it was my turn. Suddenly my stomach gave a swoop of dread.

I'd chosen a paragraph earlier on but now it seemed trite and silly. What could I possibly read out? This had turned into almost an interview: a one-to-one with someone a million times worse than my headmistress. And she could kill with a look from fifty yards.

'I'm not sure ...' I hedged.

It was the part when my heroine throws herself in front of the queen and pleads for the hero's life. Even as I read it out I knew it was half-baked. And did they actually have curtains in the sixteenth century?

'Excellent,' Helena said.

The others made encouraging noises, but I wasn't fooled.

'You're very kind.'

'Early days yet?' Oliver said.

Yes, only eleven years, I thought.

'A work in progress,' I said.

We all looked hopefully at Oliver.

He didn't wait to explain himself or set any scenes; he just dived in. I'll never forget his first sentence.

'He had loved a woman he didn't like. He had liked a woman he could never love. But this woman: she was everything. Cold hands, warm heart. She was different.'

We sat in respectful silence while he read out what I presume was Major Harry Field's new perspective on the female sex now his creator had received valuable advice from a nitwit who burned a perfectly good Victoria sponge while he was typing it out. I didn't know what to think. Did he mean it? Was he poking fun at me in front of everyone?

'Brilliant,' Vivienne sighed when Oliver had finished. 'Just wonderful.'

'Wow,' Nick said, 'she must be quite a girl.'

Oliver busied himself shutting down his work. Then suddenly he gave a funny little half-smile.

'Yes,' he said, 'I'm beginning to think she might be.'

93

And then he looked at me.

I swear to God, in that moment he saw right into me. And he carried on looking. There was understanding in his eyes, a sharp, clever knowledge. It was frightening. The hairs on my arms prickled to attention.

I couldn't breathe properly.

I was imagining it, of course I was. I was reading far too much into the situation. Why would a man like Oliver look at me with anything other than amusement? Why would he look at me at all?

I wanted to get away from him. I was used to men ignoring me. Or flicking me a glance to compliment my cooking. I wasn't used to them actually looking at me. Seeing me.

We had all been closeted together for the week – that was all it was. We had the literary equivalent of cabin fever. I was clumsy and impatient and boring; he was brilliant and bad tempered. It was time for us all to go our separate ways.

Everything was quiet for a second and then people started talking, laughing, passing around the After Eights, and arguing about whether the paper envelopes should be left in the box or not. Almost as though nothing at all had happened.

Everyone else started asking Oliver questions. How did he structure things? Where did he get his ideas? How could they make their stories more attractive to agents?

Far from being standoffish and irritated, Oliver started to unbend a bit. He was almost chatty. Suggesting things, offering advice – it was really strange.

I picked up an empty dish and took it out into the kitchen. Then I unlocked the back door and went out into the porch. After the heat and food-scented dining room it was wonderful – cold and very shocking.

The wind blew my hair across my face. I wanted to breathe out every last molecule of air in my lungs and fill them up with the storm. I could smell wood smoke, the cold scent of wet earth, and dead leaves. Back in the house I heard a burst of laughter and the scrape of a chair on the flagstone floor.

If I had been writing this story, Oliver would have left the table and come out after me. I would have seen his silhouette in the doorway and turned away, a shiver of anticipation running down my spine. It wouldn't have been a cold February evening with the rain slashing down, filling the leaf-choked gutters either; it would have been a glowing, sunny afternoon in September, maybe in Tuscany with the warm slopes of countless vineyards behind us.

He definitely wouldn't have had his leg in a plastic boot. He would probably have been in an evening suit with the bow tie carelessly looped around under his collar. Perhaps he would have a couple of champagne flutes in one hand, an open bottle of Bollinger in the other. And then he would have come towards me. He would have known what to say and what to do. And so would I.

But then I would have been someone different. I would have been taller, thinner, beautiful, more interesting. Not me at all.

*

I hardly slept that night. Around midnight I increased my theoretical lottery winnings to fifty million and even that didn't work.

I pulled out my list of things to do and clicked on my illuminated pen. I had items to add to my plan:

11) ~~Go back-packing to Thailand on my own. Join group of fun-loving students who are going to Thailand. Go to Thailand on package tour with group of elderly people in air-conditioned coach and with English-speaking guide.~~ Go on a plane by myself.

12) ~~Colour hair blue. No green.~~ Get decent haircut.

13) ~~Finish book. Get agent. Move to Monte Carlo.~~ Accept am not really getting anywhere with writing and find something productive to do with my time.

14) Become really picky about future boyfriends. Do not form relationship with selfish, penniless git with morals of failed Seventies' rock star. Even if Matt does come crawling back.

15) ~~Stop eating biscuits.~~ Restrict biscuit intake.

16) Buy new towels to replace the ones Matt took.

17) Get money back that Matt owes me.

The following morning I staggered downstairs just after five o'clock and flicked the kettle on. While I waited for it to boil I started quietly packing away the things we wouldn't need into plastic storage boxes. Then I laid the table for breakfast. I drank two cups of coffee and checked my emails. I quickly ate some toast and marmalade, went back upstairs, dressed, and packed my case. We had to be out by ten-thirty. Pippa would be here early to collect Oliver with any luck.

We got through breakfast without any sign of Oliver. There was no sound from his room either and I certainly wasn't going to knock on the door to wake him up. Actually, the way I was feeling I would happily have left him there for the cleaners to find.

Nancy and Vivienne were the first to leave, followed soon afterwards by Elaine.

Nick left just before ten-thirty. I think he was too well mannered to overstay the prescribed time. Even so he helped us load up the car. He hugged us both and tactfully I left Helena alone with him for a final farewell.

Last, of course, was Oliver.

His car turned up with minutes to spare, sweeping into the courtyard behind the house in a fine spray of gravel. At least she had remembered not to come to the front door this time. But then it wasn't Pippa who got out to help Oliver with his cases. It was a stocky, handsome man with a lot of designer stubble and hair gel.

I think I looked as though I had been awake most of the night and I had an exclamation mark of ketchup down my shirt where I had juggled a box of groceries a bit carelessly. The newcomer was immaculate of course, striding up to the kitchen door in jeans and a strange tweed jacket with coloured buttons. Designer and horribly expensive I expect.

'Hi,' he drawled, looking around him with some interest at the rural setting. 'Jake Mitchell. I'm hoping this is the right place. Have you got Oliver? I've come to take him back to civilization.'

I almost tugged my forelock. He reeked of big-city sophistication.

'Yes, he should be ready,' I said. 'No Pippa today?'

'No, she's not on good form. Fell down the staircase at work.'

'Gosh, I hope she's OK?' I said.

Suicide bid?

I imagined Pippa throwing herself dramatically down the stairs with a despairing cry at the prospect of having Oliver back.

'Just hurt her wrist. It wasn't that much of a fall either. More of a stumble. So has Oliver been behaving himself?'

'Well, you know ...' I said vaguely.

'Has he been writing?' Jake said with more of an edge in his voice this time.

Strange question – after all he was a writer who came here to write.

'Well, yes I think he has. He's been in his room quite a bit. He read us a bit of what he'd done last night.'

Jake looked at me with greater interest. 'What? Did he? Did he really? Did he say how he had been getting on? I mean the word count, you know?'

'No, not really,' I said. 'He wouldn't tell me a thing like that! But he did say he had a deadline for something.'

The newcomer followed me into the kitchen and stood, hands in pockets, as he looked around. I offered him coffee, which he refused with easy charm. Helena and I carried on packing things up and bang on the dot of ten-thirty, Oliver's bedroom door opened. He stumped out, pulling his suitcase behind him.

'Ah, you're here,' he said as he saw Jake standing in the kitchen doorway, jangling his car keys.

'Pippa said ten-thirty,' Jake said, still grinning.

'Right.'

'Well?' Jake said. 'Did it work?'

Oliver shrugged. 'Maybe.'

'Any thoughts about – you know?'

This was very weird and mysterious.

They got his case into the back of the car between them and Oliver turned to wave at us.

I waved back and followed Helena into the house.

She started wiping the kitchen table and I stood, feeling cold and empty inside, watching her.

'Well,' she said, 'he's gone then.'

'Yes,' I said, sticking my hands into my jeans pockets, 'and thank God he has. I've never been so glad to see the back of anyone in my life as Oliver bloody Forest.'

There was a noise behind me and I spun round. My stomach did an icy swoop of horror. Oliver was standing in the doorway. It seemed he had changed his mind and come back to say goodbye properly.

Bloody, bloody, bloody hell.

He shook Helena's hand and reminded her about his agent friend. She agreed she would be sending her work off very soon.

He held out a hand for me to shake. His hand was warm; mine was freezing.

He must have heard me. He *must* have heard me.

'It's been surprising – good luck with everything,' he said.

I said something; something stupid and pointless I expect and then he held my hand in his for a moment and leaned forward.

'Thank you,' he whispered.

He kissed my cheek and I felt his breath warm against my skin.

My mouth went dry and my knees were suddenly rather wobbly.

I watched as he got into the car, closed the door, and after a second Jake started the engine, reached behind him to pull on his seat belt, and drove away.

'Wow, he kissed you! Perhaps he didn't hear what you said after all?' Helena said.

I was still standing looking at the place where Jake's car had been parked only a moment ago.

'Well of course he did. Oh fuckity fuck, just great. Bollocking bollocks!' I said. 'I'll never learn to shut up will I?'

'I thought he loosened up by the end of the week,' Helena said. 'I mean he was almost OK in the end. And giving me that agent's card! Wasn't it incredible?'

'Yes, it was. Very kind. Oh well, we'd better get on with it. Have you checked the bedrooms?'

'All except Oliver's.'

My stomach gave a plunge. I couldn't think of anything worse than looking around Oliver's room, seeing the dent in the pillow where he had rested his head, smelling the last traces of his aftershave.

'Can you do it? I'll load up the last of the food boxes and start the dishwasher.'

Helena nodded. 'OK. If you don't mind?'

'I don't mind. I just want to get home.'

I went and checked the dining room one last time and replaced *The Dirty Road* onto the bookcase. I'd been dipping in and out of it and really quite enjoying it. Perhaps I should read the others?

I put my hand up to touch my cheek. Why had he kissed me?

Chapter Eleven

Finishing a successful writing retreat and being back in my odd little house were usually things to make me feel good. I think I might hide my insecurity by being a bit of a feeder, but I like people and I get on with most of them. Oliver had been an exception. And actually, if I thought about it a little bit more deeply, there were things about Oliver I had liked too; not least his good looks.

Perhaps he had been wary of us to start with, but then again the warning signs were there. He'd become famous very quickly; he was well used to people wanting stuff from him. But he did treat his PA as though she was dirt. That couldn't be excused, surely? On the other hand, he had been quite nice to us on the last evening.

And he had kissed me.

And? Oh I don't know.

I wandered around enjoying my eclectic collection of furniture and colourful junk, the sort of vintage stuff I kept acquiring even though I had decided I was going to be minimalist from now on. Somewhere I had heard it was a good idea to throw fifteen things away every week. Or was it every day? I couldn't throw fifteen things away every day, surely? Otherwise by the end of the year I'd have nothing left and would be back to slopping around in my Ugg boots and pj's.

I unpacked my case and checked the post that had arrived while I was away. There was nothing interesting; there never is. I hadn't recorded anything entertaining to watch on the television because there isn't anything and even the jolly couple in The Olde Stables next door who were usually good for a laugh during a boring evening had gone on holiday that morning. I had agreed to look after their cat and there were several tins of cat food on my back doorstep to remind me. I went and fed it before I forgot and received a dirty look from it as a reward.

Then I packed away my case, put my laundry into the washing machine, and checked my emails. Then I had a cup of coffee. And several chocolate Hobnobs I didn't need. They were ten minutes away from being stale anyway. It would have been far better if I had put them in the bin rather than me. With my 'nearly ten and a half stone' body. Bloody cheek.

I looked at the bathroom scales and almost got on but then thought better of it. Spontaneous weighing never ends well in my experience.

I checked my emails again and emptied my junk folder. Then I read my horoscope (Libra). It told me I was about to visit a magical location. As I was due back into work soon I thought this was unlikely. I decided I would be Gemini for the week instead, as they were going to have a 'wonderful surprise associated with water'. Talking of water, it hadn't stopped raining since Thursday night and I wasn't looking forward to the walk to work at all.

I read the paper online, marvelled at the size of some female celebrity's chest, and wondered if there was anything worth watching on TV. There wasn't. Another of my wildly exciting evenings stretched ahead. It was all very well saying I should do thrilling things and take chances and have adventures but what if none presented themselves? Perhaps I should start riddling out my larder?

My mobile rang; it was Helena.

'You'll never guess!' she said. She sounded as though she was about to burst with excitement.

'Go on.'

'Nick's been on the phone already!'

'Wow! What's the news?'

'We're meeting up on Thursday evening. He's going to come over and take me out for a meal. At La Mignonne.'

'On a school night? You crazy kids!'

'I know!'

La Mignonne was a horrifically expensive Michelin-starred restaurant, which neither of us had visited although we had scrolled through the sample menu on their website.

Vinny and Jade in the house next door to mine had been there for their wedding anniversary last summer and brought me back an evening's menu card: £145 for seven courses, none of them bigger than a sparrow. Actual sparrow wasn't on the menu of course. Well I don't think so. You never know these days.

'You'd better eat before you go then if what my neighbours told me was true. All delicious but not exactly filling.'

'Never mind, I'll be far too nervous to eat! What shall I wear?' she squeaked.

'Dress or trousers?'

'Dress.'

'The black lace one?'

'Hmmmm, maybe.'

'The brown one, with the squiggly pattern?'

'I've gone off it. Anyway it's too short.'

'You've got great legs!' I said. She has too.

'I mean it will be too cold. What about the flowery one? Blue and white?'

'I think it's a bit summery. You need something snuggly. Grey cashmere with a faux fur collar.'

'Not with my faux overdraft,' Helena said. 'Are there any sales on?'

'He won't care what you wear. You could turn up in your painting trousers and he wouldn't notice.'

'I'll have to go shopping. Come with me?'

'Yes of course – when do you want to go?'

'When it stops raining?' she said. She gave a hefty sigh. 'So the middle of March the way things are going. The end of our road was flooded when I got back. And the school playing fields. You?'

'I haven't looked. I've just been unpacking.'

'I haven't bothered yet. I came in and started writing. I seem to have got into the groove since Oliver gave me that agent's card. I'm going to send her my first three chapters and a synopsis when I've had a chance to double-check it.'

'Will you mention Oliver?'

'Of course! He said I could after all.'

We chatted on for a few minutes with her twittering about Nick and what she had said on the phone and what he had said and what did I think he meant by that? Exactly the sort of conversation I could have had with her when we were both fifteen.

She rang off so she could trawl through the clothing websites and fret a bit more. Meanwhile, I went into the kitchen and peered into the fridge hoping to find something nourishing and unexpected. All I found was pregnant-looking yogurt, a heel of cheese, and an exhausted head of broccoli. I'd have to go out.

Going out was not something I wanted to do as the rain was still splattering viciously against the diamond-pane windows. Instead I chipped the frost off a pizza hiding at the bottom of the freezer and chucked it in the oven with no great hopes it would emerge much improved.

I was sitting on the sofa still mindlessly chewing it when the phone rang again. It was my mother.

'So did you have fun?' she said.

'It went well,' I said. 'Very, you know, interesting.'

'Hmm, when people say a thing has been *interesting* in that tone of voice it generally wasn't,' she said.

'No, it was. We had a well-known author turn up too.'

'Oooh, who? Do I know her?'

'Him. Oliver Forest better known as Ross Black.'

'Never heard of either of them. Josie has been on the phone. She wants us to go and see the boys in their school play. You can come too; after all she has oodles of room.'

'That would be nice,' I said without any real enthusiasm.

My sister Josie likes to pretend she is almost a suffragette because she refused to marry Mark when she got pregnant with the twins, but it doesn't stop her from living in a six-bedroom house paid for by her accountant partner while she spends all her time having lunch with friends and buying handbags.

'I might stay on with her for a few days. I'm going to have

the hall decorated and you know I can't stand the smell of paint. If you got your spare room sorted out I could stay with you. I mean you've got all that beautiful bed linen from Nan and how much does a bed cost? And if you cleared out the spare room ...'

'Clearing out the spare room is exactly what I plan to do. I've drawn up a list of things I want to achieve.'

'That sounds excellent news.'

Actually, if I was honest it probably wouldn't be that much fun to visit Josie because Finnegan and Hector had spent the last eight years without any obvious discipline in their lives and were exhausting. My sister has the same lack of culinary ability as our mother and as far as the boys were concerned any food that didn't come in cardboard containers was regarded with the utmost suspicion. When I visited they liked to stand silently on the other side of the breakfast bar and watch me cooking as though I was performing some dark art.

'Excellent, that's what I hoped you would say,' Mum said. 'I expect Josie will ring you later when she gets in. So any movement on the boyfriend front?'

The first deadly question. She made it sound as though a new boyfriend could be ordered on Amazon and delivered twenty-four hours later with a forklift truck.

Sign here; solvent, reasonably well-behaved man for you, Madam.

'I don't need a man,' I said perkily. 'I have my work. You were the one with the *A Woman Needs a Man like a Fish Needs a Bicycle* T-shirt when I was growing up, remember?'

Mum made a sort of scoffing noise. 'What about taking out the recycling though? And the spiders in the bath?'

'Are you quite sane? I do both of those things,' I said.

'Well Josie doesn't. Mark does things like that. Men do have some uses. And Finn and Hector are of course lovely but I'd quite like some granddaughters before I'm too old to enjoy them.'

'So you want me to find a man so he can take the bins out and provide you with the excuse to buy tiny dresses from Monsoon?'

'Children are a great comfort and a blessing,' Mum said piously.

'Bollocks, I'll give you three hours before you are volunteering to take Josie's dog out for a walk so you can get away from the comfort of dear little Finn and the blessing that is Hector and go to the wine bar at the end of their road.'

'Nonsense. How's the diet going?'

The Diet. The second deadly question.

First The Boyfriend and now The Diet.

The Diet was almost an entity in its own right that had been following me around, tugging at my clothing like a persistent toddler for years.

My name is Billie Summers and I'm a carbohydrate junkie.

'Fine, absolutely great,' I said with more confidence than I felt.

'Good, when you lose that last stone I'll buy you a dress. You could do it by Easter if you try. Look, I'll tell Josie we'll be there, OK?'

'Fine. And you could always go and stay with Uncle Peter, if you would just make up?'

Mum ignored the suggestion as she always does when a difficult topic arises.

'You're not flooded then?'

'No, should I be?'

'Oh I just heard there had been some flooding round by you. Anyway, thanks for the call. Must dash. I'll be in touch.'

'You rang me,' I said, but she'd rung off.

The phone rang again almost immediately.

'It's me. Maybe I should wear trousers?' Helena said, continuing our previous conversation as though an hour hadn't passed.

'Yes, why not?' I said through a mouthful of cold, leathery pepperoni.

'Not jeans, obvs. But maybe some smart trousers with a white shirt? No, the last time I wore that everyone thought I was a waitress. Smart trousers with a sweater? I've got the green fluffy one with the big roll neck. But it might be boiling in there and I'd be too hot. And I could hardly take it off halfway through the meal.'

'Well not unless you want to give him the green light for later?'

'Billie! Really! What about the blue shirt?'

One advantage of being friends for so long is that I know Helena's wardrobe almost as well as my own.

'Yes it would be fine.' I flicked through a few more television channels, pausing to watch an enormously fat American woman get onto some scales and burst into tears.

I ain't eaten nuttin. I can't understand it! Them scales is wrong, sister. Plain wrong!

Yes I know the feeling, Chanisse. My scales are always wrong too.

'Or the red check shirt. No, it's a bit ...' Helena said.

'Too casual?'

'Exactly.'

I took another bite of pizza and watched the woman on television argue with the size zero nutritionist about what constituted a healthy breakfast.

'What about a plain white T-shirt?' I suggested.

'I'd spill something on it within five minutes. I'm going to be so nervous,' Helena said. 'I'll go and look again.'

She rang off and I carried on flicking through the channels, got mildly absorbed in a house renovation project where an eco-obsessed couple wrangled over how ecologically friendly their taps and floor coverings were but failed to notice their grubby child was drinking E numbers out of the can just behind them.

I returned to the American diet show in time to see the tearful reveal. The star of the show had been hauled into a corset so her bosom was propelled up around her ears like a life jacket and was wearing purple lamé and platform shoes like trotters and she came into the room to whoops and cheers.

'Hey, you is beautiful girl! Hey, Momma, you is hot!'

She cried, her family cried, I nearly cried. Perhaps that was the sort of exciting adventure I should go on? A month at a boot camp followed by some more supportive underwear? Perhaps just the underwear, after all it's many a long year since I bought any and I'm absolutely sure I'm one of the ninety per cent of women wearing the wrong size.

I did another trawl of the cupboards and with a whoop of my own found the remains of a half-bottle of brandy I had bought to add to my Christmas pudding.

I returned to the sofa with a hefty measure in a glass and continued my search for entertainment. I found a programme where women from some sort of religious commune who had never had their hair cut went to the hairdresser. You wouldn't think this would be such a cause for drama, but the tears were flowing as their Rapunzel-like tresses fell to the floor.

'I feel like I'm reborn. I'm light as air.'

I was just wondering if I too should consider a pixie crop and blue streaks when the phone rang. Yet again it was Helena.

'It's me. I'm going to wear trousers, the dark grey ones, and the top I got in the Joules sale. The pale grey one with silver stars.'

'Yes, it would look fantastic.'

'Really? Do you think so?'

'I do. He'll be thrilled. And so he should be.'

'Or I could wear the black roll neck?'

'No, stick with the other one.'

'OK. I don't want to look dull though.'

'Helena, you won't look dull. You'll look gorgeous.'

'I look so young! Ain't no one gonna tell me I can't praise the Lord with short hair. I can't believe that's me!'

'Right, so you're sorted?' I said.

'Yes. Definitely,' Helena said sounding rather uncertain.

'Good.'

'What are you watching? I keep hearing cheering in the background.'

'I'm drinking cooking brandy and watching an ex-nun having her hair cut.'

'Very funny!'

'No I mean it – you wouldn't believe it.'

'You're bored aren't you?'

'Very,' I agreed with a sigh.

'Are you missing Oliver?'

I did a double take.

'What? Oliver? No! Yes! No! Why should I be missing him?' I said, startled by the suggestion. 'And why would he look twice at someone like me anyway?'

'Because you're lovely? I just thought there was something. You know. A bit of a connection. He was patronizing. You were sarcastic. Seems like a good start?'

'Rubbish! You saw Pippa: size six, blonde, and swishy. That's the sort of stick he goes for. Not ordinary-sized women like me. Honestly just because you're loved-up doesn't mean we all are. I'm enjoying being single actually. No, I absolutely love it.'

'OK, Billie, if you say so.'

I could hear the giggle in Helena's voice.

'I'm going now,' I said with as much dignity as I could muster. 'I have an important programme about cats climbing up people's curtains to watch.'

I cut off the sound of her laughing at me and turned the TV back up.

I was glad for her, really I was. Helena is lovely: bright, kind, and pretty. Nick would be lucky to get her. She deserved someone who would be devoted to her and he seemed the sort. Slightly old-fashioned, thoughtful, and sensitive without being too wet.

While Nick didn't make the sun shine for me, I had to admit I was rather wistful watching their blossoming romance. I hoped it was going to work out for them. I hadn't been a bridesmaid since I was eleven; I quite fancied being one again, especially if I could have a nice outfit.

With that in mind I skipped through a few channels looking for one where bridesmaids choose their dresses and joined one where the chief bridesmaid was in the middle of an epic meltdown and had just slung her complimentary champagne over the bride.

A programme showing puppies in the snow followed this and by the time it finished I was well sozzled and had to go to bed.

*

The following day I woke just after ten-thirty with a headache and serve me right really. There was still no food in the house and it was still raining. Out in the garden next door's cat was hunched up under the garden bench looking bad tempered.

I dressed, went out into the cold feeling rather martyred, fed next door's cat with another of its tins of foul-smelling plap, and then walked round to Polly's corner shop where I stocked up.

'Morning, Billie! What a day eh? Nice weather for ducks, isn't that what they used to say?' Polly said.

I filled my basket with some eggs, bacon, bread, milk, and cheese and went to pay. Then I grabbed a huge bar of nut chocolate that had been reduced in price and hid it under the bread.

Polly started ringing up my things.

'Awful about the shops isn't it?'

I tried to focus through my hangover. 'What shops?'

'The shops at the end of the high street. You work in one don't you? The bookshop?'

'Yes.' I was confused. 'Why, what's happened?'

Polly looked at me as though I was simple.

'The floods? The river? The lower high street is under water, has been since Thursday morning. Going to be a heck of a clear-up. It was on the local news. Some girl turned up with a camera crew and a microphone to talk to the local peasants. Got very stroppy when everyone ignored her. Colin Pearce drove his tractor through, swamped her fancy boots. Funniest thing I've seen in ages.'

'I've been away,' I stuttered. 'I didn't know. I was due back to work this afternoon.'

Polly pulled a face. 'Well there's no chance of that, I can tell you! The water's up over the windowsills at the butcher's shop. The council came along with some sandbags, but it didn't do no good.'

Oh bloody hell. Surely Uncle Peter would have told me? Ah. Wait a minute. He only ever phoned on the house number. I hadn't checked for messages there.

I raced back and dumped my shopping in the kitchen and then after a long and irritating search I found the house phone under a pile of laundry. Yes, there were four messages. The ground-floor shop was flooded. He and Godfrey had managed to move most of the stock upstairs to the storeroom, but it was going to be some weeks until the shop would be open. Well it was certainly *a surprise associated with water*, but it wasn't exactly wonderful. That would teach me to try and cherry-pick my astrological sign.

Chapter Twelve

I put my shopping away, found some wellingtons, and went to see if there was anything I could do to help at the book-shop. I found Uncle Peter standing in the middle of the shop in a pair of rather dramatic fisherman's waders, looking absolutely devastated.

'Oh hello,' he said trying to smile. 'You're back. Did it go well?'

I sloshed through the water to give him a hug. 'This is awful. What can I do?'

He pulled a glum expression. 'Well thanks, pet, but nothing really. Godfrey's upstairs in the sitting room stacking the hard-backs we managed to rescue and making space for the stuff off the shelves. The insurance people are coming round later. I would ask you to put the kettle on but there's no electric.'

'Leave it to me,' I said and sprinted off up the street.

Well, sprinted as fast as a woman in her ex-boyfriend's wellingtons can sprint. Which isn't terribly fast. Still I was back in ten minutes with a cardboard tray and two lattes and a camomile tea from the coffee shop at the top of town, plus three overinflated lemon and poppy seed muffins. I waded into the shop and put the tray down on a beautiful table that used to hold bestsellers and was now water stained and empty except for a thin film of mud across the top.

Uncle Peter's face lit up when he saw the muffins. They always were his favourite.

'Ah, a good deed in a naughty world,' he said, patting me on my arm.

He went to yell for Godfrey who was still upstairs in their flat thumping about, and then came and took his tea.

'So how was the retreat? Good fun?'

'It went well,' I said.

None of my silly stories seemed to matter now: the gripes I had about Oliver Forest; the wonderful progress Helena had made with her book; what I had done, the funny incidents that always came out of these things; the other people there. None of it was important compared with the sad sight of my uncle standing in the shop he loved, in waders, knee-deep in muddy water.

'We had a celebrity actually,' I said, hoping to cheer him up. 'Oliver Forest turned up out of the blue.'

'Oliver Forest?'

'Better known as Ross Black. *The Dirty Road*, *The Fool in Charge*?'

'Well I'll be damned! Really? Goodness me that's a bit of a coup isn't it? We're expecting his new paperback in soon. *Glory 17*. What was he like? Godfrey, come down here, listen to this. Billie's brought you some coffee!'

Godfrey, normally dapper in tweed trousers, one of his many signature waistcoats, and a crisply ironed shirt came downstairs wearing a pair of baggy old moleskin trousers and a moth-eaten jumper.

'Buns!' he said cheerfully when he saw the muffins. 'You're

a good girl, Billie, my favourite by a country mile! Now what's all the shouting about?'

'Oliver Forest, better known as Ross Black, came to her last retreat.'

Godfrey, a mouthful of muffin hampering coherent speech, raised his wiry eyebrows to signify his astonishment.

'Go on, what was he like?' Uncle Peter said.

'Oh he was alright, a bit of a diva or should it be divo? He had come off his motorbike and had one foot in a boot thing. I think his PA just dumped him on us. He was nice enough in the end once he lightened up and realized he wasn't the centre of the universe, but he was certainly hard work.'

Godfrey nodded his grey head wisely. 'Celebrity does that to people. They start out perfectly normal and before you know it they're asking for all the red Smarties to be taken out of the bowl and only drinking coffee after it's passed through the guts of a civet cat.'

Uncle Peter finished his muffin and folded the paper up neatly before looking around for a wastepaper bin, and then shrugging and dropping it into the floodwater lapping around his boots.

'Has Mum been round?' I asked.

Peter gave me a look. 'No she's still not forgiven me. I know I should have remembered her birthday and I know she didn't think much of the present, but I would have thought a book about Cheeses of the World would have been interesting?'

'Obviously not. So what happens with the shop?' I asked.

Godfrey sipped his coffee. 'Well I suppose we dry the place out, wash off the mud, hope against hope it is indeed mud and not ... you know. Put in an insurance claim, get the builders in. Die waiting for anything to be done. Same old, same old. I mean, look at this place: all the shelving is defunct, the walls will probably need replastering and then redecorating. By the time all that has been done and we're back in business everyone will have forgotten us. The death of another independent bookseller. It's not the end of the world but – well it's a damn shame.'

He stopped at this point, obviously a bit choked. He pulled out a paisley patterned handkerchief and harrumphed and coughed for a bit and Uncle Peter slapped him on the shoulder.

'Come on now, Godders old chap. Brave soldiers. No need for that. Ladies present,' he muttered. 'And there's plenty of room upstairs to store things; that's one blessing. And if we needed to, we could always open up the barn at the back and put the furniture there while we dry out.'

'But there's never been a flood before has there?' I said. 'Why now? And why so quickly?'

'Well it's been very dry for weeks hasn't it? The driest autumn and winter on record or something, and then suddenly torrential rain for a week. The water couldn't soak away fast enough. Well I think that's the gist of what the firemen said. Lucky the school wasn't flooded too I suppose. The school playing fields are unusable, so at least the little beasts won't be out there playing football and swearing at each other like they usually do. So there's another blessing,' Uncle Peter said.

Godfrey finished blowing his nose and looked at me. 'Sorry, Billie. You know we both love you working here but there won't be much going on here for weeks as far as I can tell. Have you got any more retreats booked?'

'Not until June and that's just a weekend. But gosh, don't worry! You have far more to concern you than my part-time job and me! I'll find something else! I could get a job in the supermarket I expect. I could even spend all my time writing and get a three-book deal by the summer!'

Forgetting I had just about decided to give up writing, I pictured myself for a moment, wrapped in a duvet, eating out-of-date microwaved meals and burning old manuscripts to keep warm as I typed frantically on my laptop.

'As soon as we hear something ...' Uncle Peter said.

'Yes, yes of course. Don't worry, really,' I said.

'I still want you to have your annual bonus,' he said. 'It's due next month.'

'There's no need. Honestly.'

'I insist. I'll pop it through the door when I'm passing your place.'

'You're a sweetheart. Anyway, I'd better go. If I'm going to be job hunting ...'

'I'm going to sort out the history and self-help books. Thanks for the coffee and the muffins. You go and write!' Uncle Peter cried dramatically, flinging one arm out as he prepared to go back upstairs to the storeroom.

'Perhaps I will,' I said.

I went back home and made myself a bacon sandwich. I would have to go out and restock properly later on, maybe drive over to the next town where there was a supermarket. I preferred to use the local shops when I could, but this was different. I needed to economize, spend carefully, and budget.

Some of my least favourite words.

*

Peter Moorhouse Books was suffering from the dodgy economy and so was I. All the vacancies at Superfine

118

Superstores had been snapped up and there didn't seem to be many other jobs going for which I was qualified. I thought back over my eclectic employment career and felt a bit depressed. I'd had so many jobs and not really been any good at any of them. I wasn't stupid or lazy or stroppy. How had I got to this age and not known where I was going with my life? That was a bit pathetic, wasn't it?

Luckily, I live in one of the cutest and prettiest Cotswold towns just north of Cheltenham and up to this point there were plenty of jobs available. I'd worked in a café, an estate agent's, and a dental practice before Uncle Peter offered me a job. I have the horrible suspicion that Mum ordered her brother to take me on when I was sacked from the estate agent's, but nothing was actually said. How shaming is that? To be nearly thirty and still have your mum organizing your employment.

I went over to Helena's flat the following evening so I could paint her nails. She didn't trust herself to do them without juddering with nerves and painting her knuckles as well. She'd bought some wine too, which was very welcome.

I bent to the task, applying the second coat of the third colour she had bought. I'm pretty sure she was decided on *Russian Star*, a sort of silvery lilac colour; it would tone in well with her outfit. I think we were both a bit giddy with the fumes by that point.

'But what are you going to do for money?' she said, lifting her wine glass with stiff fingers so she didn't smudge her nail varnish.

'I'm fine for the moment. Uncle Peter says he still wants to give me my annual bonus; I have some savings. I'll start shopping at Superfine on Sunday afternoon when all the ready meals get marked down and I can fight with all the other bargain hunters for the lasagne. Perhaps I'll become a vegetarian, or maybe I'll take up pole dancing?'

I laughed. I sounded a lot more confident than I felt. We had a couple of writing retreats booked for later in the year, but they wouldn't keep the wolf from the door. I needed a job and I needed one fast. And my financial situation was far from fine. There was a water bill due in at the end of the month and my water bills were – without fail – heart-stopping. Perhaps I should cut down on washing? Or only shower once a week?

We discussed what I could do (various things including cooking, washing up, bed making) and what I was actually qualified to do (not much actually). OK I had an English degree, but no teaching qualification. I did think about it for a few minutes once, but never did anything about it. And now you can't clip kids for being rude I don't think I would be suitable anyway.

'You're hard working and funny and cheerful,' Helena said encouragingly.

'So is a circus clown but I don't want to be one,' I replied.

'Well you can cook. You make the best beef wellington ever. Any jobs at the school?'

I imagined myself for a moment behind a counter in a pink nylon overall doling out custard with a ladle as big as a bucket or slices of rubbery pizza to children who would pull a face and throw half of it away. To me school dinners meant all sorts of ghastly things. Perhaps things have changed? Anyway, wasn't I supposed to be having adventures? Perhaps I could get a job as a chalet maid in some cute Alpine village? Or a nanny to some adorable millionaire's children?

'What about those companies who need occasional staff for functions? My brother did it the summer he left school. He went to a load of really glam events. Race days in Cheltenham and private bashes – that sort of thing. He said they used to tip well too because by the end of the night the guests were all completely twatted on free booze. He stopped doing it though when he tripped and ladled gravy into someone's handbag by mistake. They didn't seem to want him after that. Still, I'm sure you wouldn't do such a thing. I'll dig out the phone number.'

'Great, it would be super.'

It sounded awful; how embarrassing would that be? Job sharing with a load of sixth formers? What was the matter with me anyway? I had a load of GCSEs and A levels. I had a degree. I wasn't thick. I had to get my act together and soon.

We finished Helena's nails and had a short discussion about whether she needed her toenails painted to match.

'But I'm going to be wearing ankle boots,' she said.

'Yes? And?'

'Well, and trousers.'

'Yes but – you know.' I jerked my head to one side and widened my eyes at her.

'Know what?'

Really, Helena was amazingly slow sometimes.

'You know,' I repeated with greater emphasis.

Helena gave me a pained look. 'I'm wearing ankle boots and socks underneath them. So how is Nick going to get to see whether I've painted my toenails or not?'

'If you take them off?'

'You can't take your shoes off in a Michelin restaurant,' Helena scoffed. The penny finally dropped. 'Oh I see where you're going with this. Honestly, Billie, I'm not going to *sleep* with him! Am I? Not on a *first date*! What do you take me for?'

I sighed. 'Well he's a bloke. He's single. He seems keen. You like him. You've been on your own for a while. Why wouldn't you?'

'Would you?'

'Like a shot! Well not with Nick obviously. Have you got new underwear?'

'No I *haven't*! Oh God, should I get new underwear? But then I'd feel like such a prat if I spent a load of money on new knickers and he didn't want to see them. I'd be sitting there all evening wondering if he did. It would really put me off. So no, I'm not going to put myself under a load of knicker-focused pressure.'

'There you are then, decision made. Are you going to have your hair up or down?'

'Up. No down. No up. Oh God, I don't know,' Helena said.

'Down, then you don't have to worry about it?' I suggested. 'And you can twirl your hair between your fingers and toss it around in a seductive and fascinating way. As long as there aren't candles on the table of course.'

'Yes. Of course. Excellent. Good choice.'

'See, we're making progress here,' I said happily.

I topped up our wine glasses and we toasted her new *Russian Star* nails. Then we talked a bit about Nick and she filled me in on the details of his latest phone call when they had apparently talked for an hour and a half about nothing in particular by the sounds of it.

'He even mentioned holidays – he said he fancied doing something different.'

'What like bog diving or painting the kitchen ceiling?'

'No nothing like that. You can be very obtuse sometimes. He usually goes to see his family or a friend in France, but he just said he fancied a change. Do you think he meant with me?'

'Well you were on the phone for an hour and a half, didn't you ask him?'

'Well no, I didn't want to seem too keen.'

'Oh for heaven's sake! How old are you? I know! Why don't you suggest you go away to a romantic hotel in Scotland together? One of those castle sort of places. You can go for long walks across the brae and kick through the heather and warm up afterwards in front of a log fire with hot toddies. You'll have kippers for breakfast every morning or porridge with salt instead of sugar. There will be a kilted retainer with a wee tartan bonnet. He'll be called Angus and he'll call you *ma bonny wee lassie* and another one called Torquill will play "Mull of Kintyre" on the bagpipes outside your bedroom window at six-thirty every morning.'

'Why would they do that? It sounds ghastly. I like the sound of the hot toddies though.'

'It's what Scottish people do. Like *I'll be seeing you just now* when they mean goodbye. *And long may your lum reek.*'

'Yours too.'

'Oooh I can just see it now. You and Nick snuggled up on a sheepskin rug in front of the fire. And you'll be getting all hot and steamy and snogging fit to burst and then Angus the kilted retainer will come in with a new tree to put on the fire. And he'll step over you both very tactfully and say, "*Have you no had your tea?*"'

We fell about laughing and Helena topped up my wine.

'You have got to tell me what happens,' I said. 'Or text me under the table.'

'I certainly won't!'

'Well nip out to the loo between courses.'

'No chance! There are nine courses! He'll think I've got cystitis.'

Helena started to fidget. 'Do you think we should do my toenails then?'

'Perhaps we should. Just to be on the safe side? You know. In case.'

'You're *awful*!'

We painted her toenails.

Chapter Thirteen

The following morning it had stopped raining and next door's cat was sitting on the kitchen windowsill watching me with an unblinking stare. I fed it again to make up for not really liking it, made a chocolate sponge, and took it down to the bookshop with more coffee and tea for Godfrey and Uncle Peter.

I found them in much the same state as they had been the previous day. Uncle Peter was standing in wellington boots in the middle of the shop although now the water level had gone down and it was only up to his ankles.

'Hullo,' he said with a brave attempt at a smile. 'More refreshments – how marvellous! You are a treasure.' He paddled over to the foot of the stairs. 'Godfrey, there's cake. Come down!'

Godfrey, still in the same disreputable trousers and jumper, came thumping down the stairs from their flat.

'You are an absolute saint!' he said. 'It's bloody freezing up there.'

'How's it going?' I said.

'I think the worst is over. The water's going down anyway,' he said, 'and the forecast isn't predicting any more rain.'

'Well that's good isn't it?' I said, cutting comforting hunks of cake and handing them out on paper napkins.

'I suppose,' Godfrey said gloomily. He gave a huge sigh. 'I got through Beatlemania and Watergate, I can deal with two feet of dirty water in the shop.'

'That's the spirit,' Uncle Peter said, clapping him on the back.

'What did the insurance people say?'

'They'll pay up but of course it will take time to sort this out and naturally the premiums will go up next year. If they will insure us at all. There's a builder coming round later and the fire brigade are going to be pumping the water out of the drains later so that will be something fun for us to watch,' he said gloomily.

'Now then, Godders,' my uncle said wagging a finger at him. 'We don't want any defeatist talk. That won't win the war will it? Buck up, man, stiffen the sinew, stretch wide the nostril and all that sort of stuff.'

'Oh all right then,' Godfrey sighed, taking a piece of cake. 'So what are you up to, Billie? Any progress on the job hunt?'

'Well nothing yet but it's early days. I'll find something. Perhaps I could sell my hair? Or one of my kidneys?'

'I wonder how much you'd get for a kidney?' Uncle Peter said. 'They wouldn't want one of mine; mine have been well pickled in brandy over the years.'

'Anyway, we'd better get on. There's a lot of stuff to take to the tip before it starts stinking the place out. The insurance people say we can; they've taken photos as evidence. I know the council will collect it at some point if I ask them.'

'Can I help?' I said. 'I've got the Land Rover. It's no trouble and it's filthy inside already so I don't mind the mess.'

'Well if you're sure?' Godfrey said looking marginally more cheerful. 'I don't think my car would allow it. I'll happily pay for your diesel?'

Godfrey had a very smart little Morgan 4/4 that he washed and valeted every week. The thought of putting muddy boxes of wet books into its weedy little boot was too depressing for words.

'I'd be glad to help. Might as well make the most of it before it falls to pieces completely. Look, I'll go and get it now and we'll make a start. And why don't you both come round for dinner tomorrow night?'

I spent the morning loading up the car and driving my soggy load to the council tip. Luckily the rather irascible man who made it his life's work to turn people away with a triumphant smirk and send them to another tip thirty miles further on wasn't around. A fair number of other people were doing much the same thing with trailers filled with sodden furniture and water-damaged appliances. It really was awful to see.

By the time I returned the fire brigade had finished pumping most of the floodwater away, and Peter and Godfrey were sweeping the mud out with a couple of heavy-duty brooms.

We went to the pub for lunch and Godfrey insisted on paying and then, filled with a glow of satisfaction, I went home. I wondered how Helena was getting on. I knew she was leaving work an hour early in order to get ready for her hot date.

Back home the heating hadn't come on and I dithered about starting it up early, but then in my new, economically sage frame of mind I decided against it and found a warm sweater instead.

Full of cottage pie and chips from lunch (approximately half a million calories so not a great start to my new, healthy-eating regime) I didn't feel hungry so I had a quick shower to rid myself of the mouldy bin smell that had settled in my hair and settled down to watch some junk TV and do the ironing. I caught the end of a programme about moving to live in the country – isn't there always one of those on? Then there was a current events programme. I turned over to the news and then ... suddenly there was Oliver Forest. On the television. In my sitting room.

I nearly dropped the iron.

He was looking exceptionally gorgeous in a sleek DJ and I registered a tiny blonde scurrying along behind him. They weren't the main point of the clip, but they had been going into some awards event where the Prime Minister had given out the prizes. The news teams were all hoping for comment on some immigration figures that had just been revealed and Oliver had been in the shot.

A closer look on pause and rewind, OK several closer looks on pause and rewind, showed it was definitely him, and with him was a wretched-looking Pippa in a straggly black dress that seemed to be in danger of falling off her skinny shoulders and her hair was in a complicated up-do.

Lucky cow. Or thinking about it, perhaps not.

I left the frozen image of Oliver on my television for twenty minutes while I finished the ironing. He was looking a bit unsettled I thought. The more I looked at his face, turned slightly to the left and looking over his shoulder at the camera, the more I thought it.

At least he wasn't wearing his plastic boot anymore; it would have ruined the look of his outfit. I even considered ringing Helena up to tell her or taking a photo of him on my phone; but to do so really did seem pathetic and rather stalker-ish so I didn't.

I put everything away and turned the television off. Then I put some music on and poured myself a glass of wine. Then I sent Helena a good luck text. And then I turned the TV back on. Oliver's face was still there, frozen, his dark eyes suspicious. Pippa was looking up at him with a wary expression. I noticed she had her right forearm in some sort of support thing. Oh of course: her failed suicide bid down the stairs.

I rewound the program and listened again to the strident shouts of the interviewer as she tried to get the Prime Minister to say something incriminating or resign or something.

I'm always amazed when they do this. I mean when an MP is going through a scandal as MPs often do, why do reporters think shouting *Are you ashamed of yourself, Minister? Have you always enjoyed kinky sex? Are you considering your position? Which position would that be then, Minister?* will provoke some sort of response?

I looked at Oliver's face for a bit longer and got a bit blue. And I remembered how only recently he had been eating my food, sitting across the table from me, and on top of that he'd kissed me and I'd seen him naked.

No, noooooooo.

I mustn't think about it. It was inappropriate and tasteless. Stop it. Stop it!

He was on his way to some bookish event. I wondered what, so I spent an hour googling overblown glitzy, literary, black tie, London. Nothing came up, so I stared at Oliver a bit more and looked daggers at Pippa. She really did look miserable.

Oooh, phone.

It was Helena.

'It's me,' she said.

She sounded as though she was inside an echo chamber so I guessed she was in a loo.

'What are you doing talking to me? How's it going?'

'Great. He's so nice. I mean nicer than I remember. He's wearing a really smart suit. I've never had anyone take me out in a suit. Ever!'

'Nor have I. How's the food?'

'Fine, I mean more than fine. I wish you were here so you could see it. I keep wanting to take pictures, but I read somewhere that's a very naff thing to do and the waiters would sneer at us. We've got to the fifth course. It's all been delicious. I had a teeny thing made of guinea fowl. I thought it said guinea pig at first and I was going to make a fuss. Good job I didn't.'

'Well go back and be charming and enigmatic and flick your hair about in a sexy and suggestive manner.'

'Oooh I'm not sure I know how!'

'Well do your best!'

'OK.'

Helena rang off and I refilled my wine glass. I wondered if anyone actually did eat guinea pigs? With salad or chips? Who knows?

I turned the TV back on and looked at Oliver a bit more and then gave up the unequal struggle and took a photo of the screen on my phone. Pathetic really.

Anyway, I saw there was a new Scandi-Noir detective series about to start so I decided to watch it. After all, nothing improves one's mood better than seeing a slightly grubby blonde girl in a red dress running through a wood trying to escape a crazed killer in a duffel coat.

And then running through an industrial wasteland – ditto.

Followed by ten minutes looking out of the window of a grimy tower block and having an unintelligible phone conversation with said crazed killer still in his duffel coat with the hood up.

Ten minutes on and the blonde was muttering sullenly into her mobile while a faceless stranger in a Volvo estate car smoked Sobranie cigarettes and watched her.

On another day I might have enjoyed it, but I wasn't really in the mood for a story that dragged along, rich with moody intensity and chunky sweaters.

I wanted to watch a classic film, something fun and light-hearted to get me in a good mood, something schmaltzy and atmospheric. So I put on *Die Hard*. Perfect!

I was about to finish my wine and go to bed when my phone buzzed with a text. It was of course from Helena.

'Good job you painted my toenails!!!!!'

Well would you believe it?

*

The following day I checked my photo of Oliver and then basically did a rerun of the previous day except this time I made a banana loaf for Godfrey and Peter and took a load of cleaning stuff with me to the bookshop. My attempts to fill my life with exciting and daring things was getting off to an exceptionally bad start. I hadn't even started on the decluttering or tidying.

I made coffee and looked in the local paper for gainful

employment. Even with my varied job history there wasn't anything suitable. I wanted to go on holiday and even 'unexpectedly cheap' holidays cost some money. And anyway, I was getting fed up with doing half-arsed jobs, patching together a full week of employment but failing to really feel needed or valuable.

That was the trouble, I realized, as though it was a Damascene moment; I didn't feel as though I was useful. Making cakes was all very well but did it really matter? Was I just contributing to the British obesity epidemic Oliver was so concerned about?

But on the other hand, people liked the writing retreats; I know they did. One day perhaps someone would mention Helena and me in their book acknowledgements.

Heartfelt thanks to Billie and Helena, without whom this book would never have been finished.

I stopped, a slice of cake halfway to my mouth. The idea was rather appealing all of a sudden. I must talk to Helena about it if I could ever prise her away from Nick. But hang on, she already had a job she enjoyed. She wouldn't want to give it up just to help me do something would she? It wouldn't be fair to ask. How could I do them on my own? I couldn't. Could I?

We spent the day scrubbing the last of the mud off the floor and washed the walls. Godfrey's builder had taken the sodden shelving and the stair carpet away and the room so recently filled with enticing piles of books, a couple of velvet armchairs, and gorgeous notebooks and stationery was now empty and had a cold, unloved feel about it. There was a rhythmic hum from two dehumidifiers in the back of the room.

132

'It's taking shape isn't it?' Peter said with more enthusiasm in his voice than I would have been able to muster. 'Now we've got everything cleared out, the builders can start. We'll be back in business in no time, you wait and see.'

'Well that's the plan,' Godfrey said, 'but let's not get too excited.'

We were standing looking at the empty room as Godfrey tried to decide where the new shelves would go and where he would find some replacement chairs. Suddenly my mobile rang. Oooh, was it Helena again with some spicy details? No.

'Hello?'

'Billie? Is this Billie Summers?'

A young woman's voice. Slightly breathless and clipped.

'Yes, can I help you?'

'It's Pippa, Pippa de Witt, Oliver Forest's PA.'

I widened my eyes at Godfrey and Uncle Peter and walked backwards out of the shop into the street where I was nearly run over by a boy on a skateboard.

'Can you hear me?' Pippa said sounding more shrill and worried than ever.

'Yes, yes of course. Hello, I was a bit confused there.'

'I don't see why – you do remember me don't you?'

'Yes, of course, sorry. How's your wrist?'

'Oh OK, I suppose. Look, Mr Forest has asked me to ring you.'

Crumbs, what was all this about then? Had Oliver left something behind after all? Or did he want my recipe for Beef Casserole *au beaucoup de Merlot*?

'Yes?'

'You know of course that Oliver, Mr Forest, is due to launch the paperback version of *Glory 17*. In Ludlow. It's been on his mind a lot. I'm sure he must have discussed it in some detail?'

Well no, not really, but I wasn't going to admit it to her.

'Yes, of course. We had a long chat about it, sounds like quite a do,' I said.

Pippa paused for a moment. 'Does it? I didn't think he wanted ... right. Well Mr Forest needs someone to do the cooking in the house where we will be staying during the event. It's four days in all. Not the catering for the *actual* launch of course. We will be having *proper* caterers there.'

I swallowed this insult and didn't blow a raspberry down the phone, as I felt very inclined to do. 'Fine,' I said.

Actually I was thinking *Just as well, he knows what I'm like. And I do tend to make things up as I go along.*

And I gave Oliver too much chocolate and cake.

Apparently there is such a thing. Who knew?

But I didn't say that because this sounded like a job offer and I was desperate for money. The electricity bill was due as well and – much like the water bill – that's never a pleasant surprise. This could be a godsend. I couldn't afford to be sarky.

Pippa was silent for a moment and I wondered if she had rung off.

'Yes, well ... um ... look, Mr Forest has told me to ring you to see if you are available. He might need you to do some other stuff if my wrist is still weak. Four days from March 16th. All travel expenses of course. Five people including Gideon and Jake and you of course, we fully expect *you* to eat.' She gave a tight little laugh.

Yes, fine, I like my food, no need to be rude – *Twig Woman.*

But Oliver had told Pippa to ring me? Really? Even after the things I'd said about him?

'March 16th,' I repeated rather stunned. 'This year?'

'Yes of course *this year*! Honestly!'

'But that's' – I checked on my fingers – 'only ten days away.'

Was that enough time to lose a stone if I really put my mind to it?

Perhaps this was the push I'd needed? Maybe I should go running too? But it really was very short notice. I usually like to work up to these things, have at least a couple of months to prepare myself. We've already established I'm not what you call madly spontaneous, and anyway doing that takes money.

'Yes. Look if you can't do it I'll tell him. I have a friend – I mean a contact who could step in. Someone with more experience than you by the sound of things.'

Flipping nerve of the woman.

I decided to try and sound more professional and sensible, wondering where this was going. Yes, it wasn't a lot of notice but I could be impulsive for a change. Couldn't I? That was what I was supposed to be doing wasn't it?

I'd been carrying a notebook with owls on the front when she phoned and now I noisily flicked over the pages next to my mobile.

'No, no it's fine, Pippa; give me just a second. Ah yes, I think I can make it! I've … um just checked my diary and if I shuffle a few meetings around I can create a window of opportunity. So yes of course I could help you out. Are there any vegans or people allergic to anything? I know *all* about Oliver's particular likes and dislikes of course.'

I added that last bit in rather a suggestive voice to wind her up.

'I'll let you know. Obviously it's not something I've ever had to think about, apart from the allergy to shellfish of course. I mean, God forbid I should have an M&S prawn sandwich in the office,' Pippa said waspishly. 'We have your correct email and your address? When I find a moment – which won't be any time soon – I'll send some details through. A car will pick you up before six a.m. on the 16th. Security is of course *very tight* on this one, so you must bring proper identification. I'm sure you understand? Your passport and perhaps a driving licence?'

'Right, um ...' I said. This was beginning to sound like something out of *Mission Impossible*.

I'll admit I was a bit distracted here because I'd just seen a picture of a Kardashian in the newsagent's and I couldn't quite believe my eyes. That *must* be Photoshopped? Surely?

Pippa was still talking and I zoned in again, hoping I hadn't missed anything important.

'... I'll be in touch with the details of fees and the menus. It will all be worked out for you.'

'How marvellous,' I said.

'Right, well I can't waste any more time. I have a heap of things to do. We're not all ladies of leisure after all!'

'Cheek!' I muttered.

'Sorry?'

'I said I'll look forward to hearing from you.'

'Hmm.'

Pippa rang off and I stood on the pavement for a few minutes, rather dazed and getting in the way of the kids who were coming out of school in tightly knit gangs, barging each other with their backpacks and shouting insults across the road.

In ten days a car would collect me! And they were going to pay me! I wondered how much. I should have asked before I agreed really. And a book launch!

OMG! This was a sign! This was the light bulb moment when I stopped messing about and got on a firm career path. In future I would credit Oliver Forest for giving me access to his address book and a long line of celebrity parties and events to sort out.

I could run writing retreats for bestselling writers *all the time.* Maybe instead of renting properties I would buy a house overlooking the sea in Cornwall. No, in *France*! I could just imagine myself, putting bowls of luscious, oil-drizzled salad onto a stone table with Monaco glowing in the distant heat haze. Jilly Cooper and J. K. Rowling would be drinking champagne together and laughing and Joan Collins would be sitting under a shady hat running a pink pen through some final edits. Marvellous.

I'd get on Twitter.

@fabulousfooddarling or

@cheftothestars.

I'd need a website and a new apron.

And against all the odds, even after everything I'd said about him, I was going to see Oliver again.

Cool.

Chapter Fourteen

The following day I messed about doing some more housework, threw out some plastic cutlery I'd been hoarding for no good reason, and baked a Swiss roll for Godfrey and Peter. Then I rang Helena to tell her about my exciting news, but her phone was turned off. Hmm, I wonder what she was up to. Her phone was never turned off. I sent her a text.

'What are you doing? Why is your phone turned off?'

I went down to deliver the cake and took some more boxes of wet paper and cardboard to the tip. Then as it was getting cold I went home.

I had checked my emails approximately every two minutes all through the day, but nothing came through from Pippa about the job until five o'clock. The subliminal message being I wasn't important or anywhere near the top of her to-do list.

All she said was I would be expected to do all the catering somewhere called The Lodge, which including myself would accommodate five people. All menus would be worked out, all ingredients would be available at the house.

Piece of cake – literally.

I would be expected to do as I was told, keep quiet and

keep out of the way of the important people. Well it didn't actually use those precise words, but I think that's what it meant. All my travel would be provided and I would be paid ... ! How much? Really? It was almost like getting a month's wages in less than a week. What's not to like? Perhaps she'd made a mistake? Well who cared, maybe she hadn't? I wasn't going to query it.

All I needed to bring was one suitcase, ID, and to be absolutely ready and on the doorstep when the car came to collect me. The implication being if I wasn't they would go without me.

I spent the next hour finding out more about Ludlow. Not exactly exciting but it looked like a nice little town on the Welsh border filled with bookshops and cafés and with a castle to explore if I got any time off. Catherine of Aragon lived there and the Tudors have always been a particular passion of mine. Maybe I could do some research and be inspired towards a new plot line? Marvellous! I couldn't wait. Now this was certainly something that qualified as an adventure.

Helena rang me as I was researching the castle and wondering how far away The Lodge was. Maybe it would be in walking distance?

'It's me!' she said.

'How did it go? Your phone's been turned off all day.'

Helena giggled. 'We had a nice time. The food was scrummy. And we had some wonderful wine too. Red and white. And then we had liqueurs with our coffee. I had Cointreau and he had—'

'Yes, but what happened!' I said. 'Tell me what happened!'

'Well we went back to his house afterwards.'

'Yes?'

'And he put some music on. Simon and Garfunkel, I think.'

'Helena!'

'And then we had some more wine and well, he asked if I'd like to stay over. So I did.'

I gasped. 'Helena!'

She giggled again. 'I know!'

'And?'

'And we, you know.'

Helena snorted with laughter down the phone.

'You lucky mare!' I said.

'I know!'

'And? And?'

'I'm still at his house. It's really lovely, not like a bloke's house at all. It's a little terrace overlooking a green. He bought it three years ago and he's been doing it up ever since. He's really tidy, just like me.'

'I bet you it's just a front. I predict the cupboard under the stairs is filled with dirty washing and black bin liners full of takeaway cartons.'

'Ha! You're so wrong, Miss Clever Clogs, because there isn't a cupboard under the stairs. He took it out when he moved in and put up a coat rack. He's gone out to get some wine because we finished it all last night. And he never has takeaways. He's made a lamb tagine for later and he didn't have to use a recipe or anything. He's so lovely.'

'Aw bless. You do sound happy.'

'I am, I really am. I just thought I'd check in so you know I'm OK. Well more than OK.'

'You'll have to go home for some clean clothes!'

'We did that earlier on.' She giggled.

'Where is my friend Helena Fairchild and what have you done with her?'

'I know! I can't believe this is me!'

'Well enjoy yourself, you deserve a bit of fun.'

'What are you doing?'

'You'll never guess. I had a phone call from Oliver's PA, Pippa. She wanted to know if I was available to do the catering for five people for four days in March, when he has his paperback launch. *Glory 17*, do you remember?'

'Wow! In Ludlow?'

'That's right. They are offering me a shedload of money so I'm not going to refuse am I? I need to get the car through its MOT in September, the gas bill is due, so is the water bill and the electricity bill, and I really don't want to ask Mum to sub me again. I still owe her for when the washing machine broke down.'

We talked about the bookshop and how things were going, and she started to tell me how Nick organized his kitchen cupboards.

Suddenly she broke off. 'Ooops better go; I can see his car pulling into the drive. He has a drive! And his car's nice and clean too. Not filled with old takeaway coffee cups and apple cores like yours is.'

'He sounds a paragon of virtue,' I said.

Helena gave a giggle and rang off.

Maybe not then?

*

I spent a few minutes thinking sentimental thoughts about Helena and Nick and then the thought crossed my mind that at that very minute they could be up to all sorts of filthy things in the privacy of his nice tidy house. So I thought about something else and went to put some washing on.

Oooh, phone.

'It's me,' Mum said. 'Has Josie spoken to you about us going to stay? They're now expecting us on March 18th because Finn and Hector are in the school play and they have tickets for us all to go. Isn't that super?'

'Hmm, school and play. Those are two words I try hard to avoid having anything to do with after last time,' I said. '*#Soblessed.*'

'Now don't be mean. It wasn't Hector's fault. Anyone can have a nosebleed. And most of the stain came out didn't it?'

'Well I've just been offered a last-minute job to do that means I won't be home until the 20th.'

'What? You're not coming? You can't be serious?' she said, her voice rather panicky.

'Sorry,' I said rather gleefully, 'I'm off to Ludlow for four days, doing private catering for a book launch.'

Mum gave a heavy sigh. 'Oh bloody hell. That means I have to go on my own to watch Finn and Hector dressed as Easter rabbits, roaring out "Bright Eyes". Well Josie will be there of course although apparently she's going to be making teas in the far distant land of *out the back*, and Mark can't go because, of course, he has a works event. Doesn't he always?'

I giggled. 'Sorry.'

'Liar.'

'Anyway, I'm going to think about packing.'

'Are you?' Mum said wistfully. 'That's nice.'

What to pack? It was March after all, so I dug out some warm sweaters and three pairs of jeans. But March can be quite mild, can't it? And after checking the weather forecast I pulled out one pair of jeans and put in some T-shirts and a couple of dresses. But we might be out in the country, and there probably would be rain. I went to find my wellingtons, realized they were Matt's and far too big, so I ditched them and put in some rather nice silver lace-up brogues I had bought in the January sales this year and never worn. I would look edgy and fashion savvy in those. Or would I look as though I was on castors?

Then I put in some Birkenstocks and took out a pair of trainers. Then I put the trainers back and took out a sweatshirt. Then I realized I might be advised to find a dressing gown. And I wouldn't want Pippa to see me in my washed-out Snoopy pj's, so perhaps I'd better get some new ones. I sat back on my heels and wondered briefly what she wore in bed and then with a cold blast of horror I wondered if she and Oliver ... if they were, like, going to be *an item* on this trip? Surely not!

I thought about the way he had talked to her and her obvious nervousness round him. Nope, there was no way Pippa would put up with him. Not unless she was a complete doormat.

Helena called again. 'You'll never guess what?' she said without preamble.

'What?'

'I mentioned the idea of Scotland and the castle and the aged kilted retainer to Nick and he's up for it!'

'Fantastic!'

'Yes! Isn't it exciting? He's downstairs now on his computer looking for places for us to stay.'

'So he's downstairs. And you're upstairs? And I bet you're not cleaning the bathroom?'

143

'No of course not! His bathroom is spotless. I'm in bed.'

'Bloody hell, still? He's got stamina, I'll give him that! Listen I'm going to be away for a bit doing this catering job. I'll be back before Easter, but I guess you'll be away in the Wee Glen o'the Kirk by then eating haggis and shortbread.'

'With any luck, yes. Oooh I'd better go, I think he's coming.'

'You might like to rephrase that,' I said before she hung up.

Bloody hell, who would have thought it? Helena and Tweedy Nick having a shag-fest! What larks!

If she could do exciting things, then so could I.

I had a list to stick to now after all.

*

I sent Pippa an email asking about the facilities at The Lodge. Was it fully equipped with all the stuff a chef of my calibre would need?

She didn't reply.

Should I take anything? My knives for example? I have a special and highly prized collection of kitchen knives stored safely in a canvas roll to take with me to retreats. Should I take them?

No answer.

Honestly, people can be so rude sometimes.

I spent the next few days cleaning the flat and changing the sheets so it would be nice when I got home.

I was about to empty the fridge when I had a brainwave, one of incredible brilliance and magnitude. So I put my coat on and immediately walked round to the bookshop.

Godfrey and Uncle Peter weren't in their flat when I arrived but there were some builders sitting outside the shop on a couple of upturned buckets, smoking roll-ups and drinking tea out of stained mugs. They directed me to the pub and I found my bosses there eating a couple of enormous steak and kidney pies and drinking beer out of the tankards they kept behind the bar.

I accepted a drink and explained my plan.

'So you can use my place while I'm away. It's not fancy but it's warm and you'd be doing me a favour looking after it while I'm away.'

They looked at each other.

Peter was first to speak. 'Are you sure? I mean we'd love to. Our flat is so cold and miserable at the moment. Our heating won't be working again until Monday. The builders have to put a new boiler in to replace the other one; it was flood damaged. I'm sure it will be fine but well, it is a bit cheerless at the moment.'

'I'm positive. As I said you'd be doing me a favour.'

'Well if you put it like that ... well yes, it would be wonderful,' Godfrey said patting my hand. 'I'm fed up with going to bed in a tracksuit. And, of course, the smell of damp is very depressing. Once the heating is going again the building will dry out in no time but until then, well yes, we'd love to. And thank you.'

'No riotous parties though,' I said, handing him my spare keys.

Peter wagged his head from side to side, his eyes twinkling.

'Well I can't absolutely promise.'

*

On the morning of the 16th March I was awake at two-thirty a.m., three-forty-five a.m., four-fifteen a.m., and five-oh-five a.m. At this point I gave up pretending I was going back to sleep, got up, had a shower, and dressed. My case had been packed, repacked, and re-repacked and I was taking a backpack with my laptop and all my other cables, pens, and stuff. Pippa still hadn't replied to my email so I took an executive decision and packed my kitchen knives in their canvas roll as well. It was as though I was going into battle. Now this *was* going to be an adventure.

At six o'clock I was waiting just inside the front door, ready to leap out and throw myself across the car's bonnet if necessary. I wondered if I was going to be sharing the drive to Ludlow with Pippa (ghastly thought) or maybe Oliver (scary thought) or possibly both of them (worst of both worlds).

At three minutes past six – just when I was starting to panic – a car with blacked-out windows, polished to impressive brilliance, pulled up and a driver got out. He wasn't wearing a peaked cap or anything, but he was obviously not a taxi driver and by the look of it this car wasn't a taxi.

He ascertained I was who I said I was and then he very respectfully placed my rather old and unglamorous bags into the boot. He then handed me into the back seat, asked about my preferences regarding car temperature, offered me still and sparkling water in pretty bottles and a crisply covered pillow and what felt like a cashmere rug in case I wanted a snooze. He then closed the partition between us and we were off.

Actually, I *was* rather tired having spent a restless and largely wakeful night, so I decided I would have a sleep. I knew the journey to Ludlow would take a few hours so it wasn't likely

I would miss anything. The car was wonderfully quiet and comfortable and my driver, whose name was Henry, drove as though he had a bucket of water on the back seat so no swerving around corners or sudden braking. It wasn't hard to just close my eyes and Mmmmm.

I woke up some time later slightly confused because we were still on the motorway. I knew from my in-depth research (I'd googled it) that Ludlow was nowhere near a motorway. I blinked a few times and took a swig of the still, designer water. It tasted just like water.

Yes this was definitely the motorway and we were passing junction 4. I sat up a bit straighter. Had Henry got lost? Was I being abducted by white slavers?

I tapped on the partition and Henry slid it open a bit.

'Ma'am?'

'I just wondered where we are?'

'Nearly there, ma'am, we won't be long now.'

He closed the partition and I took another sip of water.

And then I saw the sign.

Heathrow – Terminal 5.

I nearly spat my water out again and had to put a hand over my mouth to protect the beautiful leather upholstery.

I tapped on the glass partition and Henry opened it.

'We're at Heathrow?' I said.

'Terminal 5, ma'am. I told you we wouldn't be long.'

'But aren't we supposed to be going to Ludlow?' I said.

'I was told to deliver you to Terminal 5, ma'am. Miss de Witt will be meeting you.'

'Oh,' I said doubtfully.

Perhaps everyone was gathering here and we would go on in a minibus or something? It seemed a long-winded way of doing things. I looked at my watch; we had been travelling for over two hours.

We pulled up to the departures doors and Henry got out and went to find a trolley. Then he opened the boot and retrieved my luggage.

'If you go into the hall and ask at the information desk, Miss de Witt should be there,' he said. And then he drove off.

I felt like a right idiot. All my thoughts of medieval castles and the green rolling hills of Shropshire (I'd never been there so I wasn't sure if there were any) faded as I lugged my case into the glass and steel portals of Terminal 5.

Inside everything was noise and flashing departure and arrivals boards. People were milling about with crying children and buggies and wheelchairs. Four people were standing in the middle of the hall unpacking their suitcases, looking for something. There were fast food outlets and a bureau de change. A man driving an electric buggy loaded down with luggage and some cross-looking people nearly ran me over. It was everything I hate about travelling.

A posse of flight crew strutted across the concourse with their little wheeled bags behind them, ignoring us mere travellers. With the lift of an eyebrow they managed to convey they had just been somewhere exceptionally glamorous and were about to go somewhere even better. I bet they'd just got off the Easy Jet flight from Birmingham.

I stood in everyone's way for a few minutes and looked around for an information desk. There was a coffee shop to one side. What a great idea that would be for someone who hadn't had any breakfast. There were signs for oversized luggage. Toilets. Various time zones, a pharmacy, check-in, a newsagent.

I sent Helena a text.

'*You won't believe this, I've been driven to Heathrow. Looks like I'm flying to Ludlow. Bit weird? Private plane?*'

'Billie! Billie – over here!'

I turned to see Pippa in a tight pair of leather trousers and some vertiginous heels clip-clopping towards me. She wouldn't get far in those on Ludlow's cobbled streets.

'You're rather late!' she said as though I had encouraged Henry to go more slowly just to annoy her. I started to voice this thought, but she cut across me.

'Yes well you're here now.'

She rummaged in a capacious leather tote bag with a metal clasp bearing the name of some overinflated designer I'd never heard of. She was wearing some sort of complicated wrist support, which didn't make the task any easier.

'Can I help?'

'Take these.' She handed me a brown manila envelope with my name on the front. It was like we were conducting a drug deal or something.

I half expected a couple of burly airport policemen to come dashing towards us with cries of *Up against the wall and spread 'em* or *Right, Chummy, you're nicked*, and wrestle us both to the ground.

'What's this?' I said looking at it.

'Your travel details, tickets, information,' Pippa said in a tone implying '*duh*' at the end. 'And this is a note Oliver told me to give you when I saw you. Now look, the flight leaves at one-fifteen. You'll have to look for the gate number up there.'

She handed over a blue envelope and waved vaguely at the information board.

'I didn't know Ludlow had an airport?' I said. 'Wouldn't it be just as quick to drive?'

Pippa looked at me as though I was simple.

'Don't be daft. Look I'm off to a private lounge to find Jake and have some well-earned champagne. Knowing what the next few days is going to be like I'm going to need it. It's one-fifteen OK? Don't forget.'

'Yes fine. Um – what—'

'Look in the envelope. The one-fifteen flight to Boston BA203. Got it?'

'Boston?'

'Boston. Logan International Airport. Massachusetts.'

'Do you mean the Massachusetts in America?'

She patted me on the arm. 'Well done, you're getting there.'

'I can't go to America for four days!' I spluttered.

'Well you should have said so before now,' Pippa said looking confused. 'I did tell you.'

'Sorry, I thought we were going to Ludlow. Shropshire,' I said, trying hard to hang on to the last threads of my sanity.

'Ludlow. Vermont,' Pippa said very slowly. 'When I phoned you up to ask if you were free. Look, are you up for this or not?'

Had she told me? Surely not. I would *never* have agreed to this.

I hesitated and Pippa looked at her watch.

'Well?'

Aha! Wait a minute. Oliver had said I should seize opportunities, have adventures. Well this was deffo an adventure. The new improved Billie Summers would say yes. Absolutely!

Sometimes you have to stop being scared and just go for it.

Either it will work out or it won't. That's life.

This was going to be my new mantra.

'Yes!' I yelled, with perhaps an excessive amount of excitement.

'Right, well calm down. I'll see you later.'

She teetered off at speed towards some frosted glass doors and disappeared round a corner, leaving me with the tickets and the blue envelope in my hand and my suitcase at my feet. I stuffed the tickets in my pocket and opened the envelope. There was a single sheet of paper, a brief handwritten note written in a jagged hand.

Billie – I seem to remember we agreed you should have some adventures. Well how about this for starters? Oliver Forest.

Chapter Fifteen

It was nine-thirty and the first thing I needed to do was get rid of my case. There was of course a long queue for the check-in desk, which I joined in between a group of back-packers who were dressed for a day on the beach and another couple who were quarrelling about whether Pookie would be happy in the new cattery.

I stopped my brain from chanting 'you can't go, you can't go' over and over again and fought down the nausea I was feeling. Perhaps I was just hungry?

I was going to America for four days. How ridiculous was that? Sort of exciting though, I suppose. This was undoubtedly an adventure. I was doing something thrilling. There wouldn't be any language difficulty. Well not much anyway.

Oliver had given me something exciting to do.

Actually, I'd been thinking about this ever since the subject of my dull life had come up at the retreat and I definitely remembered doing exciting things in the past. I mean I'd been to Glastonbury a few years ago. I didn't like it much, especially the toilets which were beyond terrible, but I'd even crowd surfed until a bloke with his arm in plaster had fallen over and dropped me.

I'd shared a joint with Matt. Yes I'd been sick into his baseball cap afterwards, but I'd done drugs.

I'd been pissed more times than I could remember.

I'd even tried to snog a policeman on New Year's Eve once in Trafalgar Square. A very long time ago. So there!

As soon as I had checked in I would phone Helena and tell her all about this.

At last I got to the desk and a woman with navy blue nails to match her suit typed my details into the computer while at the same time having an arch and flirtatious exchange with one of the baggage handlers.

'Boston,' she said when she could spare me a moment. 'S'nice. Holiday?'

'Yes and a bit of cooking for some … friends.'

'S'nice,' she said again and typed a bit more, frowning at the screen.

'I'm just popping over the pond. For four days,' I added casually, hoping she'd be impressed.

Perhaps this was how Michael Palin or Bill Bryson felt when they went off on their round-the-world jaunts?

'Nice,' she said still frowning at her screen. Not impressed.

I waited as I always do on these occasions for her to say I couldn't travel. I was barred from the United States, my passport was out of date, my ESTA was invalid, I had a criminal record, I looked suspicious.

The baggage handler said something under his breath and she turned and slapped his arm. Then she rolled her eyes at me.

'Honestly, what's he like? You don't have to be mad to work here!'

I gave her a weak smile and waited for her to find out that Interpol wanted me.

At last she finished typing out the *Book of Exodus* and looked up.

'You're booked into a mid-section seat, but there is a window seat free right at the back if you wanted it?'

She turned her screen round to show me a lot of little squares.

'Wow thanks so much,' I said rather effusively although I didn't really understand where she was going with this.

She took my suitcase, weighed it, and put a long paper tag around the handle. Then she shunted it on to a conveyor belt and it disappeared through some rubber doors.

'You're right at the back, by the window,' she said. 'Safest seat on the plane.'

'Is it?' I said rather startled.

'So they say. If the plane crashes the tail section often breaks off. Have a nice flight!'

I gulped a bit. 'Thanks.'

I took my passport and boarding card and wandered off looking for something to do for three hours. Go through security I suppose. In my nervous state there seemed to be loads of suspicious-looking people wandering about – any one of which could have evil intent. Perhaps once I was through security and been X-rayed a couple of times I'd feel a bit better?

I headed towards the screens and the terrifying-looking security guards and read the thousands of notices about what I was not allowed to do or take on board.

I reassured myself I didn't have any gas canisters, explosives, animals alive or dead, fruit, fireworks, flares, or magnets and wondered pityingly what sort of moron would want to take those things on a plane anyway.

Ah.

The same sort of moron who had a canvas roll of kitchen knives in their backpack perhaps?

I froze to the spot with horror. What should I do?

I could see through to where huge security men and granite-faced women were frisking people and X-raying their hand luggage. I backed off a few paces. My knives were valuable, the tools of my trade, and I loved them. They were honed to a perfect pitch of sharpness. I could shave the whiskers off a gnat with some of them.

But I couldn't take them with me. Damn it. Why hadn't Pippa said something? Why hadn't I thought before checking my suitcase in? Trying to sneak a load of knives through Heathrow security was probably one escapade too far.

I waited until no one was looking too closely and took the canvas holdall out of my backpack. I felt the weight of them one last time and then put them into the secure bin along with the half-drunk water bottles, submachine guns, arsenic, and detonators. And then I went through security, was frisked, took my shoes and belt off, watched my bag being X-rayed, and then I stopped bemoaning the loss of my knives; after all I was into duty free!

I wandered around looking at glitzy fashion boutiques, strangely coloured handbags, enormous teddy bears, and hundreds of different neck pillows. Perhaps I should buy a neck pillow? Perhaps I needed some hideous crystal-embellished sunglasses? Or a tin of caviar? I looked at the prices; how did people afford these things?

No, it was breakfast time, and if I was going to fly the

Atlantic what I needed was a bar and a drink! If I was having an adventure, I was jolly well going to have one!

I got my phone out, plugged it into a convenient socket and rang Helena, hoping she was out of bed for once and not at work. Her phone was switched off so either of the previous options could apply. I left her a text telling her brief details of my ongoing adventure. Then I tried ringing my mother but couldn't get hold of her either, which was annoying because I could have really wound her up.

Then I ordered some Eggs Benedict and a glass of champagne because it was a special occasion and Mum had given me some spending money, which was both very welcome and slightly embarrassing. Anyway, I felt quite sophisticated, even though I was sitting next to two men in Arsenal shirts who were drinking pints of lager as though their lives depended on it.

'So why Heathrow?'

It was Helena.

I texted back.

'Apparently I'm off to Ludlow, Vermont. Flying in to Boston.'

':-o Flipping heck!'

My phone rang.

'So what's going on?' Helena said.

I explained while the two Arsenal fans next to me shamelessly eavesdropped. I swear they looked impressed.

'So I'm on the afternoon flight to Boston,' I said. 'I'm going to America for four days and I'm drinking champagne.'

'Blimey!' Helena said. 'With your new best friend Pippa?'

'She's disappeared somewhere. I'm on my own.'

Gosh, this was on my list wasn't it? I was flying somewhere on my own. I hadn't really taken that in.

'Well have fun. Buy yourself something in duty free. Some of those end-of-range designer things. You've been on that diet for ages. You deserve a treat.'

Hmm, well yes I had been on a diet and like most things you go *on* I'd also been *off*. Still I had lost a few pounds so perhaps she was right?

I finished breakfast and my champagne, grabbed all my stuff, and went shopping. I was going to be reckless and crazy. I was going to think outside the box. As a result I almost bought a skirt patterned with rainbows but at the last minute decided against it. Apart from anything else it was wrongly sized and there was no way I was going to reward myself for a week avoiding bread with a skirt labelled XXL. And I couldn't afford it. Instead I bought a giant Toblerone; well you have to don't you?

Then I went into a bookshop and bought a copy of *The Fool in Charge*. It was a very satisfying fat book with a cover rich in sandy colours, exploding starburst bombs, and a lean hero walking away, his machine gun propped over one arm.

A roller coaster ride of betrayal, courage, and loss.

Ross Black's unforgettable portrayal of one man's fight against terrorism and prejudice.

There was even a tiny picture of Oliver on the back cover. Arms folded, staring into the camera with that wary glance I knew so well. I stood looking at it for several seconds while people barged into me with their maps and neck pillows and new iPads. I suddenly felt a bit important.

There was an elderly man standing next to me looking at the same book, peering over his glasses at the blurb on the back.

I almost felt like nudging him to show off my specialist knowledge.

Oh yes that's Ross Black. His real name is Oliver Forest. By the way I know him; I've cooked for him and seen him naked.

No perhaps not.

At twelve-fifteen I saw our flight had been called to a gate that was probably five miles away and as one a crowd of people, me included, started scurrying towards the moving pavements and escalators, terrified we would be left behind.

The quarrelling couple were sitting by the departure gate, now apparently not speaking to each other at all. They sat next to each other, heads turned away at right angles like the picture of Prince Charles and Princess Diana in the back of that car just before they separated.

The group of backpackers were already there, having made their hand luggage into a defensive wall against the rest of us. They were sitting on the floor talking about someone called Jezza, with their hairy legs sticking out, a trip hazard for everyone.

There was no sign of Pippa. I assumed being in the posh seats she would not have to wait with the rest of us peasants but was already on the plane having Veuve Clicquot and a foot massage, sucking up the glamour. At last we were called up to board.

There wasn't much glamour to be had down in seat 67K. I was probably the last person to get on board and it took me practically as long to get to the back of the plane and into my seat as it did to get to the airport in the first place. Everyone seemed to be putting stuff into the overhead lockers and taking it out again including the backpackers who all had enormous bags, which could have hidden a stowaway.

It took absolutely ages. I just stood feeling resigned while the backpackers chatted to their neighbours and each other and asked everyone where Jezza was. Then they decided to take all their backpacks out of the overhead lockers again and started unpacking them to find earphones and mobiles and chargers. Suddenly they gave a collective roar of approval as a young man in cargo shorts and a ragged Coldplay T-shirt came up the aisle behind me.

'Jezza, you bastard!'

'Dude!'

They all tried to man-hug each other, overlooking the fact that I was standing in between them. Not altogether an unpleasant experience if I was honest.

Still, eventually I got past them and was delighted to see my window seat had an empty place by it. So, if nothing else, if the plane did crash I could watch the ground coming up to meet me with my bag on the seat next to me. I fastened the seat belt and sat with my hands clamped to the arms of the seat. The stewardesses bustled about shutting the overhead lockers and almost immediately people would get up and open them again.

At last the plane backed away from the airport building and started wandering across the tarmac towards other planes that were lining up. There were lots of pinging noises and a safety demonstration; I watched smug in the knowledge I was in the safest seat. Unless we landed on water in which case I was buggered.

Suddenly came the moment I'd dreaded, when the plane started sort of galloping across the tarmac and the gentle noises intensified to a roar. I did what I could to pull the plane into the air by the seat arms and shut my eyes. There was a sickening swoop and a moment when I wondered if the tail of the plane was going to scrape along the runway and actually break off. But then finally we were in the air.

I know everyone complains about airline food, but I really enjoyed it. It's not about the food anyway. Who cares what it is? It was about all those little packets and tubs. There were tiny salt and pepper sachets that I didn't find until I got to the dessert, some sort of chicken thing, and there was free wine.

The stewardess soon got fed up with trudging to the far end of the plane so she left me four mini bottles, which sat very nicely with my glass of champagne. I began to feel quite relaxed and not panicky at all. I took out my notebook, and with a flourish put a tick next to point 11 on my list.

There was an entertainment screen to investigate on the back of the seat in front with myriad films and programmes. And of course there was the interactive map to show us where we were going. Gradually we were leaving the UK and heading out over the Atlantic. Below us were thick folds of cloud and the occasional glimpse of the ocean. It was exciting but terrifying at the same time. Then I remembered I had forgotten to phone Helena and my mother again and I felt a bit guilty.

I read a bit of Oliver's book, a bit where – chillingly – Major Harry Field's new love interest was blown up on a passenger flight from London to Boston. I hoped Oliver didn't have the gift of prophecy.

Fortified by too much wine and excitement I had a sleep, my head pressed up against the window, and I dreamed of floodwater and bombs and knives and Oliver. And in my dream he kissed my cheek again and gave me a present and when I unwrapped it I found a wedge of cheese. And then I realized he was naked and I was so shocked I woke up and it was probably just as well.

*

The cabin crew brought us the airline's idea of a cream tea as local time was five p.m., but of course my body clock said nearly ten p.m. and it seemed a bit odd to say the least. How did businessmen put up with this sort of lifestyle? Drinking champagne for breakfast. Eating weird things at the wrong time? Still with a flash of the spirit that made Britain great, I managed it.

Shortly afterwards we landed in Boston out of a brilliantly clear blue sky. That was scary as we seemed to be about to land on the top deck of a cruise ship and then there was the distinct possibility we would ditch into the sea. Happily, at the last minute a runway appeared and with a gut-rocking thud we landed and I could concentrate on unclenching my fingers from the armrests.

Then there was immigration when I was glad I had dumped my knives because I think any one of the vinegary-faced officials I passed would have gladly arrested me, beaten me up, and chucked me in chains onto the next plane back to London. They made the Heathrow lot look quite friendly in comparison and they had massive guns too. By the time I had claimed my luggage and got out to the arrivals area, another hour and a half had passed and I was ready for bed. It was not to be.

A sweaty-looking man with dark glasses was waiting, holding up a card with *my name written on it*. How cool was that? There were lots of other sweaty-looking men holding cards up. Most of them read like something out of the Countdown Conundrum. *Sybilla Summers* seemed quite tame by comparison.

I went up to him with a triumphant smile, which he didn't return, and he took me out to where there was a huge red, van-truck thing waiting with Pippa and a bored-looking Jake already sitting inside.

Sunglasses man took my bags and slung them into the back with none of Henry's finesse, got into the driver's seat, and we were off again.

'Where *were* you?' Pippa muttered.

'Same as you: getting off the plane, coming through immigration,' I said.

'You took flipping *ages*,' she grumbled.

Yes because I absolutely *love* looking at my reflection in what are obviously two-way mirrors. Shuffling along at the end of a never-ending snake of people all of whom looked a bit dodgy in my opinion, even though they must have been through security too. And of course there was a group of five people immediately in front of me who hadn't ever heard of ESTAs and couldn't speak English. And two men in FBI jackets took one of them away through a mirrored door. That bit was terrifically exciting.

Jake – nice-looking, rather rumpled, and sexy in a designer stubble sort of way – leaned across Pippa and held out a hand to me.

'Jake Mitchell,' he said in an Estuary drawl, 'Oliver Forest's agent. We met very briefly? Never forget a pretty face. Better keep on her good side, Pippa, if we want to avoid food poisoning. Eh?'

Pippa made a dismissive noise and pulled her leather-

162

trousered leg away from me. I noticed some flat pumps had replaced the stilettos. Apart from those she looked just as well groomed as ever. I suppose life in business class is a bit more restful than the back of the plane, even if I was theoretically safer.

Jake talked quite briskly to me for a few minutes while Pippa yawned and sighed between us. To be fair it was nearly midnight GMT.

'How long will it take us to get to Ludlow?' I asked.

Jake pushed his sweater back to reveal an impressive, rather glitzy watch.

'Couple of hours I suppose. If we live to get out of Boston.'

'I said we should have stayed the night before the flight in a hotel. We could have avoided the early start. But no one listens to me do they?' Pippa said. 'And now we're all knackered. I don't know why Oliver had to be so stiff-necked about it.'

'Well it gave me another night at home with the kids,' Jake said.

Beside me Pippa fidgeted and fussed at her scarf.

'You're married?' I said. I'll admit I was rather surprised.

He grinned. 'Well I was. Divorced. But all very amicable. It was my turn to have the kids – Caro was at a uni reunion.'

'Wow,' I said, 'for some reason I didn't think ... well never mind.'

Jake grinned. 'Didn't think I was the marrying type? I was; I still am. Trouble was six years after the wedding she decided she preferred my best friend.'

'But you said the divorce was amicable?'

'Oh it was. Well it all worked out anyway. In the end.'

By now the van-truck thing was whizzing up a slip road,

missing other trucks and cars by fractions of millimetres. Our driver, still hidden behind his dark glasses, was chewing gum like a professional and snarling under his breath, occasionally thumping the steering wheel with the heel of his hand and making incomprehensible sounds of annoyance in Italian.

Having told me all he knew about Boston, the Red Sox, and Vermont Jake started playing a game on his mobile phone. Next to me Pippa shut her eyes, so I bundled my coat up into a pillow, rested it against the window, and tried to sleep. The car roared on through the evening rush hour and out into the suburbs. The road signs were strangely familiar. Cambridge, Woburn, Londonderry, Manchester.

When I woke up we were going through Bradford, Newbury, Newport. The scenery was still heavy-duty industrial with huge shopping malls, massive advertising boards on either side of us, and mile after mile of concrete road ahead.

Then we passed the Vermont state border and things seemed to change in the blink of an eye. Acres of dark forest stretched away to the horizon and for miles at a time ours was the only car on the road, the headlights piercing the growing blackness as we headed west.

Just as I was thinking we were going to be driving forever, we turned onto a side road where the forest crowded in on us on all sides. The darkness under the trees was dense and frightening. Occasionally I saw the reflection of an animal's eyes in the headlights' beam. From time to time I could see the lights of a house. Each one looked warm and inviting and I wished this house or *this* one was the one we sought.

Suddenly the car swung in a steep curve across the road and up a stony driveway. I saw the bright glow of windows through the trees and as we came closer a veranda or porch stretched the length of the house on two levels, illuminated by strings of lights that twinkled as the wind blew them. It was absolutely magical.

Next to me Pippa sat up straighter in her seat and gave a heavy sigh.

'That's the end of the peace and quiet then,' she muttered. 'We're here.'

I opened the car door, my legs stiff from the journey, and stepped down into the crisp, cold night air and shivered in my inadequate coat. Pippa tumbled down behind me with an exclamation of alarm and I grabbed her to stop her from falling over. Under her coat I could feel her wrist support and she winced.

'Golly, careful. Are you OK?'

She caught her breath and gave me a tiny smile.

'Yes, fine thanks.' She suddenly looked rather stressed and very young. She stopped by the side of the driver who was still snarling and battling to unwedge our cases from the boot. She reached across, took out a laptop bag, and turned to hand it to me.

'Would you mind? I don't trust many people with this.'

'Sure,' I said, hooking it over my shoulder.

Pippa looked up at the house and took a deep breath. 'Oh God. Here we go.'

'It'll be fine,' I said.

Pippa turned and looked at me. 'I bloody hope so. I'm at my wit's end.'

Suddenly the front door opened and there was Oliver Forest. He came towards the car, shielding his eyes against the beam of the car headlights.

'For heaven's sake come inside quickly – it's cold,' he said and when I heard his voice again, when I knew it was him, when I recognized the shape of him in the darkness – I shivered with excitement.

'We're trying,' Jake said with a laugh. 'Girls, go inside. We'll bring the cases.'

Pippa was at his side. 'I don't mind. I mean if there's something light. I could help?'

Jake put his arm around her shoulders and steered her towards the house. She looked up at him, the lights from the house reflecting in her eyes.

'He won't bite, Pippa. Go on, stand up for yourself.'

Jake turned away and I saw the expression on Pippa's face as she watched him. There was no doubt about it, she had an almighty crush on Jake and he had no idea.

Now this could be interesting.

Chapter Sixteen

The house was amazing. You know those photo shoots you sometimes see of rugged men in plaid shirts and lumberjack boots looking all outdoorsy and lustrous with health? They usually have a sexy wife with no visible hands because she has tucked them cutely into the sleeves of her snuggly sweater. Occasionally there are a couple of adorable children somewhere in the picture doing something photogenic with a fishing rod or a puppy. You know that family don't you? Well this is the house they would have lived in.

There was glowing timber everywhere, high cathedral ceilings with a gallery landing above us. There were massive sofas covered in tweed cushions and cashmere throws. There was a six-foot square coffee table in front of a gigantic stone fireplace where a log fire was burning with Hollywood perfection.

'Come in and get warm,' Oliver said. 'Can I get anyone a drink? Wine? Beer? Hot chocolate? Or would you like something to eat?'

'I'd like the loo,' Jake said dropping his jacket on the arm of a chair and heading off down a corridor. It looked as though he'd been here before.

I unfastened my coat and went to stand in front of the fire, holding my hands out to the blaze.

'I've been travelling for fifteen hours. I'd love a glass of champagne to celebrate getting here!' Pippa said, lifting her chin.

Splendid idea! Atta girl, Pippa, I thought with admiration. Wouldn't mind one myself actually.

Oliver looked surprised for a moment. 'Anyone else? Billie?'

'Oh I think Billie's tired. She's been snoring and drooling on my shoulder like a baby all the way here,' Pippa teased shooting me a grin.

'I haven't!' I said indignantly. 'I'd love one. You can carry your own bloody laptop next time!'

Pippa giggled and we exchanged a look. Maybe she wasn't as bad as I'd thought?

I pinched my leg to wake myself up and came into the room, looking around admiringly.

'This is a beautiful house,' I said. 'Just gorgeous. Have you lived here long?'

'My grandfather was a timber merchant and he built it. It's the family home,' Oliver said.

Golly! My grandfather worked for the council and the only thing he ever built was a shed. And the door never closed properly either; it had to be wedged shut with a brick.

Funny what people do with their lives isn't it? I wondered if in years to come my grandchildren would point out something I'd done and be proud of me. If they did it certainly wouldn't be for baking a few cakes. I needed to think a bit more about point 6 on my list. Think about the boring stuff like pensions and annuities or whatever they were.

Oliver went out and returned with a champagne bottle and four glasses. Pippa, meanwhile, had arranged herself at the far end of the sofa in front of the fire, tucking her legs up underneath her. She looked about twelve. I looked at my own reflection in the mirror over the fire. I looked knackered. Pippa looked annoyingly fresh-faced. How did she manage it? Perhaps she was just young?

Jake came back in and slumped on one of the other sofas. I went to look out of the huge windows. Outside was utter blackness.

'Gideon is arriving tomorrow; he's got the publicity department all cranked up and ready for action. The Hall is nearly ready. The caterers are going to be there the day after tomorrow. Everything is in place.'

Oliver handed out the champagne. The atmosphere in the room was rather tense. It was just what I didn't need.

I went to sit next to Pippa.

'Remind me? Who's Gideon?' I asked out of the corner of my mouth.

'Oliver's US publisher. From Marymount Books. He's Very Important,' she stressed with a meaningful look.

'Welcome,' Oliver said and we all clinked glasses.

Oliver started to talk to Jake about someone called Bruno so I turned my phone on and a battery of good luck, safe journey texts came through from my mother and Helena. Followed by one from Josie telling me how jealous she was and filling me in on how awful the twins' school reports had been. Apparently there had been an episode with some poster paint. Luckily for Hector and Finn she seemed to find this funny and evidence of their marvellous individuality. I realized my phone battery was low; I should find my charger before bed.

Across the room Jake and Oliver were talking about people called Miles, Fee, and Sonny who had been at a party where

Simon and Fizzy got engaged. Jake had recently taken on a new intern called Beatrice who was proving to be both clueless and lazy.

'Did you have a good flight?' Oliver said turning to include me in the conversation.

I sipped my champagne and wished I could have had Helena on Skype with me so she could see what I was doing.

'Fine,' I said. 'I love flying. I love airports too.'

Lies, all lies. Although to be honest it hadn't been as bad as I'd feared. I hadn't pulled the arms off the seat, the window next to me didn't crack at thirty-five thousand feet, and despite the alarming whooshing noise I didn't get sucked down the toilet.

Pippa remembered something.

'That man Wesker from *The Times* was on the phone again. He won't take no for an answer will he? I told him we were going to be out of the country for a few days. I'm awfully sorry. I'll put him off as much as I can but maybe you'll need to speak to him when we get back.'

'Wesker?' Oliver said.

'An interview. Photo session.'

'Tell him no.'

'I tell him no and he rings back again.'

Oliver gave an exclamation of annoyance. 'He shouldn't even be speaking to you. Give him Bea's number and tell him to speak to her if he can ever find her in the office and not on holiday. Jake, this is your department.'

We turned to look at Jake who was asleep among the cushions, his empty champagne flute resting against his chest.

'I'd better show you to your rooms,' Oliver said.

'Oh yes, that would be nice,' I said, trying not to whimper with gratitude.

I couldn't stay awake much longer.

He woke Jake up and I followed them upstairs and on to the galleried landing.

'I've put name cards on the doors,' Oliver said. 'Someone did that recently and I thought it was a good idea. Even if it didn't work.'

He meant me didn't he? That thing with Elaine's room when he'd been so rude?

Jake's room was first. He disappeared into it with a relieved groan.

Then we passed a room with Pippa's name on it and finally we got to my room. There was a card with my name on it and a picture of a snowman, which was a rather sweet touch. I sneaked a backwards glance at Pippa's name card and hers *didn't have a picture on at all,* and that made me feel incredibly smug.

#OhFFS.

'Anything you need let me know,' Oliver said.

'Thanks,' I said.

My only wish was there would be a bed.

There was a bed.

A huge bed with rows of pillows and a plump quilt calling me with a siren song to creep underneath it. A bay window stretched across one wall and opened onto a balcony. There was a bathroom, a walk-in wardrobe and a sitting area. I seriously thought I had died and gone to heaven.

I cleaned my teeth and got into bed. A bed high and wide and soft and warm. A bed that gave new meaning to the word comfortable.

I was asleep in seconds.

*

When I woke the room was still in darkness, only a thin sliver of light creeping between the curtains. I lay back on the pillows and stretched. I went to the loo, admiring the glass basins and marble floors and surfaces. There was a delightful selection of toiletries; piles of white, fluffy towels in a wall unit; and a lovely new pale-blue dressing gown folded up and tied with a satin ribbon, waiting for me to unwrap it. Which of course I did.

Then I tinkered about with the shower, which was more of a wet room with a giant shower rose and dozens of water jets shooting out all over the place and a black slate floor that must be a nightmare to keep clean. Perhaps I could have a shower before I started on breakfast?

I checked my watch and staggered with shock. It was half past nine. Bloody jet lag.

I raced back into the bedroom to dress, cursing myself for not setting an alarm.

I could just imagine Oliver, sitting at the table waiting for breakfast and glowering because I wasn't at my post. I dragged on some clothes (jeans; new white T-shirt because once you've worn them, spilt food down them, and washed them a few times they're never quite the same; trainers).

I went out onto the galleried landing. There were lights on downstairs, but I couldn't hear anyone moaning about me or asking where I was. I went through the glorious sitting room with the floor to ceiling stone fireplace and the floor to ceiling windows. Oliver's grandfather certainly did things on a huge scale.

I peered out at the view; it was still dark outside but – and this was very exciting indeed – *it was snowing*. The biggest, fattest flakes of snow I'd ever seen were falling and settling into a thick white duvet over the garden. Occasionally there was a gust of wind, which blew them against the windows.

Perhaps later on we could go for a walk and have a snow-ball fight? I allowed myself a brief fantasy where Pippa and Jake decided not to come with us and Oliver and I walked through the trees together, the branches bowed with snow and tipped with crystals. He would have to throw off his bad temper though.

In the kitchen I started off by having a look around to find where things were kept. Why I had thought I needed to bring my own stuff I had no idea. On the black granite worktop was a block with a selection of Henckels knives and in the drawers were every kitchen gadget, appliance, gizmo, and saucepan known to man.

I went to look in the fridge, which of course was massive. There were two doors to pull open and as I did so a blinding light came on; it was like going on stage. I paused for a moment to bow, kiss my hands, and smile modestly at the giant milk containers and the huge glass jugs of juice. There was a similar-sized freezer, a utility room with a washer and dryer big enough to cope with the England Rugby team's post-match washing, and two dishwashers. Two!

I carried on opening cupboards and finding where things were kept. Of course, the thing I wanted was coffee. There was a complicated coffee machine on the worktop. On closer inspection I saw it was loaded up with coffee beans. Bean to cup eh? I'd never tried one of those; this was going to be fun. Another adventure. Well, a small one.

I pressed a few buttons and lights came on and went out in a very perplexing way. Perhaps it needed time to heat up. I left it and went off to look in the walk-in larder. *Walk-in larder!* I mean how brilliant! It was about the same size as my sitting room back home. I admired the labelled glass jars of flour, sugar, pulses, and pasta. There were dozens. Plus enough canned and bottled stuff to stock a small supermarket.

I went down the shelves, enjoying the unusual food labels and puzzling over some of the products. I mean what was Rice-A-Roni? Reddi-Wip? Snapple? Tofutti?

Back in the kitchen a red light was blinking on the coffee machine and I pressed another few buttons. There was a sort of rumbling, hissing noise and a green light flashed twice followed by a single polite beep. To me this seemed like progress. I went back through the cupboards, found a mug, and stuck it under a metal nozzle. Then I got another one and stuck it under a second nozzle at the side just in case. Better to be safe than sorry. I didn't want coffee to flood out all over the granite.

The possibility of coffee flooding anywhere was unlikely at that moment, but I was excited to hear new noises coming from inside the machine. Sort of glugging, ticking noises. Nothing was actually happening so I went back into the pantry to see if there was any instant coffee. Or failing that, tea bags. Hmm, how complicated could tea be in America? I mean builders tea not herbal, compost teabags.

There was White tea, Black tea, Green tea, Red tea, Wild tea or Roasted dandelion root presumably for people who were tired of tea and were searching for a new tea-like experience.

By this point it's quite possible my tongue was hanging out and dragging along the floor. I hadn't been this far away from imminent coffee for about twenty years. And still no one else had come downstairs, which was a shame in the grand scheme of things because someone could have helped me with the infernal machine.

I pressed all the buttons again and the machine started grinding beans! Yes!

After my heart rate had settled down to normal I stood watching the machine, sure at any moment something would happen.

After a few minutes I decided not to watch it in case it had stage fright and went to set the table. This was a long slab of golden wood as though someone had cut a slice out of the biggest tree ever and then polished it to a mirror-like glaze. There were twelve chairs set around it and a pile of slate placemats stacked up at one end.

I put out some cutlery, crockery, and glasses and tried to decide what to do for breakfast. Would they want eggs, bacon, corn bread, grits? Whatever they were. I wondered if I had time to google 'grits' and find out. They didn't sound very appealing, but they might be the most delicious things ever?

I got the three jugs of juices out of the fridge and about six different sorts of jam and arranged everything artistically on the table. And then I put the radio on.

There was some sort of country music playing, a woman singing in a sobbing voice about Little Joe not coming home. Perhaps he'd gone out to find some proper tea?

Then there was a man's excited voice welcoming me to PXVO *The Voice of the Green Mountains* and a special showcasing the talent of The Lorna Brothers Band. This heralded a lot of banjo music and foot stomping. I wasn't really in the mood for either but if I couldn't work a coffee machine I certainly didn't feel I could retune the radio.

I went to stare at the coffee machine and after pressing a few more buttons gave it several hefty whacks with a rolled-up tea towel and pressed all the buttons again.

'You miserable, useless, lazy bitch! All I want is a bloody cup of coffee! Why? Why can't you just co-operate? It wouldn't kill you would it? You have one job—'

'What on earth are you doing?'

I spun round and almost fell over. Oliver was standing in the doorway, barefoot and in a dark-blue dressing gown. He ran one hand over his hair and blinked at me.

'I'm trying to make some coffee. Would you like some?' I said, trying to calm down and look efficient. 'Or breakfast? What would you like?'

'Neither. And could you turn that awful music down? It's only ten to five,' he said.

We stood and looked each other for a minute and the truth dawned on me. Jet lag. Time difference. The other way. Ah.

'God I'm such a ...'

'I wondered what the hell was going on out here. All that banging cupboard doors and crashing about – is this how you always work? It was just the same in the retreat.'

'No, I didn't mean—'

'Well I'd really appreciate it if you wouldn't do it here. I'm only down the corridor' – he waved towards his room with one hand – 'and I can hear every bloody sound.'

'I'm so sorry.'

How was I to know?

'Right. I do appreciate you have jet lag, but do you think you could have jet lag quietly?'

'Yes of course, I—'

'I am going back to bed, and I am going back to sleep. I don't need breakfast for at least three hours. If other people do, then please ask them to keep the noise down. Right?'

Someone's grumpy.

'Right.'

He turned away.

'Oh, Mr Forest,' I said.

He turned back with a weary sigh. 'What now?'

'Before you go, could you turn the coffee machine on? I've been pressing buttons and stuff but I'm not entirely sure …'

I needed coffee, I really did.

He looked at me and I gave him a weak smile. 'Sorry.'

He closed his eyes for a moment and then came across the kitchen towards me. He pressed one button on the side of the machine and the blasted thing sprang obediently into life, grinding beans from the hopper and making all sorts of exciting shushing and humming noises heralding imminent success. He moved one of the mugs to a different space and gave me a hard look.

'Anything else?'

'No. Sorry.'

'You're sure?'

'Absolutely sure.'

'Right.'

He went back across the kitchen and down the corridor and I heard a door close with more than a hint of a slam.

Oh well.

Meanwhile, the machine was politely dispensing coffee into my mug and releasing a glorious smell into the kitchen too. I took my drink and went to sit by the window.

On the horizon dawn was breaking over the mountains in a yellowy, snow-tinged light. I could see snow, snow, and more snow everywhere. Not the sort of pathetic sprinkling you get in England when everyone gets excited and starts panic buying bread and shutting down airports. This was deep and crisp and even.

Every tree was covered; the lawn/field whatever it was that stretched away from the house was hidden and smoothed out under an undulating white blanket. And it looked glorious. It was a childhood dream come true.

It was how winter should look and seldom does except on a wildlife special about Canada with a David Attenborough commentary about bears.

It would be the perfect backdrop to a Michael Bublé Christmas Special too. I wouldn't have been surprised if a one-horse open sleigh had come up to the house, harness jingling, filled with laughing people and huge presents.

I almost felt the need for a chunky Scandi-Noir sweater. Actually, I did wish I had thought to bring warmer clothes and some wellingtons. And thick socks. And a cute woolly hat with a giant furry bobble. And a proper coat. And a scarf. What had I been thinking? I'd brought jeans and everyone knows jeans are no use in the snow. They get wet and shrink and cut off the circulation and then your feet fall off. Oh well.

I went and got more coffee and decided – as it was only quarter past five – I'd go and find my phone charger and then see if I had more luck with the shower in my bathroom.

No phone charger. How come? I know I had packed one. I even had a handy plug adaptor tucked away that I'd bought at the airport once I realized I was going to America.

I sat on the edge of my bed and thought back to the last time when I used it.

Of course, I'd left it in the airport.

I opened the Toblerone and broke off the first chunk.

#Officiallyanidiot.

Chapter Seventeen

Eventually Pippa and Jake came downstairs for breakfast grumbling about jet lag although by my calculations they hadn't lost any sleep at all. By the time we had sorted out what they wanted (pancakes, maple syrup, and smoked bacon, bleugh – I mean who thought that was a good idea?) Oliver had joined us.

As I doled out the food – all of which to be fair looked quite appetizing, just not together on one plate – the three of them discussed plans for the day. Pippa managed to make every event, from driving into the village to talking to the caterers, sound like a world trade summit.

Apparently Very Important Gideon was going to join us at some point but before that they were going to spend time in the village sorting out the final preparations for the launch party. Although Oliver had rejected *The Times*, he seemed quite happy to be giving an interview to both the local paper fetchingly named the *Green Mountain Trumpet* and the local radio station that I'd already listened to (PXVO – The Voice of The Green Mountains), both of which were apparently run by one man and his mother.

They would all be away for most of the day so I had hours to myself. Excellent; it would give me a chance to have a poke about and explore the house and perhaps even send a couple of emails.

Despite complaining that the pancakes, etc. were like soooo fattening, Pippa managed to tuck away three and even wiped the syrup from her plate with a finger. Jake meanwhile was evidently not great at chatter in the mornings and sat at his end of the table packing away pancakes with dedicated resolve.

Huge amounts of coffee with something deadly called heavy cream were drunk. At least I now knew how to get the demon machine topped up and working, and then just as I was about to tidy up they started on some of the fresh fruit salad I had made as an antidote to all those calories.

Eventually Pippa and Jake went back to their rooms, ready to drive into the village with Oliver, and I cleared away and stacked one of the two dishwashers. Oliver seemed quite happy to stay at the end of the table as I did so.

'Your leg's better then?' I said as I wiped the syrup off Pippa's chair.

'Yes, I can't ski yet, but it's fine otherwise.'

'I can't ski either.'

'Ever tried?'

'Well, once on a dry ski slope near Gloucester, but all I did was fall over.'

'I learned to ski out there on the field. It's a gentle slope, very easy.'

'Hmm, easy for you,' I said. 'That might be an adventure too far for me before you suggest it. Going home with a broken leg isn't my idea of fun.'

Apart from anything else I couldn't see myself skiing in trainers and jeans.

'So how is this adventure going?' he asked.

I shook my head. 'I wasn't expecting it I can tell you! I thought I was going to Shropshire!'

'Not disappointed then?'

'No.'

'Were you tempted to say no?'

'Absolutely not!' I lied.

'I bet you were!'

I changed the subject. 'Will the roads be OK? I mean it's been snowing quite hard.'

'Oh this is nothing,' he said. 'Do you know what they say about the seasons in Vermont? Almost winter, winter, still winter, road construction. There's a thaw due tomorrow. Did you see I wanted you to make cottage pie this evening?'

'Yes I saw that on my instruction sheet. That's a strange thing to ask for,' I said. 'It's not exactly fine dining.'

'I don't want fine dining. I want what you made at the retreat. I liked it.'

I could feel myself blushing and I turned away to start wiping the hob. 'You're the boss,' I said trying to sound nonchalant.

'So will you be OK here on your own? There's an SUV in the garage you could borrow if you wanted to go out? I mean you can if you want to.'

The chances of me doing this were nil. I've never driven on the wrong side of the road and I wasn't about to start now. Still, I wasn't going to admit it.

'Oh yes, that's a good idea. I'll see how I get on.'

Oliver started talking about nice Vermont villages I could

visit and cute country stores that sounded wonderful if I had the nerve and the necessary insurance.

'I might just find out where everything is and how stuff works. I might go for a walk tomorrow.'

'You're a keen walker? I didn't have you down as an outdoor type.'

'Oh gosh yes, there's nothing I like better than a good walk,' I replied.

Especially if there's a wine bar at the end of it.

'It's beautiful down in the woods beyond the meadow. By the way I meant to ask—'

I never did find out what Oliver meant to ask because Pippa came downstairs with a new outfit, a fresh face of make-up, and exactly the same bobble hat I had imagined wearing in my earlier daydream.

Rats.

'Ready!' she said, standing by the door as though she couldn't wait to go.

'Oh, fine give me a moment, I'll find a coat,' Oliver said, and he went off somewhere to look for one.

Jake came downstairs in a quiet, sort of useless don't-ask-me-to-do-anything mood. I saw Pippa shoot him a quick look and I felt rather sorry for her. I mean she was such a pretty girl and Jake didn't seem to see her.

'I seem to have left my charger at the airport,' I said. 'Does anyone have one to fit this phone?'

I held up my mobile and Jake pulled a face.

'Where did you get that? *Antiques Road Trip?*'

Hmm apparently not. I'd have to buy another one. Or do without. Was it possible to be without a mobile phone these days? The idea was quite alarming.

182

After a few more minutes messing about and Pippa checking in the hall mirror to make sure her fur bobble was at precisely the right, cute angle, the three of them went out to the car.

Back home there would have been a thirty-minute delay while the snow was cleared off the windscreen, followed by someone searching fruitlessly for the de-icer and probably calling out the AA. No such problem here. Oliver's SUV had after all been nestling cosily in a centrally heated garage and it started and drove off down the lane with no trouble at all.

I waved from the balcony and waited until I was sure they really had gone and weren't about to come back for lip gloss or scarves. Then I sprinted back in and had a good look around.

Upstairs there were six bedrooms, all of them with their own bathrooms and walk-in dressing rooms. I poked my head into each of them. Jake's room was messy; Pippa's was worse. For heaven's sake they'd only been here five minutes. I took the snowman name card off my door and stowed it away safely in my suitcase before anyone thought to throw it away. Then I continued exploring. There was also an additional bathroom, in case six weren't enough.

I was surprised and rather pleased to see while all the bedrooms were lovely mine was undoubtedly the best. There was also a sitting area on the landing with a fab view out over the field and the mountains beyond.

I went back downstairs and took some ground beef – what I'd call mince – out of the freezer to defrost. Then I explored the other rooms. There was of course the big sitting room, a more formal dining room, and a book-lined study with a giant Mac computer on the desk. There was an oil painting of a grey-haired man on the wall above the fireplace in that room. He was standing with one hand on the head of his dog, and he looked rather nice and more than a little like Oliver so I guessed this was his grandfather.

Perhaps this was where Oliver wrote, sitting behind the green leather-topped desk, rocking back in the swivel chair, occasionally staring out of the window for inspiration? Perhaps he set a strict timetable for himself, with pre-determined breaks for a run, or maybe he had a personal trainer who turned up.

It would be a man of course – I wasn't going to allow any Lycra-clad, fat-burning, ripped skinny woman to bend over backwards for him. Or forwards. So to speak.

Someone muscular and monosyllabic who talked about reps and said things like: *You don't get the ass you want by sitting on it.*

What really surprised me was when I eventually found Oliver's room. Compared to the others it was tiny. A single bed, built-in wardrobe units, a chair, and that was all. No pictures or photographs anywhere, not even a stray sock left balled up in the corner. Everywhere was immaculate. This was his house. Why did he have the smallest bedroom with no view of anything other than the garage wall?

I couldn't believe he had moved out of his usual room because we were staying. There were still three bedrooms unoccupied upstairs. Weird. I suddenly noticed a Belfast sink in one corner behind the bedroom door. Why was that there? And then I saw something else. Tucked away in one corner was the plumbing for a washing machine. Oliver was sleeping in what was originally a sort of utility room, not a bedroom at all. Why? Why on earth was he sleeping in such a dull

184

little room when there were six glorious bedrooms available upstairs? It didn't make any sense at all.

I did some more food preparation and then sat down with my laptop. Wi-Fi? Password?

I hunted around in my bedroom until I found a hastily scribbled note with it on and then logged on. Nothing important seemed to have occurred in my absence, although there was an email from Uncle Peter saying how much they liked staying in my house and the builders in the shop were driving them mad with their terrible singing, and there was one from Helena saying Nick had booked somewhere in Scotland.

*

I spent the rest of the afternoon trying to discover how to work the oven and wondering what the difference was between bake and broil. Having worked it out, I made a cake and while I was waiting for it to cool I googled Oliver again to see if I could find out anything new about him.

There still wasn't much. There was more about his alter ego Ross Black including the trailer from the film version of *The Dirty Road*. I watched it a couple of times just for the thrill of seeing *based on the novel by Ross Black* in the title credits and thinking Oooh I know him; I'm making him his dinner. It made me feel rather excited and pleased. I suppose that was the sort of effect celebrities had on people?

There was a bit of newsreel from the premiere where an excessively thin actress pouted all over Channing Tatum and tried to look as though she could be some use in an emergency and not as though she would be blown away by a single puff of a sandstorm. She wasn't my idea of Selina; it was hard to imagine any of her dresses being 'tight in every place' unless her clothes came from Ladybird.

Oliver's footprint on Google was irritatingly patchy. There was some detail about his charity work and a great deal about several court cases he had undertaken in order to protect his privacy. Two years previously he had won an undisclosed settlement from some tabloid paper and donated it to charity. Well that was very unsatisfactory, but at least there weren't dozens of pictures of him with beautiful woman or tales of paternity suits and drunken evenings falling out of nightclubs.

I put the radio on – the same music seemed to be playing; a man was crooning about wanting to be back home with Momma. I went to check the worksheet I had been given and decided to make some bread. There was of course a bread maker but after my adventures with the coffee machine I decided to ignore it and do it by hand.

There's a lot of pleasure to be had out of kneading dough and while I did I thought about my list. I certainly hadn't lost a stone and the clean-eating regime had lasted for half a day until I found some chocolate I'd forgotten about. I'd have to try again when I got home. It would be a bit hard to do in a house where the fridge contained two pints of heavy cream.

PXVO – The Voice of the Green Mountains – was having a country music celebration day. There seemed to be two sorts of songs: sad (death, divorce, lost love, failure) or resolutely upbeat (love of spouse, children, country, or dogs). Should I get a dog?

His eyes looked into mine and he loves me all the time as the song said. No; let's be honest pets cost money and vets' fees were worse than any electricity bill. I'd make do with next door's cat.

*

I yawned and suddenly realized it was beginning to get dark and it was nearly four-thirty. Or nine-thirty according to my body clock. I supposed they would all be back soon, and I celebrated by having a glass of red wine from the bottle I had opened so I could add a glassful to the cottage pie. I like putting wine in things, especially me.

I went and sorted out the fire. I wasn't so particular I was prepared to clean out all the ash, but I did find some kindling and stirred the embers of last night's logs into life so there was soon a merry blaze for me to sit next to. Outside it was snowing again and as the light faded the landscape was almost luminous.

I sank back into the cushions and closed my eyes. It had been an amazing day. I definitely wasn't in Lower Bidford.

*

'So this is what you've been getting up to while we've been slaving away! Nice for some!'

I woke up with a jump to see Pippa standing in front of the fire, unwinding her scarf, her fur bobble drooping with melting snow like a wet cat on top of her head.

'I was just—'

'Asleep. Yes I could see you were. Honestly!'

She took off her coat, an expensive-looking waterproof, ski-type of garment, and shook it so I was splattered with dollops of icy water.

'It's all right for you, lazing about. I've got hours of work to do now.'

She looked exhausted. I felt unexpectedly sorry for her.

'Shall I sort your coat out?'

'Thanks.'

Pippa handed it over and I went to the lobby where there was a mudroom and hung it up. Jake was standing in there already, dripping onto the tiled floor.

'Flipping cold out there,' he said.

'Is Oliver with you?'

'Putting the car away in the garage. Is there a drink to be had? I'm gasping.'

'I've opened some wine.'

'Good idea.'

At that point Oliver came in. I went to take his coat.

'How did the interviews go?'

'Fine,' Oliver said. 'I like to do the local paper a favour. And the radio station. They have absolutely no budget. I'd rather speak to Wes Wesley from PXVO than some self-important prat from the national networks.'

'That man from Sky was OK,' Pippa muttered.

Oliver gave her a look.

'You only think that because he tried to bribe you with muffins and a trip to Vienna. I was the one who had to listen to him pontificating about hidden agendas and the morality of Harry Field and which country England should apologize to next. You talk to him if you're so keen; I've got better things to do.'

'But surely you have to do publicity?' I said.

'I do,' he said. He sent Pippa a glaring look. 'I thought you were going to get those emails sent?'

188

'Going now,' Pippa said.

I went too, not prepared to listen to Oliver grumbling for longer than I had to. When I came back in with a tray of cashew nuts and pretzels, there was someone new in the room.

'Look, I'm beginning to think this was a mistake. I don't know why I'm doing this in the first place,' Oliver said.

'Because people are excited about this book,' Jake said.

'And it wouldn't hurt your sales figures,' said the newcomer.

He noticed me coming into the room and turned and looked at me. A rather wolfish smile crossed his face.

'Well and who is this lovely creature?' he said. He came and took the tray and held my hand. 'Do introduce me, Oliver.'

'This is Billie Summers; she's looking after us. Doing all the catering here while we get on with the launch,' Oliver said. 'Billie – Gideon March, my American publisher.'

His tone had suddenly become rather cold and clipped. I think I had interrupted a fledgling row.

'Well I wish I could find someone as charming to look after me. I'm delighted to meet you, Billie,' Gideon said, squeezing my hand and covering it with his. 'Delighted.'

'I'm delighted too,' I said.

So now we're all delighted, could you let go of me so I can get back to the kitchen, please?

'Come and have a drink with us,' Gideon said, bending his head towards me.

He was good-looking in a tanned, white-toothed, American way, like a Kennedy who had escaped from the Martha's Vineyard compound. Tall, muscular, healthy – I could imagine him fussing over his diet, going to the gym as a lifestyle choice not just a way to escape from his children, taking his life and his cholesterol levels very seriously.

'No thank you, Mr March, I have things to do,' I said, tugging my hand away. 'I must sort out the cheeseboard.'

'I hope it's properly aired?' Oliver said, straight-faced. I didn't dare look at him.

Meanwhile, Gideon was twinkling at me in a practised manner I think I was supposed to find irresistible. 'And what are we having for dinner? Something smells wonderful.'

'Cottage pie.'

Gideon raised one eyebrow. 'Made with real cottages?'

Very funny.

I explained what it was, retreating a step at a time to get away from him and his rather overpowering cologne.

'Ah, what I would call a Military Special,' he said, following me.

'Either way ...'

'Well we'll talk more later then, Billie; after all, don't forget, the way to a man's heart is through his stomach,' Gideon said with a wink.

Well yes, especially if you use an upward thrust with a spear, I thought.

'Super,' I said and beat a hasty retreat.

From my place at the kitchen sink scrubbing vegetables I could hear the argument continuing even though they were obviously trying to speak quietly.

'You know I hate this sort of thing,' Oliver said.

'It's just a few idiots,' Gideon said soothingly. 'It's publicity.'

'So why should I spend time with idiots?'

'It might be fun.'

'It won't. God, I wish I'd never agreed to this.'

'You just need to show up and smile. I'll do all the talking,' Gideon said.

190

'Yes I bet you will.'

'No need to be like that; I'm on your side, Ollie. Just trust me.'

'The comment of someone who has no real answer.'

'Maybe but everything is in place now for the paperback of *Glory 17*. Let's just roll with it and see what happens, eh? And you do realize you are already months late with *Death in Damascus* don't you? I mean are we anywhere near?'

'Nearly,' Oliver said, his voice rather clipped.

'When can I expect to get hold of it?'

'I'll let you know. I'm doing some structural edits at the moment. And you're not in a position to push me. We still have that contract to sign, Gideon. I still haven't decided.'

'Don't I know it. You're killing me with this. Let's open the kimono on this one shall we? You *are* going to sign aren't you?' This last bit in a cajoling, friendly tone.

Open the kimono?

'We'll see.'

'So you've worked through the – you know – writer's block? You've made progress?'

My ears pricked up. Writer's block? *Writer's block?* Hang on a minute; I thought there was *no such thing*?

Oliver gave a short laugh.

'I've told you I'll let you know. I started to get somewhere that week I was away. I had some new ideas just coming to me and then somehow ... anyway. Let's just get this one out of the way.'

Gideon laughed. 'You'll sign. We go so well together, Ollie. I'm the pretty face and you're the brains.'

'Crap!'

'All right then you're the pretty face and you're the brains too but I'm the one on the tail of a very lucrative film right deal. It could be fun for both of us.'

'Your definition of fun is not the same as mine, Gideon.'

Gideon gave a chuckle. 'Looks to me like you have some fun lined up already.'

'Meaning?' Oliver said frostily.

'Well I always thought that PA of yours was a cute thing. And now you introduce little Betty into the mix. Hey, you have all the bases covered!'

'Don't be ridiculous. She's nothing.'

I frowned. Betty? Who was Betty? Was there someone else joining us?

Just as things were getting interesting, they came back inside and closed the door behind them.

Jake wandered into the kitchen. I grabbed a saucepan and pretended to dry it.

'Enjoying yourself here?' he said. 'Nice kitchen?'

Having got over his jet lag, which as a man was always going to be far worse than mine, Jake had become chattier. Either that or he was bored.

'It's brilliant,' I said. 'One of the best ever. Fantastic ... er ... knives.'

He went to have a look. 'Yes, you wouldn't want to clean your nails with this bad boy would you?' he said pulling out an eight-inch chef's knife from the block and eyeing it with respect. 'Are you coming to the launch party?'

'No,' I said getting the coffee tray ready and putting some muffins out in a basket.

'Poor old Cinders eh?' Jake said pulling out a wicked-looking Santoku knife and holding it up to his face so his eyes crossed slightly. 'Stuck in the kitchen, not going to the ball.'

'I'll survive,' I said. 'Put that back before you cut your nose off. Anyway, you can look after Pippa. I don't think she's having much fun.'

Jake frowned and considered this statement. 'Pippa? Isn't she? Oh well I suppose not. I hadn't really – I expect she's used to it. Do you think these cost a lot of money?'

'No one gets used to being treated like a moron, Jake. Is Oliver always this objectionable?'

Jake sat watching me while I cut up vegetables.

'I know you won't believe me, but Oliver is a great bloke. He's kind and funny and generous. OK I'm his agent so I am going to defend him but he's also one of my best friends. You don't realize how much pressure he has been under for the last few years. I know it seems as though he's behaving badly but there are two sides to every story. And Pippa should stand up to him a bit more. I've told her that. She's too nice.'

'Far too nice,' I said. 'And she's very pretty isn't she?'

'Is she?' He looked thoughtful. 'I suppose so.'

'She is and very long suffering considering how she is treated.'

Jake shook his head. 'I've explained that. I don't know why—' He stopped; I suppose he didn't want to badmouth his friend to a virtual stranger. 'What about you? Do you have family?'

'I live on my own.'

He looked up from examining his fingernails. 'Really? No boyfriend?'

'Not at the moment – I'm too busy, running those writing retreats with my best friend.' I decided not to mention the occasional cake making or the part-time job in my uncle's bookshop.

Jake smiled. 'Yeah, Pippa thought it might help Oliver. And let's be fair she was right, so good for her. But sometimes nothing is right. And she had a holiday booked anyway and the chance of a couple of days in Paris.' Jake chuckled. 'He thought he was going to be in some sort of hotel. He was like a rabid monkey when he found there were a load of old ducks there too.'

Old ducks? Really?

'I don't remember there being any old ducks there,' I said stiffly.

Oblivious to my mood, Jake came and filled his wine glass up again.

'God yes, he was bloody livid. The first night he was firing off text messages by the minute, threatening her with the sack. Luckily, she was out of the country and didn't get any of them until he'd calmed down a bit. Still he did say it had given him something to put in his latest book. From the little he told me there was a stalker-type who came into his room and made a complete tit of herself. It sounded hilarious.'

'Fascinating,' I said, wondering who was the target of his bile-dipped pen.

Hang on. That was probably me!

I went cold at the prospect. Just when I thought I could get along with Oliver, I find he's been laughing about me behind my back.

Jake stretched his arms above his head.

'Right, I'm going in the hot tub later. Lovely moon. Fancy a dip?'

'No I don't think I do,' I said. 'I have dinner to cook. Ask Pippa. Gideon has been pestering her I think.'

'Has he? What a git.'

I was surprised at the strength of Jake's reaction.

'Yes,' I said airily, 'I rather think he's taken a shine to Pippa. I mean like I said, she's a very pretty girl isn't she?'

Jake looked grim. 'I bet he's trying to poach her. He was all over her in London.'

'Yes, I think he still is. He's the sort isn't he? To make a beeline for a bright girl like Pippa. Still if she doesn't feel appreciated working for Oliver, she'll move on I suppose? I expect he will offer her a job.'

'Has she said anything?' he said.

As I was making all this up I couldn't really comment so instead I gave an enigmatic shrug.

'Do you get bored cooking all the time?' he said, suddenly changing the subject.

'Do you get bored with eating?'

'No, I guess not. What else do you do though?'

'I'm a champion wing-walker and I'm learning the saxophone.'

'Really?'

'No of course not.'

'Oh, oh that was a joke, right?'

'Right.'

Chapter Eighteen

At eight the following morning Oliver turned up asking for apple juice and poached eggs on whole-wheat toast. He was freshly showered in jeans and a black polo neck sweater that made the most of his broad shoulders and muscular chest and ... Hmmm. I could just imagine what his arms would feel like under my hands. Sort of hard and ...

For God's sake, woman, what the hell is the matter with you?

I went into the larder, my new go-to place when I wanted to make myself scarce, and straightened up a couple of boxes of Rice-A-Roni, pretending to find something so I could calm down and not dribble in the food.

I had to remind myself of all the mean things he had said about our writing retreat (Old ducks? Stalker?) so I could dislike him even if he did look exceptionally handsome and more than a bit sexy. No he didn't, he looked like a bad-tempered man but with just the right amount of designer stubble and dark shadows under his beautiful dark blue eyes ...

Oh shut up.

I went back into the larder and shifted some bottles of passata about. Then I pretended to check on how many eggs remained in the earthenware bowl with the chickens painted on the side.

When I came back out into the kitchen, Oliver was shrugging on his coat and winding a soft blue scarf – exactly the same colour as his eyes – around his neck.

'Right,' he said, 'I'm off to see Gideon. We'll be back for lunch. Tell Pippa and Jake I'll expect to see them there very soon.'

'Is Betty coming today?'

He stopped and looked at me, his expression blank. 'Betty?'

'I heard someone mention her the other day, said she was joining the lunch party.'

Oliver flushed. 'No, Gideon was being stupid. Forget about it.'

'Well OK if you say so. I just need to know—'

'Forget he said anything; he's an idiot. Forget I said anything.'

Didn't make any difference to me. Very Important Gideon was his publisher; Oliver could say what he liked about the man.

I watched as he went out to the garage and drove off towards the village. The sun was brilliant this morning. I could see grass out on the meadow now, and most of the trees had lost their snowy hats.

I cleared away and wondered how long Pippa and Jake were going to be. While I was waiting I started making Minestrone soup for lunch. Then I turned on my laptop and caught up with the news from Uncle Peter and Godfrey and a hasty email from Helena whose grasp of the English language got increasingly erratic the more excited she became. By Easter I anticipated she wouldn't know how to spell Scotland never mind get there.

At nine o'clock I heard the slam of a bedroom door and Jake came downstairs, followed seconds later by Pippa.

I poured fresh coffee and passed it to them.

'Oh what a shame,' Pippa said, walking to the window to look at the view. 'The snow has gone.'

She stood sipping her coffee and glancing back at the table. She put one arm up to rest on the window frame and sighed.

'It's so lovely here isn't it? I mean so pretty and restful.' She stifled a yawn. 'A real change from London.'

Jake looked up at her and smiled, then carried on shovelling in toast and peanut butter while he read the back of the Cap'n Crunch packet.

Pippa went to sit next to Jake and he winked at her.

'I'm starving,' she said with a cat-like smile.

'I bet,' Jake said.

'Anything else you would like for breakfast?' I asked, glancing at the clock. It was nine-fifteen; surely they had things to do? 'Oliver wanted to see you as soon as possible, and that was nearly two hours ago.'

Pippa shot out of her seat. 'Jesus he'll kill me. Jake, have you got those notes I had last night? Hurry up! Think! Where did I leave them?'

'In my room,' Jake said.

Hello.

They left the house ten minutes later, Pippa still jamming her shoes on in a blind panic. I went back to my tasks and when I'd done everything I could I decided to go for my walk.

There were plenty of assorted coats and boots in the

mudroom by the back door, and having found some that fitted I set off.

The air was so clean and clear – that was the first thing I noticed. And there was no sound apart from the occasional flutter of bird wings or the distant crack of a twig. I walked down the garden towards the trees, my boots crunching on the gravel path. At the bottom was a metal gate leading into the woods.

The air was different here, denser as though it had been trapped under the trees for the winter. I could smell pine and dark earth and hear the sound of running water somewhere. I walked on, my boots collecting a decorative collar of mud and pine needles.

Puffing slightly, I reached the top of a rise where there was an old stone bench overlooking the valley and the river below. I brushed the pine needles off the seat and sat down with a grateful sigh. Somewhere in the hills, far off, I heard a couple of shots. Hunters out shooting something? Or maybe bank robbers at a stand-off? Perhaps I'd go back to the house soon.

The grass on the field below the house was vibrant and green and I took a deep, invigorating lungful of crisp mountain air. This was the life; perhaps I should move to somewhere really rural? Like West Wales or Yorkshire. That would be an adventure wouldn't it? To live the simple, country way, have chickens, grow my own vegetables, bottle fruit, and make jam. Clean eating. I could stop worrying about being fashionable and wear plaid shirts and cute dungarees. Like a cross between Felicity Kendal and Nigella Lawson. I wasn't sure I was ready to be a vegetarian though. I'd tried that and let's just say tofu and I will never be friends.

A thin film of mist drifted above the water, which suddenly evaporated as the sun rose above the trees.

I saw something moving by the riverbank. A deer? A moose? Or a bear?

Jeez! What if it was a bear?

What if it was a bear?

What would I do?

My enthusiasm for exploring – never great – rapidly faded. I could just imagine the headlines.

Tragic British woman mauled to death on adventure holiday.

Celebrity chef eaten by bear.

'I should have taken greater care of her,' said heartbroken writer Ross Black. 'She was a wonderful woman. I'll never forgive myself.'

Another distant shot echoed, far off. Maybe the bank robbers were caught in a Butch Cassidy and the Sundance Kid drama?

I held my breath, and watched as the deer (yes it was a deer) wandered away from the river and back under the trees.

'Ah there you are!'

I leapt to my feet and turned to see Oliver walking towards me. I felt a weird mixture of excitement and relief.

'I wondered where you had got to,' he said.

He wasn't out of breath at all, I noticed. He looked quite relaxed and even a bit smiley. Nothing like the man who had left this morning.

'Is anything wrong?' I said, rather flustered.

'No,' he said, a bit surprised, 'I came back early and fancied some exercise. I see you had the same idea. I was getting rather stressed with everything.'

He sat down next to me, his hands on his knees. I didn't dare look at him.

'Gorgeous isn't it?' he said. 'Sometimes I wonder how I can ever bear to leave it.'

'Speaking of which, are there bears around here?' I said, my voice slightly panicky.

'Oh yes,' Oliver said. 'Not at this time of year of course.'

'Of course not.' I laughed. The very idea. 'Have they all gone to the Caribbean on holiday?'

'At this time of year they're probably still hibernating,' Oliver said patiently.

Probably. That's a weasel word isn't it?

What the hell was I doing out here in the back of beyond in the middle of bear country? Hungry bears too if they had been hibernating.

I thought about the distance between where we were sitting and the house. It suddenly seemed a very long way, even if it was downhill.

How fast could a bear run? How fast could I run? The woods were the absolutely ideal place for a massive grizzly or two to be lurking.

I looked behind me. Over there for example: was it actually a fallen log or was it a crouching bear? Possibly with a bowler hat on? And a taller bear on a chair next to it? With an umbrella? No it was a fallen tree. Even so.

'You're sure? Absolutely sure? I mean could there be a couple with insomnia around here? Wanting a bit of a change?'

'I'm pretty sure there aren't,' he said.

Pretty sure. That's not a reassuring statement.

He was wearing a thick, padded gilet over an Aran sweater. He stood up and walked forward a few steps. He stuck his hands in his pockets and I had to look away quickly to stop myself admiring his arse.

'On a scale of one to one hundred, how sure?' I said, inspecting my nails.

'I don't know. Ninety-nine. Ninety-nine point five.'

'So there's a nought point five per cent chance there's a bear in these woods?'

'I guess so.' He turned back, scratching the stubble on his chin. 'Is that a problem?'

'What do we do if we did see one?'

'You make a lot of noise and walk backwards away from it,' he said.

'And then run?'

'Only if you can run faster than thirty miles an hour.'

Hmm that seemed very unlikely; could anyone run faster than thirty miles an hour? Could Usain Bolt? I bet I couldn't.

'Well what about playing dead?' I said.

'Only if it's a grizzly.'

'How can you tell the difference?' I was starting to seriously panic.

He gave me a comical look. 'The grizzlies wear straw hats and ties. Haven't you seen Yogi Bear? You could always distract it with a picnic basket, Boo-Boo.'

'What about climbing trees?' I said.

'They can climb much faster than you can.'

I trawled about my brain to try and remember the few things I had read about bears.

'And they only attack if they have cubs and you get between them and the mother? Is that true?'

'No, black bears attack to eat you.'

'What sort of bears do you have round here?'

Oliver thought for a moment. 'Black bears.'

It wasn't reassuring, let's be honest. Could Oliver run faster than I could? Of course he could. Everyone alive between the ages of five and eighty can run faster than I can.

'Perhaps we should go back if you've had enough excitement?' he said, and he grinned as though he knew exactly what I was thinking.

'Well if you think so,' I said casually. 'I'm easy. No, I didn't mean to say that, I'm not easy at all. I mean I don't mind.'

He looked as though he was trying to stop laughing and led the way back down the hill to the house. Every few steps I turned to make sure there wasn't a bear following us. Nought point five per cent chance was still a bit much for me to be honest. You don't have to think about that in Lower Bidford.

We reached the house without incident and Oliver disappeared into his study. I went to resume my duties in the kitchen. I heard a car come up the drive and looked at my watch – five to twelve. A bit early for lunch? I began to look efficient and busy. The back door opened and it was the last person in the world I was expecting or wanted to see.

It was Very Important Gideon.

I stood with a large wooden spoon in my hand, dripping soup onto the floor.

'I think Mr Forest is in the study,' I said.

Gideon unzipped his bulky jacket and favoured me with a white and gleaming smile.

'No matter,' he said. 'I wanted to have a word with you anyway. Is that OK?'

'Well yes, no, yes of course,' I said, rather flustered.

He slung his coat over the back of one of the kitchen chairs and sat down.

203

'Can I get you anything, Mr March? Coffee?'

'Well now aren't you nice? Call me Gideon. What I'd like is bourbon. Will you join me?'

'No thanks, it's a bit early for me.'

He gave me a wink. 'I know where Ollie keeps it. I'll help myself. Sure I can't tempt you?'

'No thanks.'

I wiped up the mess I'd made and began washing fruit to put into the bowl on the table.

Gideon poured himself a chunky-looking drink, helped himself to ice from the dispenser on the front of the fridge, and sat down again.

'Are you happy in your work, Billie?' he said.

Odd question.

'Yes absolutely,' I said.

He chuckled and shook his head. 'I just love the way you talk! What is it about the English accent that is so adorable?' He took a sip of his drink and tried to imitate me. 'Yes absolutely. Yes absolutely.'

I laughed along with him.

'So what happens when you go home?' he said.

'Well I suppose I'll carry on doing what I do.'

'And what's that?'

'I run writing retreats, I cook, I help out in a bookshop.'

'Busy girl,' he said admiringly.

'Well it keeps me out of trouble I suppose.'

'That's a pity,' he said, and gave me a wink that made me feel a bit uncomfortable.

I looked at my watch.

'The others will be back in a minute,' I said, although I really wasn't expecting them until one o'clock at the earliest.

204

Gideon stood up and walked around the table.

'You're a pretty girl too,' he said. 'Clever. I admire you enormously.'

'Well thanks,' I said, wondering if it was time to escape to the pantry again. Hmm maybe not, I wouldn't put it past him to follow me.

'How about coming to work for me?' he said suddenly.

'What?'

'Well I can always use someone like you,' he said. 'Someone pretty and clever. And adaptable.'

'Oh I'm not adaptable,' I said. 'I'm well known for being very un-adaptable.'

Was there such a word?

He laughed. And knocked back his drink.

'Well think about it,' he said. 'We can keep it quiet for now, but I'll be in touch.'

He had eyes like ice chips: pale and cold. I suddenly wasn't sure I liked him. I moved away from him and began chopping up an apple for no better reason than I felt better with a knife in my hand. It made a dull thudding noise on the wooden board and he watched me; calculating, disturbing.

'Ah well, we'll see what happens,' he said. He put his glass down on the granite worktop without a sound. Then he came and put an arm around my shoulder and hugged me. 'Think about it, hey?'

'I don't think I would be a very good—'

'Yes you would, Billie. I know you would.'

He pulled me against his side. I could smell his cologne. I stood not knowing what to do, the knife still in my hand.

If I stuck the knife in him it would ruin his beautiful

cashmere sweater. Perhaps that particular aspect wasn't the first thing I should worry about?

'Sorry, am I interrupting something?'

I turned to see Oliver watching us.

I could have wept with relief. Then I realized I was probably making something out of nothing. I've watched every episode of *Friends*. Americans were friendly people; they didn't have the same reserve as we did. They weren't as obsessed with the notion of 'personal space' as English people.

Gideon was unruffled. 'Ah, Ollie, there you are. I'll stay for lunch if I'm invited?'

'Did you want something particular?'

'No, just thought I'd have a last run-through with you about tomorrow if you have a few minutes?'

'I suppose so.' Oliver's face was expressionless, but I knew he was annoyed. 'You'd better come through into the study.'

Chapter Nineteen

The following day was the book launch. Oliver came out of his room at eight dressed in dark chinos and a grey cashmere sweater and stood and looked out of the window at the sky. It was heavy with rain clouds, whipping across the horizon.

'Are you all right?' I said. 'You don't look it.'

He didn't either. He looked a bit rocky to be honest.

'Oh I don't know ... I'm not really looking forward to today,' he said at last.

He didn't look at me. In fact, he rested his forehead on the windowpane.

'Why ever not? You must have done these things before,' I said, trying to be reassuring.

'Nope. I did the first one and then – well something happened that meant I didn't do any other big launch events. Until now.'

'Well you must have missed out on some great parties! Don't you like people telling you how marvellous you are? I would. I'd love it.'

He shook his head against the window then came and sat down at the table and reached for some apple juice.

'It's just a book, that's all. What matters is getting the next one out there.'

I stood and looked at him, my hands on the back of a chair. 'But you've made it! Doesn't that thrill you?'

Oliver sipped his juice. He still hadn't looked at me. I wanted him to look at me; I wanted him to talk to me properly, not just see me as a woman waiting to make his breakfast.

He flicked me a quick glance. 'What's your favourite thing? Don't think about it – just say the first thing you think of. My favourite thing is ...'

'Do you mean—'

'Just say anything.'

'Toblerone,' I said. 'I mean the giant ones you get in airports.'

I was three-quarters of the way through the one I had bought on the way out. Perhaps I should get another one when I went home?

'What if I said you could have a giant Toblerone at every meal for the rest of your life? After breakfast? After lunch? After dinner?'

'I'd pretty soon get sick of them.'

'Being well known, having people telling you you're fantastic is eventually the same thing as Toblerone three times a day.'

'I don't believe you,' I said. 'What about the money?'

'In the end money means nothing.'

'Ha! Funny how you never hear poor people saying that,' I said.

Oliver shook his head. I went to put the toaster on.

'The launch is just people wanting me to sign books for them. And photographs. Random journalists taking pictures with me as though we're mates. And all of them asking the same questions. Am I like Major Harry Field? Why does he

208

always try to save someone who can't be saved? Can't I write anything else? Always avoiding – And Gideon.' He stopped suddenly. 'Oh yes, Gideon. He'll be there, schmoozing and glad-handing people like the old pro he is.'

'He offered me a job,' I said.

Oliver's head came up. 'You're not considering it?'

'Well—'

'You mustn't!' Oliver said. 'I absolutely forbid you – you mustn't.'

'Forbid me? You can't forbid me.' I laughed. Who was he to tell me what to do? 'That might be an adventure, don't you think?'

'Don't be ridiculous,' Oliver snapped.

I started polishing the worktops. They didn't need it, but it was something to do.

'And?' he said.

'And what?'

'You can't possibly take a job with Gideon. You're not nearly ... Didn't you say you work for your uncle?'

'It's temporary and part time. I'm thirty soon. I need to find a proper career. I've got an English degree. I'm not an idiot you know ...'

'I never suggested you were!'

'Well I could start working in publishing couldn't I?'

Oliver spluttered.

'God forbid. Not for Gideon. Do something else, anything else! Forget about Gideon; write your nice little book. Is your main character like you? Does she make cakes? Or knit perhaps? Or do needlepoint? Most books seem to have heroines who do. Or they talk to their cats. I bet you have a cat?'

Cat? Nice little book? Patronizing sod!

I pulled back from the pleasing mental image I had been constructing of myself, having somehow dramatically lost weight and learned how to straighten my hair, in a tight, designer suit and stilettos wafting around a glass-walled office, organizing Gideon's diary with a Mont Blanc pen.

I was outraged. 'Actually no I don't have a cat. Occasionally I borrow the cat from next door to talk to and he talks more sense than many men I've met. The rest of your prejudiced nonsense is so not true!'

He wasn't listening to me.

'And they have friends who are so cutely crazy they are almost certifiable. And usually there's a similarly cute dog. Or a house rabbit. Every book seems to have cupcakes in the cover and some mention of a village fete. And there's always a dotty old aunt. And a handsome vet or doctor. Why is that?'

I was fuming and suddenly I didn't feel like sucking it up any longer.

'You don't have a very high opinion of contemporary women's fiction then? Or women for that matter. Just because you're in a bad mood about this launch, don't take it out on me. You're making a sweeping bloody generalization if ever I heard one! Maybe the women's fiction you buy is like that' – hurrah, thought of an acidic retort immediately rather than at half past two tomorrow morning – 'but there's plenty of choice. Some wonderful psychological dramas, historicals, sagas – it's endless.

'You might just as well say all men's fiction had pictures of submachine guns on the front and buildings on fire and a lantern-jawed hero coming out of a sandstorm with a scarf round his face carrying a woman with a twisted ankle. I mean what's the one you're bringing out next? Death somewhere?'

He raised one eyebrow. 'It was originally called *Death in Damascus*. It was about a man fighting as a mercenary in Syria but then ...'

'I bet he has a drippy girlfriend who falls over all the time? Why don't you write about a woman who saves him for once instead of the other way round?'

He glared at me furiously and then looked away.

'That would be interesting,' I said. I knew I'd overstepped the mark. 'Sorry.'

'No, by all means carry on! I mean this sort of conversation is just what I need,' Oliver snapped. 'And after all what would you know about it? What would you know about producing a book every year? What would you know about the stress? The criticism? Unreasonable deadlines? What would you know about the pressure?'

He was getting very annoyed now but in my state of mind at that moment I didn't care.

'Oh please!' I said. I should have shut up, but the worm had turned and I couldn't stop myself. 'Try having no job and no money and no pension. Try working overnight in a supermarket stacking shelves. Or in a hospital dealing with the worst that life can chuck at you. Think how that feels.'

'I was a teacher for many years. I know all about the worst life can chuck at you!'

'What? Don't make me laugh! Try having a car that any day soon is going to vomit its engine up onto the road and collapse forever. Come to think of it, imagine how awful it must be for Pippa to work for a boss who never says thank you, or treats her with any sort of respect. Even when she's got her arm in a splint. You should be able to remember how difficult that can be.'

'What? I don't! Has she said something?'

'She doesn't have to. You talk to Pippa as though she's dirt,' I said.

I was probably tired. Or, as my mother would say, overtired. I still had jet lag. I'd been on my feet for the best part of three days. But I was going home tomorrow. I had a return ticket in my handbag. Maybe Oliver wouldn't pay me after all? Maybe he would deduct fifty per cent from my fee for sheer insolence?

'You're talking rubbish! You don't know what it's like! Forcing yourself to think, to write … You don't have people door-stepping you when they see you talking to any woman under fifty. And writing rubbish about me and how I get my inspiration, and Jessie—'

He stopped and drummed his fingers on the table.

'Who's Jessie?' I said.

He made an exclamation of annoyance. 'No one, forget I said anything.'

I felt I was on the edge of a cliff. Not a real cliff obviously, but a sort of metaphorical cliff, and if I took a step more something would happen.

The silence between us stretched on until I could almost feel it throbbing in my ears. I'm not one to let a silence go unfilled; anyone who knows me will tell you that.

'It doesn't matter,' I said at last, re-wiping the worktops for the third time.

I chucked my cloth down and went to stand in front of him.

It was time to lighten the atmosphere.

'Now, what do you want for breakfast?'

'Nothing.'

'Don't sulk. I'm going to make you scrambled eggs,' I said,

willing him to join in, to allow himself to be encouraged into a better mood.

He glared up at me for a moment. It was not to be. 'I'm not sulking. I have a job to do and I'm going to do it. I suggest you do the same.'

I took a deep breath and held it.

I wasn't going to say anything else was I?

Was I? I was. Of course I was.

'Tomorrow I will be going home and the chances of us ever meeting again are between nil and zero. On that basis I'd like you to know that you are the rudest man I've ever met. I don't care if your book launch is today. You're a self-obsessed nightmare. No wonder your PA is permanently on the verge of a nervous breakdown.'

He stood up. 'And you are the noisiest, most maddening, interfering woman I've ever met. You did warn me that hardly anything shut you up didn't you; I should have paid more attention. You're a walking migraine.'

'Right.'

'Right. Tell Jake and Pippa to take the other car. I'll see them in the village. And I don't expect to be kept waiting.'

He stamped out of the house and I heard his car start up and drive away.

About ten minutes later Pippa and Jake came downstairs.

'Is Oliver about?' Jake asked, taking a bagel from the hot plate and buttering it. 'I thought I heard his voice earlier.'

'He's gone,' I said. 'We had words.'

Jake laughed and Pippa drew in a horrified breath.

'But it's his launch day!' she said.

'Doesn't excuse him for being a rude git,' I muttered, 'or for talking to you as though you're a moron.'

'It doesn't matter, I'm used to it,' she said.

'Well you bloody well shouldn't be!' I said furiously.

'But he must be so tense,' she wailed. 'Oh God he's going to be impossible. What did you say?'

'I told him he was rude and self-obsessed and he didn't know the meaning of the word stressed. If he wanted to find out what real stress is go and work in a supermarket stacking shelves overnight for the minimum wage.'

Jake roared with laughter and Pippa gave a little moan of distress.

'Well that's been a long time coming,' Jake said. 'Come on, Pippa, we'd better go and smooth his feathers down.'

'Oh God, what shall I do?' she said, clenching her hands together so tightly that her knuckles showed white.

Jake went over to her and kissed her forehead. 'Pip, calm down. Oliver is my oldest friend, but he has become rude and self-obsessed. It won't hurt him to hear the truth from someone.'

Chapter Twenty

Apparently, despite my outburst the launch went well. I guessed this when they all returned after midnight, Pippa spectacularly drunk and held up by Jake. He helped her across to sit at the kitchen table and I went to fetch her a glass of water. She slumped, the full skirts of her beautiful red dress crushed like flower petals.

I nudged the glass towards her and she looked up at me.

'Oh look, it's Betty,' she said and hiccupped.

'What?'

'Oh didn't you know? Gideon calls you Betty. You know Betty Crocker? Because you're always making cakes and you're such a whizzy creature in the kitchen. Always such a feeder aren't you? Always running after Oliver. He really should have bought you one of those frilly aprons.'

'Pippa, stop it,' Jake said, shaking her shoulder.

She turned, buried her face in his side and burst into tears.

'Oh, Jake. I'm so miserable. He's gonna sack me. I know he is. But if he does I'll – hic – *neverseeyouagain*.' This last bit came out as a sort of wailing sob.

Jake looked at me over the top of her head. 'Sorry, she's a bit ... you know.'

'Pissed? We'd better get her to bed, Jake. You need to be up early tomorrow. The car is coming to collect us at midday. You have to be up, packed, dressed, and ready. And it's not going to be much fun with a monster hangover is it?'

Pippa looked over at me, her eyes unfocused and tearful.

I followed her upstairs and helped her into her room, leaving the door open. She stood and swayed a little, before she rushed into the bathroom and vomited rather dramatically.

I waited until I heard her groaning '*Oh God, I'm never drinking again*' and I left her to it.

Downstairs Jake had disappeared and Oliver was wandering around the sitting room, putting out the lights.

He looked exhausted. I felt terrible, remembering the way I had spoken to him.

'Is she OK?' he said. 'She was on a mission tonight.'

'She's throwing up. Probably the best thing she could do,' I said. 'I'm going to bed now.'

As I walked past him he took hold of my arm and looked down at me. 'Billie, look I wish—'

I stood and looked at him for a moment. 'I'm sorry I spoke to you like that this morning,' I said.

He shook his head. 'I'm trying to apologize to you.'

Well that was a shock. I didn't reply immediately; I just stood there enjoying the feeling of his hand on my skin. His thumb rubbed backwards and forwards over my wrist.

'Well go on then.'

'Go on what?' he said.

'Apologize.'

'I'm not very good at that,' he said.

'You don't get enough practice. Look I talk too much. I'm well known for it.'

'You don't say,' he said.

I looked up at him. He smiled and I felt the most incredible jolt of attraction shoot through me. I swear I nearly fell over.

'Are you OK?' he said at last.

OK in what way exactly? I wondered.

OK in that I was looking forward to going home?

OK because I had enough clean clothes for tomorrow?

OK that I fancied the pants off one of the most successful writers of the last decade? Who had sneered, ridiculed, and irritated me just about every time I'd been in the same room as he was?

'Great,' I said, my mouth suddenly dry. 'I'll apologize if you do?'

'OK, I'm sorry,' he said, and we shook hands. His grip was warm and strong and – bloody hell, I felt a bit light-headed for a moment.

'And I'm sorry,' I said, my voice rather wobbly and funny.

There was a tiny beat then. A moment when I could convince myself he was going to kiss me. He just needed to take one step towards me and I would probably have flung myself at him. But he didn't and the moment passed.

'I hope you have a good trip back. Now I must check the garage is locked up.'

He let go of my hand and I watched him go off into the darkness.

Perhaps he would come back in and ask if I wanted a nightcap? And I'd say yes and he'd stir up the fire and we would sit and drink bourbon in crystal tumblers and the flames would flicker off the glass. Although it might be something else, because I don't think I like bourbon. And then he would be kind and funny and perhaps this time he really would kiss me.

The minutes passed and none of these things happened and I wondered – not for the first time – whether this particular adventure was worth having and if it wasn't, what the hell I was doing.

I woke up several times during the night unable to get comfortable. The pillows – so soft before – were lumpy as old socks. First my hands and feet were cold; an hour later I was too hot. It was like having Reynaud's Syndrome and the menopause at the same time.

I watched the clock crawl round until it was five o'clock and then I made myself a cup of tea and went to sit in bed and wait for the alarm to go off at six. Then I would go downstairs and make them all breakfast for the last time.

I sat and thought about Oliver and felt a bit fluttery and annoyed and silly in a way I hadn't felt – well ever I think.

I went back through the events of last night like a fourteen-year-old with a strange crush. His face, his voice, what he had said, the feel of my hand in his. The way his thumb had stroked my wrist.

Could I imagine him fancying me? Hmm. Most of the time I'd spent with him I had been in jeans and sweatshirts, red-faced from the oven. Not much to fancy there I would have thought.

Outside, the first fingers of a new dawn were brightening the sky, throwing the mountains into sharp shadows. The snow had all gone now and the pine trees at the edge of the garden were tipped with funny little tufts of juicy, green growth. I thought about the spring, the fresh life in the world. It was a time of surging growth and new birth.

I hadn't had sex for … well ages. I couldn't actually remember. Probably when Matt and I got pissed together because we knew we weren't really going to go the distance. And that was two weeks before we were supposed to go to New York, and three days before he dumped me and took sodding Dee instead.

Still, I think I had a grasp of the basics when it came to the finer points of bedroom cavorting? I bloody well hope I remembered when the opportunity next arose, so to speak. What if I'd forgotten? What if I did it wrong? *What if I'd always done it wrong?*

It was quarter to six. I needed to get dressed and finish my packing then search under the bed for lost socks and T-shirts. Maybe Oliver would stand on the balcony waving us off? Or maybe he would come in the car with us, muttering about how glad he was that it was all over and looking forward to getting back to civilization? I imagined him crowding me into a corner with his huge leather laptop bag and his mobile phone bleeping away like a Geiger counter as all his emails rolled in.

Pippa was going to be horribly hung-over.

Hung-over, embarrassed, and resentful.

Hung-over, embarrassed, resentful, and … well never mind. I was a bit sad about Pippa. I'd tried to stick up for her too and that was the thanks I got for it: abuse. Betty Crocker indeed.

Still, perhaps I should go to her room and make sure she hadn't choked on her own vomit. That would be the kind thing to do.

I pulled on my dressing gown and tiptoed along the corridor. Her door was open. From inside I could hear the sort of snoring I might have expected from a dinosaur asleep on its eggs, not a size six, adult woman. I deduced she wasn't dead and went back to my bedroom to shower and pull on some warm clothes.

When I am hung-over – which of course is hardly ever as my body is a temple and I adhere strictly to a clean-eating policy – I like a full English, orange juice, and as much toast as I can get my hands on. Perhaps Pippa and Jake would be the same? I'd get everything ready, and fix a smile on my face.

*

Jake was up and dressed and practically ready by eleven o'clock, which was pretty impressive. There was no sign of Pippa. I left Jake eating scrambled eggs and mushrooms, as apparently the other alternatives were 'too noisy'.

Pippa was still in bed, still snoring, and her room was an absolute tip. It was reminiscent of scenes from *Lord of the Rings* after the Orcs had been through. I wondered not for the first time how Pippa could emerge from such devastation looking as flawless as she did. I opened the curtains and admitted the sunlight. Then I opened the windows and let in the fresh air. Pippa gave a grumbling squawk and pulled the duvet over her head.

'Time to move, Pippa,' I said brightly. 'It's eleven o'clock. You've got an hour till the car comes to take us to the airport.'

'I'm dying,' she said with a rather pathetic sob in her voice.

'Quite possibly but you still have to get up.'

I pulled her case out and lifted it onto her bed. Pippa moved her legs and grumbled a bit more.

'I'm packing your case,' I said. 'There's breakfast downstairs. Jake is eating scrambled eggs. If you're quick, he won't have eaten them all. Or I could do some bacon?'

Pippa gave a whimper and shot out of bed and into the bathroom where I could hear her retching and complaining.

I carried on folding up her clothes and stuffing them as tidily as I could into her bag. Luckily, as she had come business class, she had a bigger baggage allowance and there were two cases instead of one. Even so she seemed to have brought enough clothes for a month. I took an executive decision and left out a pair of sweat pants, a cashmere hoody, and a T-shirt for her to wear. I was guessing those tight leather trousers would not be the way to go.

Seconds later I heard her shower running so I took her bags out onto the landing and went downstairs to make sure Jake hadn't fallen asleep in his breakfast. He was still sitting there, drinking coffee and looking a bit white around his mouth.

'OK?'

'Never better,' he said. He put his mug down and his shoulders drooped as he sat looking washed out, his mouth slightly open.

The back door opened and Oliver came in. I hadn't even known he was awake.

'Everyone up and jumping?' he said. He didn't look at me.

'Well I'm up.' Jake rubbed a hand over his face.

'Job done,' Oliver said. 'Where's Pippa?'

'Last heard of in the shower,' I said. 'I packed her bags and they're on the landing.'

'I'll go and get them.'

Oliver went upstairs and returned with her cases.

'I heard her on the phone to someone so she's still alive,' he said. 'Let's have some coffee.'

Luckily at that moment Pippa came out of her room and came very carefully down the stairs, holding on for dear life to the banister.

She sat down next to Jake.

'Where's my stuff?' she said through stiff lips.

'All here!' I said cheerfully.

Pippa pressed her fingers onto her forehead. 'Coffee and two aspirin,' she whispered, 'please.'

'Not feeling well?' Oliver boomed.

Pippa winced. 'I'm dying. Sorry.'

I passed her a mug of coffee and went to get the aspirin. 'Breakfast? Eggs, bacon, French toast?'

Pippa blew her cheeks out a little. 'I know you mean well but please shut up.'

'OK,' I said cheerfully. 'You need to finish your packing I'm afraid. It's twenty to twelve.'

Pippa finished her coffee and slunk back off upstairs. We could hear her on the phone muttering into her mobile and thumping around slamming doors to convey her misery to the rest of us.

'Got all your stuff? Charging cables, adaptors? Got all your washing out of the dryer?'

'Bloody hell, it's like having my mum here,' Jake grumbled.

'The van is just pulling up,' Oliver said a few minutes later. 'Any sign of Pippa?'

I went up to her room and found her curled up on her bed asleep.

'The minivan's here!' I said.

She moaned and turned away from me.

'You can sleep on the drive back to the airport,' I said.

'Tell me when everyone's got their stuff in and you're about to go,' she said.

'You've got about five minutes.'

Downstairs Oliver had put Jake's cases in the back of the van and Jake himself was standing next to it looking vague. He got into the seat at the back of the van, made a pillow from his coat, rested his head on it, and closed his eyes.

'Pippa?' Oliver said.

'Wants to be called at the last minute.'

'This is the last minute.'

'I'll go and get her,' I said.

Pippa was fast asleep and didn't appreciate being woken up. I got her downstairs and into the back of the car and Oliver put her bags in.

She slumped across the next row of seats and then realized perhaps it wouldn't work. She sat up and moved across to let me in. I caught her eye and passed her a bottle of chilled water.

'Thanks,' she said in a tiny voice.

'You're welcome,' I said.

'Sorry,' she whispered.

'It's fine,' I said.

I took a last look around before I got in beside her. The sun was high in a dazzling blue sky, the air was clean and cold and filled with energy. This had definitely been an adventure. I'd seen a tiny part of a huge country I knew hardly anything about. It was vast and beautiful and different. I promised myself I would come back one day, I would explore.

I would get fit what with clean eating and losing weight. Perhaps I'd hike the Appalachian Trail? I could almost imagine myself triumphantly breasting the brow of a hill and looking down on a verdant valley filled with red grain silos and black and white cows, where American people made quilts and had yard sales. Whatever they were.

Then I thought about the bears. Perhaps not.

Chapter Twenty-One

I got back to my house the following day to find everything spotless. Of course it would be. With Godfrey and Peter staying there, every surface from the skirting boards to the fridge had been cleaned and polished. They had left a bunch of flowers in a vase on the worktop, a welcome home card, and a helium-filled balloon decorated with the Stars and Stripes.

I dragged my case in, shut the door, and slumped down at the kitchen table. Then I found my spare phone charger and put my mobile on to charge.

Of course, a barrage of texts, emails, and messages arrived within seconds. Lots from Helena with a blow-by-blow account of the journey and how she was enjoying herself in Scotland. One from my mother who was back home from Nottingham. The twins had brought some of the scenery down at their school play but other than that everything had been great. And lastly, an email from Gideon March. Offering me a job. Unbelievable.

I clicked on the reply button and then hesitated. Would I accept or decline or even bother to reply? Perhaps it was a joke? I deleted it.

Nothing from Oliver at all. Why on earth had I imagined there would be? What would he say?

I went to empty my case and then, seeing the beautifully made bed with its fresh, clean, ironed sheets, I just kicked my shoes off and got in. After all what bloody time was it anyway? Who cared? While I was trying to puzzle it out I went to sleep.

I woke up some time later to hear someone knocking on the front door. I dragged myself out of bed. 'Who is it?'

'It's me, it's Peter. Are you decent? Come on, open the door, petal.'

Godfrey and Uncle Peter stood there with a bag of groceries.

'We've brought you some milk and some bread and stuff,' Peter said.

Godfrey stepped forwards. 'Can we come in? Have you had fun? Are you all right?'

'Thank you for leaving this place looking so lovely and clean. I can't thank you enough,' I said.

'Pish! It's the least we could do,' Peter said. 'We found some interesting things at the bottom of your fridge, including something that may be a form of life not previously encountered. I hope you don't mind we had a bit of a clear-out?'

'God no I don't mind!'

'Good. Now let's have some wine and then we'll have the chicken casserole I've made,' Godfrey said.

'Oh you didn't need to—'

'No but we have. And you can tell us all your news. Well some of it. You know, just the edited highlights. You're not that fascinating,' Godfrey said with a wink.

We sat around my kitchen table and talked, and I had no idea what time I thought it was or even whether I wanted chicken. We drank some more wine and I told them about the job offer I'd had from Oliver's publisher Gideon.

'Gideon March? Now that rings a bell. We heard something about him didn't we? Godfrey's friend works in some seventh circle of hell all to do with publishing and apparently the hot rumour was your Oliver was looking for a new American publisher.' He pulled a face.

'What happened to Gideon March?'

'Let go. Sacked. Something to do with creative differences. That's what they always say. I googled Gideon March. His eyes are too close together. He looks like a well-groomed weasel.'

Yes, I could agree with that.

'Your Oliver looked nice though; very handsome,' Godfrey added.

'He's not my anything,' I said.

'And muscular,' Godfrey added, 'but in a good way.'

'Oh shut up!' I said not knowing if I was going to laugh or cry.

*

I went back to see how they were getting on a couple of days later when my jet lag was just about sorted out. Peter and Godfrey were in relentlessly good form, chatting effusively with the few customers who came in. It was obvious they really didn't need me there too. There were only so many cups of tea and cakes they could get through and the chap fixing the shelving only drank diet cola and ate chewing gum as far as I could tell.

I wandered around, straightening piles of books and dusting shelves for a bit, and then went to see Helena.

She looked exceptionally happy and had enjoyed her trip to the frozen North a great deal. Scotland had been delightful. The scenery unrivalled, the hotel romantic, and of course Nick had been wonderful.

We were having coffee and biscuits in the cupboard officially known as her office, while she pretended to catch up on work emails. She was still filled with a happy wonder about Nick and wanted to go over all the details.

'He made me tea in bed every morning we were there. And did I show you the photos? He wants us to go back there next year too. Our room was covered in tartan. I mean plastered. Tartan curtains, tartan carpet, and tartan mugs, and there was even tartan trim on the towels.'

'But there wasn't an aged retainer called Angus? That's very disappointing.'

'There wasn't; all the staff were Polish I think, absolutely charming of course. Dressed in their kilts and frilly shirts. They must think we are absolutely mad over here.'

'And Nick? Is he still Mr Wonderful?'

Helena blushed and giggled and wriggled in her chair a bit. 'He's lovely.'

'And?'

'He's coming over at the weekend. I'll have to tidy up a bit.'

'Helena, your house is always immaculate. Unless you've discovered some new way to torment yourself cleaning moss off the roof tiles.'

'Well I'll have to change the sheets then.'

'Good one. And all is still well in that department?'

'Oooh yes, I should say. Do you know last weekend I was still asleep and I was really surprised when he—'

The door opened and I never did find out what Nick had

done to surprise her. Perhaps it was just as well.

It was one of the other librarians, a worried-looking girl with her hair in several plaits.

'Helena, has *The Duke's True Love* come back yet? Only Miss Timpson is out there kicking off. You'll have to come and calm her down. I can't lay my hand on the Jackie Collins title she's looking for and she doesn't like Barbara Cartland because there's no sex.'

Helena rolled her eyes and shoved in the last of her shortbread, brushing the crumbs off her skirt as she stood up.

'I'd better go.'

'Me too. I've got work to do. I'm going to expand the writing retreat business.' I was making it sound like a multinational takeover. 'But first I need a book on building a website. Can you point me to the right section?'

*

I wandered back down the high street, picking up milk on the way and stopping at the bank. I stuck my card in the machine to check the balance. I hate doing that. I'm nearly always disappointed or confused why there's no money in my account. And then I have to go through the depressing business of reconciling trips to coffee shops and book purchases on Amazon. Usually there was a balance of a few hundred pounds; sometimes it dipped into the red.

Today there was nearly a thousand pounds in there.

I checked it three times and even went to use the machine inside the bank too. Then I got a mini-statement and checked it. Then I did a full printed statement and took it into the nearest café.

When I was settled with a cup of mint tea and a toasted teacake, I spread the papers out on the table and looked over them to make sure.

Payment for some birthday cakes I had made had gone in and another from the writing retreat to reimburse me for groceries I had bought. But on top of that there had been a bank transfer for six hundred pounds, two days ago, from the account of Ross Black Limited, HPGD Bank, Chelsea Branch.

I sat there for some time looking at the figures. This was surely more than I had been offered to do the job. Why would Oliver do this? Was it some sort of fat-finger mistake?

I drank my mint tea but after a few sips I realized it was tepid, unpleasant, and I pushed it away. The teacake wasn't much better. The butter had soaked into it and now it was cold and greasy. I couldn't eat it, and I have never in my life left a toasted teacake uneaten. Perhaps this would be a good time to start point 2 on my list, my clean-eating plan? Well, when I'd finished the new Toblerone I'd bought at the airport …

I felt tired and a bit sad, not even the sight of a load of unexpected money in my bank account cheered me up. In fact, it made me feel a bit worse. Why did it make me feel worse? It was like charity. I wanted to get my life back on track by my own efforts. I didn't need or want charity.

I'd done the job and now I was being treated like a broken-down old warhorse being put out to pasture.

Well more like a young-ish horse being put into a paddock.

No, what was I talking about?

A young, attractive horse being escorted to a lovely, flowery field where it would have a pleasant and fulfilled life.

There was no doubt about it I was losing my mind.

I wasn't a horse of any sort. I wasn't being put out anywhere. I'd just been paid more than I was expecting.

I paid my bill and, after a moment dithering about, decided this was the day when I would buy some new bras. Point 3 on my list. Now this was an adventure I hadn't expected when I woke up this morning. I'd been meaning to do this for years.

The bra fitter was nice but very determined I was not going to leave the shop without at least three. She brought me armfuls of the things, something I'd always avoided doing because putting the right one back on the right hanger in the right way is almost impossible unless you've been on some sort of training course. She didn't seem to mind though, and was delighted to find how badly my existing underwear was fitting. Or not fitting. I felt I had given her plenty to use at the next Bra Fitters' Seminar she attended.

There was a great deal of strap hauling and whispered conferencing with her colleague behind the curtain and when she had finished I was surprised to find I did actually have a waist. Who would have thought it? When I looked down I also seemed a bit reminiscent of Madonna in her Jean Paul Gaultier phase but I was assured it was OK. I'd get used to it. Well if nothing else I had somewhere new to rest my book.

'Now do you need a sports bra?' she said just as I was thinking I was past all my pain.

Sports bra.

'I'm not sure,' I said. 'Do I?'

She pursed her mouth. 'Well do you do any sport, play tennis, running – that sort of thing? All you young girls seem to go running these days; it's very bad for your bosoms though, without a sports bra. You need firm support.'

Sport. Tennis. Running. No of course not.

I took a breath ready to tell her how unlikely I was to do any of those things and then stopped.

I might? After all I was trying to do different things wasn't I? Perhaps running could be my new pastime.

'Yes, I absolutely do need a new sports bra,' I said confidently. 'Mine is almost worn out.'

She brought back some garments that were apparently made from old wet suits in neon shades with thick straps and a lot more hooks and eyes than I was used to.

'Give me a shout if you need a hand,' she said and swished the curtain closed again.

In less than five minutes I understood why people like Serena and Venus Williams need a team of people to follow them around the world. They probably have one designated person to help them into their sports bras every morning. No woman could put one on unaided in my opinion. Not unless she had no bosom to start with.

I wrestled with the wet suit off-cuts for several minutes.

'All right in there?' my fitter called encouragingly through the curtain.

At this point I was red-faced and sweating. I had one hook done up and the straps were flapping around my ears.

'Fine,' I said cheerily.

'Well let me know if you need help adjusting the fit,' she said. 'They can be a bit tricky. I'll be back in a minute.'

By the time she returned I was exhausted.

My fitter looked around the curtain and handed me some wet wipes.

'Hot work isn't it,' she said.

She hauled at the straps as though I was a horse and she

was adjusting my saddle girths. Then she tugged at the back for a few minutes before she was satisfied.

'That's really lovely,' she said, admiringly. 'You won't get better than that. They need to be tight, do you see?'

'Yes,' I said, gasping for breath. It was quite possible I was going to pass out. Still it was another tick on my list.

*

I made good my escape and celebrated by buying some Kat Treatz for next door's cat who had evidently appreciated being fed too often during his owner's holiday and had taken to loitering in my garden. Then I went back to Uncle Peter's bookshop where the young gum-chewing shelf-fitter had downed tools and gone for the day. The shelves he had been fixing seemed no further on than they had last week. Peter and Godfrey were in the shop, muffled up against the cold wind howling under the door and through the rickety window frames.

'How are you getting on?' I asked. 'How's it going?'

One look around showed me it wasn't good. This time there was no one in the shop. Peter was sitting behind the desk with a pile of paperwork while Godfrey leaned over his shoulder and gnawed at his thumbnail.

'Oh you know,' Godfrey said.

'It's a bugger,' Peter said.

'It's just a bad time of year,' I said, trying to sound positive. 'Things will pick up when ... when they pick up. In the warmer weather.'

'Maybe,' Uncle Peter said, 'but it's not just us. The big booksellers are playing with all the Aces. They do it their way.

233

Not to mention Amazon. There always used to be space for us little independent shops too, but these days, well, not so much. There are so many books out there and people have never bought so many, they just aren't buying them from shops like this one. They like to pick them up with the sodding potatoes and their horrible cheap wine.'

'Calm down, remember your blood pressure,' Godfrey murmured.

'What can you do?' I said.

They both looked a bit blank.

'Coffee and cake? People like to sit and browse and relax in bookshops these days.'

Godfrey shook his head. 'We don't have the room; we thought about it when we had the flood and the chance to reorganize. But if you do you open yourself to breaking all sorts of rules and regulations. Health and safety, food hygiene, bloody *Human Rights Act* for all I know.'

'You need a USP,' I said.

'Like telepathy?' Godfrey said.

'No, you're thinking of ESP; USP is a unique selling point. I've been reading up about it. Like buy one get one half price.'

Godfrey looked doubtful. I decided to tell them my idea; if nothing else it would make me sharpen up my thoughts. Once it was out there I'd have to do it.

'Look, I've been thinking about things. I'm going to get a website up and running this evening. I don't need the wages you pay me. I've got some money to keep me going. I'll be happy to work here for nothing if it would help? But what I want to do is expand the retreat business. Helena can't spend any more time on it – she's got a full-time job – but I certainly can. It's what I like doing and I think if I was more organized

234

and went about it more seriously I could make a go of it.'

'Really?' Uncle Peter said.

'Yes really. I'm nearly thirty; it's time I stopped messing about with student jobs and did something.'

'Good,' he said. 'You're right. It is about time.'

My mobile vibrated in my pocket and I took it out: a number I didn't recognize.

'Is this Billie Summers?'

Well it might be; it depends what you want.

'Who is this?'

'My name is Jeff Ford-Wilson; I'm ringing on behalf of my wife Kitty. She would like to come to you for a week's retreat. She has edits to do and the kids will be home from school soon and they'll drive her mad.'

This was beyond weird! Kitty Ford-Wilson? Why did I know that name? How had she found me?

Hang on! The Kitty Ford-Wilson? The bestselling writer and internationally famous Kitty Ford-Wilson? The one who wrote *Life's Not Bloody Fair* and *Not in Your Size, Madam*?

'Um, yes of course. When did you have in mind? And how did you get my number? If you don't mind me asking?'

'From Oliver.'

'Oliver Forest?'

'Yes, he's a friend of Kitty's, says you organize everything a knackered writer could need. And as soon as possible really. What do you say? I'd be really grateful. Oliver said a hundred and fifty pounds a day; I don't care what it costs. I don't care where it is within reason ...'

A hundred and fifty pounds *a day*? I never said that!

'... she's not fussy, she just wants somewhere quiet and comfortable with somewhere to write, no distractions, and intravenous coffee. And soon. Please. I'd be really grateful. And so would the twins. It's nearly the school holidays. If I get Kitty settled somewhere I can take them to Center Parcs.'

He was beginning to sound a tad panicky by now. His voice was getting a bit high-pitched. It sounded as though Kitty Ford-Wilson would make Oliver Forest look like a pussycat.

'Perhaps a hotel?' I suggested.

'She hates room service – all that bowing and scraping over a pot of tea. She hates hearing other guests when she's editing. If she hears a loo flushing it drives her nearly mad.'

'A rented cottage?'

'Yes, but she can't cook. Well she can but she doesn't, if you see what I mean?'

'Oh, yes I see. Look, I'm sure I can do something. Can I get back to you in the morning?'

Jeff gave me his number and email address and rang off.

I looked up to see Uncle Peter and Godfrey watching me.

'So what was all that about?'

'Oliver has recommended me to Kitty Ford-Wilson,' I said. 'I rather think that's my first client.'

Godfrey went over to the shelves and fished out *Not in Your Size, Madam.*

'This Kitty Ford-Wilson?'

I nodded. 'She needs somewhere quiet to finish editing. Somewhere she can't hear people or loos flushing.'

We stood and looked at each other for a few minutes. Then we discussed the various options. Holiday cottage? Hotel? Yurt in a field?

'Spare room,' Uncle Peter said.

'I haven't got a spare room,' I said. 'Well not one I can use.'

'So make it useable,' he said. 'What's the point of having a spare room if it's just storing junk? Or if you can't be bothered, I suppose she could stay here with us. Although ...'

'She can't stay with you! You'd drive her mad. You are up all night playing Scrabble and listening to Gilbert and Sullivan!' I said. 'And your spare room is a tip as well so don't get funny with me. Last time I looked it was full of paperwork and books. And a broken filing cabinet.'

'Ah but if you sorted out *your* spare room, you could have that bedstead we've got in the garage. You've been marvellous helping us out; now it's our chance to help you. You've got a downstairs loo so she wouldn't get annoyed every time you need a wee. She could have the upstairs bathroom and the box room to work in. The walls are so thick she'd never hear anything.'

'I suppose so,' I said thoughtfully. 'It was on my list to get it sorted. I need to go and see.'

Uncle Peter came with me.

My house, old and odd as it was, did have thick, stone walls and it was as quiet as any temperamental writer could hope for. It would take a bit of doing but it was feasible. And I had money to buy a few nice things and some new towels. I didn't think someone as sophisticated as Kitty Ford-Wilson would appreciate Ninja Turtles bath sheets.

Out in the garden I could see Not My Cat sitting on the garden wall. I hoped Kitty wasn't allergic or anything.

Chapter Twenty-Two

Kitty Ford-Wilson arrived six days later. I had spent several days cleaning and painting the spare room, assembling the bed (brass bedstead, porcelain knobs, really rather lovely) dressing it with crisp white bedding and plump pillows. There was a new towel stand laden with white bath sheets. The bathroom had been decluttered and cleaned and supplied with new toiletries. The box room, which might have been big enough for a cot or a tiny single bed, had been turned into a writing room for her.

I'd managed this by decanting all my junk into Uncle Peter's garage. And I do mean decanting; I'd practically hurled all the boxes of old books, kitchen equipment, and Christmas decorations in through his door – something he wasn't too thrilled about.

I'd then painted the box room a soothing sort of pale grey, put up new curtains, organized a chair, table, and armchair and even bought a coffee maker – the sort I'd always wanted, where coffee is kept on a hotplate. The day she was due to arrive I put a kettle, mug, sugar, tea, and a basket of home-made cookies in there and hoped for the best. She'd either like it or she wouldn't.

I'd been googling Kitty Ford-Wilson for days to find out more about her. She was obviously very successful, prolific, and important. From the few personal details I found out she sounded rather tricky.

(She was quoted as saying she didn't suffer fools gladly. But to be honest I've never met anyone who did.)

More accurately she sounded impatient, bad tempered, and fond of a drink. Great.

Having got into the clearing-out groove I decided to declutter my wardrobe and create the stylish palette of elegance I'd promised myself. After a couple of hours it became obvious I didn't have the necessary garments to be either stylish or elegant. But I did have a lot of T-shirts with random food splatters across the front that no amount of washing would remove, ten pairs of jeans, none of which I could bear to wear for an entire day because they were too tight, and six shirts that didn't button over my new sculpted and supported bosom.

In the end I shoved some stuff into a black bin liner for the charity shop and the rest into the back of the wardrobe. It wasn't exactly decluttering, but it was a start.

A car pulled up outside my house just before three in the afternoon and Kitty's husband – a small, worried-looking man – brought her bags in. He put them down to shake my hand.

'Jeff Ford-Wilson. Pleased to meet you. I can't tell you how grateful I am,' he said, rather breathless. 'Kitty is on such a tight deadline and things are going from bad to worse. I keep telling her it will be all right in the end, it always is, but that doesn't seem to help. She gets very … The girls are back from boarding school tomorrow. I don't think I could deal with … well let's just say Kitty needs some space. I mean teenage girls are a nightmare aren't they? It's in their job spec. But still …'

He kept up a continuous stream of apology and explanation until he had put all her stuff into the room.

'She'll like this,' he said looking around. 'She likes white bed linen and towels. And she takes up lots of space in bed so just as well it's a double. That's why I sometimes sleep ... well never mind.'

'Um where is she?' I said when I could get a word in edgewise.

Jeff looked up startled and for a terrible moment I wondered if he had forgotten to bring her or left her somewhere. He looked at his watch.

'Oh she wouldn't come with *me*. She doesn't like my driving. She'll be here in a few minutes. Can we put the coffee maker on? That will settle her. I'm not sure about the cookies; Kitty is a bit weight conscious, like all you ladies. I don't know why, because she's a lovely shape.'

He picked up the basket of cookies and looked at them rather doubtfully before putting them back.

'Don't be surprised if she throws them out. It's no reflection ... So you're Billie, a friend of Oliver's? What a nice man. He's such a laugh isn't he?'

Laugh? Oliver Forest *a laugh?*

'Oliver Forest the writer?' I said as I followed him back downstairs. 'A laugh?'

'Golly yes, he has us in stitches when we go over for dinner. Kitty has such a crush ... well never mind. Now then, I think we're all set. She has lunch at one, tea at three-thirty, dinner at seven. Did I tell you she only eats off white china? I'd better go.'

Jeff hurried out towards his car.

'Don't you want to wait and make sure she gets here OK?' I said.

He got into his car and lowered the window. 'Crumbs no,

240

she won't want to find me here interfering with her chakras. I'll be off. You've got my number haven't you? Any emergencies let me know otherwise I'll see you on Friday. Good luck, I'm sure it will be fine. Better than fine, I mean great.'

He drove off with a jaunty wave through the window and I watched until his car turned the corner. Wow, Kitty sounded terrifying. I hardly knew what to expect. She appeared ten minutes later, and I wasn't disappointed.

*

She arrived in a red Maserati, its twin exhausts booming a warning as she drove up the road to my house. Then she sat in the car apparently talking to herself until I realized she was finishing a phone call. By her expression someone was getting a tongue-lashing. She got out and stood looking around for a moment. I hurried out to greet her.

The thing that struck me first was how ordinary she looked. Without the trademark crimson jacket, artful make-up, and bouffant hair styling of her book covers she looked like quite an ordinary, slightly stout, middle-class housewife. Apart from the knuckle-duster diamond on her ring finger. And the Gucci laptop bag.

'Mrs Ford-Wilson?'

Just in case there was any doubt.

She shook my hand. 'Kitty.'

I showed her to her room and she glanced around. Then we went to the makeshift writing area and she stood looking at it.

'Yes,' she said after a long, terrible pause, 'it'll do.'

'The coffee is on. Would you like to help yourself? Would you like a cookie? Or some cake? Or both?'

'No, no, no, and no thank you,' she said, dumping her laptop bag on the table. She opened one of the bags that Jeff had left in the bedroom and pulled out a bottle of gin, which she handed to me. 'Have you got any tonic? Full fat not slim-line. Ice and lemon? I'm not going anywhere else today and I need a pick-me-up before I start work. I'll be down in ten minutes, yes?'

I scurried off to the corner shop to buy some tonic water and made up a rather stiff drink for her. Thirty seconds after the ice had hit the glass she came downstairs in an ugly housecoat and some raddled old slippers and sank down on my sofa with a sigh of pleasure. She had scraped her blonde hair back into a ponytail and she looked every one of her fifty-four years.

She downed half the drink in one gulp.

'That's better. Now then,' she said, 'I know Jeff has sent you some advice, but I'll just run through. Dinner at seven, no pasta – it's too heavy. Salad, steak, bread – I love bread. Cheese, any. Red wine, not South American. OK?'

'Fine.'

'Breakfast, seven-thirty. Toast, Marmite. Proper butter too, not that ghastly grease.'

'Fine.'

'Lunch – any soup but not oxtail. Tinned is all right by me. French bread.'

'Fine.'

I took her glass away and refilled it; she looked at me with a sideways glance. There were deep wrinkles around her mouth that spoke of a lifetime's disapproval of everything.

'You're not what I was expecting,' she said.

'Nor are you,' I replied.

'What were you expecting?' She narrowed her eyes at me. 'Someone older.'

This is always a good answer to questions like this I think. You can't go wrong with it unless it's a policeman.

Kitty pursed her lips at me thoughtfully.

'I smoke.'

'I know.'

I could tell that from the stains on the first two fingers of her right hand. And the faint nicotine smell that permeated the air around her.

She raised her chin and glared. 'Aren't you going to tut and forbid me and send me to the end of the garden?'

'Not unless you feel the need. They are your lungs. Just not in the kitchen.'

The answer pleased her and she nodded. 'True. Right, I'm going to unpack. I'll see you at seven. Oliver warned me you make a lot of noise. Let's not do that hmm?'

She heaved herself to her feet and went upstairs. After a few minutes I heard the door to her writing room close and I tiptoed out to the kitchen. And very quietly opened the back door to let the smell of her cigarettes out of the house. Not My Cat was sitting on the doorstep and it looked up at me with its silent meow until I fetched it some Kat Treatz.

'You don't know how lucky you are, cat,' I said. 'All you do is sleep and wait for someone to spoil you.'

By the time two uneventful days had passed I began to relax. Kitty Ford-Wilson, despite her fearsome reputation, was no trouble at all. Mind you, I came to suspect she might have been borderline alcoholic and she never seemed to wear anything other than the housecoat and slippers, but she ate everything I put in front of her, and didn't once complain about any noise as I tiptoed around downstairs, cooking in an exaggeratedly quiet manner.

On day three, like a rather cumbersome poltergeist she unexpectedly wandered downstairs, obviously wanting company. She poured herself her customary G&T sat silently at the kitchen table watching me cooking. It was rather unnerving, but I wasn't going to start the conversation unprompted.

'What are you doing?' she said at last.

'Making scones.'

'Why?'

'Because I like them and I thought you might too. I was going to give you a cream tea. When you have your afternoon break.'

'I've never had that,' Kitty said.

'Never? You've never had a scone with cream and jam? Never?'

'No, too fattening. I have a problem with my weight do you see?'

'Do you? Why?'

'Why what?'

'Why do you have a problem with your weight?' I said.

'Isn't it bloody obvious? I'm greedy. I'm fat.'

'No you're not.'

Kitty flared her nostrils at me. 'I think I'll be the judge of that.'

'Suit yourself,' I said.

I affected a casual air but inside I was quaking.

She patted the pockets of her dressing gown and drew out a cigarette packet and a lighter.

'So now then, Oliver,' she said.

'Yes?' I said carefully not looking at her.

'Was he all right? I mean when you saw him?'

Was he all right? Well, apart from being rude and patronizing?

'I suppose so, he had an injured leg. I don't think that made him any more cheery,' I said.

'Oh yes, he fell off my stepladder.'

I frowned. 'I thought he came off his motorbike?'

Kitty gave a throaty laugh and slapped the table with the flat of her hand.

'Ollie? On a motorbike? Don't make me laugh. He can't ride a pushbike let alone a motorbike! No, he was trying to get my cat out of a tree and he fell off the stepladder. Hahaha! Ollie on a motorbike? Hahaha!'

She was one of those people who actually do say 'Ha Ha' when they laugh too. It was very unexpected after two and a half days of near silence.

'I'll never forget the time my brother had a unicycle and Ollie tried to ride it—'

Kitty almost choked with laughter and wiped tears from her eyes. 'He ended up in the hedge and the girls were hysterical.'

The thought of this was so far removed from the man I knew that I couldn't process it.

Kitty sparked up her lighter and I frowned at her.

'Oh all right, I'll stand outside,' she grumbled. Not My Cat came and wound itself around her feet. She nudged it away but not unkindly.

'So how long have you been doing this malarkey?' she said.

'A couple of years,' I said, patting out the scones.

'Why?'

'What do you mean why?'

It was like having a six-year-old child to stay.

'Well no one grows up wanting to run writing retreats for bad-tempered writers like me,' she said.

'No,' I said carefully.

'So you *do* think I'm bad tempered?'

'Kitty, will you stop it? And stop blowing your cigarette smoke in here.'

'Tetchy aren't we?' She moved a few steps away. 'Why aren't you asking me questions?'

'Because I was told you wanted peace and quiet.'

'Yes, but people usually ask *some* questions. Or they want a book signed for their mother. Do you want me to sign any books?'

'Well not at the moment, thanks.'

'Why not?'

'Kitty, will you stop going on?'

'I don't do any cooking. Jeff does it all,' she said. She stubbed out her cigarette on the wall and looked around for a bin. When she couldn't find one she chucked the stub into the hedge.

'Don't do that!' I said.

'What?'

'Don't chuck your fag ends around my garden.'

Kitty huffed and went to pick it up. 'Ollie was right – you're bloody bossy,' she said.

I couldn't resist it. 'What else did Ollie say? Did he say anything about me?'

Kitty smirked. '*Did Ollie say anything about me?* I guessed as much,' she said.

'What?'

'Never mind. I'm never wrong with these things. I said as much to Jeff.'

'Said what?'

'Ha ha,' she said wagging an annoying finger at me.

I put the scones onto a baking tray and put them into the oven. Kitty watched me.

'I won't eat those you know,' she said.

'OK, that's fine,' I replied.

I think I was getting the measure of her. She was so used to people walking on eggshells around her that she seemed to enjoy a little bit of normality. Even so I was wise enough to know I could push her so far and no further.

She lit another cigarette and watched me through the door as I cleared up the kitchen and set the tea tray with some pretty china, strawberry jam, and a small bowl of clotted cream.

'Why aren't you married?' Kitty said. 'You seem nice – you're domesticated and friendly. You'd be quite pretty if you made a bit of an effort.'

'Well thanks,' I said, trying not to laugh.

'I didn't mean that. I meant why isn't someone like you attached to someone?' She peered at me. 'You're supposed to have two distinct eyebrows and your top lip needs waxing.'

'OK, thanks – perhaps I'll do that.'

'Are you a lesbian?'

'No.'

'You don't mind me asking?'

I shrugged. 'No.'

'No boyfriend?'

'Not at the moment; I had one but he dumped me for someone with a chest measurement larger than her IQ.'

It was true too; Dee was what you might call over-blessed in the chestal department and was thick as a brick. I wonder what the bra fitter would have thought of her? Perhaps she would just have brought out two of those pop-up tents people take to the beach and can never wrestle back into the covers. Still, if she made Matt happy...

Kitty snorted. 'I might use that one in my next book if you've no objection?'

'Feel free.'

'And you write?'

'I have done but I don't think I've got what it takes to be a successful writer. I get distracted.'

The oven timer pinged and I went to get the scones out of the oven. The smell was fantastic and Kitty inhaled with delight, her eyes closed.

'Maybe just one small one?' she said.

We ate our cream tea out in the garden with Not My Cat meowing silently for cream under the table. Two scones later and after a heated discussion about the need for butter, and whether the cream should go on top or under the jam, Kitty went back upstairs to carry on writing.

As I was putting the last plates away my mobile rang.

'It's me,' Helena said. 'Have you got a minute?'

I hadn't heard from her for a few days. 'Yes of course, what's up?'

'How is the famous writer? Is she as awful as she sounded?'

'No actually, she's a bit prickly but she's growing on me.'

'Can I come and meet her?'

I hesitated. There was no way Kitty was going to hold court to random visitors in her housecoat and slippers.

'I'll ask,' I said.

'I've got one of her books for Mum's birthday present. Do you think she would sign it?'

'I'll ask,' I said again, not entirely sure what Kitty's reaction to this would be. I'd heard enough to know she didn't enjoy that sort of thing.

'I know we have the retreat to do in June, but it will work if Nick and I go to Barcelona in September won't it?' Helena said.

NickandI had become an entity all of its own these days, almost as if they were one person. And I suppose they were come to think of it. NickandI were together every weekend and some weekday evenings too.

'Yes of course, fine. Sounds fun,' I said. 'D'you know, Kitty says Oliver is a great laugh. And he didn't fall off a motorbike; he was trying to rescue Kitty's cat from a tree and fell off a stepladder.'

'Huh?'

'I know.'

'Perhaps it's a different Oliver?'

'Hang on, I can hear Kitty coming down the stairs. I'd better go.'

'I need some fresh air,' Kitty said when she came into the kitchen, almost as though she was expecting me to produce some for her. She was at least dressed though in an aggressively floral shift dress that made her bosom look like a shelf. 'I think perhaps a walk to the shops? You'd better show me the way.'

It was less than half a mile down a straight road, but I nodded obediently and went to get my purse.

'I could take you in to see my Uncle Peter,' I said as we reached the high street.

'The one who owns the bookshop? I'm not doing any signings or reading or anything,' Kitty said rather defensively.

'No one wants you to,' I said, 'but it's near the newsagent's and I suspect that's where you want to go for more cigarettes?'

Kitty snorted and didn't reply.

I was right though. She went and stocked up on cigarettes and then, still grumbling about the price, followed me warily back down the street and into the bookshop. Godfrey was wandering about with a pile of paperbacks and he came over to say hello.

'And this must be Mrs Ford-Wilson? How delightful to meet you. Would you like a cup of tea?'

'No, just had one,' Kitty said. 'And scones. Billie forced me.'

'Yes, she is a bit of a feeder isn't she? I hope she's looking after you?'

Kitty gave me a sideways look. 'Adequate,' she said with the suspicions of a twinkle in her eye.

'Peter will be sorry to have missed you. He's gone to the doctor for his prescription. I hope the writing is going well?' he said.

'Surprisingly so,' Kitty said. 'Funny how a change of scene can do that. A friend of mine recommended her.' She noticed the empty bookshelves at the end of the room. 'This is a charming little shop, but what's happened here then?'

'Oh we had a flood. I'm afraid the chap doing the refurb is a tad unreliable. But we're getting there. Bookshops like ours are getting to be a rarity these days. We're not cash rich even if we do stock literary treasure.'

Kitty sniffed her disapproval at the state of the world. 'So do you have any of my books you want signing? They generally go pretty well.'

I looked at her in astonishment. 'You said you wouldn't.'

Kitty flared her nostrils at me. 'When did I say that? Utter nonsense.'

Godfrey pulled out half a dozen copies of Kitty's books and she signed them with a flourish. She picked one up and flicked through it.

'*Not in Your Size, Madam*. My God if I had a pound for every time I've heard that.'

'Ditto,' I said.

'You? You're a twig. Don't be ridiculous!' Kitty snorted.

'Ah but my generation are supposed to be thin, voluptuous, ripped, sculpted, muscular, feminine, and androgynous all in the same week. You can't win. It's like *Dressing Up Dolly*. The many faces of the modern woman.'

Kitty looked pensive as she handed the books back to Godfrey, and then she shook herself.

'That's a very interesting thought, Billie. A very, very interesting thought. Look, I can't hang about here. I have work to do,' she said. And she sailed out of the shop and back up the road to my house without another word.

When we got home she scooted upstairs, returning five minutes later in her housecoat and slippers and an empty glass.

'Gin,' she said. 'Stiff. Plotting.'

*

Kitty barely spoke to me for the rest of the week. I even had to nudge her gently to come down for her meals. She was up in her writing room typing fit to burst, the air thick with cigarette smoke and gin fumes. I'd never get the reek out but of course it was too late now to change the house rules. Kitty came downstairs on the last day, dressed in her trademark red jacket, her face carefully made up for the first time since she'd arrived.

'Right, I've packed my bags. Jeff should be here later on to pick them up.' She checked through her handbag and looked up, satisfied.

'I have all my things; I'll be off. It's been real.'

'Real?'

'I mean fine. Great. Excellent. I'm going to recommend you to a couple of friends of mine. Thank you for ... You'll be hearing from me.'

With a cheque I hope, I thought as I waved her off. I waited until the Maserati was out of sight and went back in to open all the windows. I might have to shampoo the carpets in her room. I'd certainly have to wash the curtains.

Jeff Ford-Wilson arrived half an hour later.

'So she's fine?' he said. He looked like a different man from the one who had dropped Kitty off a week previously. From his suntan I guessed he'd been out in the fresh air for most of the week. He was wearing some disreputable old shorts and a sweatshirt that was covered in grass stains.

'Yes I think so – she didn't say much,' I said.

Jeff smiled. 'That's an excellent sign. I couldn't be more pleased.'

He swung her bags into the boot of his car and handed me an envelope.

'From Kitty. Thank you,' he said. 'I mean really, thank you. I can tell she's been smoking like a chimney in there. You might need the extra for – well you know.'

After he'd gone I opened the envelope to look at the cheque. Bloody hell! She must have been pleased!

*

252

The following day found me having another sort of adventure, on the fourth floor of our local department store, lying on a paper-lined couch while someone called Jools smeared hot wax over my brows and top lip. There was soothing whale music playing in the background, which might have soothed any whale lying on the couch but didn't do much for me.

I'd avoided doing this for years but if Kitty Ford-Wilson thought it was a good idea, who was I to argue?

'Will this hurt?' I said.

It was rather too late to ask this if you think about it.

'Oh no,' Jools said airily, adding another layer and some gauze and humming along.

She was quite blessed in the chestal department too; her boobs kept banging up against the top of my head. I almost felt like slipping her my bra fitter's card. I wondered if she wore a sports bra. Perhaps it was time to try mine out? I needed to find something sporty to do that was free. So no point joining a gym or a tennis club. Apart from anything else I can't play tennis, have no interest in learning, and have the upper body strength of Pingu.

'Going anywhere nice on your holidays?' she said airily.

It should have set off alarm bells that she was up to something.

'Not really, I went to America earlier this year.'

'Oooh *lovely*.'

She gave an almighty tug at one of the eyebrow things and I yodelled in pain.

'Oooh you're such a baby!' she said, ripping the other one off while I was distracted and trying to climb off the table. 'Now then, last thing and then we're all done.'

The wax on my top lip was yanked off with complete disregard for my yelps.

'Oooh look at that,' Jools said holding the gauze out so I could see. 'That's brilliant! Come and look at this one, Hayley!'

I had apparently been growing a small badger under my nose without noticing.

'You could come and have something else done if you like,' Jools said. 'Second visit you get fifty per cent off. Special offer on at the moment.'

She handed me a leaflet describing how she might introduce me to a landing strip somewhere in Brazil. I handed it back with a whimper and fell away, a broken woman.

I staggered as far as the overheated shoe department on the third floor and suddenly felt the need to sit down. Of course you can't do that in a shoe department without someone homing in on you. At least there was a sale on.

'Can I help?'

It was a tall, very thin girl in a black jumpsuit accessorized with blue hair so I knew I was in uncharted territory. Should I dye my hair blue? I'd considered it. Maybe not, up close it looked a bit weird.

'Something adventurous!' I said, casting my fate to the winds.

Half an hour later I had been persuaded into some shoes that would do perfectly if I was ever invited to a Gladiator Fetish party. They had the highest heels I've ever worn, and several rather complicated suede straps that went up my legs to the knee. The whole thing was accentuated with the sort of studs normally only seen on Rottweiler's collars. They weren't as uncomfortable as I thought they would be and the best thing about them was they were reduced by seventy-five per cent. I wondered why.

Blue hair girl disposed of my battered ballerina pumps and

I teetered off to catch the bus home. By the time I got there I was almost crying with pain. They were the sort of shoes made for nipping from a car to the safety of a barstool and no further. I slung them into the back of the wardrobe with the black bin liner of discarded clothes. It was that sort of day, evidently. Well at least I'd tried.

*

I spent the next couple of days scrubbing and cleaning to try and get rid of Kitty's nicotine miasma. The spare room was so nice I almost felt like moving in there myself, but I suddenly felt a little skip of confidence. Perhaps I *would* be able to make a job out of this? I mean I had my food hygiene certificates; I could get additional insurance. Perhaps I needed more towels and bed linen, but when I thought about running a retreat for one author at a time, I felt rather excited. But how would they find me?

I needed to work on my Facebook page. I needed to add some extra tweets and think about a new Twitter page. What was Instagram anyway? And Pinterest? I needed to finish that website and get all the free publicity I could. But I wouldn't take any mug shots until the swelling and inflammation on my face had died down.

That evening I sat down with my laptop and opened a new Twitter account @writerscottage.

Chapter Twenty-Three

It took me a while to get things going I don't mind admitting. I had more than a few sleepless nights, wondering if I had the courage or the stamina to do this on my own. Even though Helena didn't cook when we did retreats she was always encouraging and supportive and did her fair share of washing up.

I spent hours on Twitter and Facebook updating my profile and my availability. I'd even started a blog, describing what I did and adding a couple of nice comments from Kitty Ford-Wilson. I emailed every writers' group in the country and when Helena gave me a list of addresses I sent posters to all the libraries. Many times – when I was juggling my finances and wondering how I was going to cope – I considered giving up and getting a job in the supermarket but something stopped me. This was the new me. This was the me with ambition and determination and properly fitting underwear.

Helena and I did our June weekend retreat and it went well. We had four quiet, sensible people who enjoyed themselves and appreciated the peace. Nothing went wrong, no one got food poisoning or fell down the stairs, so it was a success but this time it was different. All the time my mind was on ways to advertise my one-on-one retreats, how to make them attractive to writers. And, of course, Helena was missing Nick.

I got back home to an email asking for availability in the next month. Caroline Bennet, recommended by Kitty.

I began to get more requests for information. The number of enquiries I'd had was increasing every week, and I was thinking of producing a brochure.

When I looked over my diary (yes, I had one now, a proper one that Uncle Peter had been given by a stationery rep and never used), I could see things were changing.

And the funny thing was although it was tricky keeping track of who had phoned for details, who was thinking of coming, and what they would or wouldn't eat, it was the most exciting thing I'd ever done.

There were so many things I liked about my new business. Occasionally I was contacted by a writer who was already successful, sometimes even a household name. They were nearly always friends of people who had heard of me.

I had all sorts of people contact me and they began to book. Most of them were women who were doing final edits, and some had school-age children or elderly relatives to consider. The story was always the same; they had a deadline to meet and they were panicking. Instead of worrying about other people, they needed looking after. It gave me a great feeling.

I bought catering-size tins of coffee beans and tea bags; I made cakes and fresh soup and bread. I used pretty china and vintage glasses from the junk shop and put fresh flowers in their room. (Unless they had hay fever or asked me not to of course.)

At this rate I would be able to do more than one or two a month. Perhaps I would be able to move to that house overlooking the sea in Cornwall. Or the stone *longère* in Brittany?

*

The weeks were starting to slip past. Nick and Helena were just about inseparable and had morphed into *NickandHelena* – the ultimate badge of coupledom – and were about to head off to Barcelona together. Both of them were so keen to defer to the other's choices that it would be a miracle if they ever decided where to go, what to eat, or what to see while they were there.

The summer months had been disappointing but, as is often the way, late September was turning out to be glorious. The flowers in my small and largely ignored garden were still blooming. I don't know what half of them were – they were there courtesy of my grandmother. There was a pink rose tumbling over the garden wall, and the purple thing that grew alongside the house had lost its blossoms. It could have been wisteria. Or lilac? I kept meaning to find out.

One afternoon I was standing outside my back door with a mug of tea and I suddenly remembered the straggly, wet garden at our February retreat when Oliver had arrived so unexpectedly. Ha! I wondered what he would think of me now. Now I was used to bossing well-known writers about and not putting up with any nonsense. I'd deal with him very differently now if he turned up and that's a fact!

Why was I thinking of him all of a sudden? I'd not heard from him at all since our last meeting. A couple of weeks back

Godfrey had showed me an article in one of the trade journals he received. Ross Black had officially left Marymount – his American publishers; I bet Gideon March was furious. He had signed with Appalachian – a small publisher based in Vermont.

There was even a picture of Oliver shaking hands with the managing director, a bearded man in a checked shirt who looked like a lumberjack. He was about to produce Oliver's next book – presumably the long-awaited *Death in Damascus* – and he looked as though he had won the lottery, which in a way I suppose he had.

I waited until Godfrey wasn't looking, cut the picture out, and put it in my purse.

*

My mobile rang: unknown number.

'Billie Summers?' A woman's voice, with a slight London twang.

'Yes, can I help?'

'My name is Fee Gillespie. I've heard about your retreat services from a friend of mine, Imelda Collins. I wonder if I could book in for a few days really soon? There's some final editing to run through and I'm told you can offer privacy and peace and quiet.'

'That's what we do,' I agreed, rather pleased with how things were working out.

I thought back; Imelda Collins had been a dream. She had come along having been recommended by Pippa, which was unexpected and rather nice of her. Imelda was a tiny little woman who had needed time to finish her latest bonkbuster

259

– *Filthy Linen*. I'm not making it up – that's what she called it.

She liked to read out snippets to me over her tea breaks and some of the things she came up with almost made me curl up with embarrassment. Vivienne would have loved her.

'Yes, but does that *scan*?' she'd asked me on one occasion, her face creased with concern. 'Does that *sound* right?'

'I'm not sure it's physically *possible*,' I'd replied and we spent an interesting half- hour thinking about the logistics, and she happily changed things a bit to accommodate the space available for three sex-starved people in a single train berth on the way to Scotland.

But back to my latest call; Fee was still there.

'Fabulous. How soon can I book in? It is an *actual* emergency,' she drawled.

I'd heard this before. Usually from writers who had missed their deadlines and who had irate editors on their backs.

'Just putting you on hold while I check. Is that OK?'

I clutched my mobile to my chest, resisting the urge to hum 'Greensleeves', and eventually found my proper, grown-up diary; it was in the vegetable rack for some reason. Not My Cat was sitting on the kitchen windowsill meowing silently as usual. I turned my back on him. Fee and I discussed dates and cost and her particular requirements (definitely no shellfish) and she rang off having booked a long weekend. I went back to my tea with a glow of satisfaction.

*

Meanwhile, in the bookshop things seemed to be perking up. Uncle Peter and Godfrey had pulled themselves back from

260

the brink of destruction and they credited Kitty Ford-Wilson and her signed books with the first bit of good luck they had enjoyed for some time.

Since then I had got into the routine of getting all of the published writers who stayed with me to sign some of their books and they had proved very popular. Uncle Peter had a special shelf to display them, and that morning when I went into the shop with their elevenses (raspberry muffins) they had sold quite a few but they still had a lovely selection.

Hot Summer Daze and *Getting into You* by Imelda Collins. The titles said it all really, unmitigated rudeness and generally based in the Lake District.

Tears for Araminta and *The Last Wish* by Caroline Bennett – Regency sagas of betrayal, abandoned babies, destitution, and dukes. Thrilling stuff.

The Best Christmas Ever, *Christmas Bride*, and *Sleigh Ride to Love* by Polly McKenzie. Self-explanatory: Christmas stories with gorgeous covers, masses of snow, and fairy lights – compulsive reading.

Pride of place went to the latest treasure: *Tudor Propaganda* by Mary Starcross, a weighty tome heavily tipped for the Booker Prize. That wouldn't stay on the shelf for long.

'Any more for us?' Godfrey asked, seeing me nosing around the shelves.

'Not yet, I have someone booked in for the weekend though. Fee Gillespie. Ever heard of her?'

Godfrey did a bit of googling and then shook his head.

'Never. And there's nothing on Amazon, but then she might write under another name. What genre?'

'I forgot to ask. Anyway, she's coming to do some final edits. I'll let you know. Where's Uncle Peter?'

'Upstairs, bit of an upset tum. I told him not to eat the leftover curry, but he wouldn't listen.'

'Is he ill?'

'Oh I'm sure he'll be fine. But I think I'll eat his muffin all the same,' Godfrey said with a wink.

I went upstairs to see my uncle and found him sitting in his favourite chair sipping iced water. I know he is over seventy but today for the first time he actually looked it.

'Are you all right?' I said. I went over to feel his forehead. His skin was cool and dry under my fingertips.

'Just old and bad tempered,' he said with a brave smile. 'Bit of a gannet when it comes to curry. You know me.'

'Have you seen the doctor? Can I get you anything?'

'No, I'm fine, pet. The doc has no cure for greed as far as I know. How are you? How's business?'

We had a nice chat for a few minutes and I made him some peppermint tea and left him watching daytime TV and tutting. That evening he rang to say he was feeling much better and eating scrambled eggs on toast. Phew.

*

On Friday morning I was busy putting the finishing touches to the two rooms upstairs I had started to think of as 'the writers' rooms'. Everything looked fine. There were fresh flowers in the cut-glass vase by the bedside, some bottles of still and sparkling water. The coffee machine was primed and ready to go.

The sun was shining. There were a few birds tweeting in the garden. I'd made a dish of chicken liver pâté for lunch, and a broccoli and cashew nut quiche for the evening meal.

I'd baked a beautiful loaf of bread too. I felt sure Fee Gillespie would have nothing to complain about. I did a little bit more tidying up and mopped the kitchen floor. I may be a good cook but, as we know, I'm not a tidy one.

Then it was just a question of waiting for Fee to arrive; I expected her any time after midday. I updated my website to include a couple of nice reviews I had been sent and did a bit of tidying.

I knew the weekend would go well, but there's always that little bit of doubt isn't there? What if she arrived and she hated me on sight? Or didn't like quiche? (She should have said something.) Or what if she had terrible BO, or halitosis? Or chewed gum all the time (pet hate) and left it stuck under the chairs? (Justifiable homicide.) You think that doesn't happen? Think again.

No. I would do something I'd been meaning to do for a long time. I had downloaded a new app on my phone called *5k – No Sweat*. I had a few hours spare, I would go for a run.

I went and found my sports bra and wrestled myself into it. By the time I'd done that I felt I'd done 5k already. I didn't actually have any running gear so I wore some tracksuit bottoms I'd found in the wardrobe when I was continuing my clear-out, and a fleece.

There was an Annoying Woman on the app who told me to *spend five minutes warming up those sleepy muscles*. I went out into the back garden where no one could see me and swung my arms about. Then I went out into the road where I had to walk briskly for five minutes. I'd been going for less than a minute when my mobile rang.

'Hi, Billie, it's Mum. What are you doing? You're panting.'

'I'm going for a run.'

'Why?'

'Because I can. And because I've got a sports bra I've never used and it's so tight I can hardly breathe. What do you want?'

Mum laughed and started rabbiting on about what her neighbour had been doing. Something to do with a jumble sale to raise money for the church.

'She said they needed a new organ and I said don't we all, dear. I don't think she quite got the joke. Anyway—'

At that moment, Annoying Woman on my mobile broke into our conversation.

Now run slowly and smoothly for one minute. Feel the blood flowing around your body. Think how great you are, how fantastic you are.'

'Who's that?' Mum said.

I stabbed at my phone. 'No one – just a mobile app.'

'Anyway as I was saying ...' Mum kept up a long complicated description of a dress she had bought, how she felt about the Bake Off, and whether it would be cheaper to go to Greece or France.

Swiftly realizing I wasn't expected to say much I left Mum on speakerphone and tucked the mobile into the top of my bra. I staggered on, swinging my arms and breathing hard. I paused at one point to lean on someone's wall and draw breath. Annoying Woman started up again.

Now walk for twenty seconds as fast as you can. Think about how well you are doing.'

Mum was now on to a story about her immersion heater, and the man next door, and was asking whether Peter was any better.

Now run for two minutes,' said Annoying Woman.

Well I tried, but I seemed far better at the walking than

the running bit. I was boiling too. I made the mistake of thinking I could pull the fleece off over my head while I was still running. The mobile pinged out of my bra, down my T-shirt and out, and I managed to kick it into the gutter. I stumbled, my ankle turned over, and I dropped like a tree trunk onto the ground where I lay panting for a moment, still able to hear my mother squawking on about some curtains she'd had dry-cleaned.

'The linings just disintegrated. I think it was only the dirt holding them together.'

You have now finished the first part of your 5k – No Sweat regime. Isn't running wonderful? Everyone loves a trier,' chortled Annoying Woman.

I crawled across the pavement and retrieved my mobile before it could be run over.

'Billie, Billie, are you still there? The reason I'm ringing. Do you have a fish kettle?'

I pulled myself up onto a handy bench and tried to draw breath. 'Yes, I have a small one, but I have no idea where it is. Probably in Uncle Peter's spare room.'

'Why on earth – well never mind. I have Josie and the boys coming to visit. It's nearly half term. Can you believe it? They've only been back five minutes. It serves her right for sending them to that pretentious private school. Do you know their school blazers are ninety-five pounds each? And an extra twelve pounds for the badge? Have you ever heard anything so ridiculous? I told her she would be better off letting them go to the local comp and investing their fees in a personal pension. But what would I know?'

I was feeling a bit dizzy to be honest, not filled with the wonder of running at all.

'So the fish kettle?' I said weakly.

'Oh yes, Josie says she's been reading about fish as a brain food and she wants me to ram as much fish at them as I can while they are here.'

'Does she know about the toxins ...?'

'Don't! I don't want to know. If Josie wants the young lordlings to have fish out of a fish kettle, then that's what I shall cook. But you'll have to tell me how because I have no idea. Last time they came to stay all they seemed to eat was chicken nuggets. I tried one – like no chicken I've ever encountered. It could have been hedgehog for all I know. Anyway, I'll pop over on Sunday morning and pick it up, OK?'

'Well, just remember I will have a writer staying here,' I said.

'Oh I'll be in and out before you know it. You'll hardly notice me. I'll be as quiet as anything. As quiet as a little mouse in slippers.'

The possibility of this being true was nil. My mother, unlike her elder brother Peter, is not known for doing anything (sleeping, talking, standing, shopping, having a cold, washing up) quietly.

'Let me know what time you will be here,' I said, 'and then I will have it ready for you. Or you could just go to Peter's and pick it up there?'

'Hmm, no perhaps not.'

'Oh, Mum, go and see Peter. You know he's been a bit under the weather; you have to forgive him some time. He'd absolutely love to see you.'

By the time I put the phone down it was twenty to twelve and I was red-faced, knackered, and starving. Well not actually starving but very hungry. I'd also had a text message from Fee

266

to tell me to expect her for lunch at one-thirty exactly. I limped home, went upstairs, spent an energetic ten minutes getting out of my sports bra, and had a shower.

I laid the table for lunch in the garden as it was an unexpectedly lovely afternoon and I found one of my grandmother's embroidered cloths and moved the cutlery and glasses to the shady arbour in the corner. Fee Gillespie couldn't fail to love it.

I put out a jug of iced lemonade with a beaded cover over the top to protect it from the flies, a basket of my freshly baked bread, a fresh pat of butter in a glass dish, a little terracotta pot of home-made pâté, and a wedge of crumbly cheddar. I draped a linen tea towel over the lot. All I needed was to serve the soup.

I heard the sounds of a car pulling up round the front of the house and the door slamming as someone got out. Someone rang the doorbell.

I flung open the front door with my best welcoming smile on my face.

Cheerful but not completely insane. I've actually practised in front of a mirror.

'Hello! Welcome ...'

My voice stuttered and faded. Not what I had expected at all. Not a middle-aged woman with incipient writer's arse and sensible shoes. Not Fee Gillespie then.

'Hello,' Oliver said. 'What on earth have you been doing? Can I come in?'

'What do you mean ... ?'

I looked at the hall mirror and realized I was still puce, my hair was wet and needed brushing, and I had mascara splodged under both eyes. He, of course, was Mr Super Cool, wearing a blue chambray shirt that made his eyes sparkle, and he watched me with a broad grin on his face. He looked great, far less tense than the last time I had seen him at the airport when he could barely speak to anyone. He had lost the sort of grey, clenched look he'd had. Who am I kidding? He looked bloody gorgeous.

I stood, hanging on to the doorframe for a moment, wondering what to do.

'I was told you were expecting me?' he said, raising his eyebrows a little.

'I'm expecting someone called Fee Gillespie ... ah.' Light was dawning.

'My new PA,' Oliver said. 'I got her to make the booking. I thought it might ensure you let me in. Speaking of which, may I come in? You're very good at keeping me hanging about on doorsteps, I've noticed.'

I moved to one side, and watched as he brought his bags into the hallway. My house is quite bijou and compact and the arrival of a man who was quite so tall and broad-shoul-dered *oooh focus, woman, focus* made it look even smaller. I swear Oliver might have actually grown a couple of inches too. I felt a bit light-headed for a moment and I don't think it was anything to do with my attempts at *5k – No Sweat*.

I showed him up to his room with the distinct feeling that Oliver really was too big for the stairwell. He seemed to fill the space. What the hell he would think of the bedroom with its pretty details, pale walls, chocolate truffles, and crystal vase of flowers was anyone's guess. At least he didn't laugh.

'I hope you will be comfortable in here,' I said.

'This is fine,' he said. He looked at his watch. 'One-thirty. Lunchtime?'

'Of course. Lunch at one-thirty. No shellfish. I've put it out in the garden.'

How could I have missed the clues?

My voice seemed a bit squeaky and I cleared my throat a couple of times and tried to breathe properly.

'Excellent. Lead the way,' he said.

He followed me downstairs and out into the garden where I had left the table perfectly set up, looking delightful. Almost like something from an *Elle* Home Décor magazine photo shoot. He couldn't fail to be impressed.

The first thing I saw was the tea towel on the grass and the back view of Not My Cat's furry arse settled over the vintage dinner plate. It had knocked the cutlery off the table and having eaten the butter was now busy champing away at the pâté, eyes closed in ecstasy.

I gave a strangled scream and Not My Cat licked its chops and leapt for the garden wall, knocking the jug of lemonade flying.

'You little bastard,' I yelled up at its retreating bum as it disappeared into the foliage of the purple thing, back legs scrabbling. 'I'm never buying you Kat Treatz again. That's it!'

Behind me I heard Oliver laughing. I surveyed the damage and started picking up the broken china and shuddered at the needle-shaped fang marks in the surface of the pâté.

'I still have home-made soup and bread,' I said, scarlet with embarrassment.

Why today? Why did that flaming moggy choose today of all days to sabotage my attempts at gracious living?

'I'm so sorry, that blasted animal! I always wanted a cat, do you see, but I never felt sensible enough to have one, so I've been borrowing next door's instead.'

'Very wise,' Oliver said, choking back a laugh. 'Always best to have a practice run first.'

'Well I won't bother in future! I'm going to buy a water pistol. Bloody creature. There was brandy in that pâté too. I expect it will throw up on the doorstep this evening!'

Oliver picked up the broken handle of the lemonade jug and its muslin cover, which he looked at rather blankly.

I took it from him. 'It's to keep the flies off and cats out,' I said.

'Doesn't work then,' he said. 'Look, don't worry, soup will be fine. Can I help?'

'Absolutely not. I'll go and sort everything out. Perhaps you would like coffee while you are waiting? Black? No sugar?'

'You've got a good memory,' he said.

How could I forget?

I went to make some and returned with a cafetière to find him sitting with his face turned up to the sun, eyes closed.

'Peaceful,' he said.

'That's the plan anyway,' I said. 'By the way I always turn off the Wi-Fi during the day so you don't have any distraction. And the mobile signal here is pretty rubbish too. It's part of the charm of the place.'

'I'll cope,' he said with a wry look.

I went back indoors and splashed my red face with cold water and tried to calm down. Oliver Forest was in my garden! When had I last seen him? Weeks ago. Months. Why was he here now? What about Pippa? What had happened to her?

I reheated the soup and took it out to him with some more of my home-made bread. I found him wandering about the garden looking at my pathetic attempts to tie up the trailing thing.

'Healthy-looking wisteria,' he said (ah, so that's what it is).

He sat down at the newly tidied table. I made noises about having an urgent call to take and scurried back into the house so I could clean the tea stains off the sink and surreptitiously watch him through the kitchen window.

There was no doubt about it – he looked frigging sensational. His dark hair was gleaming in the sunlight and he looked lean and muscular and rather hunky and ... *shut up, woman.*

This is the man who practically drove Pippa to a nervous breakdown. Who was impossible to please, who would spend hours arguing about nothing and on top of that I'd once seen him naked.

By mistake obviously but still ...

No, no don't think about that.

No!

Think of something else!

By the time Oliver had finished his lunch my sink was gleaming. So were the taps and the top of the cooker. I was almost tempted to start cleaning the kitchen windows. Especially the outside where there was a snail trail of cat nose prints courtesy of Not My Cat. Suddenly Oliver appeared in the doorway carrying a tray with his dirty dishes on it.

'You don't have to do that,' I said hurrying forward to take it from him.

'It's all right,' he said. 'I'm quite capable of ...'

'I'm not saying you aren't, it's just not how I do things,' I said.

'Well you're the boss.' He jammed his hands in his pockets and turned away from me to look around. 'This is a lovely place, typically Cotswolds. All this beautiful stone.'

'Yes, I suppose it is,' I was suddenly flustered. I looked away too. He really did have a fantastic arse.

I picked up my tea towel and patted at the sweat on my top lip.

'Would you like a glass of wine?' I said.

He turned back to look at me.

'I'd love one, but I have a rule: no wine before seven o'clock, otherwise I'd have to go to bed for an afternoon nap and I don't think I'm quite old enough for that yet, do you?'

Mmmmm. I don't know. Oliver Forest in bed for an afternoon nap …

'Well I won't keep you,' I said, my voice rather shrill. I dabbed at the worktops with my cloth, sweeping non-existent crumbs into my hand. 'Perhaps I could make you some coffee?'

'That would be great; I'd prefer that to the coffee machine in the writing area if I'm honest. Let's just leave it for an hour or so. I have to take something down.'

Stop thinking rude thoughts, woman, for the love of God …

'Well anything you need …' I said.

I listened to his footsteps going upstairs and felt quite odd and jittery to think that he was under my roof and that he would be sleeping in my spare room. His bed just a wall away from mine.

I busied myself with my ongoing project: tidying out one of the kitchen cupboards, the one that held the dry goods. I found five different sorts of sugar, two of them rock hard and unusable. There were numerous jars of herbs and spices to be sorted, a couple of them best before September 2014. Hmm, who knew cardamom pods could go off?

An hour later to the minute I took up a tray of coffee. I hesitated outside the closed door to the little box room I had converted to the writing area. I waited for a moment but couldn't hear any noise from inside. I knocked.

'Yep?'

I went in. Oliver was sitting at the desk, his laptop open in front of him.

'Thanks,' he said and carried on typing.

I stood like a spare part wondering whether I should do anything else.

He turned his face towards me, his eyes still on the screen. 'Yes?' he said.

'I just wondered if you wanted anything else?'

Biscuits? Or fruit? Or perhaps a back rub or a shoulder massage?

'Hmm? Nothing. Dinner at eight?'

'Yes fine. Ok, I'll just ...' I gestured towards the door and went out, closing it behind me.

I went back to my cleaning, finding among other things three jars of Marmite that had their lids welded on. I love Marmite. I've always thought there was the potential for industrial adhesive in that stuff. Perhaps one day with a bit of chemical engineering it could be adapted to putting up shelves or mending windscreens? I wonder if Oliver liked Marmite. Not that it's a deal breaker but it's good to know.

Chapter Twenty-Four

Of course, the first thing I'd done was text Helena.

'Oliver Forest has just arrived here. For a weekend writing! Can you believe it? Don't ring me, he's upstairs working and I'm scared he might hear me.'

After a few seconds Helena replied.

'What???? The Oliver Forest? The same one???'

I smothered a laugh. The more I thought about it the more overexcited I became.

'Yes, that one. I'll phone you when I get a chance. X'

I tidied away the remains of lunch, made myself a cup of tea, and had a couple of broken Hobnobs. I mean they don't count do they? All the calories have leaked out.

I heard a noise behind me. I spun round, my mouth still stuffed with biscuit. Oliver was standing there with his laptop under his arm.

'I think I'd like to work outside in your lovely garden if that's OK?'

I wiped the crumbs off my chin, choked a little, and chewed frantically. 'Of course, I mean yes of course it's fine. Please go on.'

I'm not sure but I think he was trying not to laugh at me.

God would I never get it right with him? He must think I'm a right prat. In the last six months I'd managed to keep a belligerent Kitty Ford-Wilson happy; I'd impressed self-obsessed Marnie Miller so much she had tweeted about me; Imelda Collins had sent flowers; even Vanessa-Mary Dell had accepted my friend request on Facebook. Not once had I dropped a plate or a clanger.

Oliver Forest hadn't been in my house for two hours and I already looked like a nitwit. I needed to sharpen up my act and concentrate. I was not going to do anything stupid or fall over or poke myself in the eye. I was going to be a grown-up. I was not going to snarf up biscuits in future unless I knew exactly where he was.

I went to the window and peered out at him. He was already typing at high speed. It looked as though he was doing it properly too, using all his fingers. I wondered how he was getting on with his latest book. Was Major Harry Field still blasting away with his submachine gun or whatever he used? Was Selina still bursting out of her unsuitable frock or was there a new, sleeker love interest?

I cleaned the taps again and filled the kettle. I assumed he would want more coffee before too long? This was all very well but was I ... oh dear, hang on. I'd been quite happy to sit and eat my evening meal with my other guests. Kitty had been as amusing as any television comedian; Marnie Miller had been happy to talk about herself, particularly her upcoming stint on board the *Atlantica* liner in America. Imelda liked to eat in relative silence thinking about sex. Occasionally she would throw out a random thought like: 'Do you think spanking is over?' or 'Which is worse, sand or pine needles?' Actually, she seemed to think about sex most of the time – it must have been quite a party in her head. Vanessa-Mary had talked about her ex-husband quite a lot, her tongue dripping with venom that occasionally translated on to her laptop and resulted in a great many exasperated screams and supressed fury.

But what would I do with Oliver? What would I talk to him about? Would he prefer to eat alone? I believed I was slightly more sensible than I'd been in February but let's be honest I was still noisy.

Perhaps I would lurk upstairs in my bedroom and creep downstairs when I thought the coast was clear? And who would go to bed first? Me or him? And would he leave the bathroom *in a fit state* or would he leave his bristles all over the sink and toothpaste on the mirror? I think I'd be better off sticking to the downstairs loo. Perhaps I should sleep on the sofa?

Oh FFS, calm down, woman.

Right, do something useful. Make dinner. What was I going to do? I had been planning to make some individual chicken and ham pies, but I wasn't sure I could eat that in front of him. He'd think I was a pig. He'd give me a look and he'd be thinking no wonder she's a bit ~~lardy~~ voluptuous. Perhaps I should do a salad and some new potatoes and some cold roast chicken instead. And make sure I kept Not My Cat out of the kitchen.

I started getting things out of the fridge and, after checking that Oliver was still working in the garden with his back to me, ate another biscuit.

My mobile buzzed. It was Helena.

'How's it going?'

I replied: *'He's in the garden.'*

276

'Is he as bad as ever?'

I thought about it. Actually no, he didn't seem as bad as he'd been. In fact, looking at things rationally he'd been perfectly pleasant. He hadn't been rude or unreasonable. I texted back.

'He's OK so far.'

I watched him for a few more minutes. He was leaning back in his chair, looking at the garden wall. Perhaps he was thinking calm, flowery thoughts?

I put on a clean white apron so I looked efficient and professional and got on with preparing the chicken. Then I washed some new potatoes and thought about dodging into the utility room (posh name for a cupboard with a washing machine and ironing board in it) for a small glass of wine. I felt I needed the boost.

I took another glance at Oliver and went to find the red wine. I slugged a bit into a glass and went to pretend I was fiddling with the tumble dryer.

The wine was just what I needed. I stood with my eyes closed feeling the warmth of it working down to my stomach. Ooh that was better. I took another mouthful.

'Any chance of some more coffee?' Oliver said behind me.

I spluttered a bit, holding my hand over my mouth to stop myself from spitting at him.

'Of course!' I said brightly hiding my wine glass behind the iron; I think I got away with it. 'I'll bring it out.'

It was only after I'd taken the fresh cafetière out to the garden that I realized I had a big splodge of wine down the front of my apron. Oh for God's sake.

*

277

We ate our evening meal in the garden after a fabulous sunset that streaked the sky with pink and apricot silk. It was beginning to get chilly, but it was his idea after all, and I lit some candles in a couple of storm lanterns I'd found in the junk shop. He ate tidily and without any fuss and expressed genuine pleasure at the crème brûlée I'd made. That always goes down well. Men are supposed to like bread and butter pudding too but just the look of it turns my stomach for some reason. We shared a bottle of wine and eventually we seemed able to talk without any sort of awkwardness.

Mind you he did start with the ghastly question: 'So tell me about yourself. Have you found exciting things to do? Since we last met?'

It was as though I was seventeen again when an aged great-aunt had asked me what I was going to do when I finished my Matriculation. I think she meant A levels.

I mean I'd had my eyebrows and my top lip waxed (agony), had a couple of manicures, and a proper bra fitting since I last saw him, but I wasn't going to share any of that with him. Nor was I prepared to discuss how many blouses and skirts I'd given to the local charity shop in the last few weeks because they didn't fit properly.

'Well I'm doing this now,' I said. 'I've realized it was the catering side of things I enjoyed about writing retreats, not the writing bit. So I've created a business, and I seem to have found my niche. I enjoy it. And thank you for sending Kitty to me; she was the start of it all. Writers are interesting people and they have some fabulous gossip. I do all my advertising online and it's so much easier than dealing with a house full of people.'

'Who might and might not get along with each other?'

'Exactly. And my clients are generally people who want to be left alone to get on with their work. They don't need much entertaining; up to now they've all been very appreciative.'

He gave a funny little half-smile. 'You think I'm going to be different?'

'Well I don't know do I? You haven't been here long.'

Six hours thirty-eight minutes actually. Not that anyone's counting.

'I'm not planning on being difficult,' he said.

He leaned across the table to top up my wine glass and I took the opportunity to look at him. He was without doubt the best-looking man I'd ever seen let alone shared a bottle of Pinot Grigio with. He looked up and caught my eye and I felt myself blushing.

'Nor do I need much entertaining,' he said.

Hmm. How could I entertain a man like Oliver?

I stood up rather suddenly and knocked the table, so the crockery rattled.

'I'd better clear away and leave you to it,' I said. 'Perhaps we should go in? It's getting cold.'

He reached out and caught my wrist. 'You don't have to do that,' he said. 'You don't have to keep avoiding me. I won't bite.'

I looked down at his hand on mine and felt rather faint.

'Sit down,' he said. 'Will you just talk to me?'

'I don't like looking at dirty dishes,' I blurted out.

God, those idiot pills I'd been taking were still working then?

'Just for once let me help you.'

He stood up and started to gather together the dessert bowls and the other bits and pieces on the table and we tussled for a moment about who was going to take the table-cloth. He helped me load the dishwasher and waited until I was satisfied with the state of things and had found a woollen throw to wrap around my shoulders. Then he put a gentle hand in the small of my back and steered me back into the garden.

By now it was dark and the sky had deepened like navy blue velvet and was studded with stars. He poured me the last of the wine and then of course I had to go back inside to find a second one because his glass was empty. I'm usually OK about drinking on my own but it would have been a bit rude this time. While I was hunting for another bottle I took the opportunity to knock back a slug of vodka from the freezer.

No, I don't know what I was thinking either.

What was the matter with me? I could feel my heart hammering in my chest. I looked at my reflection in the dark window. My hair was behaving for once – I didn't look as though I'd been wrestling.

I felt an odd tremor of excitement; I was alone with Oliver Forest. He wanted to talk to me; he wanted to spend time with me. He wouldn't bite me.

Bloody hell, I wish he would.

I had a terrible mental image of his mouth on me, his tongue tasting me, his teeth grazing my neck ...

Stop it. Just bloody stop it.

Outside he was sitting watching the local bat swooping about. There was a leafy sort of scrabbling in the wisteria and Not My Cat dropped off the wall into my garden. I was about to chase it away with a few well-chosen oaths when Oliver bent down and stroked Not My Cat's tabby head. It wound itself around the table legs in a fervour of feline excitement and favoured him with a silent meow.

'You've found a friend,' I said as I went to sit down again.

'Well we got off to a bad start, but I hope so,' he said and he looked at me in a way that made me shiver.

'Not too cold?' he said.

'No, I'm fine. Honestly.' I pulled the throw more tightly around my shoulders.

'You can have my sweater if you want?' He made a move to indicate he'd be happy to take it off.

Oh my God. The thought of that. I could just imagine it, pushing my arms down the sleeves still warm from his skin.

'No, I'm all right.'

We talked a bit more, about his new publisher and the way Gideon had fumed and raged and threatened to sue him.

At last he stretched his arms above his head. I yawned.

'You don't have to stay up,' he said. 'I'm planning to work late.'

'I can't do that.'

'Of course you can. You don't have to tuck me in you know.'

Oh boy, just give me half a chance!

'Well if you're sure,' I said.

'Absolutely sure. Sleep well. Thank you for a great evening.'

I went to bed, my head buzzing with alcohol and confusion. Was this the same Oliver Forest who had been so difficult? What had happened to change things?

Still puzzling it out I fell asleep and I did sleep well, foolishly happy to know he was going to be in the next room.

*

By the time I came downstairs the following morning, Oliver was already in the garden with a cup of coffee. His hair was wet from the shower and he was dressed in a deep purple shirt and jeans. He looked bright-eyed and fighting fit.

'Gosh couldn't you sleep?' I said.

'I'm an early riser,' he said. 'Always have been.'

'Breakfast? Let me see if I remember. Whole-wheat toast, apple juice, and poached eggs?'

'Would be ideal,' he replied.

After we had sorted that out he went back upstairs to the writing room with a fresh cafetière of coffee and closed the door behind him. I had already pretended I needed more milk and I made good my escape. Halfway to the bookshop I phoned Helena.

'He's writing,' I said.

'Is everything OK?' she said. 'You sound a bit funny. Are you out of breath?'

'I'm just hurrying. Perhaps he's on his best behaviour. Or he's on new medication. It can't last. By the time I get back he will be snarling. Next door's cat ate his lunch but he even dealt with that without throwing a wobbler. And then we sat in the garden and drank wine until it was dark.'

'Wow, perhaps it's his identical twin brother, Arnold?'

I snorted with laughter. 'I don't think so. How's Nick?'

'Lovely,' Helena said, as she always did.

'Yes, but apart from that?'

'He's getting very excited about our holiday. He's packed already and made me a list too.'

'Really? How bizarre.'

'Passports, insurance thingy, phone charger, that sort of thing. Not how many pairs of knickers I need to take.'

'Not long now then?'

'Three days, I can't wait.'

We chatted for a bit longer and then I reached the shop and had to end the call. I picked up some milk, a French stick, and a bar of chocolate, which I intended to hide for emergencies. I already had some somewhere but in all the excitement I'd forgotten where I'd put it. Typical. I found a Mars bar the other day that I'd hidden in a kitchen drawer. It had gone all funny and grey and was inedible. Even for me.

Back at the house everything was quiet and Oliver's door was still closed. I listened at the bottom of the stairs for a bit but I couldn't hear anything. Perhaps he was deep in his plot? Perhaps he was asleep?

I went into the kitchen and started making lunch. Some of the crusty bread, ham, and fruit. No cheese – that I did remember.

At one-thirty he came downstairs almost as though he was on automatic pilot.

It was another nice day so I had set the table outside again, but minus any food that Not My Cat might take a shine to.

'How has your morning been?' I asked.

'Pretty good,' he replied helping himself to mustard, 'but it's been going well for a while.'

'That's good.'

The easy companionship of yesterday evening had gone and we were back to being formal with each other. I cast my mind about to think of topics to discuss.

'So your next book is due out soon isn't it? *Death in Damascus*? What's that about?'

'The title has changed but it's still about Damascus, and ...' He tilted his head towards me.

'Let me guess, a death?' I said.

'Several deaths actually. And sundry bombs, grenades, and burning tanks. You'd probably disapprove.'

'I might not,' I said.

He shook his head. 'But you'll be glad to hear there isn't a – what did you call them? – walking pair of tits in this one, so that's an improvement isn't it?'

I flushed. 'Sorry about that, I don't know what came over me.'

'It's fine.' He paused to butter his bread. 'You were right. You were right about a lot of things actually.'

'I was?'

'You were.'

Like what? I wanted to ask, but I didn't dare.

Perhaps later we would share another bottle of wine and I would keep his glass topped up so he got a bit pissed and he would tell me then.

Chapter Twenty-Five

He spent all afternoon writing and came out for coffee and a brisk walk around the garden at about three-thirty. He'd only gone a few steps when Not My Cat hurled itself down from the garden wall and trotted after him, lifting one beseeching paw when he stopped to drink his coffee.

I busied myself making my signature dish, Beef Casserole *au beaucoup de Merlot,* but I just put in half a bottle this time, which meant I could stash away a sneaky couple of glasses for later. Well, the rest of the afternoon was going to be doing the ironing, which is the pits isn't it? I deserved a reward.

After ten minutes Oliver came back inside, the cat hot on his heels. I think it would have followed him back upstairs to his room if I hadn't dissuaded it with a well-placed foot. Instead it leapt up on the kitchen windowsill, pressed its nose against the clean glass, and glared through it at me. I glared back. I'm more than a match for a cat who nicks other people's food and can't even meow properly.

By five-thirty the Merlot casserole smelled wonderful and I'd finished the laundry and put it away. There was a knock on the front door and I went to open it.

'Hiya, sexy!'

I was aware my mouth was hanging open.

'Matt! What the hell are you doing here?'

'Well that's not very friendly, Billie; aren't you going to ask me in?'

I stood looking at him. He was as good-looking as ever, with his thin, clever face, bright eyes, and tousled curls. He leaned on the doorframe and grinned down at me.

'You're looking great, Bills – you lost weight?'

I made some vague blathering noises and he bent to kiss my cheek.

'I was passing. I thought I'd drop in and see how you are.'

He made to walk past me into the house but I stood my ground until we were almost nose to nose.

'What are you doing here?' I said.

'I wanted to see how you are,' he said, rather surprised. 'I missed you.'

'How's Dee?'

'Who?'

'Dee. Dee with the enormous tits. The one you dumped me for. The one you took to New York instead of me.'

'Oh Dee. No idea, we split up.'

My heart did a sort of jump in my chest. Once this news would have filled me with unreasoning joy. I would have felt that I was in with a chance. That I might get my boyfriend back or get laid or something. And God knows how long ago that latter event had been on the cards.

'Oh, really,' I said.

'Well she wasn't a patch on you, Bills. I mean she couldn't boil an egg without burning three pans. Do you fancy a drink?'

He had a duffel bag slung over one shoulder; he opened

the drawstring and pulled out a bottle of Barolo. He had remembered; my absolute favourite wine that I never bought because it was always over my price threshold even in Superfine Supermarket.

'Wow, you've got a good memory,' I said.

'I remember a lot of things, Bills,' he said with a wink. He was just so cute, and he was getting around me. I could feel my resolve weakening for a moment.

'No thanks, Matt,' I said.

His dark eyebrows shot up in surprise. 'What?'

'I said no thanks.'

'Why?'

Because you're a tosser?

'I'm not in the mood, Matt. Have you got the money you owe me?'

'What money?'

'The money you took from me in this very house that was supposed to be paying for my trip to New York that never happened,' I said, spluttering slightly.

'Ah well, now I thought I could do the skirting boards and the architrave around the back door instead. That would just about cover the cost.'

'I don't want you to come and do the sodding skirting boards,' I said furiously.

He shrugged. 'Well I've offered and if you think about it you've already paid for them to be done. Seems a bit daft to say no doesn't it?'

'I don't want you coming round here,' I said. 'You'll be moving in before I know it—'

Matt grinned. 'Nice of you to offer, Billie. You don't hang about do you?'

287

'I don't want you in my house for any reason!'

'I can come back later? Or is it, y'know, *wrong time of the month*? Ooops, I know how crabby you used to get.'

'Crabby?'

'God yeah, you were an absolute mare. Perhaps I'll leave it a few days.'

'You are unbelievable, Matt. Do you know that?' I said.

He grinned. 'So I've been told.'

'No, I wasn't paying you a compliment, you prat, I mean it. Your bare-faced cheek is unbelievable. You dump me for someone with no obvious signs of intelligent life, I lose my deposit on that holiday that you said you were going to pay me back for and never did, and then nearly a year later you turn up as though nothing has happened. Are you in the real world?'

'Aw come on, Billie, it wasn't like that. Don't be miserable, eh?'

'It was exactly like that, you sod. It was exactly like that, plus you never returned my cashmere scarf, the pale green one, and you still owe me at least six hundred and fifty quid I gave you for that holiday. So not only did I *not* go to New York, I also by default paid for Dee frigging Henderson to go and also *you*!'

'Oh you're in a mood, I see.' He took his foot off my door-step and gave me a sad look as though I was having a tantrum that was nothing to do with him.

'What do you mean I'm in a mood? You're still not getting it are you?'

Matt snorted with laughter. 'Nor are you by the sounds of it. You always got bad tempered when you weren't getting any. Let me in and I'll give you a good seeing to – that'll cheer you up.'

'Look, Matt, are you always an idiot or is it just when I'm around?'

'What?'

'I just want my money back.'

'I don't have it, Bills. That's what I mean. Let me come and sort out your architraves instead.' He managed to make this sound vaguely obscene which annoyed me even more.

'You can take your architraves and stick them—'

'Excuse me, is there a problem?'

Oh great. Oliver was standing behind me, his face like thunder.

'I'm sorry, Oliver, he's just going.'

Matt pulled an unpleasant smile. 'Oh I see. Oliver is it? Well you should have told me shouldn't you. Typical.'

'Well from what I've heard, Billie has made it clear she would like you to go,' Oliver said.

Matt hesitated for a second, obviously wondering if it was worth taking the discussion further. I think he must have clocked Oliver's superior height and muscle power and thought better of it. With a last sneer he turned away.

I closed the front door. 'I'm so sorry about that,' I said. 'I didn't want you to be disturbed.'

'Doesn't matter,' Oliver said. 'I'm guessing that's your boyfriend?'

'He was,' I said. 'A long time ago. I can't think why, and I don't know why he's turned up here after all this time. I'm so sorry.'

'Stop apologizing and tell me what that fantastic smell is in the kitchen.'

'Your dinner,' I said. 'Beef in red wine.' I looked at my watch. 'But it's going to be at least another hour, maybe longer. Sorry.'

'For heaven's sake, woman, will you stop apologizing for everything?'

'OK then, it's not going to be ready for another hour so don't start moaning. You're the one who wanted dinner at eight o'clock.'

'That's more like it. I've come to a convenient break in proceedings and I fancied a drink. What do you say?'

'It's only six-fifty,' I said. 'I thought you didn't drink before seven?'

'Rules are made to be broken occasionally,' he said. 'Let's go mad.'

*

It was another lovely evening and we sat out in the garden again with next door's cat sitting at Oliver's feet, adoring him with such passion that its whiskers trembled.

'So what have you been doing today?' Oliver said once we were settled and halfway down our first glass of wine.

'Cooking, ironing,' I said, 'spoke to Helena. She's about to go to Barcelona with Nick. Do you remember them? They met at the retreat you came to.'

'I do – and they are still together?'

'Going from strength to strength.'

'That was a special week then wasn't it?'

'It was? I mean yes it was.'

'I don't think I was in a very good place then. Do you remember?'

I sat mesmerized by his beautiful eyes for a moment, wondering what to say.

'I do,' I said.

This sounded embarrassingly wedding-y and I could feel myself blushing even more.

'I tried being a vegetarian recently,' I said.

'And how did that go? Not very well by the aroma coming from the kitchen.'

'I didn't last very long. I tried before actually but this time I found a couple of cold sausages in the fridge, which didn't help. And then three days later I was going out with friends and they ordered steak and chips. I meant to have the spinach and ricotta pancakes but then, well I didn't. So I did give it a go. But then I sort of fell off the wagon. But I've started this new business,' I said defiantly. My voice had gone a bit funny at this point and I sounded odd even to myself. 'It's going brilliantly.'

'I thought it would when I heard back from Kitty. She was well impressed with you.'

He smiled and topped up my wine glass.

He lifted his glass and tilted it towards me. 'Here's to doing unexpected and exciting things,' he said.

His eyes locked on to mine and there's no other way to describe it, I felt a bolt of lust firing through me for the first time in oooh ages I suppose. It was a good job I was sitting down because I don't think my legs would have supported me. And it was a very good job the light was fading because I could feel myself blushing; I was probably crimson all over. Can your knees blush? It felt as though mine were.

I wished I had thought to change out of my work clothes because it felt like an exotic moment. Instead of jeans and a fleecy sweatshirt, I should have been in a flimsy tea dress with my hair in swooping curls or maybe a slinky satin number like Selina. No maybe not, it wasn't that warm and I didn't have the figure for it any more than Selina did with her 'tight in every place' frock.

'Any more carnage today?' I asked to break the ensuing silence.

'Only a couple,' he said. 'Nothing significant.'

'How many do you usually get though on a daily basis?'

He laughed. 'Half a dozen? It all depends how I feel. Sometimes there aren't any. Occasionally there is mayhem.'

I shook my head. 'I hate to think what the body count is then. Ross Black must be responsible for the death of thousands.'

'Ah well, Ross Black is dead, new publisher, new contract, new name.'

'Really? That's exciting. What are you going to be called this time?'

'I can't tell you just yet. There are a couple of possibilities out there.'

We carried on talking as the shadows lengthened. As I'd hoped, he had loosened up a bit and we seemed to be getting on quite well. I found my woollen throw and I brought the beef casserole out in bowls with some crusty bread and Not My Cat inched closer, its eyes crossed with longing.

'Cupboard love,' I said.

Oliver laughed. 'Cats do seem to like me. I've no idea why.'

'I expect Kitty Ford-Wilson's cat is your most devoted fan!'

Oliver looked at me and laughed. 'She told you then? How I hurt my leg?'

'She did. Motorbike accident? She roared with laughter at the very thought.'

'I was trying to sound more interesting.'

'Silly.'

292

Oliver reached down and scratched the cat's head. It rolled over, its paws in the air.

'I think he likes you,' I said.

Oliver looked across at me, his eyes dark. 'I like you,' he said.

I could hardly breathe. 'Do you?'

'Oh yes,' he said.

*

We finished the bottle of wine and Oliver went to get another when I took the dishes in. I switched the kitchen light out so that it didn't shine out and spoil the beauty of the night. Without a word we went back into the garden. This time he pulled my chair around to be closer to his and I sat with my thigh touching his, stunned by the intensity of my feelings.

I was drunk. That was all. No that wasn't it. I was a bit tipsy but I wasn't drunk. Was he? He didn't seem it. He just seemed relaxed and different from the tense and unhappy man he had been when I first met him.

We discussed books we had read recently and what his new publisher in America was like. We compared childhood holidays – Devon for me and Cape Cod for him.

But then he took my wine glass and put it down on the table with his. And he turned towards me, his eyes glowing in the soft light.

'Billie,' he said, his voice very low, 'come here.'

And then he kissed me.

I mean I've been kissed before – of course I have – but not like this.

Not in a way that turned my insides to molten lava. Not

in a way that quite possibly would melt the zip on my jeans and the buttons on my shirt.

I gave a little whimper in the back of my throat and he pulled me round so I was sitting in his lap. I hoped the chair would take the weight. But then I stopped worrying about that and began to enjoy myself. Bloody hell it was fantastic. It made me realize what I'd been missing all these years with stupid types like Matt who didn't always associate the joy of kissing with oral hygiene or taking his gum out first.

I could feel his hands on my breasts, warm through my shirt, and I shuddered with pleasure.

I hoped he realized how well my new bra fitted. I still had a definite muffin top, but he didn't seem to mind. It certainly didn't put him off. I pushed my fingers into his warm hair and kissed him back.

I could feel his hands on my skin and I began to undo the buttons of his shirt. I don't think I really knew what I was doing but I knew I wanted him. I wanted him now. As quickly as possible. Here in the garden, on the cold, sweet-smelling grass.

Suddenly Oliver pulled back. He was trembling. 'I'm not sure I meant to do this,' he said, his voice a bit shaky. 'I just couldn't resist you any longer ...'

Resist me? Any longer? Crumbs!

'... and you just looked so beautiful, so glorious sitting there. Believe me I've been wanting to do that for quite some time.'

Me? Glorious?

He bent his head down and kissed my breasts, his breath warm, his tongue tasting me just as I'd hoped he would. Then he smoothed back my hair and took my face in his hands and kissed me again.

I could feel the muscles in his shoulders hard under my hands.

'Oh God, Billie. I'm sorry. I'm going in before I say or do something stupid,' he said.

'Oh,' I whispered, my spirits plummeting.

No go on, say something stupid. I might like it.

Whatever he was thinking of doing or saying I bet I would have been completely fine with, but I didn't have the nerve to say so. Instead, like a muppet, I watched him going inside, and the light in his room shine out into the darkness before he closed the curtains. Then, shivering, I went in and locked the back door and finished my glass of wine, cursing my reticence.

Chapter Twenty-Six

I think I fell asleep just after midnight, my legs jumbled up in the bedclothes as I tried and failed to get comfortable. My thoughts were equally as tangled.

He thought I was glorious? Happy and Glorious. That was in the National Anthem wasn't it? And beautiful; he thought I was beautiful too. And he had found it hard to resist me.

Since when?

Since when did he find it hard to resist me? That was the question I wanted to ask. Had he been fighting the urge to kiss me, to touch me since the first time I saw him when I couldn't unlock the front door and I was yelling at him and he was standing outside in the rain? Or when I'd gone into his room with the jug of iced water and seen him ... nooo! No, I mustn't think about that.

At all!

Bad, stop it!

Perhaps it was when he caught me stuffing in broken biscuits in the larder or spitting wine down my front? Oh God perhaps he was teasing me? Perhaps it was all a silly joke? Had he gone off upstairs to have a good laugh, muffled by his pillow? I fell asleep remembering the feel of his hands on my skin.

*

I woke up and it was very dark. I had kicked the duvet off and I was cold. I heard something. I sat up in bed, my ears straining to hear the sound again. Nothing.

I reached over to find my phone and see what time it was: four-thirty.

There. That was the noise. I heard it again. Downstairs. What was it? It had better not be that bloody cat from next door chomping through the remains of the beef. Had I shut the kitchen window properly?

I pulled on my dressing gown and went to open my bedroom door. Oliver's door was still closed and there was no sound from his room. He didn't snore then?

Shut up. You'll be thinking about what he wears in bed next!

I went to the landing and listened again. There! The noise had come from downstairs, definitely. I put the landing light on and went down a few stairs and listened again. It was a sort of cry. A quiet shout if that makes sense.

At the bottom of the stairs I opened the door to the sitting room. There was someone in there, someone on the sofa. Someone in distress, someone turning and twisting with a nightmare.

'God, God no, please!' The voice was a tortured whisper. It was Oliver.

I hesitated in the doorway. What should I do? Perhaps I should just go back upstairs and leave him to his bad dreams, but somehow I couldn't. I trod carefully into the room, my bare feet silent on the rug.

There was a muffled noise from Oliver. I was standing next to him. In the gloom I could just see his face and the tears staining his cheek. He was crying in his sleep. I should leave; I should turn and leave him. He might be embarrassed to know I had heard him? But he was in distress; I couldn't just leave him.

I crouched down beside him and put a gentle hand on his shoulder. He flinched. He gasped and woke up.

'Are you OK? I heard you. I came to see you. Why are you down here? What's the matter?'

He reached out from under the duvet he had wrapped around himself and took my hand.

'Billie,' he said. He was looking at me.

'I'm here,' I said.

He pulled my hand to his mouth and kissed the palm. 'Thank God,' he said.

I could feel the tears on his face and my heart contracted with emotion.

'I just wanted to help,' I said. 'What's the matter?'

'Come here.'

He pulled me towards him and somehow I was lying with him under his duvet, his body warm, his hands pulling me close to him until we fitted together. It's a good job I've got a big sofa.

He kissed my cheek, my temple, my eyelids and then he pushed my hair back off my face and kissed me properly.

'Oh, Billie, Billie,' he whispered. 'Thank God. I thought ... Billie.'

His hands were pushing my dressing gown off my shoulders. I reached down and untied the sash. I could feel his naked body against mine. Nothing but nothing had ever felt so good.

His shoulders, his chest was warm and hard under my fingers. We explored each other, his touch tender, gentle.

'I want you, Billie, so much,' he said. He stopped, raised himself up on one elbow, and looked down at me, waiting for me to say something. To pull away? I don't know.

'Billie?'

I couldn't speak. I wanted him with every last bit of me. Yes, I hadn't had sex for quite a while but this was different somehow. Was it passion? Need? Lust? Want? I couldn't say, I just knew I couldn't and wouldn't stop.

'Yes,' I said, 'oh yes.'

I felt the muscles of his back moving under my fingers, the hardness of his thighs, the willingness of him. His fingers were warm and strong as he held me in the darkness, his mouth gentle on my body, delivering the lightest of kisses. His teeth grazed gently against my stomach, then I felt the trace of his tongue, as he tasted me. Tested my responses. He waited and I closed my eyes and gave myself up to the feel of him. The kindness of his touch, the warmth of his breath on my body, my hands buried in his warm hair. The pleasure mounted until I cried out, helpless in his arms. Then he held me and turned me while he whispered in my ear.

Yes, yes, oh yes.

He pulled me down underneath him and suddenly in one wonderful moment my world was complete, just like that. His breath warmed my throat; his kisses traced a path down my neck. He called my name and rocked against me as I trembled and cried out in the darkness.

*

299

I don't know how long we lay like that, together, breathing in and out, not speaking. The first grey light of the dawn was lighting the window.

'Billie,' he said, his mouth against my cheek.

I turned to look at him. 'Are you OK?' I said.

Now that's a stupid question isn't it? I think even I know enough about men to know they are generally OK in this sort of situation.

He smiled down at me and raised himself so I could move my leg, which was in danger of going numb.

'That was ...' He didn't finish the sentence.

I wondered what he was going to say.

That was fine? Average? Entertaining?

'... absolutely mind-blowing.'

Phew that was a relief. I hadn't forgotten how to do it then.

'I've imagined what it would be like so many times, wondered how it would feel,' he said.

Blimey, had he?

He kissed me and smoothed his hands over me again.

'Why are you downstairs anyway?' I said at last. 'Isn't the bed comfortable?'

'Of course, it's fine. Really don't worry.'

'Then why are you down here? Sleeping on the sofa?'

He gave a funny sort of laugh.

He pulled me back against him so we were spooned together, and rested his chin on the top of my head.

'I'm not a great sleeper.'

I could feel his voice rumbling against my back. It was lovely, sort of comforting.

'I used to get these nightmares all the time. These days not so much.' He ran a hand over my breasts with a groan of

300

pleasure. 'You are fantastic. That ex-boyfriend of yours must be a copper-bottomed idiot to let you go.'

We lay entwined for a few minutes and I wondered if he had fallen asleep but then he kissed my shoulder and I shivered.

I was desperate for a cup of tea. But if I got up I'd probably need the loo and then the mood would be completely wrecked.

How did people manage to do things elegantly in these circumstances? If I got up I'd need to find my dressing gown and no one needs to see me with my arse in the air first thing in the morning, let's be honest.

'Can I make you a cup of tea?' he said. 'I'd really love one.'

I breathed out a sigh of relief. A kindred spirit. And it would give me a chance to find my dressing gown too.

'Yes please. That's a brilliant idea.'

He got up, pulled on some boxer shorts, and went out to the kitchen. I scrabbled around until I located my dressing gown hanging over the back of a chair and dashed to the loo.

He was back in a few minutes with two mugs of tea.

'I thought you only ever drank coffee?' I said.

'Not all the time.'

He sat down next to me and put an arm around me.

'I think I've taken your hospitality a bit too far, Billie,' he said.

'Have you? I didn't notice,' I said with a sort of laugh. Jeez was he regretting it already? That would be a new record, surely?

'I let my feelings get a bit ahead of myself,' he said. 'Sorry.'

'You don't have to apologize,' I said.

'Are you sure?'

I felt a bit odd; the atmosphere was stalling by the second.

'Oliver, I'm positive.'

We sat and drank our tea in silence. What had I done wrong? I'd definitely done something.

Outside the sky was the palest grey tinged with pink as the sun rose over the garden and Not My Cat leapt up onto the windowsill and mouthed through the glass at the object of its desire. I felt like closing the curtains. Or chucking something at it.

'I want to explain something,' Oliver said at last. 'I think I owe you that much.'

I didn't move but I could almost feel my ears pricking up. 'You don't owe me anything, Oliver.'

'Once I leave here I might not see you again. I know I'm going to be spending more time in the States in future,' he said.

My heart sank.

I've been given the 'morning after' brush-off before now; I know how it works.

You're a lovely girl but …

I'm still in love with my ex …

I've even had *It's not you it's me …*

Even so I'd never had someone plan to leave the country even before they've put their clothes back on, in order to get away from me. Perhaps I had forgotten how to do sex after all. Or maybe I'd *always* done it wrong. I'd always suspected as much. There should be books, or advice manuals about men. Like those books on Ford Cortinas you see in Halfords. *The Haynes Guide to Men's Bits.*

Actually, there are loads of self-help books. It's just I've always been too embarrassed to buy them. Perhaps that's why Kindles are so popular: people can read that sort of stuff

302

without someone else looking at them and snorting with laughter.

'I was engaged,' he said.

'Ah,' I said, and I actually bit my lower lip to stop myself from talking and asking embarrassing questions.

Like *Why are you telling me this*? What am I supposed to do with this information?

Obviously you wouldn't expect a man of his age not to have had significant others. Or even a wife. He's gorgeous, he's intelligent, and as I now know bloody fantastic in bed. But I wanted to ask who, what happened, what was she like, did she go off with another man, or did you have an affair, where is she now?

'Her name was Jessie. She was bright and very clever .'

Ah Jessie. Yes he'd mentioned her. I remembered.

But she ran off with the milkman?

Had an affair with your father?

Dumped you for her karate instructor?

Was a hopeless alcoholic?

'She was independent, feisty. She worked for a charity helping homeless kids.'

Oh God, do a quick back-pedal.

She's a living saint, clever, compassionate. I bet she has legs up to her armpits and because-you're-worth-it hair.

I bet she's never owned a pair of Spanx.

'But six months after we got engaged – the night of my first book launch – she died.'

Oh bloody hell! Bloody bloody hell! I wasn't expecting that.

'My God, what happened?'

'She was at a conference in Thailand. There was a fire in the hotel. She was on the top floor. She couldn't get out.' His voice suddenly faded. 'She couldn't get out. She was trapped.

The nightmares started then. Not about her, just a terrible feeling of panic, of being powerless.'

I felt physically sick for a moment imagining it.

'Oh Christ Almighty. I'm so sorry. Oh, Oliver, how awful. When did this happen?'

'Nearly six years ago. It's been a long six years. I didn't think I would ever get over it.'

I suddenly realized something.

'Is that why you prefer to sleep downstairs? In Vermont in that little room, not upstairs? Why you had to have the ground-floor bedroom in the writing retreat? It was nothing to do with your ankle was it? And it's why your books are so sad, the heroines always die or leave Harry Field for someone else. That's why.'

'I don't know. It doesn't matter. Just ignore me, forget what I just said. I'm an idiot to even tell you. I've never told anyone before.'

'I'd never tell anyone!'

'I couldn't stop you anyway.'

'Oliver, I know I'm noisy and a bit on the crazy side on occasions, but I don't lie and I don't let friends down.'

He looked at me. 'Am I a friend? You hardly know me.'

'But I want to.' I took his hand between both of mine.

'I'm not used to trusting people,' he said. 'I've been alone so long.'

'I know.'

He pulled his shirt on and went into the kitchen, putting his empty mug in the sink. I followed him. He opened the back door and we walked out into the pale, clear morning. The wet grass was cold under my bare feet. I watched him.

'It's beautiful here,' he said. 'I've felt more chilled in the last two days than I have for years. I wonder why that is?'

'You don't have to worry about anything here,' I said. 'That's the point isn't it? You sent Kitty here, she spread the word, and the others followed. It wouldn't have worked if it hadn't been for you. She even came and signed some books in my uncle's shop. And then so did my other guests. I was hoping you would too?'

He took my hand and squeezed it.

'Yes, you're good at looking after people. I just got the ball rolling. I think I need someone like you, Billie. Now Pippa has gone, and Fee is just a temporary solution.'

Somehow my heart sank. He didn't need *me*. He needed someone *like* me.

'What happened to Pippa?'

'She left. She and Jake fell for each other. Didn't Kitty tell you? They've moved in together. That's the triumph of hope over experience.'

'Oh but I'm so glad! Not that Pippa left, but that she and Jake realized they would be good for each other.'

Oliver turned to look at me. 'How did you know? You hardly knew either of them?'

I shrugged. 'It was obvious.'

'Was it? Not to me! I couldn't believe what they had been up to in Vermont.'

'Good for them I say! And what about Fee?'

'Temporary contract. She'll be leaving soon. I don't suppose ...' Oliver spun round to look at me, his eyes bright with hope. 'What?'

'I don't suppose you'd like to come and work for me?'

I laughed. 'Not a chance!'

His face fell. 'Why not?'

'It wouldn't work, Oliver – you know it wouldn't. As you

said, you don't need me; you need someone like me. Anyway, I have my own stuff to do.'

'You could go back to writing? I could help you. I could put your stuff on the right desks, get you going.'

I held my breath for a moment, thinking about what this might mean.

'Of all the ideas I've heard that is one of the worst, Oliver. I know you mean to help but that's not the way is it? Think about it!'

He dropped my hand and walked away from me to the end of the garden. Not My Cat came slinking out of the long grass and sat staring at him.

I went back into the house, my feet freezing. Should I wait for him? Should I go back out? What was the right thing to do?

What I wanted, what I needed, was a hot shower.

I went upstairs, found a clean towel, and went into the bathroom, locking the door behind me. Much as I might have wanted Oliver to come in after me and share the experience, I was suddenly shy again. Just for a brief moment I hadn't cared. I had felt sexy and desirable. Now I was only too aware of the faults in my figure. I looked at myself in the bathroom mirror and blushed.

When I came out of the bathroom Oliver's bedroom door was open. He was dressed.

'Are you ready for breakfast?'

He hesitated. 'No, but thanks. Bit early perhaps. I need to go back to London. I've had a call from the office. I'd like to deal with it from here, but I think it would make more sense to drive there.'

'Oh.'

306

We were strangers again. I went downstairs, my wet hair hanging limp and unbrushed, still in my dressing gown that smelled of Oliver and sex and sweat. I didn't think I would ever wash it again.

At last we stood looking at each other in my little hallway next to the front door.

My sadness had settled like a stone in my throat. Oliver bent to kiss my cheek. A cold, dry kiss of brief acquaintance.

'I'll see you,' he said.

I wanted to throw my arms around him, beg him to tell me what I'd done but I didn't. At that moment the doorbell rang.

I opened it. My mother stood there, rattling her car keys in her hand. She was dressed in her gardening clothes and a disreputable old fleece hat.

'Sorry I'm so early. I've come for the fish kettle. Oooh!' She visibly jumped when she saw Oliver and her eyes flicked from him to me and back again, taking in my dressing gown and wet hair. 'Sorry, am I interrupting something? Do introduce me!'

'Mum, this is Oliver Forest. Oliver, this is my mother ...' For a moment I couldn't remember my mother's name and I screwed my eyes up in my attempts to remember.

Mum leaned forward and they shook hands.

'I think Billie's having a senior moment. I'm Penelope, always delighted to meet any of Billie's ...'

Don't say it. Don't say it.

'... many boyfriends.'

Oh great. So now I sound like the town bike. Thanks, Mum.

'Sorry to rush off but I must be going,' Oliver said. 'Nice to meet you, Penelope.'

He walked past her, got into his car, and drove away.

'Have I spoiled a tender moment? Did I say I'd be calling in? He looks nice by the way,' Mum said with a thoughtful look. 'Is he special?'

'I don't know,' I said.

Chapter Twenty-Seven

I went to look for the bloody fish kettle and eventually found it in the lean-to shed by the back door. It was covered in dust and spider's webs and I had to give it a good scrub before Mum would even touch it but at least it gave me time to calm down. Then we had an infuriating half-hour when I told her how to use it and she refused to listen or understand and I had to write out a recipe for her. With diagrams. Why she couldn't just look on the Internet like everyone else I don't know.

All the time I wondered where Oliver had got to.

'Come over and see the boys. They'll be arriving round about lunchtime. They'd absolutely love to see you,' Mum said.

This was so unlikely that I thought I was going to cry.

Hector and Finn would be far more interested in their X Box than a dull aunt mooning around with a face like a wet week. And was watching them play some shoot 'em up game enough to distract me from remembering how this day had begun: with the best sex I'd ever had with the handsomest man I'd ever known?

No was the answer I was looking for.

'I'll be over sometime, Mum,' I said.

Mum was wandering around picking things up and putting them back in the wrong places, which meant I had to wander around after her. I wished she would leave but she had other ideas.

'Shall we have coffee?' she said, opening the back door. Next door's cat shot in and straight out again in a scurry of flying paws. Even it seemed to know that Oliver wasn't there anymore.

I began to think I was losing my mind. I didn't talk much. All I could see was Oliver sitting next to me, his fingers curled around his wine glass, talking about the body count in *Death in Damascus*.

'So that good-looking man who was leaving, tell me about him,' Mum said as we settled down with coffee and a full biscuit tin.

'Oliver Forest, also known as Ross Black,' I said.

'He's the chap who took you to Vermont isn't he? He must be keen!'

'He's not keen, Mum. He's just another writer who needed a space to write without interruption.'

'So do you always look so miserable when your writers leave?'

'Very funny.'

'Are you in love with him?'

'Oh don't be ridiculous, Mum. I hardly know him,' I said.

I pulled out a broken Hobnob and ate it. Why did I do that? Did I think I didn't deserve the whole ones? Did I really believe that two broken halves were less fattening than one biscuit?

I threw the pieces into the bin and took a Mint Club.

'But you like him,' Mum said, determined to pry as always.

'He's a bit difficult, moody, clever.'

Brilliant in bed.

'Sounds like your father,' Mum said, unwrapping a KitKat. 'When are you seeing him again?'

'I've no idea. He had to go back to London. Unexpectedly.'

'He likes you,' Mum said. 'I can tell.'

'You can't possibly know that on a ten-second acquaintance,' I said, irritated.

Mum laughed in that annoying way she does sometimes.

'I'm never wrong. Anyway, I'd better get on with things. I have a fish to cook after all. Come round later and you can see how I manage. And I know Josie would like to see you. She and Mark are thinking of selling the cottage in Cornwall and buying a place in France for holidays and weekends. She's had a load of stuff through from French estate agents. You wouldn't believe how cheap property is over there.'

I felt exhausted just thinking about it. I wanted to go back to bed, bury my head under the duvet, and sleep.

*

It was awful being in the house remembering Oliver wasn't upstairs writing or out in the garden so I accepted her invitation and spent the afternoon at Mum's house. I could distract myself listening to my sister's tales of Hector's brilliance at cricket when he had bowled someone out who was almost County standard apparently; unlikely for someone on an under elevens team. Finn had staggering ability at coil pots – an example of which stood filled with cocktail sticks we didn't need on the dinner table. And, of course, there was the prospect of a French bolthole to consider and discuss.

Josie was looking fantastic. I mean she always has been taller, thinner, and prettier than I am but she was also looking toned and tanned and altogether buffed. As the day wore on it became apparent she spent most of her time in the spa or the gym, so that would explain it. I bet she didn't have to worry about her electricity bill. I expect elves came round at night to service her car too.

'So what do you think of the salmon?' Mum said later, poking at her plate.

'Lovely,' I said obediently.

'It hasn't got any breadcrumbs,' Finn said, his mouth an arc of dissatisfaction, 'and where are the fingers? They're the best part.'

'We're working up to actual *fish* fish,' Josie said sotto voce.

'And there aren't any fries,' Hector added.

'Well maybe later,' Mum said. 'It's my favourite thing ever for dessert ...'

Across the table the boys brightened up.

'... Butterscotch Angel Delight. I saw it in the supermarket the other day. I didn't know they still made it. I'd assumed it was banned under European law.'

The boys looked blank as well they might. I hoped they didn't get their hopes up too high.

After we had parked the boys in front of the TV for the rest of the afternoon the three of us went into the kitchen to drink wine and – in my sister's case – complain about her husband Mark who had discovered fishing as a hobby and now spent most of his spare time sitting by the side of a river near Worcester. In my opinion it seemed a reasonable exchange for a French holiday home and a lifestyle of doing not much, ably assisted by a gardener and a cleaner.

I sort of zoned out while she discussed his fishing habits and friends and only came to when my mobile rang.

'It's me, Helena,' said Helena. She sounded as though she was about to burst with excitement.

'You sound happy – what's happening?'

'I've just had an email from that agent. Do you remember? Oliver's friend who was setting up a new agency? Maryam Delaney. And he said give her a try when the book was ready?'

'Yes?'

'Well I did. I sent off some stuff to her last week and she's just been on the phone. She wants to be my agent!'

'Wow, that's fabulous news! Well done you!'

'I know! I'm so excited! I can't believe it! Is Oliver still there? I mean apart from wanting to tell you, I'd like to speak to him and thank him. If he's not busy?'

'Well, no actually.'

I explained as best I could about Oliver's sudden return to London while my mother and sister shamelessly eavesdropped, their eyes boggling with interest.

'I don't understand why he would leave early. You said he was OK, that you were getting on with him? What happened?' Helena said.

Oh God.

'I'll tell you another time,' I said. 'I'm at Mum's and I have Mum and Josie earwigging at the moment.'

'We aren't!' Mum said indignantly.

'Well I am,' Josie said.

'Did you have a row?' Helena said.

'No.'

I stood up and walked off out into the garden where they couldn't hear what I was saying.

'Look I know you're going to tell me off, and I probably deserve it. And I don't know what I was thinking but I did all the same. And it was probably the most stupid thing I've ever done. Well not *the* stupidest, I mean you were there when I looked down the hosepipe to see what was blocking it. But actually it wasn't that stupid, not really. I mean ...'

'What are you talking about?' Helena said.

'I slept with him,' I hissed.

'Oliver? You slept with Oliver Forest? You didn't!'

'I did. I woke up and he was downstairs having a nightmare and I went to see ... anyway one thing led to another.'

'Flipping heck. I can't believe it! He slept with you? I'm assuming you mean you had sex?'

'Well I didn't have to persuade him or anything. Yes we did.'

'And?'

'And it was fantastic. But then the next minute he's packing his bags and saying he has to go. He needs to think, all that usual bollocks.'

'Flip, what are you going to do?'

'I've no idea. Nothing I suppose.'

'Seems a shame. And I mean it; I really would like to thank him. But that doesn't matter. I would pop round to hear all the details but Nick's coming round after work to go through our travel stuff one last time.'

'It's fine. Anyway, I'm thrilled you have got an agent. We'll have a drink when you get back from holiday.'

'Sure you're OK?'

'Yes, I'm great, like I said I'm at Mum's and Josie and the twins are here.'

I felt a bit depressed all of a sudden. God, I was such a wuss.

'OK, speak soon.'

I took a deep breath and walked back into the kitchen where Mum and Josie had opened another bottle of wine. I'd forgotten what they are like when they get together.

Mum was ready for me, her eyes like gimlets.

'You *slept* with him? You told me you hardly knew him!'

Oh great.

*

The rest of the afternoon passed with my mother and sister casting knowing looks in my direction and talking in a strange sort of cryptic language whenever one of the twins turned up looking for more food or bleating on about the *weird pudding* Granny had tried to fob them off with.

'More wine? I mean have you had *enough* generally or would you like some *more* of the same?' Josie said at one point.

'I'm fine *thank* you and yes I would like a top-up. After all *too much* of a good thing is *marvellous*,' I said. I think I was a bit squiffy at this point. It's a good job I wasn't driving.

Hector looked at me from under his dark fringe. 'Why are you talking funny?' he said. 'It's like you're talking in code.'

'Is it? How strange – perhaps it's because Mummy and Granny are a bit deaf.'

'Is that why she said she didn't hear when I asked if we could go to Alton Towers?' he said, leaning on the back of my chair and rocking it.

'Probably,' I said.

'Can I have a biscuit?' Hector whined.

'Ask Granny,' I said.

'*May* I have a biscuit,' Josie corrected him.

'I don't know, ask Granny,' Hector said, kicking my chair leg.

*

I was feeling quite mellow. Well a bit pissed actually. But it was a good thing to be. It went with the way I felt. I needed to get my act into gear, focus on the future, and stop wishing stuff.

Wishing I were thinner, had better dress sense, or more money. Wishing I had some sort of love life and perhaps the prospect of children. I mean Hector and Finnegan were fine in small doses, but I was sure my children would be better behaved, want to cook with me, and would sleep through the night from six weeks. And not poke about looking for biscuits.

My children would have nutritious, home-grown vegetables and fruit on a daily basis. They would not think Chinese takeaway menu B was the same thing as Sunday lunch. They would not steal my chocolate. They would not pull the scenery down at school plays or roll round on the floor in the supermarket kicking each other.

Buoyed up by this pleasing scenario I got home without thinking about Oliver once. But then of course I had to wonder who was going to be the father to these exceptional children. And then I was plunged into gloom again and the first thing I did when I got my shoes off was knock back a slug of vodka. Because that helps.

Chapter Twenty-Eight

I spent the rest of the week tidying up and moping. I was expecting a writer called Patsy Poole on Friday evening. She was a vegetarian and gluten intolerant and needed absolute peace in order to finish her twenty-sixth book. I'm assuming it was going to be like the previous twenty-five, all of them sweet Georgian romances, rich with dimity dresses, blushing maidens who shook their curls and said *Fie, Lord Winchester, you may not kiss me 'til we are wed.* The dark-browed heroes generally crushed the heroines to their broad chests with lines like: *You are my destiny, Seraphina. I will speak to your father.*

Patsy only drank decaffeinated coffee. I mean what's the point in that? And thinking about it from my personally caffeine-rich environment, when they take the caffeine out where does it go? Do they shove it in other things? Add it to petrol? Sell it on the black market to shady-looking blokes in raincoats?

Anyway, bang on the dot of six, Patsy Poole – a statuesque redhead – arrived, parking her *it's got everything* Range Rover in my drive. She was only going to stay with me until Monday morning but had brought enough luggage for a transatlantic crossing and had what can only be described as a ghetto blaster under one arm. I didn't know they still made such things.

She settled in very quickly, ate the broccoli and tomato quiche (gluten free) she had requested, and told me lots of wonderful gossip about well-known authors, none of which I can repeat as I can't afford the legal fees. I mean who knew a much-married, surgically enhanced writer of a certain age was actually a bigamist? Or a famous historian had been cautioned for shop lifting dog outfits?

Patsy declined more than one glass of wine and went up to her room to write 'in peace'. I decided that I too would have another go at being a vegetarian. After all Patsy looked ten years younger than her actual age. Her skin was as smooth and rosy as a child's. Perhaps she'd had cosmetic surgery – I didn't think of this until later.

Still, she had a wonderfully slim figure that often seems to go with people who don't eat pies and mechanically recovered meat products. Perhaps I would google vegetarian recipes when I got a moment and give it another go.

A few minutes later I was washing up and enjoying a cheeky Merlot when suddenly Whitesnake started blasting out from upstairs at such a volume that it shook the windows. It's a good job I have thick walls and no near neighbours who could hear 'Come An' Get It' in all its glory. This continued until nine-thirty when there was a merciful silence, and something called 'Slide It In' was stopped mid-riff. Thank God. So much for absolute peace and quiet.

Patsy came downstairs with a bottle of Sailor Jerry in one hand.

'God, that's better, I've been writing up a storm in the last hours. There must be something in the air here. You're awfully good at this.' She shook the bottle at me. 'Care to join me?'

I declined and poured another glass of Merlot. She joined me at the kitchen table and took off her shoes (Pink Converse trainers).

'I meant to say, I saw Ollie a few weeks back. He was the one who said I should come here. He said you were the best person at this by a mile. The food always good, always plenty of booze. I rather think he likes you.'

'Really?' I blushed as convincingly as one of Patsy's dimity-clad heroines. 'What did he say?'

'Just that. He was coming here. Has he been?'

'Last week. He left a bit suddenly though,' I said trying not to sound too pathetic.

'Oh yes the thing.'

'What thing.'

'The thing with the next book. I heard he was going back to the States. Wasn't due to come back here until the New Year.'

That was about four months away and I felt a sudden plunge of disappointment. Why? He meant nothing to me and I obviously meant nothing to him.

Bloody hell, was I really that crap in bed that a man not only went home early but *went to a different continent too*?

'He's OK though?' I said trying to gee the conversation up.

Patsy knocked back her drink and refilled her glass. Golly a lot of these writerly types seemed real piss artists. So why wasn't I more successful? I could do alcohol just as well as the next woman.

'Ollie? Yeah he's fine. Well he was when I saw him.'

'And still single?'

Cringe.

'Yeah, I thought he was gay but apparently not. Perhaps he's asexual,' Patsy said airily.

I don't think so!

'Or one of those people that deliberately don't do sex because it stops their creative urges.'

'Hmm.'

'Which is a shame isn't it? A man as sexy as that? I would wouldn't you?'

I made some vague noises and slewed back my wine.

'Anyway, I'm going out for a fag. You don't do you?'

I shook my head.

'Very wise.'

So she was gluten intolerant and a vegetarian but she drank neat rum out of tumblers and smoked. How did that work then?

She went up to bed soon after that and I didn't hear anything from her until the morning.

My phone rang just after Patsy had finished her (gluten free) breakfast toast and Nutella, and had gone back upstairs to write accompanied by Iron Maiden.

She'd told me a bit about book twenty-six and it was indeed a Georgian romance between a delicate heiress and a pirate. Evidently she was revving up the romance to the strains of 'Charlotte the Harlot' and I went out into the garden so I could hear who was trying to talk to me.

'Billie? It's Elaine. Elaine Weston. Remember me? I came to the retreat ...'

'Of course I remember! How are you? How is the arthritis?'

'Oh much the same. Listen I rang you to tell you some good news.'

'Oh that sounds exciting – go on!'

'I've won a writing competition!'

'Oh wow, that fantastic news!'

'I know, I can hardly believe it. All these years and I've not made a single penny out of my writing, and now I've won two hundred pounds!'

'I couldn't be more pleased, Elaine,' I said.

'And it's all thanks to Oliver Forest. Do you remember? No, you wouldn't remember. He said I should enter some writing competitions and I did. Well the first few nothing and then I entered one called *Weird Words* and I won! I had the email this morning and I wanted to tell you straight away. I don't suppose you have a contact number for him do you?'

'I can dig one out,' I said. 'I have his PA's details somewhere.'

'Oh yes, poor Pippa!'

'Well it's not actually her anymore …'

We chatted for a few minutes and I brought her up to speed with the business and she told me about her kittens before she rang off to ring someone else and tell them the good news.

So, another nice thing Oliver had done. First Helena and now this. He really was having a change of heart or character or something.

Back in the house Iron Maiden had given way to Black Sabbath and 'Fairies Wear Boots'. How the hell could she manage to write with that row going on? And what about her urgent need for absolute peace and quiet?

Other than being a vegetarian, Patsy ate just about anything and was – apart from the noise – no trouble at all. She left on Monday morning with double air kisses and promises to recommend me to all her friends.

After she'd gone I sat drinking coffee letting my eardrums settle before I went to clear her room and change the beds.

My phone rang.

'Hello, petal, can you come round? I've got something that might interest you.'

'Hello, Uncle Peter, what would that be then?'

He wouldn't be drawn, just chuckled a bit, so I found some shoes and went off to the bookshop. There I found a veritable scrum of customers. Very unusual. Godfrey was behind the till and Uncle Peter was trying to organize people into an orderly line while they queued up with their purchases.

I looked over at him. 'What on earth is going on?'

Uncle Peter laughed and beckoned me over.

'You couldn't make it up really. The most amazing thing happened. Just after I opened up the shop a van pulled up and delivered these boxes.'

He waved at some stout cardboard cartons.

'Take a look,' he said.

Naturally enough it was books, hardbacks straight from the publisher by the look of things. I peered in. *The Girl from Damascus*, loads of copies and all of them signed by the author; not Oliver Forest or Ross Black but what was apparently his new incarnation – Sam Steel.

'Wow,' I said.

'I know, it's not due out until Friday. I thought there must have been a mistake but there was a note with it – look.'

He handed over a piece of paper with dark, strong writing on it.

'I believe I owe you these? You're getting them a few days early and I'm going to announce as much on Twitter. Let me know if you need more. Hope it helps, Oliver Forest.'

I gasped and pulled one of the books out, inhaling that gorgeous smell that is so distinctive. I pressed it between my palms and then opened it at the title page. There's something about a brand-new book, isn't there? That exciting moment when you know you are the first person to look inside it, the funny little crackling noises as the spine opens.

The Girl From Damascus
By Sam Steel.
Dedicated to the Cheese Airer.

'Strange dedication isn't it?' Uncle Peter said. 'I wonder what it means?'

I took the book and went to the back of the shop, hardly able to breathe.

It was me surely? I was the cheese airer. How could it be anyone else?

The stream of people continued all morning until the last volume was snapped up. Godfrey said they had sold a hundred and taken orders for as many again.

'I really didn't expect this,' he said. 'I must write and thank him. He left your house early I understand? What a pity, I would love to have met him.'

What was I going to do next? What was the right thing to do?

*

That evening I sat looking at the emails I had received from Pippa and then from Fee. I could imagine where they worked, from glossy offices in Central London with views over the

Thames I expect. But Oliver? Where was he? He was going back to America; he wasn't coming back until the New Year.

I couldn't bear it. I wanted to see him again. Whether I was too noisy or said stupid things at the wrong moment or even if I was so bad at lovemaking that it drove men away, I needed to see him one last time.

*

Astonishingly at nine o'clock the following morning, just as I was about to ring her, Fee Gillespie rang me.

'Mr Forest has asked me to contact you. He has a parcel he wishes to pass on and needs to get it to you.'

'OK, what do you need me to do?' I said rather enthusiastically.

'Fine, no need to shout,' Fee said rather tetchily. 'There should be a car arriving outside.'

'Outside where?'

'Outside your house,' Fee said with a definite 'duh' in her voice.

'Now?'

'Soon.'

'But I might not have been in. I might have been on holiday. I might have gone shopping.'

'And where are you?' Fee said.

'At my house.'

'Well there we are then, no harm done,' she said and rang off.

Ten seconds later my phone rang again. Had she forgotten some vital information?

'Billie? Is that you?'

'Godfrey?'

'Oh thank heavens; I've been trying to ring you. You always seem to be engaged or not available. Why don't you answer the house phone? I'm in a bit of a state. I'm afraid it's Peter.'

I went cold. 'What's happened?'

'He's really not well. That tummy upset never did clear up but he wouldn't go to the doctor. You know what he's like. I don't know what to do. You know we don't drive, and I've called an ambulance but apparently there's been a pile-up somewhere the other side of Cheltenham and they can't get to me for thirty minutes at the earliest.'

I went back into the house, grabbed my car keys and ran. I got into my Land Rover and floored the pedal. This sounds dramatic but it only meant I did about forty miles an hour. But very loudly so it was quite impressive.

When I got to their flat I found Uncle Peter sitting on the side of his bed, looking very grey and ill. He bent over with a groan of pain as I cannoned in.

'What is it? Have you called the doctor?' I said.

Godfrey grasped his hands together and paced around.

'I don't know what to do. I did try the surgery but they weren't much help. They suggested I ring for an ambulance, and I did but ...'

I looked at my uncle's face. He was beginning to sweat and he looked awful. I took a decision.

'Come on, Uncle Peter, we need to get you to hospital. Godfrey, go and get a quilt or something. Help me get him into the car.'

'God, I think I'm going to be sick,' Uncle Peter said in a weak voice. 'Sorry and all that.'

He made it to the bathroom where he was violently ill and

sank to his knees, white and trembling. Behind him Godfrey started whimpering and biting his fist.

After a few minutes Uncle Peter managed to get to his feet. He put out an arm towards me, his eyes wide with fear.

'I'm awfully sorry, Billie, I think this is it. I think I might be dying.'

'No you're bloody not. I'm not going to let you. Now come on, let's get you to hospital,' I said.

I don't know how we did, it but between us Godfrey and I got him into the back seat and set off for the hospital, praying that the car wouldn't start playing up. The Land Rover had already shown me it realized that its MOT was up in two days' time. It always had a slightly spiteful streak, failing to start at inopportune moments and occasionally leaving its lights on so the battery went flat. Only last week it ran out of petrol despite the gauge claiming to be half full.

We roared through the narrow streets, causing a large silver car to swerve into the kerb as I wrestled with the gears and cursed in language that would have caused Uncle Peter to blush if he had been in the mood to listen. Gunning the car through the main gates and ignoring the one-way system, I skidded to a halt outside the main doors, much to the fury of a woman in a tight dressing gown who was standing by a litterbin smoking.

'You can't park here, hospital policy. My husband has to park miles away. Over there,' she said waving with her cigarette towards the car park.

'Really?' I said.

I ran past her to find a wheelchair and when I returned she was standing berating poor Godfrey as he tried to help Uncle Peter out of the car. I carefully ran the wheelchair

326

wheels over the back of her feet, making her yelp and scuttle out of the way.

'If you've got mud on my new slippers …'

'… then my living will not be in vain. Can't you see he's seriously ill? Get out of the way, woman, if you can't be helpful,' I shouted. 'And stop smoking! It's a frigging hospital!'

She shambled off sulking and muttering about human rights and we got my uncle into the wheelchair and into A&E.

Half an hour later Uncle Peter was in the operating theatre. Godfrey was sitting looking shaken with a cup of something that might have been tea, or possibly oxtail soup – he might have hit the wrong buttons – and I had a parking ticket.

Chapter Twenty-Nine

Uncle Peter was back in the ward by midday by which time I'd moved my car three miles away to the hospital car park and parted with the gross national product of Belgium for the privilege. I found Godfrey and we went to have two dramatically awful sandwiches in the hospital canteen. I have no idea what they were. By a process of elimination we decided the only thing worth drinking from the machines was the hot chocolate. Or more accurately the scalding brown beverage that appeared when button C9 was pressed.

We sat beside Peter's bed, watching as he lay log-like under the thin blue counterpane that had been tucked tightly round him. A stout nurse wandered up and put a paper plate with a banana and a cheese and pickle roll on the locker next to him.

'Dead men's dinner for you,' she said lugubriously. 'Tea or coffee?'

'Tea for me please, two sugars. It's been a bit of a day,' Godfrey said, looking up at her with a weak smile.

'I meant for him,' the nurse said, curling her lip.

'Well I'm sure that's what he would like,' I said cunningly.

She wasn't fooled. 'There are machines you can use on the ground floor. You'll need the right money and don't ask for change at the shop. They get very shirty about that.'

'Why?' I said.

'Why what?'

'Why don't they like giving change?'

'It's not what they're there for,' stout nurse said, flicking a meaningful look at the watch pinned upside down on the straining bosom of her lilac uniform.

'What, making life for visitors a bit more bearable?'

Godfrey nudged me with his knee. 'Don't,' he muttered. 'She might take it out on Peter. We'll get him home as soon as we can, and we can look after him there.'

'Visiting hours finish in five minutes,' she said.

'OK,' I said sending the stout nurse a fierce look as she swayed off.

'What are you arguing about,' Uncle Peter said.

'Ah so you're back in the land of the living!' Godfrey said with a glad cry. 'How are you feeling?'

'Pretty rubbish actually,' he said, his thin fingers plucking at the bedspread. 'Where am I?'

'Hospital. It was appendicitis,' I said, reaching out to put my hand over his.

'Really? Thank God, I thought it was something far worse,' Uncle Peter said with the smallest of smiles.

'The surgeon said yours was the worst he's seen for ages so well done,' Godfrey said.

'I do my best. Can I go home please?'

'I think we should wait for the doctors to tell us. If there are any around,' Godfrey said looking vaguely around as though expecting to see a *Carry On Matron* gaggle of medial staff wending their way towards us. Instead there was just a woman with a cleaning trolley who was leaning on her mop by the nurses' station complaining about the rota.

'I'm sure they will be along soon.'

'You have a Dead Man's Dinner,' Godfrey said. 'If that's any consolation.'

He picked up the paper plate and prodded the roll that was hermetically sealed in several layers of cling film.

'I'll wait,' Uncle Peter said. 'Somehow I can't quite fancy that.'

We heard the sound of some sort of argument further down the corridor. The grumble of the stout nurse and unmistakeably the more strident and challenging tones of my mother.

'I've brought my brother some home-made soup. I'd be grateful if you would direct me to his room ... No, I'm not interested in knowing the visiting hours ... Well I will be in and out in a flash ... I was speaking to my cousin the Chairman of the Local Health Authority about this only last week ...'

Peter looked up at me and rolled his eyes. 'Guess who?' he said.

Mum came sweeping triumphantly into the room and up to Uncle Peter's bedside, a thermos flask in one hand.

'Hello, you old fool,' she said, tears in her eyes. 'What have you been up to now?'

*

Instead of having two weeks in hospital followed by a month's bed rest as Godfrey's father had done when he had his appendix out, Uncle Peter was home the following afternoon.

330

He made the most of being officially an invalid, requesting Ben and Jerry's Phish Food ice cream and my home-made tomato and basil soup for his dinner. Then the following day he had scrambled eggs on toast for breakfast, smoked salmon sandwiches for lunch, and asked for chicken casserole and lemon meringue pie for his evening meal.

Godfrey voiced his suspicions that Peter might be pushing his luck and the following day resolutely ignored the tinkling of the little bell Peter had found. Within a couple of days, life was pretty much back to normal except Mum popped in again as she always used to, their feud forgotten. It was only then I remembered Fee Gillespie and her mysterious message. The package, the car, nothing had happened.

By then I was looking forward to the return of Kitty Ford-Wilson for another weekend while Jeff took their children to visit his mother in nearby Upper Slaughter. As before Kitty's luggage arrived before she did but this time their daughters were in the car too.

Jane (after Austen) and Bridget (after Jones) seemed delightful girls, nothing like the delinquent fiends Kitty had described. They accepted a glass of orange squash, a slice of cake, and half an hour in the garden where they made the acquaintance of next door's cat, safe in the knowledge that their mother was over an hour away thanks to their phone tracking app.

'Mummy's nearly finished her book edits,' Jane said, coming up for air after a long pull at her drink. 'She says another sweep through and she'll be done. Then we can go on holiday.'

'What's this book called?' I said.

'It's called *Dressing Up Dolly*,' said Bridget. 'It's all about fashion and how no one can find decent clothes these days.'

'Sounds about right,' I said.

Jeff finished his coffee and checked his phone. 'Come on, girls, Mummy's just past Andoversford. We'd better go.'

They finished their drinks, thanked me politely, and got back into the car without any cajoling. Mummy must be absolutely terrifying.

'Where are you going on holiday?' I asked as Jeff shook my hand and thanked me profusely.

'Florida. Disneyland – Kitty loves it.'

'Really?' That seemed unlikely.

'Oh gosh yes, we went there on our honeymoon. We go back once a year if at all possible.'

I tried to imagine Kitty on the Big Thunder Mountain Railroad and failed.

'Well have fun,' I said. 'I'll look after her.'

'Oh I know – she was saying to Oliver the other day, she really—'

'Oliver?' I felt like jamming my arm in the car window to stop him from driving off. 'Oliver Forest?'

'Yes, he phoned up. He's been in Boston for a few days, but he's supposed to—'

'Daddy,' Bridget shouted from the back seat, 'Mummy's only fifteen minutes away.'

'We must be going,' Jeff said with a jaunty wave.

Bang on cue, Kitty arrived fifteen minutes later, the Maserati roaring its return to the rest of the town.

'Kitty,' I said, holding out a hand to welcome her.

She swept me into an unexpected hug.

'Thank you so much!' she said. She reached into the back of the car and brought out an extravagant bouquet. 'These are for you.'

332

'How absolutely lovely! Why?' I said, more than a little confused.

'Your plot idea. The book practically wrote itself. It just poured out. My editor wept with laughter. I told her what you'd said; she wants you to come to the launch.'

What idea was that then?

'Did it? That's incredible,' I said.

'OK there are some edits to be done and I need to cut a couple of scenes and add one about going to the doctor when she gets a STI, but apart from that ...' Kitty finished with a jaunty thumbs-up sign.

'Sorry but remind me, what did I say?'

'*Dressing Up Dolly*: the many faces of the modern woman. A main character trying to be thin, voluptuous, androgynous, feminine, all at the same time. I can't remember the exact words, but anyway it set me going. I just know this one is going to be great. Women having to be all things to all men and never, ever being able to find the right outfit. It's such a laugh; I've been chuckling away. Especially the scene where she gets a tattoo.'

A tattoo.

I should get a tattoo.

Yes, that would be a real adventure. If I was brave enough?

Had that been on my list of things to do? It had been ages since I had thought about it, I couldn't remember. When I had Kitty settled I went to check. Yes it had been, point 8. A small tattoo I could hide from my mother.

I re-read the list and was quite surprised to see how many things I had achieved. I had even sent Matt packing when the old me would have been seduced by his return. I still hadn't got the money back that he owed me, but it was a start. I'd done loads of things, I was in a better place. Little by little my life had changed after all.

*

Kitty was a new woman this time round. She was a delight, ate everything, never once complained about her weight or her size, and worked for nearly all of the weekend until Sunday afternoon when she came downstairs, triumphant.

'I've only bloody finished!' she said, waving a bottle aloft. 'I thought I might – I brought this specially. Let's crack it over the bows of my new book!'

So we did.

We sat in the kitchen knocking back prohibitively expensive champagne, eating cheese straws, and discussing her forthcoming holiday.

'Of course Jeff proposed at Disneyland Paris so it holds a special place in my heart. I'd just been on Space Mountain and I'd thrown up over his trainers. You wouldn't think it was a romantic moment but it was. Hmm. That was fifteen years ago.'

She looked a bit wistful for a few minutes and then came to so she could top up our glasses.

'You should go,' she said. 'It's enormous fun. Not the Paris one obviously. The French are hopeless at customer service and pretending to be jolly whereas the Americans – well it comes naturally. They can't help themselves. And, of course, the weather helps in Florida. Disneyland is marvellous but let's be honest it's so much better in the sun.'

'I'm thinking of getting a tattoo,' I blurted out.

'Why?'

'It would be a new experience?' I said, suddenly not quite so sure of myself.

'So would banging yourself on the head with a brick but it doesn't mean you should do it,' Kitty said. 'I don't suppose I could have one of your cream teas before I go?'

'Of course.'

'Jeff's coming to get my stuff tomorrow,' Kitty said. 'What would you have tattooed and where?'

'I don't know and somewhere hidden. There's a tattoo place in town. I might go there tomorrow.'

Kitty sighed. 'So why do it if you need to keep it hidden?'

'Just as a statement. Someone once challenged me to do unexpected things. Getting a tattoo would be great.'

Maybe it would after all?

'You're crazy – imagine what it would look like when you're seventy. How old are you?'

'Nearly thirty.'

'Exactly,' Kitty snorted. 'That's forty years of yo-yo dieting and skin sag you have to look forward to. You'd start off with a unicorn and end up with a manatee. Anyway, it's a very immature thing to do. Now let's open another bottle. I feel like getting smashed.'

'And that's not immature?'

Kitty winked at me. 'You don't need to get laser surgery to remove a hangover.'

*

She left the following day and the first thing I did was go along the back streets near the bookmaker to look for the tattoo parlour I'd heard about.

A vague-looking chap who introduced himself as Kev showed me some examples of his work. Terrifying photographs of bulldogs playing snooker across someone's back, American eagles, Marilyn Monroe in a bathing suit on someone's bicep, a classic heart with *Mum* inked across it.

'Something small,' I said. 'Something I could cover up.'

So my mother doesn't see it.

'So your mother doesn't see it?' Kev said, taking a long drag at an e-cigarette and puffing out rose-scented smoke.

An e-cigarette? Perhaps I should try one of those? No perhaps not.

I smiled weakly.

We agreed I would have a small one on the back of my right shoulder and after checking the spelling three times and getting me to sign an agreement that I wouldn't sue him, he set to work.

It blooming well hurt. Don't let anyone tell you it doesn't. Like a lot of tiny needles rattling away on my back. Which of course is exactly what was happening.

Kev kept up a long rambling stream of stories about the evils of Brexit and tattoos he had seen that had gone wrong – maybe not the best thing to entertain me with. A favourite was someone who came to him last year wanting him to correct *Nowlige is Power* on one thigh and *No Ragrets* on the other.

Anyway, just as I was about to get to the end of my pain threshold and ask him to stop, the doorbell tinkled and someone shouted through the modesty curtain Kev had pulled across.

'I'm looking for Billie Summers; is she here?'

'Police after you?' Kev said mildly. 'I can tell him to piss off if you like?'

'Absolutely not! Yes, I'm here.'

I stood up and pulled on my T-shirt before I peered out through the curtains.

There was a man standing there, vaguely familiar.

'Who wants to know?' I said, rather bolshie.

I think an hour in Kev's company was wearing off on me. The man's face cleared when he saw me.

'Ah, Miss Summers, I came to collect you a few days ago, and you weren't at home. Are you available now?'

'What for?' I said.

Kev came to stand next to me, wiping some ink off his hands. 'Bailiff? Want me to see him off?' he said narrowing his eyes.

'No, I think I know him. How did you know I was here?'

'Henry,' the man said, 'Oliver's driver. I have my methods. He told me to give you this. He said you would understand.'

He handed over a copy of *The Girl from Damascus* and I opened the title page.

Please forgive me? Oliver.

I felt a prickle of excitement up the back of my neck.

'Oh God yes! Of course!'

That's right, Billie: play hard to get.

'Ready?' Henry said. 'We'll only be a few hours.'

'I haven't finished,' Kev warned. 'I've only done a bit of the outline. I haven't even started inking in and you've paid for the whole thing.'

'I'll come back,' I said.

I knew I wouldn't. That was fifty quid wasted. How do people afford these huge tattoos? Like those massive roses on Cheryl Cole's bottom? They must cost thousands.

Kev patched me up with a dressing, gave me a couple of

paracetamol and some after care advice. Then I collected my bag and coat and followed Henry out of the shop. His car – silver and shiny with darkened windows – was waiting. He helped me in to the back.

Henry was courtesy itself with the same cashmere rug, bottles of water, and apparently an utter lack of curiosity. It was just like last time. He didn't ask any questions apart from was I warm enough and then he closed the partition between us and the car powered on towards the M40 and the motorway. He drove me to Terminal 5 of course, the same terminal as last time, and this time he held the door open for me.

'I think you are just in time, Miss,' he said.

'In time for what?'

He didn't answer. He didn't even smile.

I went into the terminal building and waited to see what would happen. It was like being a secret agent. I didn't have my passport so there was no way I could be drugged and whisked off anywhere. I looked around at all the people who were going somewhere with their suitcases and bags. Above me the arrivals and departure boards flickered and changed. Planes going to Greece and France and Rio and ah yes to Boston.

'Hello, Billie.'

A familiar voice just behind me. I turned and he was there. Oliver Forest was there, looking at me.

We just stood and stared at each other for a moment. And then somehow I was in his arms and he was holding me very tight. We were getting in everyone's way, causing travellers to dodge around us, some of them muttering at us irritably.

Oliver bent his head down to kiss me. I honestly thought I was going to cry.

'I can't believe it's you,' I said at last.

He held me tight again, and laughed, the sound rumbling through his chest and into my head.

'Thank you for coming,' he said. 'I didn't know if you would.'

'Of course I would,' I said.

'I hoped ... it was short notice. After what I said ...'

'I know. Is it? What are you doing here? Short notice for what?'

'I've flown overnight from Boston to see you. But I'm going back in' – he looked at his watch – 'just over an hour. I've waited as long as I could but I have to go back.'

'Are you?' My stomach did a plunge. 'Do you mean you've flown over just to see me? Why didn't you just ring me?'

Why would anyone do that?

'Yes, I couldn't do this over the phone or by email. And I wasn't going to risk that ex-boyfriend of yours steaming in. Do you want a drink?'

'I think I need one,' I said.

He took my hand and steered me to a private lounge, which was gorgeous and comfortable and apart from everything else, nearly empty. He brought back some champagne and we sat at a table overlooking the runway. In front of us a continual stream of planes were taking off for far-flung destinations but I didn't care. I just wanted to sit there with him, with his thigh touching mine. I wanted to sit there looking into his beautiful blue eyes and seeing such wonderful kindness and desire reflected there.

'Thank you for everything,' I said. 'Especially the books. Uncle Peter was thrilled. And then he had appendicitis and everything was going wrong.'

'And now?'

I looked at him and he smiled.

I didn't want to sit here being polite. I wanted him. I wanted to put my arms around him and feel his body next to me. To know the touch of his skin against mine again.

He reached over and put his hand over mine. It felt right and wonderful. I had the awful feeling that when he went I was going to miss him in a way that crying and a bottle of wine a night would not alleviate.

'I'm sorry, Billie.'

'For what?'

'For rushing off. For being an idiot. Were you doing something important when Henry found you?'

'I was getting a tattoo,' I said.

Oliver shook with laughter. 'Well I wasn't expecting that! Why?'

'It was a new experience. You told me I needed to do things that were different and adventurous.'

'Where and what? Anywhere I can see without both of us being arrested?'

I pulled the neck of my T-shirt down and moved the dressing a bit.

'Can you see? On my shoulder?'

Oliver looked puzzled. 'Why have you had the word Carp drawn on your shoulder? Do you like fish? Is this a particular passion I need to know about?'

I blushed. 'When I go home I've got to go back and let Kev finish it. It's supposed to be 'Carpe Diem' but when Henry came into the shop to find me I just rushed off.'

Oliver laughed and hugged me. 'You're crazy. I've never known anyone like you. So special.'

I looked up at his wonderful face and tried to force the image of him onto my brain. I didn't want to forget this moment. Perhaps if he thought I was special ...

'Anyway, go on,' I said.

Now it's not like me to let someone else do all the talking but he'd been travelling all night so it seemed only fair.

'I've been fighting it for a very long time. Fighting the way I felt. You're the first person in a long time who ...'

He paused.

What?

... *has been rude to me?*

... *has given me a migraine?*

... *has seen me naked?*

'What?'

'... has made me want to go on. Has made me laugh.'

I grinned. 'Did I? I'm a bit of a clown – I know I am.'

Oliver shook his head. 'No, it's more than that, Billie. When I met you I was a mess. I couldn't think straight; I couldn't write. I can admit it now; I had writer's block. Remember how dismissive I was about that in the retreat? I was really at my lowest ebb that week. I know I was being impossible. I knew I was being rude and stupid, but I didn't care. I was sick of everything.

'And then suddenly you were there. Not taking any nonsense, making such a racket, being so kind, so beautiful, being so damned funny. I'd never had such well-aired cheese in my life. Did you see the dedication? And for some reason the book that had been keeping me awake for months took a new direction because of you, because of what you said. Do you remember?

'Because of you the blackness lifted. Everything was OK.

341

For the first time in months I felt there was something ... I started writing again. I did what you suggested. I made a woman save my hero. *The Girl from Damascus*, do you see? No stilettos, no rushing around in a dark house with a killer after her. Just a brave, feisty, funny woman like you.'

He stopped and shrugged and gave me a lopsided grin and my heart did a swoop.

'I wish you didn't have to go,' I said.

I touched his hand and he took it and kissed my fingertips. 'I'll be back.'

'In the New Year? That's ages away.'

'I'll be back next week. I'm not giving up on this. On us.'

'Us?' I said.

Wow I was part of us.

OliverandBillie.

BillieandOliver.

No Billie and Oliver would do just fine.

'You matter to me a great deal. Do you know what I mean? I'd like to see a lot more of you,' he said.

He was looking at me with an expression that made my insides clench with lust. I leaned across and kissed him.

'I thought you'd seen all of me already?'

He grinned. 'And you're gorgeous.'

For once, just for once, I didn't say something stupid like I usually do.

Oh I'm a bit tubby. I can't manage my hair. I have no sense of direction.

Instead I just said, 'Thank you.'

And he put his arm around me and kissed me properly again.

'Are you completely sure you don't want to come and work

for me?' he said at last. 'Is there nothing I can do to persuade you?'

His breath was warm on my cheek and it would have been so easy to say yes, to give in, to take the easy option, but somehow I didn't.

'Positive. I've got such a lot to do here. I've been going through a bit of a rubbish time too. But now, for the first time in ages I'm really getting somewhere. I'm doing something I love. Something I can be proud of. And I'm good at it too – I know I am.'

'I know you are. So how are we going to work this?' he said. He kissed me again. 'I'm not going to lose you, Sybilla Summers.'

For the first time in my life my name wasn't embarrassing or weird. It sounded exotic and rather lovely. I felt suddenly glamorous and fascinating and a bit thinner – I swear I did.

He took my hand and kissed my fingertips one after the other as he spoke.

'When I get back from Boston I want to take you out for dinner. Let's think of it as our first date. I'm going to take you somewhere wonderful and decadent and buy you champagne. And afterwards I'm going to take you to bed and make love to you and show you just how much I've been thinking about you and missing you. Would you like that?'

'I'd like that,' I said rather faintly. 'I'm not going to sleep very well tonight.'

'Good.' He softly bit the pad of my thumb. 'I've lost enough sleep over you in the last few weeks. I think it's your turn.'

I couldn't stop grinning; I must have looked quite crazy to the waitress who was hovering at a discreet distance, probably wondering if we wanted anything other than each other.

'In the meantime, I've got something for you.' Oliver reached into a briefcase down by the side of his chair and pulled out a package. He handed it over. 'If nothing else works I think this will keep you lusting after me. I know the way to your heart.'

It was, of course, a giant Toblerone.

I smiled up at him, suddenly a bit weepy that he had remembered.

'You know how to impress a girl.'

He rubbed a tear from my cheek with his thumb.

'That's what I'm hoping.'

Acknowledgements

Thank you to the team at Avon UK for their help and advice especially Victoria Oundjian, Rachel Faulkner-Willcocks, Helena Newton and Michelle Bullock and, of course, to Annette Green my agent.

Thank you to all those who read and reviewed my debut *The Summer of Second Chances* and helped to make it a bestseller. A lot of them wanted another book, well here it is, I hope you enjoy it.

The writing journey wouldn't be quite so much fun without the LL's who have helped, advised and cheered every step of the way, so a big thank you to them.

To Beth and James for a fantastic launch party.

To my family, who continue to be rather surprised.

Finally, and most importantly, to my husband Brian, who has provided all the enthusiasm, encouragement and Mint Clubs I could wish for. x

An irresistibly funny read about never giving up, whatever the world throws at you.

Out now!

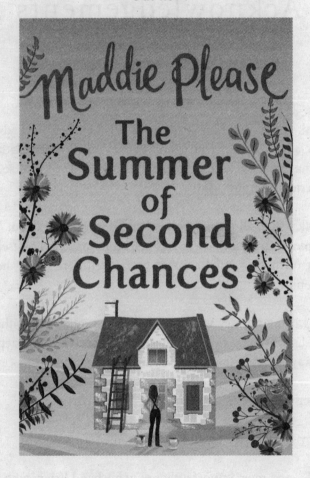